Rescue

A Derrick King Novel: Book 4

By Daniel L. Copeland

"Derrick, Miriam, Rebekah, and now, many more, face tremendous challenges. Rescue's storyline and pace are intense. And yet, Copeland's gift with character development and plot twists continues to impress. Great book. Outstanding series. Must read."

Rod Leonard

Text Copyright © 2020 Daniel L. Copeland
Cover Copyright © 2020 Daniel L. Copeland
All Rights Reserved
No part of this publication may be reproduced, stored in a retrieval system, or transmitted in any form or by any means—electronic, mechanical, photocopying, recording, or otherwise—without the prior written permission of the copyright owner.

This is a work of fiction. The names, characters, incidents, places, and plot are products of the author's imagination or are used fictitiously. Any resemblance to actual persons, agencies, companies, or events is purely coincidental.

Rescue
A Derrick King Novel, Book 4
Published June 2021
First Edition

ISBN: 978-1-970773-05-7
Ingram Spark Edition
Published by Chipping Away Press

Dedication
The work is dedicated to the kind hearts and gentle souls who make the world a better place.

In the Beginning

Miriam King escaped from Pacific Edge.

Rebekah Ford became her companion.

Together, they found Derrick King.

Together, they saved Potterville, California.

Together, they disabled a robot sent to capture them.

Together, they faced an unknown future at the hands of the Potterville student council.

Together, they learned Rebekah's younger sister, Anna, had also escaped from Pacific Edge.

Together, they must rescue Anna Ford.

Part One

1

Sunday, April 4, 12:43 p.m.

DERRICK AND MIRIAM HAD GONE INTO THE HALL FIVE minutes ago, but it felt longer. Derrick had asked to have a private conversation with Miriam. Nyx allowed it—no surprise there. Their exit left Rebekah alone in an unfamiliar classroom, in an unknown school, in a strange town, waiting for Derrick and Miriam's return from their impromptu hall conference. Derrick had not included her, and it pissed Rebekah off to no end. *We're in this together,* they had said, but she was not in the hall with them. She was in here with strangers. Rebekah wanted to march out and demand answers, but here she sat, turning redder by the second.

They could not stop her from leaving, although it felt as if they might. Nyx could try to block her path. Rebekah felt confident she could handle Nyx, but Nyx could slow her down, and the others could prevent her exit. The attempt might prove futile. Derrick and Miriam might have already escaped. They excelled at that.

Rebekah scanned the room, hoping to cool her growing anger. It wasn't helping. Everything here looked old. The room smelled odd. The boys wore undershirts—not a collar among them. And weird-looking faded-blue pants—not one of them wore slacks. They all wore athletic shoes, not a polished shoe in the room. Even the girls wore undershirts, faded-blue pants, and athletic shoes.

Rebekah wanted out of Pacific Edge, where the polished facade grated on her nerves until she could not endure another day. However, she did not think she could grow accustomed to this place either.

Along with anger, fear filled Rebekah's thoughts. Angry because Derrick and Miriam left her out of their discussion. Scared because her sister's whereabouts were unknown. Prime wanted Anna, and Rebekah didn't even know what Prime was, had never heard of it, and only knew people here thought it was more formidable than the Chosen. But as the seconds ticked by, she recognized her fear was layered. She did not want to look beyond the surface because there existed thoughts she'd rather not contemplate.

Not the least of which, "*Why did I escape with Miriam in the first place?*"

Rebekah's obvious anger seemed straightforward. Derrick and Miriam left her alone with strangers, kept her out of their conversation.

Silence did not help. Alone time was unnecessary. Rebekah didn't want time for thoughts, deep or otherwise. But she couldn't avoid thinking, and it exposed a hidden resentment that could not be unseen.

Rebekah was furious because she was on Derrick's list for The Choosing.

And she wanted him to pick her.

She wanted him to want her.

But Derrick would not have picked her. He didn't want her.

There it was. Floating around in her head. Unwilling to hold still for examination. It wasn't because she loved Derrick. She did not. She wanted him to pick her because she was competitive. Truth? She hated The Choosing. Hated that her life held no significance beyond being a prize in a contest that would define her life. Having spotted that little detail helped. In Pacific Edge, she had no voice. The only thing she could control was trying to win the contest of The Choosing.

Had she drawn a worse potential husband, she might have tried to escape sooner without Miriam's help. But Derrick was okay as far as forced marriage candidates go. She thought him not abusive, which was important because, in the world of the Chosen, they never blame husbands for marital problems. It's always the wife's fault. Wives were often banished for complaining about an abusive husband.

Derrick would have been an okay husband by Chosen standards. Arrogant enough to earn a decent living, which meant he could afford a companion or two to satisfy his lust. She had some control over that. Be just cold enough that he needed a companion or two. That would give her time to do whatever Chosen women do, which, near as she could tell, was limited to buying clothes and getting their hair, fingernails, and toenails done.

Derrick was self-centered. He would have been more interested in himself, how he looked, how he felt, what he had, what he wanted—the perfect Chosen husband. Derrick was a simple soul but not aggressive. When he decked Marcus Carver, it surprised her as much as a person can be surprised. She would have never thought it possible.

Now it was coming into sharp focus. She wasn't mad at Derrick. She wasn't even mad at Jana Somersworth. Rebekah wanted to win. But Derrick did not want her. He wanted Jana Somersworth.

No, the person she hated was herself. Because she was just as self-centered as Derrick. She wanted to win because it was in her own best self-interest. She had tried to snare Derrick to serve herself.

Why? That posed an interesting question. Was she just being selfish?

Rebekah closed her eyes. Selfish, yes, but more than that. Unsatisfying though it would have been, life with Derrick would have provided her a slight taste of freedom. Not much, just a little.

Miriam and Derrick kept asking why she had escaped. Derrick thought it was about him, which she anticipated, and there was a little truth in that. But there were other things she wasn't willing to share. Some things she wasn't sure of herself.

Beyond wanting to win at The Choosing, beyond wanting the life he would have provided—she liked him. Somewhere under his self-centered shallowness, a decent person lurked. In Pacific Edge, could anything have scratched the surface hard enough to free Derrick's inner self? She did not know. Now, she sensed Derrick was free, and she liked what she saw.

But it was too late for her. She saw how Derrick looked at Nyx. Even when Nyx seemed pissed at him, he could not hide his feelings for her.

Why did I escape? Freedom?

And there it was. Freedom is what she wanted. Now, she had it. But the cost was too expensive. Yes, she was mad.

Livid.

With herself.

Because of her selfishness, because she focused on her own freedom, she forgot Anna. Now, Anna was lost, hunted. Freedom sounded great, but had she known the price, Rebekah would have stayed in Pacific Edge.

Miriam and Derrick were not out of the room for long, but long enough for Rebekah to make a decision. She was going for Anna, with or without them.

But when the door opened, Rebekah saw they had additional problems. AJ Patel followed Derrick and Miriam into the room.

Patel walked straight to Rebekah.

Rebekah jumped to her feet, unwilling to let Patel tower over her.

"Hello, Rebekah. I trust you have a stun gun in your bag. Please don't use it on me until I explain why I'm here," Patel said.

Patel then walked to the back of the room. Coach Browning and Sheriff Collins greeted Patel with smiles, handshakes, and hugs. From the beginning, Rebekah had a bad feeling about this hearing. With each passing second, those bad feelings grew worse.

Miriam sat, separating herself from Rebekah, forcing Derrick to sit in the middle. Derrick did not know AJ Patel, except for what Miriam had said about him. Whether his presence was good or evil remained unknown. It seemed odd that Patel showed up looking for Miriam but stranger still that everyone here knew him. Patel had connections with the people here long before his contact with Miriam.

*　*　*

Since leaving Pacific Edge, Derrick had learned how little he understood about pretty much everything. But of one thing he was certain: AJ Patel's involvement was no coincidence.

As Derrick tried to make sense of things—from the punch that started it all, to Miriam finding him in the middle of nowhere, to the vast complex hidden in the mountains, even to the robot named Charlie—a discussion in science that he'd paid little attention to suddenly seemed relevant.

Because James Carver Academy did not teach science and the Chosen considered it blasphemy, Derrick tuned the discussion out. Tuning out proved unnecessary most days because he was in Earth science: rocks, plants, weather patterns, and other natural processes, which were not quite as evil as Derrick had envisioned. However, Mr. D., the teacher, taught other science classes and tolerated, if not enjoyed, venturing into other science-related discussions.

One day the class got off-topic, tumbling into a rambling discussion that Derrick could not follow. Something about multiple universes. Now, he wished he'd paid closer attention. Because it seemed someone had transported him to a different dimension. He could make little sense of what was happening here. Perhaps he had been transported to an alternate universe, not just a new town. That would be easier to accept than the reality before him.

2

A LOUD BANG SOUNDED AT THE front of the room. Derrick startled. Turning toward the racket, he watched Nyx smack the podium with a wooden hammer for a second time. He flinched even though he saw the blow coming.

"Allen, welcome and please sit. We are in session," Nyx said.

Patel nodded. "Sorry, I am late." He held up the case in his right hand. "Akira asked me to bring a few items." Patel sat next to Sheriff Collins, placing the case on the floor.

Derrick glanced at Miriam. Miriam stared at the case. Turning his head to the other side, Derrick looked at Rebekah. Rebekah looked angry. Derrick grew more confused, which seemed impossible.

Henry Clark stood. "I motion we vote on the proposals before the council."

"Wait!" Akira stood.

Nyx banged the hammer. "Out of order. Akira, sit down. There is a motion before the council. Do I hear a second?"

"I will not sit down," Akira snarled, fists to her side.

This was new. Derrick had not witnessed Akira angry. That her anger was not directed at him was the only good thing about this situation thus far.

"I have some things to say before we vote, and you are going to listen to me," Akira said.

Nyx looked perplexed. Antonio gave a slight nod. Derrick's confusion did not improve.

Nyx said, "Go ahead, but be brief."

Akira tossed her hair to one side. "I have learned something about where Rebekah, Miriam, and Derrick were before returning."

Henry Clark interrupted. "Where were they?"

"I can't say," Akira said.

"Won't say," Clark scowled.

"That too. We should let them stay. Or perhaps a more accurate description is to let them use Potterville as a base for supplies and such. I want to support them, but not just because we've become friends, but because it is the safest thing for Potterville."

"How can allowing them to stay, make Potterville safer?" Henry Clark asked.

Clearly, Henry Clark, quarterback, had extended his leadership to this meeting. Derrick doubted anyone would consider Akira's suggestion unless Clark embraced it, and that seemed unlikely. Derrick appreciated Akira standing up for them, but he did not understand why she put herself in such a position. Derrick felt more confused than ever.

"I can't tell you that. But I'm serious. Our safety depends on them," Akira said.

Derrick scanned the back of the room. Coach Browning's brow furrowed. Sheriff Collins's face looked twice as angry/concerned/confused as did Browning's. Patel's head cocked to one side, nodding as if it made sense.

"This is nonsense," Clark said, standing.

"Sit down, Henry," Nyx said, "It's not nonsense. What Akira says is true."

"Then tell us where they have been," Clark said.

"I can't and I won't," Nyx said.

"Then back to my motion to vote," Clark said.

Larry Kinkead said, "I second the motion."

Nyx looked at Akira. "Sorry, Akira. We must vote now. Those in favor of allowing Derrick, Miriam, and Rebekah to stay, raise your hands."

Akira sat and lifted her right hand into the air.

"Those in favor of them leaving but helping them relocate?"

Nyx scanned the room. She glanced at Derrick and then raised her hand.

"Those in favor of making them leave immediately?" Nyx asked.

Henry Clark and Larry Kinkead raised their hands. Henry glared at Malcolm Cross. Malcolm let out a long breath and raised his hand.

"Let the record reflect that Henry Clark's motion has the majority vote," Nyx whispered.

Malcolm looked at Derrick. "Sorry, bro."

"The student council's meeting regarding Derrick King, Miriam King, and Rebekah Ford is now closed," Nyx said.

Antonio Morales stood, groaning. "Not so fast, my friends. We are not done here."

3

ANTONIO LIMPED TO THE FRONT OF THE ROOM, backed up to the teacher's desk and hoisted himself to a sitting position. A bead of sweat formed on Antonio's brow. Derrick assumed from the pain in his leg and wondered why he didn't use his crutches. Although perspiration glistened on Antonio's forehead, Derrick felt a chill, a cool breeze because the air condition unit had activated. Something Derrick had not thought about in Potterville was the up and down cycle of heating and cooling. The equipment here was not as sophisticated as in Pacific Edge. Derrick was like the equipment here, unsophisticated. He had no idea what was happening.

"Nyx, take a seat. I'll take it from here." Antonio looked over his shoulder. "Derrick, Miriam, Rebekah, take seats with the others."

Frowning, Nyx walked to Antonio and held the wooden hammer out to him. Antonio waved her off. "No need," he said.

Derrick, Miriam, and Rebekah took seats together near the front but off to one side. Glancing to the back of the room, Coach Browning gave Derrick a weak smile.

"I have a few questions," Antonio began, "to clear some things up in my head. First," Antonio looked to the back of the room, "Allen, what are you doing here?"

"Hello, Antonio. I am here filling in for Ms. Donna," Patel said.

"Cut the crap, Allen. These are serious decisions we are making. I'm going to ask one more time. Why are you here? And your answer best ring true if you want to remain in this meeting."

Derrick had never heard Antonio speak to anyone in such a manner or with such authority. Resisting the urge to turn and look at Patel was futile. Fortunately, everyone else turned to watch his response.

Patel cleared his throat. "Very well. I am here because of Miriam and Derrick. And I brought supplies Miriam requested." He paused for a moment and then added, "As it turns out, I'm here because of Anna Ford as well. Sorry, Rebekah. I'm certain you are worried about Anna, as we all are."

Rebekah started out of her seat. Miriam grabbed her arm.

"What do you know about Anna?" Rebekah demanded.

"More than you," Patel said with more boldness than seemed warranted.

"What's that supposed to mean?" Rebekah snarled.

"Tell her, Miriam. She has a right to know," Patel said.

Rebekah glared at Miriam. "Tell me what?"

Miriam looked at Patel. "Now, is not a good time."

"It will never be a good time," Patel said, "So now is as good as any. Besides, Antonio should know as well."

Turning to Rebekah, Miriam said. "I've wanted to tell you, but it never seemed like the right time. AJ is right about one thing. There will never be a right time. And what I'm about to say should not change how you feel about Anna or your relationship with her."

Rebekah's chest heaved. "What? What are you saying?"

Miriam said, "Anna is not your sister. I suspect, deep down, you may already know that."

Rebekah said, "Take that back. Anna is to my sister. We grew up together."

Miriam studied Rebekah. "When did Anna come to live with you?"

Tears started flowing down Rebekah's cheeks. "Okay. My parents adopted Anna when she was in the third grade. But she's, my sister."

Miriam glanced at Akira and then turned to Patel. "Akira, AJ, have you ever heard of an adoption in Pacific Edge?"

Neither Akira nor Patel spoke for a few moments.

"I have not, but I left Pacific Edge at a young age," Akira said.

Patel took a deep breath. "You know the answer, Miriam."

"I do, but Rebekah does not," Miriam said.

"There are no adoptions in Pacific Edge. Or any other Chosen Community," Patel said.

"You're lying," Rebekah cried.

"We are not," Miriam said. "I know how you feel."

"You don't know everything! And you can't know how I feel," Rebekah said through sobs and a fountain that had erupted from her nose.

Miriam reached out to her, but Rebekah pulled away.

Tears ran down Miriam's cheeks. She turned to Derrick. "I know exactly how you feel because I felt the same when I learned Derrick is not my brother."

4

SEVERAL TIMES DURING THE PAST FEW DAYS, Derrick felt certain his life could not worsen, only to learn another level of despair existed below what he thought was the bottom. Yet, he had suspected this. He hated to admit it, but even in Pacific Edge, he wondered how he and Miriam could be related. When he learned they shared the same nightmares in which he was Number 7, and she was number 6, that's when Derrick knew, but he forced the thought from his mind.

Miriam looked at Derrick. "I'm sorry to tell you this way. I was afraid this might happen. But you will always be my brother."

Antonio said, "This is disturbing, especially for you, mi amigo." Antonio looked at Derrick. "But you still have not answered my question, Mr. Patel. Why are you here?"

Patel held up one hand. "Just a little patience, please, Antonio. The fate of these three is a perilous decision, and I don't think you realize just how serious—although I appreciate you understand it is important—more disclosure may cast additional light." Patel looked at Rebekah. "Rebekah, why are you here?"

Rebekah wiped her face on her sleeve, not ladylike, but Derrick had witnessed it before.

"I don't see why that is important," Rebekah whimpered.

"Honesty is important," Patel said.

"It's complicated. Mostly, I wanted freedom. Had I known Anna would follow us, I would not have left," Rebekah said.

Patel nodded as if he understood. "So, it had nothing to do with Derrick?"

"No," Rebekah snapped.

Nyx frowned at Derrick, and had he not known better, he would have sworn her eyes changed color. Then another layer of despair overtook him. The student council voted three to two that Rebekah, Miriam, himself be removed from Potterville immediately. He would never see Nyx again. Antonio's actions were irrelevant.

"So, that you were on Derrick's list for The Choosing had no impact on your decision?" Patel whispered.

"No. Not really. Maybe a little. It's complicated," Rebekah said.

"What's this Choosing?" Nyx asked, still glaring at Derrick.

"Why don't you explain it, Derrick," Patel said.

Earlier, Derrick felt cold. Now, sweat formed on his face. Derrick cleared his throat, then looked at the floor. "It's how the Chosen select their wives. Rebekah was on my list."

"And you felt that was unimportant? Not worth telling me? Even after Rebekah showed up here?" Nyx demanded.

"I did not know how to tell you. I did not plan to pick Rebekah. Sorry, Rebekah. And I didn't think it was important because I was no longer in Pacific Edge. It became a moot issue." Derrick paused, still looking at the floor. "When I was in Pacific Edge, I thought The Choosing was a perfect system. Now, I'm embarrassed I did not see how unfair and degrading it was. I felt ashamed. And…"

Rebekah interrupted. "It's not Derrick's fault. It was how they did things there. None of us had a choice in the matter. Derrick was just doing what they taught him. Besides, I wasn't Derrick's pick, and I knew it."

"Yet, you came here," Nyx said.

"I did," Rebekah replied. "Like I said, it's complicated."

Derrick continued staring at the floor, hoping this would be the end of it, knowing it was not.

"So, who was your choice?" Nyx asked.

Derrick looked up, although he could hardly bear seeing Nyx's expression. "Her name was Jana."

Nyx glared at him.

"I know I've lied many times, but I'm speaking honestly. I loved The Choosing, the power of it, that I was in control of it, but now, I see it was a despicable way of doing things. I've apologized to Rebekah, but I'm certain it isn't enough. It will never be enough. Jana Somersworth was my pick, not because I loved her or even liked her, but she fit the criteria. If you hate me, I understand. I hate myself most of the time."

Akira said, "Derrick, don't hate yourself. You did the only thing you knew to do."

"Thanks, Akira, but I should have known better," Derrick said.

"Stop!" Antonio stood and then, grimacing, sat again. "This is not helping…"

Patel held up his hand. "Ah, but it is. We are getting to the core."

"How are we getting to the heart of anything?" Antonio asked.

"We are starting to understand how Derrick thought and how he was supposed to behave. He endorsed the Chosen way. Yet, he failed to act as they anticipated. Derrick's failure is the key."

5

FOR MIRIAM, NONE OF THIS WAS NEW information, but perhaps she failed to understand the implications. She knew Derrick had failed the test, but she did not comprehend the importance. In focusing on Derrick, she had not considered they were also testing her. Not just after they exiled Derrick, but her entire life. Had she failed too? And what was the purpose of the tests? She did not know. Then there was Anna Ford. Miriam had only recently recognized Anna was also a test subject.

Henry Clark stood. "Mr. Patel, you arrived late. We already have three motions before the student council, and we have voted. There's nothing left to discuss."

Antonio cleared his throat. Waving his hand, he said, "Excuse me. When did you take over the council, Henry?"

Henry faced Antonio. "Sorry, just trying to help."

"Henry, if I need your help, I'll ask for it. Now, sit down and shut up. Got it?" Antonio asked.

Henry sat.

Jim Priest jumped up. "Henry is right. You guys voted, and these three gotta leave town. Me and my friends would be happy to drive them outside of town and dump them."

Antonio remained calm, but Derrick saw Antonio was not calm under the surface. While he had not been here long, and reading people was not his strength, Derrick never suspected Antonio pulled any weight in this process. That no one challenged him, told Derrick that the others knew this side of Antonio already.

"Jim, Nyx has warned you once. Sheriff, escort Jim and his friend out, and if possible, can your deputy escort them home and ensure they stay put?"

"Sure thing," Collins said. He motioned Jim's friend to his feet and then pointed to the door. "No problems from either of you, or you'll spend the night in a jail cell. Understand?"

Jim Priest sulked to the door. Derrick didn't like him already. Once Priest left the room, he swore the oxygen level increased by 20%.

"What about Red?" Malcolm asked.

"What about him?" Antonio asked.

"Well, should he get to stay? I mean, he comes with Jim."

"Has he done anything wrong?" Antonio asked.

"No," Malcolm said.

Antonio paused, then looked at Derrick. "What do you think, Derrick?"

Stunned, Derrick sat straight. Glanced at Red, and then back to Antonio, and then at Miriam. "It's your meeting."

"You have a gift of stating the obvious. But not so good at answering questions," Antonio said, a slight curl formed at the corner of his mouth.

Derrick looked at Red again, remembering when Red protected him after football practice, not because they were friends, but because he was a teammate. Not that Red could protect him here because Red had no vote. Turning back to Antonio, Derrick said, "I would like for him to stay."

Antonio nodded. "Works for me. Mr. Patel, is there anything else? Or can we proceed?"

"Yes, just one thing. It's rather important," Patel said.

Antonio waved his hand in a hurry-up gesture.

"Miriam, did you discover why the Tribunal wanted Derrick back?" Patel asked.

Typically, Miriam felt confident making decisions. That's because, typically, she was in control of the situation. Not the case here. How much to say? She did not know why Derrick was significant, or why his failed test so angered someone of importance.

"Well? Did you learn anything or not? Let's start there. It's a simple yes or no answer," Patel said.

"Yes,"

"And why did they want him back?"

Miriam stared at Patel. "I don't know why."

"Let me rephrase the question to Derrick. Derrick, what did that man, I believe his name is Bruce Bolden, promise you if you returned to Pacific Edge?"

"That I would receive a full pardon and apology," Derrick said.

Patel said, "Generous offer. Yet you refused. Why?"

Derrick looked at Nyx. "Because I wanted to stay here."

"Best decision of your life, too, I might add," Patel said, and then added, "Miriam, did you learn their actual plan for Derrick?"

Miriam exhaled. "Yes."

"Explain, please," Patel said.

Miriam started crying. With her voice cracking, she said, "They planned to deconstruct him."

Nyx said, "They what?"

AJ Patel walked to the front of the room. "They planned to take him apart, piece by piece, while he was still alive until his heart stopped. It's a living autopsy. The technicians wear noise-canceling headphones and listen to their favorite music. They attach instruments to the test subject to monitor bodily functions, including pain level. So, the test subject does not die too soon, they administer drugs to keep the heart beating and the subject conscious. The procedure takes hours. They are in no hurry."

Now Nyx, Akira, Antonio, L. Linda, and even Mr. Patel were crying. Derrick felt tears flowing down his cheeks but did not wipe them away, fearing it would bring attention to the fact he was crying.

"That's murder. It's not allowed in Chosen Communities," Rebekah stammered.

Patel said, "I agree. It's murder in the most sadistic way possible. But the Chosen don't call it murder because they don't recognize Derrick or Miriam as people. They are test subjects and therefore merely property."

Patel turned to Antonio. "I am sorry for taking the council's time. You recognized that this was a serious decision before I arrived, but I thought you should understand just how serious."

Patel returned to his seat.

Derrick resisted the urge to look at Coach Browning.

Through sobs, Akira said, "Can we reconsider our vote?"

Antonio stood, grimacing. "You may not."

"But…"

Antonio held his palm toward Akira. "A new vote is unnecessary because I made my decision before AJ enlightened us further. But what we've learned has increased my resolve."

Antonio used one hand on the desk to steady himself as he rose to his full height. "As council president, I veto your decision. But first, I have a few questions and comments about the process. Nyx, why did you not vote with Akira?"

Nyx wiped her tears away with both hands. "Because I hoped someone would vote with me to at least give them support in leaving."

Antonio nodded. "Okay. I can accept that." Then he stared at Malcolm. "Malcolm, I'm disappointed. I thought I knew you better."

Derrick did not look at Malcolm.

"I'm disappointed in myself," Malcolm said, voice trembling.

"Henry, you're the leader with these two. That's clear. You have the skills to lead, but you don't have the heart," Antonio said.

Henry said, "I was thinking of what's best for the town. I didn't like sending them away, but it seemed best for the rest of us."

"Best for the rest of us?" Antonio limped toward Henry. He placed his hand on Henry's shoulder. "Brother, what makes Potterville special?"

Henry squirmed in his seat. "I don't know. The councils, I guess."

"You repeat the words, but they have become meaningless. Potterville is special because we came together to make our lives the best they could be under Chosen tyranny," Antonio said.

Antonio continued, "Potterville is special because it took courage to come together and coming together strengthened us."

"Strength," floated on whispers through the room and then with louder voices followed, "Courage."

"My friends, because of our strength and courage, we fight against injustice and greed."

Everyone said, "Fight."

"But they are not from Potterville," Henry offered.

Antonio walked back to the desk and sat. "True. Derrick wasn't invited here, but he had little choice in the matter. He lied to us. But he admitted his mistake. When Derrick twisted his ankle and fell near the end of the cross-country race, most people, including the people in this room, would have called it a day. Maybe hobbled to the finish, maybe not. Did Derrick show strength getting up and not limping but pushing himself to the finish?"

Derrick looked around the room, saw nodding heads. Malcolm said, "He did."

Antonio continued, "When Derrick went from a limping stagger to a running pace, did we not witness courage? And then to push on to win, we saw fight, unlike anything I've ever seen. On that day, Derrick King embodied the Strength, Courage, and Fight we hold dear. And on that day, Derrick became a Bearcat. That's how I see it."

Henry turned to Derrick. "I'm sorry, man. I screwed up. Forgive me?"

Before Derrick could speak, a phone sounded at the back of the room. Everyone turned to see Sheriff Collins retrieve his phone from a black leather pouch on his belt.

"Sheriff Collins —"

A long pause and then,

"I see. Not good.—

Thanks. I owe you one."

Collins stood. "We have problems. That was my brother-in-law. He is stationed at the Carver Military Base Number 27. They are gearing up for a major deployment."

"Where to?" Browning asked.

"Here," Collins said.

6

MURMURS, WHISTLES, AND WHISPERS FILLED THE ROOM to the point Derrick heard no actual words, but the implications were clear. Things had changed and not in a good way. One thing remained the same: Miriam, Rebekah, and he must still leave regardless of Antonio's intervention. Although he deemed avoiding deconstruction important, protecting Potterville was essential.

Coach Browning stood. "Coming here? Why? When?"

"I think we know why. My brother-in-law knows they are to surround Potterville tonight and check every vehicle coming in and out. Special forces will send search teams at dawn to execute orders. Only the search teams know the specifics, but I suspect it's about finding Derrick, Miriam, Rebekah, and Anna," Collins said.

Henry stood, but before he could say anything, Antonio said, "No, we are not taking another vote, but I am open to discussing a plan."

Henry said, "Uh, I was going to suggest ordering pizza. I think we'll be here for a while, and I'm starving."

"Accept my apology. Pizza is an excellent idea. Sheriff, I don't suppose you'd waive the law and let us order beer?" Antonio paused for a moment and then smiled. "I didn't think so. Malcolm, would you take up a collection?" Antonio asked.

"No collection is necessary. I'll pay for it," Miriam said, and then continued, "Can Derrick, Nyx, Akira," Miriam paused, "Rebekah and I have a few minutes in private?"

"You may not unless you include me. I'm out on a limb here," Antonio said.

Miriam looked at Derrick, then turned to Nyx. Nyx nodded.

"Sure. Is there a room we could use?" Miriam asked.

Antonio hobbled to the desk where he'd sat and gathered his crutches. "Malcolm, order pizza and sodas. Get plenty. We'll chip in if needed."

Again, Miriam said, "Chipping in will not be necessary." She handed Malcolm several bills. "I don't know what things cost. There's more if that's not enough."

On crutches, Antonio said, "Follow me."

Larry Kinkead said, "Why a secret meeting?"

Without turning to look at Larry, Antonio said, "If you want to leave, you can. If you want to stay, shut up."

Antonio led them to a classroom. Derrick knew the place. It was the living-room-style Mandarin classroom.

As everyone found chairs or sat on the sofa, Akira said, "I'll prepare tea."

"We don't need tea," Antonio said.

"It is custom here," Akira said.

Antonio looked at Akira. "Tea would be perfect."

Miriam remained standing. "Okay, if I start?"

Antonio waved his hand.

"Rebekah, I know you won't like this, but we must return to… the place we can't talk about."

"I know that. I'm not stupid," Rebekah said.

Miriam said, "You are not." Miriam scanned the rest of the room. "To protect Potterville, we must leave before the military arrives. We have work to do and can't risk being caught or followed."

Nyx held up her hand. "Miriam, Antonio is the only one here who doesn't know what you are talking about."

"I don't want to put him in danger. The less he knows, the safer he is," Miriam said.

Nyx glanced at Derrick and then said, "I appreciate you want to protect us. I understand how dangerous the place might be, but you can't do this alone. Think about what Antonio said. Why Potterville is special. Strength, courage, fight. It's possible the only people able to defeat whatever threatens us are in the building. You can trust Antonio. I believe that with all my heart," Nyx said.

Miriam looked at Antonio. "So, we found something in the mountains. It's dangerous, but we also might find something there to help defend ourselves and Potterville. We have to go back," Miriam looked at Rebekah, "We have to go back before we can find Anna."

To Derrick's surprise, Rebekah nodded.

"And to make that happen, I must keep a promise," Miriam said.

Akira returned carrying a tray with cups and tea. No one spoke as she served each person. Derrick thought tea was unnecessary but realized he was wrong with one sip. Tea was precisely what he needed. Something simple, grounded, traditional.

Miriam said, "I'm sorry to be cryptic, Antonio, it's just that…"

Antonio sipped his tea and then waved Miriam off. "No worries, continue. I'm a big boy."

Miriam said, "Nyx is right. The place we found is dangerous. I can't explain how it is dangerous."

Antonio asked, "Like destroy the entire planet dangerous?"

"Exactly," Miriam said.

Antonio's eyes widened. "Oh. I see."

"So, as I was saying, we must go back. First, I must fix a hard drive. Akira, I did not know it was AJ Patel bringing the hard drives. As you probably have gathered, I know him from Pacific Edge. He helped me there, but I am unsure of his motives. I'm not sure I can trust him." Miriam paused. "And the last time I saw him… well, things didn't go well."

Akira set her cup on its saucer. "What does that mean?"

"Uh, I zapped him with the stun gun."

Akira said, "You've zapped several people. Three are sitting in this room."

Miriam studied Akira for a moment. "You trust AJ?"

"I do. We know him as Allen here. Plus, working on the hard drive is a mechanical process. It isn't connected to a computer. Allen can either fix it, or he can't. But he won't know what's on it," Akira said.

"Okay," Miriam said, "I also need to copy the old hard drives to new ones. They must be exact copies. Can you help me do that?" Miriam asked.

"You want clones. Yes, I can do that," Akira said.

Miriam smiled. "Fantastic. How long will it take?"

"Depends on the computer. Derrick has a decent machine. A few hours, depending on the amount of data. We could use his laptop too," Akira said.

Miriam took a deep breath. "Then we can be out of here tonight before they close off the town."

"Who is 'we'?" Antonio asked.

"Derrick, Rebekah, and I," Miriam said.

Derrick thought about this for a moment before speaking. It made sense, yet it didn't. They agreed to stick together, and yes, the fewer who knew about the hidden complex, the better, yet… "When they come looking for the three of us, who is at risk here?" Derrick asked.

"What does that mean?" Miriam demanded. "They want us."

Derrick said, "But who might they arrest for helping us? Who might they use as leverage against us? Plus, we need to fix things. We got lucky the first time."

"What do you mean, 'you got lucky'?" Antonio asked.

Rebekah said, "We fixed something that might have made people here sick—or killed them."

No one spoke for a moment. What an incredible situation to be in. Derrick considered for a moment how his life had changed in such a short time. A few weeks ago, he thought he had it made. He had a perfect life. Now, his life was far from perfect. Yet, he liked it better.

"There are others who will be at risk because we disappeared. How do we keep them safe?" Derrick asked.

"Amazing," Miriam said.

Derrick said, "What's amazing?"

"A valid question. You are right. They might hold people hostage to force our surrender," Miriam said.

Derrick didn't like the way Miriam said that, although she had stated his concern accurately.

"I'm not sure I understand," Antonio said.

"They might think we've grown close enough to certain people here that they will threaten them if we don't surrender," Derrick said.

"Like who?" Antonio asked.

"Like Nyx," Rebekah said.

Antonio nodded. "Oh. Right."

"And Akira," Miriam added.

They were right about Akira and Nyx, but something else nagged at Derrick, just out of reach at the edge of his thoughts. Then he realized. "We still need to fix stuff. Next time, it might not be so easy."

A knock sounded at the door. From the hallway, Henry said, "Pizza will be here soon."

"Be there shortly," Antonio said and then added, "Save us some."

Antonio held his finger to his lips and waited for a few moments. When he was confident Henry was gone, Antonio said, "So, those that go, Akira, Nyx, Derrick, Miriam, Rebekah, and me. Anyone else?"

"You?" Derrick asked.

"Yep. I would not miss this for the world."

"But you're hurt. You need to heal. I heard surgery might be necessary," Derrick said.

"You are correct, but surgery is out of the question," Antonio said.

"Why is that?" Rebekah asked.

"My family is not what you call privileged. Mom is a cook at Potterville High, and dad works in the fields. They don't have medical insurance, few people do. I'll heal okay without surgery."

"But you won't compete again," Rebekah said.

"Probably not. But I'll never be a professional athlete."

"But don't you need a scholarship to go to college?" Derrick asked.

Antonio shrugged. "How did you know that?"

Derrick said, "I don't know. Someone mentioned it."

"I'll find another way."

"How much does the surgery cost?" Miriam asked.

"I don't know. Too much. Thousands," Antonio said.

"I'll pay for it," Miriam said.

Everyone stared at Miriam.

"What? It's their money," Miriam said.

"What about school?" Derrick said.

"What about it?" Nyx asked.

"Tomorrow's Monday. You should all be back in school," Derrick said and then added, "I should be back in school."

Nyx said, "It's spring break. Were you not paying attention? Someone must have mentioned it."

Derrick didn't know what spring break meant. Someone might have mentioned it, but he had not paid attention. "Maybe someone said something, but I missed it, or didn't pay attention, or didn't understand, or all of those things."

"Spring break means no school next week," Nyx said.

"What about your parents?" Derrick asked.

"Good question. We'll figure it out," Nyx said.

Derrick said. "What about fixing stuff? We don't know what we are doing. Antonio might be able to help. The rest of us…"

"What?" Nyx said. "We're just girls?"

"No. Well, yes. It might take heavy lifting and other skills we don't have," Miriam said.

"And Derrick has skills?" Nyx asked, her voice a higher pitch than normal.

"She has a point," Derrick said.

"So, who can help?" Antonio asked and then added, "We need solutions."

Derrick thought for a moment and then remembered something Mr. Fletcher had said. "How about Red?"

"The big kid who wasn't supposed to be in the meeting?" Miriam asked. Derrick said, "Yes."

"Red tried to take your head off the first day of football. Bro, that dude don't like you. Why would you think of taking him to the place you can't tell people about?" Antonio asked.

"Mr. Fletcher said Red is his grandson. He said Red can fix things," Derrick paused, glanced at Miriam, "And Mr. Fletcher can impress upon Red the need to keep this quiet."

"That makes little sense," Antonio said.

Miriam said. "But can we trust him? He's not even on the council. Right?" Miriam looked at Antonio.

"He is not. He's friends with Jim Priest, and I don't trust Priest."

"I trust Red," Derrick said. "After football practice, Priest tried to pick a fight with me. Red stood up to him. Said it was because I was on the team."

Akira said, "That's true. I was there. Red stepped in and Priest got pissed. Brought up their years of friendship and how Red was ending it. But Red didn't back down."

"Humph." Antonio drank the rest of his tea. "He's the backup left offensive tackle. He could start there, but he likes defense. No person is more important to a QB than left tackle because the left tackle protects the quarterback's blindside. The QB has gotta trust the person in that position. Henry keeps trying to convince Red to play left tackle. Perhaps you are on to something, Derrick."

"Maybe we should ask Coach Browning first," Derrick said.

Antonio cocked his head to one side. "Browning? I don't understand."

"Malcolm said Browning has a sixth sense about people. At least with sports. Perhaps it extends to other things as well," Derrick said.

"Is that it?" Antonio glanced around the room. "Derrick, Miriam, Rebekah, Akira, Nyx, Red, and me. That was easier than I thought."

Rebekah said, "I don't see how Antonio can go. He's on crutches and there's a lot of walking."

"We can reduce the walking," Miriam said.

Rebekah said, "But how…"

Miriam held up her hand. "Trust me. I have a plan."

Rebekah frowned. "But he needs surgery, and what if he makes the injury worse?"

Miriam studied Rebekah, and then a slight smile formed on her face. "We'll take care of him. If we survive, we'll figure a way to get his surgery done."

"That sounds great but unlikely," Antonio said. "Let's get back to the others. I hope there's some pizza left."

"Not done yet," Derrick said.

"What now?" Antonio asked.

"Families. What if they do something to Nyx's mom, or Akira's and your parents? They could hold them hostage as leverage," Derrick said.

Antonio said, "But how would they know…"

"Duh. It's obvious," Rebekah said.

Miriam said, "True. And our Keepers had Nyx and Akira's names listed in their work area."

"Our Keepers?" Derrick asked.

"Sorry. Something else I didn't tell you. Father and Mother did not live in our house. They worked there. What we thought was their bedroom was a monitoring station for watching us," Miriam said.

Derrick nodded. He should have known this, but he had not thought about it. It didn't surprise him, but it still hurt. *So, who are our parents? Maybe we don't have parents. Incubated in some sort of oversized test tube.*

Not people.

Just property.

Derrick did not ask who their parents were or how they came into the world. He didn't want to know. Someday, he'd learn the truth, but not today.

"Ideas?" Antonio asked.

"The sheriff can monitor them," Miriam offered.

"Not good enough. He only has one full-time deputy," Antonio said.

"Could they stay at home until we get back? Maybe the sheriff has some volunteers who would help," Rebekah said.

"Volunteers? Against military personnel? Not good enough," Derrick said.

"They need someplace safe. Someplace secret," Antonio said.

"My mom will not go for that. She won't let me disappear for a few days either. I'll have to sneak out and pay the consequences later," Nyx said.

"Same here," Akira said.

Rebekah said, "At least we don't have parents to deal with. So, we have that going for ourselves."

"Exactly," Miriam said and then laughed.

"You have a sick sense of humor," Nyx said.

"You have no idea," Derrick said.

Antonio stood, grabbed his crutches. "We need adults to help with this, and I need pizza. We are in agreement. Right? They need to hide someplace safe, even if Collins has to arrest them. Damn, my mom is going to be so pissed."

7

DERRICK HEARD AN ODD SOUND, faint and far away. He recognized it but didn't know why, yet he knew it meant danger. He did not know why he understood that either. His thinking had changed after the robot did the hypnosis thing. He could not explain it, and he didn't want to acknowledge it. Soon, ignoring it would be impossible.

As Rebekah and Miriam entered the classroom, Nyx grabbed Derrick's arm, stopping him in the hallway. "Can we talk?"

"Sure," Derrick said.

Nyx said, "I'm hurt you didn't tell me about you and Rebekah, but I understand. I won't get in the way."

"What do you mean, get in the way?" Derrick paused. "Oh. It's not like that. There is no Rebekah and me. I should have told you. I didn't know how… I was afraid that… I didn't want to…"

Nyx smiled. "Shut up." And then she gave him a quick kiss, spun around, and disappeared into the classroom.

Derrick stood in the hall, staring at the classroom door. After a few moments, he went inside.

"Dude," Malcolm said, "Want to share the good news?"

"What good news?" Derrick asked.

"Whatever has you smiling like that," Malcolm said.

Derrick felt sure he turned several shades of red. He looked at Nyx and realized he should not have, but she gave him a sly smile. "Oh, uh, nothing really. Only glad we've made some decisions." Then Derrick said, "Where's Coach and Collins?"

"Fetching pizza," Henry said.

Miriam said, "I was going to buy. Where are they? I'll catch them."

"No need. Pizza is free. When the owner of the Flyn' Pie learned it was for the student council, he said no charge," Malcolm said, and then added, "You three have more support than we expected."

Collins and Browning returned, each carrying flat cardboard boxes. The aroma of pizza filled the room. Derrick's stomach growled. Then the sound Derrick heard earlier grew louder, its source closer. Everyone rushed to the pizza, causing a ruckus. But their banter did not conceal the sound.

"Does everyone hear that?" Derrick asked.

"Hear what?" Browning asked, stepping back, allowing the kids to grab pizza.

Derrick pointed in the sound's direction, toward the western corner where the wall met the ceiling. "That noise. Whop, whop, whop."

"I don't hear anything." Browning said.

"Amigo, your imagination has run amuck," Antonio said, limping to the closest desk with two slices of pizza draped over a paper plate.

Collins said, "I don't hear anything." He walked to a window, turned a metal handle in the center, and tilted the window outward.

To Derrick, the sound flooded into the room, yet no one seemed to notice.

Collins held his head to the window opening. "Nothing. No, wait. I can hear it. Faint. Helicopter."

Derrick knew what helicopters were, although he had never seen one in person. He saw them on New America Media news stories about the urban wars of the commoners. Now, he knew there were no commoner wars. The videos must have been from old wars. But these were real, and he could distinguish the sounds. Three of the machines—approaching fast.

"How many?" Browning asked, leaning his head toward the window.

"Can't tell," Collins said.

Derrick said, "Three."

"You don't know that," Rebekah said. "I can't even hear it." Rebekah joined Collins and Browning at the window. "Okay, I can hear it now. Just barely."

"If Derrick says there are three, believe it," Miriam said.

"Does he have supernatural hearing?" Rebekah asked.

"No, but he has specialized training," Miriam said.

"I don't have special training," Derrick said.

"You do, but you don't remember. That's why you could compete on the track team. You already had conditioning," Miriam said.

Rebekah said, "How is that possible? Derrick never left the house. He didn't even walk to James Carver Academy."

"He left several nights a week. I didn't know until I saw his file," Miriam said, then added. "Sorry, Derrick. More stuff I wanted to tell you when the right time came. You have skills we'll need. You gotta figure out how to access your memories and soon."

Derrick knew Miriam was correct. Not because he had an insight into his mysterious training, nor could he remember it, and he had no idea how to access it. He believed Miriam because she was always right.

Plus, she read his file.

His brain had leaked memories, like a dripping faucet. The seeping started when he learned Miriam shared his dreams. At the house in Pacific Edge, the faucet in his bathroom operated by the motion of his hands. The water temperature was exactly right, the flow abundant. But this faucet wasn't like that. It was unpredictable and he could not access it. This faucet was hidden deep in some dark corner of his mind. Memories dripping here and there. Part of him wanted to lock those memories out; part of him knew he could not.

Henry Clark joined them at the window. Larry and Malcolm followed.

"I don't hear anything," Henry said.

Sticking his ear next to the window, Malcolm said, "I hear it. Faint. Far off."

Browning motioned them away from the window. "You all best eat. Things may change quickly. L. Linda, your job is finished here. You need to go. The fewer we have here, the better. You can take a slice of pizza with you."

"I don't need to get home. I should stay. You know, take notes and such."

Collins said, "Not open for discussion, L. Linda. Now, grab a slice and scoot."

L. Linda packed her things into a backpack. She did not go to the pizza, but with her lower lip in a pout, she went to Derrick, put her hand on his shoulder, and said, "Please be safe. I'll wash dishes at the Bistro until you return." Then she kissed him on the cheek, stared at Browning, and huffed out the door.

Miriam glanced at Rebekah, shrugged, took one slice of pizza, and sat next to Akira.

Derrick noticed Red Badowski remained seated at the same desk he was in during the council meeting. Derrick looked at Nyx and nodded toward Red.

Nyx said, "Red, the meeting is over. Have some pizza."

Nyx put a slice on one plate and two on another, then motioned for Derrick to join her at the far side of the room. As they sat, Nyx whispered, "I'm scared and excited at the same time."

"I'm scared too. Not excited," Derrick said.

Nyx stuck her lower lip out.

"What?" Derrick asked.

"You're not excited about going on this adventure together?"

Derrick thought for a moment. He felt happy and sad that Nyx was going with them. Happy because she would be safe there, at least for a while. Sad because she would also be at substantial risk, and he did not know if he could protect her. "I would be happy if it were not dangerous." He took a bite of pizza, and then added, "I don't know if I can protect you."

Nyx frowned. "More likely, I'll be saving your ass. Besides, I'm not your responsibility to look after."

Carrying a plate with a single slice of pizza, Red approached the table. Nyx kicked out a chair. Red sat but said nothing.

Miriam walked up behind Derrick, placed her hand on his shoulder. "Akira and I are going to the next room with Mr. Patel to work on the hard drive. We should leave soon, not wait until tonight."

Derrick said, "Agreed. Those helicopters spell trouble. They might be sending an advance team. We can't let them find or follow us."

"I'm thinking the same thing and working on a plan," Miriam said, then walked toward the door where Akira and Patel stood waiting.

At some point, Derrick had to ask Red to join them on a dangerous mission he could not explain. Taking Red sounded simple when he said it. Now, the idea made little sense, and Red probably would not even consider it. They ate in silence. The silence became uncomfortable.

Red cleared his throat. "Thanks for inviting me, but I feel like a third wheel here."

"Third wheel?" Derrick was puzzled.

Red stood.

Nyx said, "Sit. We need to talk."

Red sat. Derrick thought he somehow looked smaller than usual.

"What about?" Red asked. "I know the rules. I won't say anything about the meeting, never have and never will."

"We know. I suspect that's why Antonio let you stay," Nyx said.

"But you let me stay," Red said.

"Only after I got a signal from Antonio."

"I don't understand," Derrick said.

"You and me both," Red added.

"Antonio is the council president, but he doesn't like to be in front of the room, keeping order and enforcing procedures. Says he thinks better when he just listens. The president doesn't vote, but he can veto the council's decision. He's never done that until today. You might call me the sergeant-at-arms. I keep things in order. Enforce procedures," Nyx said.

Derrick didn't understand the term, but Red nodded.

"We've never been friends," Red said, staring at Nyx. "So, why am I here, and I don't mean why was I allowed to stay. I mean, why am I here?" With both hands, Red pointed at the table.

"Because we need to ask you something," Nyx said.

"What could I possibly know that you don't?" Red asked.

"We want to ask you to do something," Derrick clarified.

Red did a slow turn of his head. Despite Derrick's lack of emotional insight, it was clear there was no love in Red's eyes.

Nyx said, "Derrick, Miriam, and Rebekah must leave. Akira, Antonio, and I are going with them."

"Explain," Red said, taking his last bite and sitting back. The chair groaned as if it might come apart.

Nyx said, "Derrick, Miriam, and Rebekah found something. It's hazardous. Just knowing about it is dangerous. They showed Akira and me so we would understand. They must go there for their safety and to protect Potterville. Miriam said the Chosen were monitoring us and had identified Akira and me as Derrick's friends. That makes us potential targets…"

Red interrupted. "Targets for what?"

Nyx said, "To be taken hostage. Pawns to force Derrick and Miriam's surrender."

"Okay. I follow. What about Antonio? Why would he go?" Red asked.

Nyx said, "Because he is Antonio. He has to be in the middle of things."

Red nodded. "What does that have to do with me?"

Nyx was about to take a bite of pizza but returned the slice to her plate. She looked at Derrick. "Maybe you can explain."

Derrick remained silent for a moment. "Miriam could explain it better."

Nyx took a bite of pizza and then mumbled, "I don't see how. It was your idea. Besides, Miriam's not here."

"True," Derrick admitted. "Okay. This place is sorta like a big, uh, not sure what you call it. Like a place where things are built…"

"Like a factory?" Red asked.

"Yeah. Kind of like that. And things are wearing out. When they do, the place becomes dangerous. So, we need to go there and make sure everything is running okay," Derrick said.

"Why are you asking me?" Red asked.

"Because Mr. Fletcher told us you're a brilliant mechanic," Derrick said.

Red rocked forward. "You talked to my grandfather?"

Nyx said, "Last night. Sheriff Collins set it up. Derrick, Miriam, and I talked to him. He invited us in for tea. He is a nice man."

"Doesn't sound like my grandfather. You sure you have the right guy?"

"Does he have a picture of a 1963 Shelby Cobra on his wall?" Derrick asked.

"I'll be damned. You were in his house. How did you manage that?" Red asked.

"It wasn't easy. Miriam convinced him," Nyx said.

"How?" Red asked.

"She mentioned the name of a man he knew when he was young," Nyx said.

"That doesn't clear things up. When would we leave?" Red asked.

Derrick glanced over at the pizza boxes, stood, and extended his hand toward Red. "Want more?"

Red hesitated and then handed his plate to Derrick. "Sure. Three if there's any left."

Derrick turned to Nyx. "You want more?"

"I'm good," Nyx said.

Derrick thought of her kiss, almost said, "you sure are," and then caught himself. He decided "I'm good" meant she didn't want more pizza.

After Derrick walked away, Red said, "Things have gotten strange since Derrick showed up."

Nyx nodded and said, "True. Perhaps even stranger than you know."

"What's that mean?"

"Oh, nothing," Nyx said as Derrick returned, sliding a plate with four slices in front of Red.

Derrick looked at Nyx, her cheeks slightly pink.

"I said three," Red said, grabbing a slice from the top.

"I can eat three. You probably need four." Derrick took a bite.

Red studied them both as he chewed. When he swallowed, he said, "So, when would we leave?"

"Not sure. Soon. Miriam's working on a plan," Derrick said.

"Would we be back tonight or tomorrow?" Red asked.

"I don't know. Not tonight and not tomorrow. I hope this week sometime. Maybe you can come back sooner than the rest of us. The Chosen don't know about you," Derrick said.

"I'll have to ask my parents," Red said.

"You should not do that," Derrick said.

"I can't just run off," Red said.

"Safer for your parents if they don't know," Derrick said.

Red looked at Nyx. "What are you and Akira telling your parents?"

"I don't know. We need Collins' and Browning's help with that. It won't be safe for them here," Nyx said, her voice cracking.

"Could you talk to your grandfather?" Derrick asked.

"My grandfather? Why would I do that? Not safe for him either," Red said.

"He already knows about the place. Tell him you're going with us. He'll understand why your parents can't know. Maybe he can tell them you're staying with him to work on cars," Derrick said.

Red took two slices, putting one on top of the other, like a pizza sandwich, and took a bite. "We always work on cars. Plus, it's spring break, and we planned on doing some major rebuilds. I don't stay at his house, but I've slept at the shop when I work late."

"Perfect. He can tell your parents you're staying at the shop," Derrick said.

"I don't know. It all sounds fishy," Red said.

Nyx said, "Talk to your grandfather. He'll help you decide. If you're not back within an hour, we'll assume you're not coming. We'll understand." Nyx paused, "But we need you, Red."

Red finished the pizza sandwich, grabbed the last piece, and then stood. "Is there food at this place?"

"Yeah. Not as good as here, but edible," Derrick said.

Red said nothing more and started for the door.

"Red," Nyx called out. "Don't tell anyone and don't call us. If you head back here, turn your cell phone off. Not just on vibrate. Off."

"You make this sound like scary shit," Red said.

Nyx said, "That's because it is."

8

DERRICK KNEW THE HELICOPTERS WERE JUST outside of Potterville. Their beating blades grew louder, and he concentrated on estimating their location. The others' faces indicated they heard them as well. Nyx gripped Derrick's hand on the tabletop.

"Someone should step outside and see what's happening," Henry said.

Nyx said, "Better they don't see any activity at the school."

Akira walked in, followed by Miriam and Patel. Derrick wanted to know what happened but knew it could wait. Miriam's smile said volumes. Now, it was time to get out of town.

"Nyx," Antonio nodded toward the front of the room, "Time to wrap this up."

Nyx motioned to her chest and mouthed, "Me?"

Antonio nodded.

Stepping to the lectern, Nyx raised the wooden hammer but then laid it down. Clearing her throat, she said, "We've made another decision, but we need help with details."

"What sort of decision?" Browning asked.

"For everyone's safety, it's important that Derrick, Miriam, and Rebekah leave Potterville for a while."

"Is this about the thing they found they won't tell us about?" Collins asked.

"It is. Plus, the military will search the town for them. There's no way to hide them in Potterville. And anyone helping them would also be in danger," Nyx said.

Henry said, "Wait. We voted for them to leave, but Antonio vetoed it. Now, they are leaving anyway?"

"Correct. I know it sounds contradictory, but it's not," Nyx said.

"How is it not?" Henry asked.

"Because Akira and I are going with them," Nyx said.

Derrick mouthed, "Red," but Nyx gave a slight shake of her head.

"Whoa, hang on now," Browning began, then said, "I can't support this. You all need to stay here so we can protect you."

Nyx said, "Things at this place must be, uh, let's just say, fixed. Plus, it's too dangerous here. The Chosen already had Akira, and my name listed. So, they will come for us to use as leverage. We are no safer here than they are. Besides, you can't protect any of us against the military."

Antonio twisted in his seat to face Browning. "I am also going."

Browning said, "What? Why you? That makes little sense. I can see why it makes some sense for Nyx and Akira, because they have been associated with Derrick. But you have only talked to him in school, and that's not uncharacteristic. You talk to everyone,"

"I'm going because I can. I'm the council president, and I make such decisions. Besides, the council members who are going are not—unbiased. Decisions affecting Potterville will be required. Therefore, I'm going," Antonio said, and then added, "Red might be going too."

Browning said, "We need more discussion on this…"

The helicopters passing overhead drowned out Browning's voice. Everyone covered their ears. The machines were just above the trees.

Nyx waved her hand toward the din. "No time for discussion about us. Our families won't be safe. When they can't find Derrick, Miriam, and Rebekah, they will start looking for Akira and me. When they discover we are also missing, they'll find our families. We can't tell our families where we are going, but we must get them someplace safe. Antonio's family, too. Although the Chosen may not associate Antonio with us, we can't take that risk. So, how do we keep them safe?"

"My deputy and I can keep an eye on them," Collins said.

"Not good enough," Nyx snapped. "An army will be here within hours."

Browning said, "Calm down. We can handle this. And you guys can't run off without your parents knowing where you're going."

Nyx stomped her foot. "You're not listening. We can't do that. You don't understand how dangerous this is."

Derrick wanted to intervene but thought it best to let Nyx handle it. He glanced at Miriam. Miriam seemed content to let it play out with Nyx in charge.

From the back of the room, an unexpected voice chimed in. "What does Miriam think?" It was Allen Patel.

Derrick heard movement as everyone turned to look at Miriam, who had pulled her desk close to Akira, which Derrick thought was odd.

Miriam cleared her throat. "Nyx is right, and we are running out of time."

"Why are we letting her have a say in this?" Henry Clark asked.

Without emotion, Patel said, "Because Miriam is the smartest person in this room and knows more about the situation than the others."

"What about you, Allen? If this is so dangerous, what about you and your family?" Collins asked.

"You raise a good point," Patel said. "I do not understand the dangers of this secret place of which Miriam speaks. But if she says it is dangerous, I trust her judgment. I understand the danger of the Chosen's search for these three, four if you include Anna Ford. I have taken great care to isolate myself regarding my trip here today. Yet, I fear my best efforts are not good enough. My wife and daughter are waiting in a car that cannot be associated with me. We are vanishing the moment I leave this meeting. The sooner, the better."

"You're leaving Pacific Edge? You have influence there. That's a little dramatic, don't you think?" Browning said.

"It is not. Plus, we no longer live in Pacific Edge, and I agree with Nyx. You are not listening," Patel said.

The beating blades of the helicopter shook the building. Everyone covered their ears. The windows shuddered, and debris flew into the room from the opening.

"What the hell," Browning shouted.

"Get to the back of the room," Collins yelled as he dashed to the front.

Derrick started for the back but then turned, facing the front, ushering Miriam, Nyx, Rebekah, and Akira behind him. Silhouettes appeared outside the frosted glass of the classroom door. At least three men, Derrick judged. He did not know what to do, yet something circled just outside his consciousness—drip, drip, drip, like a leaking faucet, circling back to what Miriam had said about remembering his training.

Collins put his hand on his gun. Derrick wished Collins would pull it out. The door exploded inward, spewing splinters of wood into the room. Collins and Browning both ducked, holding their hands up to shield their faces. One man dressed in black stood in the doorway. Two more stood behind him on either side. Before Collins or Browning could react, the first man shot them both, lifting them off their feet, tossing them back into the front row of desks.

9

THE WEAPON WAS A SUBSONIC BLAST GUN. It fired an inaudible sound wave. At close range, it could stun, cripple, or kill. Derrick did not understand how he knew this information. It was just there in his head unexpectedly. Like a faucet dribbling memories. Blood trickled from Collins's left ear. Derrick did not think Collins was dead, confident they would have set the blasters to stun. Collins and Browning would survive, but they would remain unconscious for 10 to 15 minutes. Both would have head and body aches and ask people to repeat themselves for several days. The stun gun's setting revealed the rules of engagement. Derrick did not know how he knew that either.

The three soldiers stood at the front of the room. Derrick felt hands around his waist. It was Nyx. He felt certain of that. She should be in the back of the room. He didn't need her here. Although he did not know what he needed. The adults, who might have provided protection, lay incapacitated on the floor.

They had not shot Mr. Patel. Perhaps Patel had led them here.

Nyx stepped in front of Derrick. "What do you want?"

"Those three." The man pointed at Derrick, Miriam, and Rebekah. "Then we leave, and you go back to whatever it is one does on a Sunday afternoon in Potterville."

Before Derrick could react, Nyx launched herself at the lead man.

He fired.

Nyx flew back into Derrick's arms. He eased her to the floor.

Rage, not unlike what he first experienced when he decked Marcus Carver, flowed through him. Time slowed, not unlike it did in the track meet when exchanging the baton. Yet, something else happened that was unlike anything he had experienced.

Time did not just slow. It stopped.

And then Derrick heard a voice in his head.

It was the voice of his instructor. He called himself by many names, sometimes sensei, sometimes sabom. There were others, but Derrick called him Master. Thoughts flowed through his mental faucet, and memories flooded into his mind.

His Master explained what Derrick must do. It would be difficult, and chances of success, limited. Perhaps 10%. Probably less. Execution was critical.

Derrick held Nyx. He felt her breathing. She did not need his help but holding her bought him time. Time for master's instruction, happening in Derrick's head from years of teaching.

And practice. Mostly on the beach.

The lead person had fired all the shots and was best prepared to fire again. Fortunately, he was closest to Derrick. Poor decision. Take him out first—but the other two posed problems. Farther away. Harder to reach. Derrick ran several assaults through his mind. Picked the best, held on to the others should things change. It would be a fluid situation.

A distraction would help. But he had no ideas.

Unless.

He looked over his shoulder at Miriam. She gave a slight nod.

Derrick asked, "Was that necessary?"

The man said, "It was not, but her choice."

"Will she be, okay?" Derrick asked, trying hard to appear shaken, which he was not.

A man standing next to the door said, "Probably, but that's gonna change. Sergeant, set your weapon to 75%."

"Lieutenant that…"

The Lieutenant said, "Gives the next person a 50% chance of survival. Do it."

The sergeant made an adjustment to his weapon.

Derrick eased Nyx to a comfortable position and then stood in such a manner that he positioned himself closer to the sergeant. Running a new calculation through his head, important that the sergeant did not fire a blast striking anyone in the room. The distance between himself and the sergeant was doable now.

Derrick noticed the sergeant's eyes shift.

"What about Anna Ford?" Miriam asked from behind Derrick.

The sergeant shifted, putting him 18 inches closer to Derrick as he tried to get a clear shot at Miriam.

Damn, that girl is smart, Derrick thought. One would think she was also combat trained.

Perhaps she was.

"What about her?" The lieutenant asked.

"Prime gave me an offer if we turned her in," Miriam said.

From the back of the room, Patel said, "Miriam, you mustn't."

Miriam held up her hand to silence Patel.

The lieutenant said nothing but looked uncomfortable. "We don't work for Prime."

"Who do you work for?" Miriam asked.

Derrick eased a few inches closer.

"That is none of your concern," the lieutenant said.

"Perhaps not, but someone here can tell the robots, and the robots can tell Prime," Miriam said.

"What robots?" the lieutenant asked.

"Robots on the street. You did not see them? There's one on the corner outside the school," Miriam said.

The lieutenant lowered his weapon a little. "We didn't see any robots."

Miriam said, "Not my problem. You should pay closer attention to your surroundings."

"You're a cocky little…" the lieutenant paused. After a moment, he looked to his right at the third man. "Go check around the school. Don't approach any robots. Report straight back."

The third man left. Miriam did better than Derrick expected.

Derrick said, "So, we go with you, and nothing happens to anyone here?"

"That's what I've been told," the lieutenant said.

"You believe that's true?" Derrick asked.

"Not my job. I just follow orders."

"Convenient," Derrick said.

Miriam said, "Not going to happen. I'm ready to give Anna Ford to Prime, and I expect Prime to make good on his deal."

Derrick heard a desk crash to the floor behind him.

"You lying bitch. I'm going to rip your face off."

It was Rebekah. The situation wasn't funny, but Derrick could not suppress a smile. These two formed a potent combination. He was glad they were on his side.

More than he could say for these two chumps.

As with football practice and passing the baton, everything slowed down for Derrick. With a step forward, he kicked the blaster out of the sergeant's hands, sending it spinning through the air and then it crashed to the floor. Next, Derrick spun, jumping at the same time, creating enough centrifugal force to send the sergeant sideways when Derrick kicked him in the head. Sideways put the sergeant in front of the lieutenant just as the lieutenant fired. The sergeant was out before he hit the floor.

That's one.

However, the lieutenant was farther away, a more difficult target to neutralize, the strike more difficult to execute. Poor odds. Standing was the worst option because it made Derrick a larger target. Instead, he fell to the floor and rolled toward the lieutenant. The lieutenant fired, hitting the floor space Derrick had occupied a split second earlier. Important information because it revealed the lieutenant's lack of training or his lack of fighting experience, either worked to Derrick's advantage, and it mattered not which the man lacked.

Derrick was within striking distance, but the next decision would determine success or failure. He could break the man's leg. That would be easiest, and it might be enough, depending on the man's pain tolerance. Since the man appeared to lack combat experience, breaking a leg wasn't a bad option, and it was easy to execute. A roundhouse kick, properly implemented, striking the man in the elbow would break his arm and move the weapon to the side, sending the next shot, if the man got one off, wide, and even a rather poorly executed kick should move the weapon off-target long enough for a second blow, but Derrick had not planned a second blow.

Derrick spun on his back, raising up enough to deliver a kick to the man's arm.

SNAP.

The man's elbow bent in a direction it was not intended to bend. The lieutenant screamed, which was not good, but he also dropped the weapon, and that was good.

The lieutenant stumbled toward the door, but Derrick swept his legs out before he got that far. The man landed on his broken arm, which was Derrick's intent. Still on his back, Derrick raised his leg straight toward the ceiling and then delivered a hammer kick to the man's face. No more screams.

Derrick heard desks scraping across the floor and a jumble of voices behind him.

"Well, done, brother," Miriam said.

Malcolm stood over the sergeant, holding the man's weapon in his hands. "I'm glad I treated you decent from the get-go instead of picking a fight. Where did you learn to do that?"

"That part is unclear to me," Derrick said. Turning around, Derrick saw Henry checking Coach and Larry checking Collins. Akira kneeled beside Nyx. Rebekah stepped over the lieutenant, picked his weapon off the floor, and then checked the hallway.

Derrick pulled the lieutenant away from the door and dragged the sergeant next to him. "Fast thinking, Rebekah. Glad you're on our side. Shoot them if they move."

Miriam said, "We need to secure them. I used a gray tape on the security guards when I escaped."

Larry Kinkead said, "You mean duct tape?" He rummaged through a cabinet. "Like this?" Larry asked, tossing a roll of tape to Miriam.

"Exactly like this. It's great stuff." Miriam looked at Derrick. "Help me?"

Rebekah sat facing the door, resting the blaster on the desk's top. "I've got the next guy. You guys have fun. I know I will."

Derrick and Miriam bound the two military men's hands and feet, and then Miriam added a piece of tape over each man's mouth.

She glanced up at Derrick. "So, they can't scream for help or alert the third soldier."

"You're scary," Derrick said.

"As if what you did wasn't," Miriam said, then smiled.

Groaning came from the back of the room. Henry helped Coach Browning into a sitting position. "What the hell?" Coach said.

"Those two barged in and shot you and Sheriff Collins." Henry pointed toward the two soldiers bound and gagged at the front of the room.

Browning rubbed his forehead. "I remember. But how… what?"

Henry said, "Derrick took them out. That dude is scary. It was like a movie, only much faster. The one guy has a broken arm. That much is certain. One guy blasted the other, but Derrick caused that too."

Collins stirred.

Derrick kneeled by Nyx, stroking her hair. Her eyes flickered open. She squinted, grimaced, then smiled.

"Are you okay?" Derrick asked.

Nyx sat. "I've been better, but I'll live. I think."

"Welcome back," Rebekah said.

Before Derrick could turn, Rebekah fired the blaster and knocked the third soldier into the hall. She rushed to the doorway, but instead of peeking out, she pointed the blaster in one direction and fired and then did the same in the other direction. Then she eased out, looked both ways, and said, "All clear."

Rebekah grabbed the third man's legs, Patel joined her, and they dragged the man into the room. Patel locked the door and then helped Rebekah secure the man with duct tape.

A thin voice came from a rectangular black box fastened to the lieutenant's belt. "Base to Scout 1. Status report. Over."

Miriam grabbed a name tag clipped to the man's shirt. She held it out. "Someone has to answer."

Collins struggled to his feet. "I'll do it. I have some experience. What should I say?"

"Tell them you didn't find us," Miriam said.

Collins staggered to Miriam and took the microphone. Holding his hand between his mouth and the microphone, Collins said, "Go for Scout."

"Do you have the subjects?"

Collins thought for a moment. "Negative. Building is clear." He paused. "Except for a handful of kids. They said the three we're looking for went to the mall."

"Roger that. It will take time to search the mall."

"Roger. We'll meet you there. Set up a perimeter first. Don't go in until we arrive." Collins shrugged and made a face.

"We can pick you up."

Collins said, "Negative. We'll walk. Might see them along the way."

"Roger. See you at the mall."

Miriam touched Collins' on the shoulder. "Quick thinking."

Browning struggled to a nearby chair. "Damn, that hurts like hell. Now what?"

Derrick said, "I don't know, but for sure, we aren't going to the mall."

10

DERRICK EXTENDED HIS HAND, INTERLACED his fingers with Nyx, and helped her to stand. He felt as if everyone in the room stared at them, waiting to hear their exchange. When the blast sent Nyx flying, Derrick's feelings prevailed. He could not remember what he said when he held her. Whatever it was, Nyx didn't hear it. But everyone else did. Except Sheriff Collins and Coach Browning because the soldier shot them first. Normally, it would have bothered Derrick to have exposed his feelings in front of people, especially this group. Now, he no longer cared.

Derrick said, "What were you thinking?"

Nyx wobbled to the nearest unoccupied desk. "I was thinking you needed help." She studied the soldiers wrapped in duct tape. "Looks like it worked. What happened to them?"

Henry said, "Derrick happened to them."

Derrick stood by Nyx, taking her hand. "Why did you do that?"

"I'm not sure. They pissed me off. Shooting Coach like that for no reason." Nyx paused. "I thought you might try something… so, well, I thought a distraction might help."

Derrick wasn't sure he believed the distraction part, but he believed the anger part. Nyx was small but feisty. "You helped me get closer to the shooter. You helped—a lot."

Nyx rubbed her forehead, then frowned at Derrick. "I don't understand how it helped you get closer?"

Akira stepped behind Nyx, rubbed her shoulders. "I'll explain it later. But now, I think we should talk about how we get out of here. Soldiers are already in town, and helicopters flying overhead. I don't see how we are going to get out of town without being seen."

Malcolm said, "They are looking for three kids. Perhaps split up. That might throw them off. You guys need to decide where and when to meet."

"Not going to happen," Rebekah said. "We stay together. Plus, remember, there are seven of us now if that big kid comes back."

Sheriff Collins said, "They don't know there are seven. Question is, how did they know we were here? They must have known Coach, and I were here. They were ready for us. Someone tipped them off."

"Sure as hell," Browning said.

Larry said, "Must have been Red."

"Damn it. I'm afraid you're right. He had just left," Browning said.

"I don't think so," Derrick said. "I trust Red."

Akira said, "Duh. Are you people brain dead? It was Jimmy. Had to be."

Henry said, "Crap. I forgot about Jimmy. I'm going to kick his ass soon as I find him."

Nyx said, "You're not. That's not how we do things, and you know it. We'll find out who did it, and the council will deal with it. We don't know it was Jimmy."

"It could have been Red," Larry said. "Like Nyx said, we don't know for sure. Letting Red stay was a bad idea. He's been friends with Jimmy for years. You might have invited a spy into our group."

Akira said, "I hate to say it, but Larry is right. Can we trust Red? I mean, if he gives us up once we are… well, you know, in the place where we are going, then it will be too late."

Derrick looked at Patel. "What about him?" Derrick pointed. "Maybe he led them here. I heard he insisted on being here and was never a voting council member until today. Plus, they didn't shoot him, did they?"

Patel's expression remained passive. "I understand your concern, but I did not lead them here. I took great care to avoid detection coming here."

"You never answered Derrick's question. Why *are* you here? And why should we believe you?" Miriam asked, then added, "The truth this time."

"I am here for the same reason you got into Technical Services. I am here to help you and Derrick. That, and after what I've done, I can't go back to Pacific Edge."

"Why help us? What's in it for you?" Miriam asked.

"Perhaps I will tell you one day, but today is not that day," Patel said, glancing at Rebekah.

"What do you mean, you have nowhere to go?" Miriam asked.

"More accurately, no place to go that's safe," Patel said.

"What about your family?" Miriam asked.

"I already told you. They are waiting down the street in a car that does not belong to me, and the Chosen cannot trace it to me. As soon as we are done here, we must try to find a safe place. Unfortunately, I don't know where that might be. Especially now that the roads are likely blocked. I risked everything to help you."

"We don't know that's true," Rebekah said.

Patel looked hurt. Derrick did not understand why.

"This is all speculation," Nyx said, "And we know where that's led in the past. That's why we have the council. Derrick asked Red to go. Derrick decides if that's still the deal. As for Patel," Nyx looked at Browning, "He's your problem."

Derrick knew someone had told the soldiers where they were, and that Browning and Collins were in the room. That limited it to Jimmy, Jimmy's friend, or Red. They might have seen Red leave, captured him. Threatened him or perhaps threatened his family. Red could be in danger. But the soldiers did not shoot Patel. Perhaps because he posed no threat. Perhaps for another reason. "I'll decide about Red when I see him."

"If, you see him," Larry said.

Collins said, "It's going to be tough getting you out of the building, and I have no clue how we are going to get you out of town."

Miriam said, "I had an idea, but that option may no longer exist."

"What do you mean?" Derrick asked.

"The soldier said they did not see any robots. I thought we might appropriate their aircraft. They must have left when the military got close."

"Who controls the military?" Derrick asked.

"The President, we think, or the Chosen," Akira said, "But that was before we learned that Prime was not a fairytale."

Miriam looked at Patel. "Someone has been watching us or trying to. We've found cameras at Derrick's condo. Who put them there? Pacific Edge or Prime. Or is there someone else we should be concerned about?"

Patel sat on the edge of the instructor's desk. "Pacific Edge security placed cameras in Derrick's condo and a couple of other locations." Patel looked at Akira and then Nyx. "I noticed someone disabled those."

"What about the second set?" Miriam asked.

"What second set are you referring to?" Patel asked.

"We found a second set of cameras after Rebekah, and I arrived."

"I do not know. It could be Pacific Edge, but the system was still down when I left. Because the system is down at Pacific Edge, cameras would not be of value. Perhaps the military."

"What about Prime?" Miriam asked.

"You keep mentioning Prime. What makes you think that Prime exists?"

"Because there was a Prime aircraft parked on the street and Prime robots scattered around the town," Akira said.

"Fascinating," Patel said.

"Fascinating? Is that what you think it is?" Derrick said.

"Yes. Quite thought-provoking. We believed Prime was a myth the Chosen invented to deflect responsibility. Or a clandestine unit of the Chosen. If Prime sent an aircraft and robots, that would be most interesting indeed. To my knowledge, the Chosen don't have robot technology. Why do you think they were here?"

"Looking for Anna," Rebekah said.

Patel grew pale. "How do you know that?"

"Because that's what the robots said to everyone who approached them." Rebekah moved her arms up and down stiffly, deepened her voice. "I mean you no harm. I must locate subject three, known as Anna Ford. And a robot recognized Derrick and Miriam. It tried to bargain with Miriam," Rebekah said.

"Bargain?" Patel asked.

"It said the three of us could go free if we gave Anna to Prime," Miriam said.

"And what did you say?" Patel asked.

"Said, I'd think about it. I asked for a written contract," Miriam said.

"This is worse than I thought, and it is my fault," Patel said.

"What is your fault?" Rebekah said.

Patel paused, looked at the floor, and then raised his eyes to Rebekah. "I let Anna escape."

11

THE ROOM GREW SILENT. THE BEATING OF the helicopter rotors faded. Derrick struggled to grasp what was happening. Understanding the entire situation seemed impossible. Anna had escaped by following Rebekah. Okay, got that part. Rebekah vacillated between what appeared to be homicidal rage and complete collapse. Miriam looked perplexed, and that was disconcerting right there. Patel had revealed he was involved in Miriam's escape and Anna's disappearance. To confuse the situation more, Akira went to Patel, put her hand on his shoulder.

Akira looked at Derrick as if to say, "I need your help," and instead said, "Allen, just tell us what happened."

Patel pulled a handkerchief from his pocket, dried his eyes, and blew his nose. "As I awoke, after Miriam and Rebekah zapped me, I'm not angry with either of you. I understand. Anyway, Anna burst through the door. She was running toward the exit, and the gate guard would have spotted her. I grabbed her. She struggled, but I got her calmed down and walked her so she could see the guard. She accepted I was telling her the truth and understood I could help her. I put her in my car's trunk and took her to my house. When Miriam zapped me, I remembered my tests on 1984…"

"What's 1984?" Collins asked.

"It's a tracking device. The Chosen all have them. Back to Anna. I did not know Miriam had crashed the entire computer system. I assumed they would soon learn that Miriam, Rebekah, and Anna were gone, and using 1984, they would locate Anna at my house. But Miriam had figured out how to defeat 1984. It was brilliant. It's why she and Rebekah had stun guns. I also had a stun gun issued to me for protection. Even Pacific Edge security believes commoners are dangerous, even though most of the guards are commoners themselves."

"What are commoners?" Henry asked.

"It's what the Chosen call anyone who doesn't live in a Chosen Community," Browning said.

"Sounds derogatory," Henry said.

Derrick said, "It is, but we don't understand that until we leave and learn differently."

"Humph," Henry grunted.

Akira said, "Can we get back to Allen? What happened?"

"I was saying. I had a stun gun and decided I had to zap Anna before they tracked her. I tried to explain it to her, but then a siren sounded. And within seconds, a knock at my front door." Tears flowed again, and Patel wiped his eyes. "Hardest thing I've ever done. I asked her to turn around. And then I zapped her. Caught her in my arms and put her in a closet. No time to hide her, but it wouldn't matter if they had already tracked her to my house. It was a security officer at the door, but he wasn't looking for Anna. He was looking for me. He demanded I go to work immediately. I had already called in that I'd be late. I tried to tell the security officer I was ill, but he said the commander insisted I get to work. Then the power failed, and I understood." Patel looked at Miriam. "You should be pleased with how well your computer crash worked."

Miriam said, "Tell me later. What happened to Anna?"

"The officer grabbed my arm and dragged me to his transport." Patel held his arm out as if being dragged. "I didn't have time to leave Anna a note." Patel hung his head. "When I got home, she was gone. I must have scared her to death."

Rebekah said, "She followed us. I should not have left her. I caused this."

"You did what you thought was right," Miriam said. "Stop beating yourself up. It won't change anything, and it doesn't help."

Patel said, "I'm sorry, Rebekah." He looked at Derrick and Miriam. "I failed all of you."

Miriam said, "They haven't found her, or they wouldn't still be searching. There are many things I don't understand. I get why they want Derrick. Well, sort of. Rebekah and I caused a lot of problems and embarrassment. So, no mystery why they want us. But why Anna? I know she's a test subject, but she brought out Prime, which, from everything we've heard, is incredible."

Antonio cleared his throat. "This is all interesting and important, but we should go. And what are we doing with those three?" He pointed at the military men, still unconscious, or so it appeared.

Henry picked up one of their weapons. "I'll set this thing at 75%, shoot each of them, and see how many we have left. That's fair. Isn't it?"

The sergeant opened his eyes. Shook his head.

"So, you're awake. How about the other two?" Henry put the weapon against the lieutenant's head. His eyes opened. Henry nudged the third man with his foot. He groaned but did not move.

"I don't know what to do with them," Nyx said.

Coach said. "Any ideas, Bill? This is more your area."

Collins said, "Damned if I know. I can't lock them up. Well, not legally. But others will come looking for them."

Clark said, "They know who we are, and they'll come after us. We are as good as dead. They give us no choice. We have to kill them and bury the bodies where the military can't find them."

The third man opened his eyes, moaned, and sat with his back against the wall. All three men stared wide-eyed.

Miriam stood. Studied them. "Check them for identification."

Nyx said, "Do as she said. Henry, you keep the weapon on them. Larry and Malcolm, search them. Do a thorough job. Put everything on the desk."

Larry and Malcolm did as Nyx ordered. The sergeant groaned loudly when they rolled him over. Soon they piled three wallets, three identification badges, and an assortment of odds and ends: keys, lip balm, a guitar pick, and coins on the desk.

Larry opened a wallet. "Hey, there's a wad of cash here."

"Put it back," Miriam said.

Larry looked at Nyx.

Nyx said, "You heard her."

Miriam walked to the desk, started sorting through the wallets and identification. She pulled pictures out of a wallet. "Cute little boy, Sergeant Davis, and a lovely wife."

Miriam spent five minutes going through the wallets, searching, and returning each item to its original location. When she finished, she kneeled in front of the soldiers. "I have a proposal."

Miriam stared at the lieutenant. "I'm going to remove the tape from your mouth. If you scream or call out," Miriam motioned with her thumb, "this fellow is going to shoot you. Understand?"

The lieutenant nodded.

Miriam ripped the tape off. "Sorry. I think faster is better. Now, Mr. Beaverton, or should I call you Todd? You live on the base, but your wife, Mary, and your daughters, Karen and Kary, both spelled with a K, live in Modesto. Thirteen eight-five 23rd street. You don't want anything to happen to them, just as I want nothing to happen to my family or friends. Am I right?"

"You're threatening my family? How dare you! I'll take you out myself. You hear me?" Mr. Beaverton struggled against the tape.

"Actually, you will not. We have not yet reached a deal, which means there's no guarantee you're even going to see your family again."

"You won't kill us. You're just kids. And the sheriff is standing right there." Spittle flew as Beaverton spoke.

"Won't I?" Miriam held her hand out. "Give me a weapon."

Nyx handed a gun to Miriam. Miriam studied it for a moment, slid a lever, causing a small light to change from yellow to red. Then she pointed the weapon at Beaverton's chest. "Feel good about your chances? I think the odds of cooperation from Sergeant Davis will increase if I fire this weapon. I'm going to guess your odds for survival are low. Am I correct?"

Beaverton's eyes grew wide. "Don't pull that trigger. Please, my kids need me."

"I'm sure they do, but they are not my concern," Miriam said.

Derrick felt a shiver up his back. At first, he thought Miriam was bluffing. Now, he was convinced she was not.

Nyx said, "Should I take a picture of his ID?"

"If you want, but I don't need it," Miriam said. She recited the man's driver's license number, military number, and three credit card numbers.

The color of the man's face changed from red to white. "What is your proposal?"

"Simple. You never saw us." She paused. "Any of us."

"But I have to tell them something."

"Let me finish. Searching the school, a robot confronted you. Before you could react, another robot came behind you and used something to knock you out. When you woke up, the robots had tied you up with tape. You never saw them again. The robots took your weapons and radios. Simple."

"And their money," Henry Clark said.

Miriam said, "We are not taking their money. You heard the man. They have families. Plus, we are not robbers. We are the good guys. Understand?"

Henry turned red and said nothing.

Nyx said, "She asked you a question."

"Yeah, understood," Henry hissed.

"Don't ask about their money again, and don't touch their wallets."

"But you told command we were going to the mall," the lieutenant said.

"So, you heard that. But who told them?" Miriam asked.

The lieutenant looked puzzled. "Oh, the robot told them."

"There you go. See? Simple."

The lieutenant said, "I don't know. Do you understand the trouble we'd be in if they discover we lied?"

Miriam shook her head. "Are you braindead? If you haven't noticed, you're already in trouble. Without an agreement, someone will carry your bodies out of here, which means your wife won't have a husband, and your kids won't have a dad. I don't want to do that, but you leave me no choice. Look, I get it. They want us, and people may die trying to find us, or we will die if they do. I accept the facts of our situation. I'm just not in a rush to die, nor do I believe you three need to be the first casualties. Mr. Beaverton, you're the leader, so I look to you for an answer, but understand if any of you don't follow the script, you all face the same penalty. Plus, I will find you, and you will pay a far greater price than the military will dish out. I assume even if the military gave you the death penalty, it would not extend to your families."

The lieutenant contemplated Miriam's words for a moment. "I don't believe you?"

"What don't you believe? That I won't find you or that I won't kill you?" Miriam asked.

The muscles in the lieutenant's jaw rippled. "Both."

Miriam said, "Have it your way."

Then she pulled the trigger.

12

DERRICK SAW THAT COMING. HE WASN'T SURE HOW. Perhaps the tone in Miriam's voice telegraphed her intentions. It was a bad situation—no question. Still, he didn't believe she had killed the guy. However, the guy looked dead.

Sheriff Collins started toward Miriam. "Stop! You can't just shoot people."

"Seems I already did," Miriam said.

"I'm the law here. Now, drop that weapon," Collins said.

Derrick turned toward Collins to see him pawing at the leather device that had once carried his firearm.

"Looking for this?" Rebekah held Collins's gun, barrel pointing toward the ceiling.

"What the…"

"The soldiers took it from you after they shot you. The soldiers proved you don't have control. You'll get your gun back, probably. But for now, Miriam is in charge," Rebekah said.

"She's right," Browning said, putting his hand on Collins' shoulder. "Sit. Let them handle it. We failed to protect the kids. They protected us. Whatever happens, the soldiers have it coming."

"But…"

Browning interrupted. "I said sit. It wasn't a request. Sorry, Bill. We failed. The kids didn't. In case you're still foggy in the head, we are in deep shit."

The sergeant stared wide-eyed, shaking his head and moaning.

"Derrick, I think Sergeant Davis has something to say," Miriam said. "You understand if you scream, I'm going to blast you just like I did your lieutenant?"

The man nodded.

Derrick kneeled, peeled the corner of the tape back, hesitated a moment, and then ripped it off like Miriam did.

"Don't shoot me. I'll do whatever you say. Anything you want. My kids are more important than any damn job."

"That's more like it," Miriam said.

"But… well, they won't believe that story. You know, what robots? We don't have robots. Commoners, uh, I mean people who live here don't have robots. Plus, why would robots attack us? They'll get the truth one way or another," Davis said.

A voice squawked over the radio. "Lieutenant Beaverton, report."

Davis said, "That's the mission commander. We need to check in. Bring me a radio. I can handle it." Davis paused. "Trust me. I don't want to end up like him." He nodded toward the lieutenant.

Sheriff Collins brought the radio, held the microphone near the man's mouth, and pushed the button on the side.

"Mission command, this is Sergeant Davis, over."

"Where is Lieutenant Beaverton?"

Without hesitation, Davis said, "He and Caldwell are questioning some locals. They may have information. We'll report when we know more."

"Roger that," the radio squawked.

Miriam studied the man for a moment. "Why won't the robot story work?"

"Like I said, we don't have robots that could do something like that. I suppose we have things you could call robots. Like you can ask a box that's hooked to your computer to play a song or ask what the weather is in San Francisco. I guess that's sort of a robot. Maybe the Chosen have robots like that. But I've only seen Chosen security staff fly those hovercraft things, which is unlike anything we have. But I have never heard the Chosen have robots like that. Where did you come up with that idea?"

Miriam said, "Not important. The military doesn't have hovercraft like the Chosen? Does the military have self-driving vehicles?"

Davis said, "No. Nothing like that. What makes you think these things?"

Miriam said, "Movies. We are in such a small town here. Figured the Chosen and the military had things we don't."

Davis stared at Miriam for a minute. "Well, that story won't work, and when things don't add up, they are going to put us on a damned lie detector or something worse."

"Worse?" Miriam puzzled.

"Sometimes they skip the lie detector and use what's called a serum test. It's a mix of psychoactive drugs. Effective, but people rarely recover from it."

"Okay," Miriam said. "Let me think."

Derrick had an idea, but Miriam was the smart one, so he remained quiet. Miriam thought for several minutes. But his idea sounded viable, at least, in his head.

"I have a suggestion," Derrick offered.

Miriam looked at him.

Derrick said nothing.

"Let's hear it then." Miriam gave him a hurry motion with her hand.

"They are looking for the three of us. We know that. So, these guys found us. But we got the better of them. Which is true. They can tell that part of the story like it happened and pass the lie detector test. We told you Anna Ford was in the building. The lieutenant sent this guy," Derrick pointed at the third soldier, "to look for her. I attacked you. Got the better of you. This guy got shot when he returned. We tied you up. All you must do is not mention seeing anyone else. None of the other people needs to be involved. Just keep them out of it."

No one said anything for a moment. Miriam nodded. "Not bad, brother. A few questions." She looked at Davis. "Can they tell if this weapon has been fired?"

Davis nodded. "All the discharge information is recorded. The number of shots and the level at which each blast was fired."

Miriam said. "So, your story has to match the five blasts—three blasts when you shot the Sheriff and the Coach. Coach fell to the floor, causing you to miss once. One shot hit this girl," Miriam pointed to Nyx, "because she charged you, which is true. That's four. A final blast hit this soldier," Miriam pointed, "after Derrick took the weapon. Can you remember that?"

The lieutenant moaned. The sergeant pulled back, trying to distance himself from the now stirring corpse.

Miriam said, "I dialed it back a bit before I pulled the trigger. I didn't want to kill him. Not yet."

The lieutenant groaned, "You… You shot me!"

"I sure did. Next time you won't wake up."

"But why?"

"Because you were not taking me seriously," Miriam said. "I hate it when people do that."

"Serious about what?" Beaverton asked.

Miriam said, "Serious about hunting you and your family down if you don't cooperate. Do I have your attention?"

Beaverton nodded.

Miriam continued, "Good. You have been relieved of command. I've promoted Sergeant Davis to lead negotiator. Fortunately, he was ready to discuss the situation. We have a better solution."

Miriam explained the changes. Beaverton nodded, but Miriam made each soldier repeat the story. Beaverton agreed to Miriam's conditions.

Derrick thought Beaverton was being honest. However, he had no way of knowing that for sure.

Miriam said, "You need to contact your control person. Tell them you headed back to the school. Pass this test, and we leave you here alive. But don't underestimate me. You may have heard that I escaped Pacific Edge and crashed their computer system. I'll hunt you and find you. First, I'll take your money, then I'll stalk you. Your death won't be fast or painless."

Beaverton nodded.

Davis told Beaverton about the last transmission.

Beaverton said, "Bring me a radio."

Collins held the microphone to Beaverton's mouth. "Mission control, Lieutenant Beaverton."

A voice responded, "Go for mission control."

"We have intel from locals that the kids headed back to the school. We are en route to that location."

"Roger that. Do you request assistance?"

Beaverton glanced at Miriam. "Negative. Will advise if assistance is needed."

"Roger that. Notify us upon your arrival at the location."

"Roger."

Beaverton stared at Miriam for a moment. "This isn't going to work out for you."

"You might be right. But why do you say that?" Miriam asked.

"We are using a private channel. Turn it to the operations channel, which is 12."

Derrick studied a radio for a moment and then twisted a knob. The radio went from silent to a chaotic rapid-fire of overlapping transmissions. From the chaos, Derrick learned a couple of things. Helicopters were flying back to monitor the high school, and a second assault team was en route.

"How long before the second team gets here?" Derrick asked.

"Ten minutes tops. Maybe sooner. They'll see you leave the school, and they'll track you down. They will capture you," Beaverton said.

Miriam said, "Your situation will be worse if you double-cross me. Let us worry about our escape. I'm rather good at it, as is my brother. When they discover we have disappeared without a trace, your situation won't look so bad."

"You need to move fast, but you need to secure us better," Beaverton said.

Miriam looked at him.

"This isn't good enough." Beaverton held up his two hands, which were taped together. "We would be out of this within minutes."

"Okay. Add more tape," Miriam said to no one in particular.

Beaverton said, "Not just more tape. First, sit us in chairs. Then tape our arms to each chair and our legs to the chair legs. Be quick about it."

Holding up half a roll of duct tape, Nyx said, "We don't have enough tape. Coach, is there more?"

Browning stood. "Probably, but we don't have time to look for it. I have an idea." With that, Browning went to a cabinet, returning with rolls of white fabric that looked like something a doctor might use. "Use this."

Nyx said, "Someone bring three chairs."

Henry grabbed a desk.

"Not a desk. Chairs!" Then Nyx looked at Browning. "Bandage wrap? That won't hold them."

"Strong enough with several wraps. Then we'll wrap it with duct tape. It'll be plenty strong. Now hurry."

First, they put each man in a chair, and then the kids followed Beaverton's instruction on binding them. Beaverton proved himself useful. He believed his life and his family's safety depended on this ruse. Beaverton was wise to trust Miriam meant what she said.

Just before Derrick placed the tape over Beaverton's mouth, Beaverton asked, "How are you going to get out of here without being seen?"

Gathering her bag with her back to Beaverton, Miriam said, "The less you know, the better. Escaping is our problem, not yours." And with that, she picked up a weapon, stepped to the door, and eased it open. "Clear. Take the radios and weapons."

"What about their wallets?" Henry asked.

Nyx said, "Leave them. But should we take their IDs?"

"Unnecessary. I have all their info in my head," Miriam said, stepping into the hall.

The whop of helicopter blades echoed down the hall, rattling the windows. Derrick could smell the jet fuel exhaust. He wondered how he knew it was jet fuel. Thoughts kept streaming through his head for which he could not account.

Derrick said, "Wait here."

Derrick ran to the front lobby. Easing toward the large glass doors, he saw a helicopter hovering over the front lawn, men sliding down ropes. He ran toward the back of the school, through the gymnasium, up the bleachers to the top, where he pulled himself up and peered out a window. A helicopter hovered over the football field, more men sliding down ropes. He did not go to the sides of the building. It was unnecessary. They were trapped.

Derrick sprinted back to the others, set his feet as he approached, and slid, almost crashing into Coach. "Too late. the strike team has arrived."

Collins said, "Which side of the building?"

"They have us surrounded," Derrick said.

Patel grabbed his briefcase, glancing at Browning.

Rebekah handed the pistol back to Collins. "You may need this."

Henry held up a soldier's weapon. "We'll fight our way out."

Derrick said, "Won't work. We might get by the first guys, but not without casualties of our own. We are outnumbered and can't win."

Miriam turned to Collins. "Sheriff?"

Securing his pistol, Collins said, "Damn it! I shouldn't do this, but there's no choice."

Collins sprinted to the stairs. Looking back, he said, "Don't just stand there. Follow me."

13

THREE ADULTS AND SIX KIDS FROM POTTERVILLE—their lives at risk because of three kids from Pacific Edge. It felt unfair, and Derrick didn't like it, but he could not change it. All of them running down the stairs into a basement. It made little sense to trap themselves. But even if there was a way out, which there wasn't, it seemed impossible to get out of Potterville without being seen, followed, and captured.

At the bottom of the stairs, Nyx whispered to Miriam, "We should have sent Henry, Larry, and Malcolm away earlier. No reason for them to be here, no reason to put them in this situation."

Miriam said, "Hindsight being 20/20, you're right. But it's too late now."

Collins led them down a narrow stairway, deeper into the basement and into the boiler room, where students were not allowed. The place smelled of dampness, aging pipes, spilled chemicals, and crumbling concrete. Dimly lit by three light bulbs mounted on the ceiling. Dark corners made it a decent hiding place, but not good enough. A locked door would do little to slow the soldiers. Coming down here was a mistake. Derrick should have stopped Collins. But he didn't. Derrick knew better but had done nothing.

If he was ever in a similar situation, he'd take charge. Before that could happen, they had to get out of the current predicament. It seemed doubtful he would experience anything like this again. Unlikely he'd survive this time. He could fight, give the others a chance.

Inside the boiler room, Collins said, "After being elected sheriff, someone showed me this, and I swore to keep it a secret. I've done that until now, and you wouldn't see it if there were another option. I'm asking you to keep this a secret. It's important to Potterville that you do."

Derrick said, "Give me a weapon. I'll create a distraction so the rest of you can escape."

"You'll do no such thing." Collins walked to a shelf lined with paints, solvents, and other chemicals. Reaching deep into the cabinet, he pulled something, and then swung the entire shelving outward, revealing a narrow tunnel. Collins stood to one side and motioned the others in. When everyone was inside, he pulled the cabinet closed, slid a bolt into a hole, which secured it from the inside. "Little chance of them finding this, and if they did, they'd have to tear the cabinet apart or use explosives."

Miriam said, "They have explosives."

Collins nodded. "True. Let's get moving in case they decide to blow the place up."

Rebekah looked at Miriam. "Oh, great. Another tunnel."

"What is this place?" Browning asked.

"The hot springs tunnels," Collins said.

"Those are just a legend," Henry said.

"Let's keep it that way," Collins said.

Browning said, "The tunnels are probably impassable."

"They're passable. In fact, the hot springs still work. A good percentage of our heating comes from the hot springs. The school's boiler is a booster. Because the school is near the end of the pipeline, the water has cooled to 65 degrees. Needs a boost to heat the building but still saves a bunch of money. I inspect the tunnels weekly."

"I'll be damned. Who knows about this?" Browning asked.

"As few as possible," Collins said, counting on his fingers. "Before today, three people. Me and two city maintenance guys."

"Why the secrecy?" Nyx asked.

"Because if the Chosen knew we had it, they'd charge us for it," Collins said.

"Good point," Nyx said.

"Where will this take us?" Browning asked.

Collins said, "Lots of places. Mostly to city and county buildings, but many buildings downtown."

"How was it kept secret if it heats so many buildings? Especially, private businesses?" Akira asked.

"It's not easy. The business owners think we have big boilers in the city buildings that make excess steam, which we sell to them cheap. That's how we pay for maintenance and the workers. So, far, it's worked," Collins said.

The lighting was sparse, the tunnel narrow, damp, musty, and cluttered with pipes wrapped in thick coverings. Insulation, Derrick assumed. Derrick followed Antonio. The obstacles slowed Antonio as he negotiated the labyrinth. How Antonio would get to the complex worried Derrick. Plus, Antonio would slow them down. Slow could prove fatal.

At an intersection, Collins stopped. "Hold up. Decision time."

Browning said, "Fortunate this thing exists. Getting out of the school any other way undetected would have been difficult."

"Not difficult. Impossible," Derrick said.

Collins said, "Henry, Larry, and Malcolm should go now. If Miriam's threat works with the soldiers, their involvement will remain unknown. The sooner we part company, the better for them."

Collins pointed left. "Malcolm, go that way. Go up the first ladder you come to. It takes you to a valve station in the alley near the Bistro. They disguised it as an electrical station, and it's plastered with high voltage signs. You'll see a tool belt and cap near the door. Put on the tool belt and a cap.

Leave as if you belonged there. I'll come by your house later to get the belt and cap. Understand?"

Malcolm said, "No worries."

Antonio said, "Uh, Sheriff. That doesn't sound like a good idea."

"How so?" Collins asked.

"Well, Malcolm looks the least like an electrician of anyone here. No offense, Malcolm."

"None taken, bro," Malcolm said.

Derrick wondered what Antonio meant by that but would ask him later.

Collins said, "Good point. Larry, you go."

"Will do," Larry said.

Collins said, "Malcolm, you and Henry go this direction." Collins pointed to the opposite tunnel. "It comes out in the library basement. Just walk upstairs and leave like you belong there. No disguise needed. The library is open."

Browning said, "Much better. Malcolm's presence will make Henry being in the library less suspicious. No offense, Henry."

The Potterville kids laughed.

Malcolm, Henry, and Larry made the rounds, saying goodbye and good luck. There were hugs and fist bumps. Browning and Collins got handshakes, but Coach hugged each of them after shaking their hands.

Henry had said nothing to Derrick, which didn't surprise him, but it hurt just a little. But as Henry and Malcolm started toward the tunnel leading to the library, Henry paused and whispered something to Malcolm.

Henry stepped in front of Derrick, staring at him for a moment. "So, uh, well… Okay, here's the deal. Nyx is our star runner. Don't let anything happen to her. Okay. And… well, I want you in my backfield this fall, so take care of yourself as well."

"I'll do my best." Derrick paused. "You guys need to listen."

Henry looked puzzled. "Okay. I'm listening."

Derrick said, "At the door before you open it."

"Got it. For helicopters," Henry said.

"Yes. And voices," Derrick said.

Miriam said, "Hold on." She gathered two radios. "Listen to each channel. You might learn where the soldiers are before you step out. Then shut them off and toss them in the trash. In case they can track them."

Henry took one radio and handed the other to Larry. "And what if we hear there are soldiers where we are?"

"Find another exit," Collins said.

Derrick extended his hand, which Henry grasped, but then Henry hugged Derrick. "Good luck."

After the three boys left, Collins said, "Allen, I think this is as good as any for you." He pointed to a ladder on the wall. "Get your family someplace safe."

Derrick said, "Wait. Miriam, did you get what you needed?"

Patel stepped to Derrick. "She did. I transplanted the old disk into a new hard drive. The old disk had physical damage, so it will need more work and may never work properly. Miriam can clone the other hard drives. Akira can help." Patel held out the briefcase he'd been carrying. "You can carry this for Miriam. Yes?"

"Yes, sir. Good luck to you and your family." Derrick paused. "Thank you for helping Miriam. She would not be here if not for you."

Patel looked at Miriam and then at Derrick. "It is important you are together."

Patel grabbed the ladder.

Rebekah said, "Wait. What about Anna? You were the last one to see her. How am I going to find her?"

"I would like to help you. But I don't know how I can. It's my fault she is missing. I messed up." Patel paused. "I am truly sorry, but I have my family I must put first."

Miriam pulled a burner phone from her bag. "Take this. Beginning tomorrow, turn it on at six p.m. for ten minutes. I'll call if we need anything from you."

Patel turned the phone over in his hand. "But…"

"Don't worry. I won't call unless it's absolutely necessary."

Patel nodded. "If I can help, I will."

Collins led them farther down the tunnel. Derrick estimated they had traveled half a mile. Miriam could probably tell them how far they had traveled, but he did not ask. When Collins stopped, he said, "We are under the public safety building. You know—courthouse, jail, and my office. It's not open to the public today. My deputy is on duty, but she should be on patrol. We can discuss a plan to get you out of town. Any objections?"

"What should we do with the weapons?" Nyx asked.

Miriam said, "Leave them here, for now, hidden up on the pipes. We'll decide later if we need them. They could have tracking devices, but they shouldn't be able to track them underground."

Derrick stepped up on a pipe, taking the weapons and placing them behind the top pipe. "Can you see them?"

Miriam said, "No. That will work."

There were no other objections or questions, so Collins started up the ladder. Derrick stepped to Antonio's side. "Can you make it up the ladder?"

"I'll manage. Can you help with these?" Antonio held out his crutches, balancing on one leg.

"I can," Derrick said.

Antonio waited for the girls to finish their climb and then motioned for Derrick to go next.

"I'll go last," Derrick said.

Antonio offered no argument and started up the stairs, using one leg and then pulling himself up with his arms. Derrick noted Antonio's strength, which made sense because he was an athlete like the rest of his friends, other than Akira. Perhaps Akira also played a sport. Derrick didn't know. He had not yet learned how to pay attention to other people's lives beyond how they affected him.

When Derrick started up, he realized the crutches were more troublesome than he expected. After trying a couple of methods, he settled on lacing his arm through both crutches and letting them dangle as he climbed. He used his hand opposite to carry the briefcase, which limited its use but not so much that he couldn't get up the ladder.

The others waited for him in another boiler room. As at the school where they entered the tunnel, the entrance was concealed behind a case that held paint cans and chemicals. Collins led them up the stairs, down a long hallway—across a large open area, one side boarded by large glass doors that opened to the front of the building—on the opposite side, a wide staircase led to Courtrooms One, Two, and Three. Derrick wondered what they did in such rooms but did not ask.

As they reached the Sheriff's Division entrance, Derrick turned to see two soldiers on the sidewalk. His hope, what little there was of it, faded. Escape seemed impossible.

14

IMPOSSIBLE. THAT THOUGHT BOUNCED around in Derrick's head. He edged through the group, tapping Collins on the shoulder. Raising his finger to his lips for silence, Derrick pointed toward the street. Collins nodded and then continued down the hallway. They entered a room containing several desks, not unlike those at school except larger, and then down another hallway.

Collins stopped at the door embossed with a gold shield over the words Sheriff William Collins. Collins unlocked the door and then motioned everyone inside his office. "Sorry, there aren't enough chairs."

Nyx said, "You old guys take the chairs. We can sit wherever." Nyx sat on the floor with her back to the wall.

Derrick felt uncomfortable choosing a place to sit, which should have been the least of his worries. He wanted to sit by Nyx but wasn't sure. Perhaps the girls should sit together. He could stand. He glanced at Nyx, hoping for a clue. She furrowed her brow a little. Then, to Derrick's relief, she patted the floor next to her.

"It appears we don't have as much time as we hoped," Collins said. "Soldiers on the streets. Any ideas?" Collins addressed the question to the group but looked at Miriam.

Miriam gathered papers that were spread on a counter along the wall, stacked them in a pile, and then sat. "Yes, turn on their radio."

"Good idea." Collins turned on the radio, set it to the command channel. They listened for several minutes. They heard nothing good.

Miriam motioned to turn it off. "First thing, we need to find Patel and Red Badowski and bring them here. Patel will never make it out of town, and Red is heading back to the school right into their primary search."

Collins paled. "Right. I'll call my deputy." He pulled his radio from his belt.

Miriam said, "Stop. Don't use the radio. They are probably monitoring it."

Collins blew out a deep breath. "Good point. I'll leave, and once I'm away from the office, I'll radio her to meet me. Then we can talk directly. Two officers meeting shouldn't raise any suspicions. One of us will find Patel, and the other will find Red. Problem is, I don't even know what kind of car Patel is driving or which way he's going."

Miriam said, "Look for an orange four-door called a Camry. Check gas stations going east."

"How did you come up with that?" Collins asked.

Miriam said, "I saw that car parked a block from the school. A woman and a girl sitting in the back seat scrunched down as if to conceal themselves. Patel said his family was waiting in a car. Patel drove here from Pacific Edge and was late, which means he'll need fuel before leaving town. He also said he was in a car that could not be traced to him. The orange car had Idaho plates. East is the fastest way to get to Idaho." Miriam looked at the others. "Am I the only one who noticed them? We all walked past them. You guys need to pay attention. Seriously."

Derrick did not remember seeing the car. He dared not glance at Nyx because he assumed she would not take being scolded well. Akira was looking at the floor. Rebekah looked angry. It surprised him when Rebekah said, "She's right. We need to do better."

He was equally surprised when Nyx said, "I'm sorry. I'll try harder."

Collins stepped to a metal cabinet, spun a dial right, then left, then right again, then opened the door, and pulled out a long gun with a large barrel. "Coach, take this just in case. Don't leave. I'll assume you'll have a plan when I return."

Collins stopped at the door, then over his shoulder, he said, "Wish me luck. We are going to need it."

No one spoke after Collins left the room. After a few minutes, Antonio said, "I need a soda and a candy bar. Anyone else?"

Browning said, "Collins told us to stay put. Besides, you just ate."

Antonio shrugged. "But we didn't have dessert. There are vending machines in the next room. I'll be careful, and it would not hurt to see what's happening outside."

Browning scratched his chin. "How do you know there are vending machines?"

Antonio said, "I've been here before. When I was younger, before I got my act together."

Nyx said, "I remember those machines. Good times, eh, Antonio? Get me something with chocolate, caramel, nuts, and a soda. I don't care what kind."

Browning shook his head then said, "Derrick, go with him. Stay away from the windows and be careful."

Antonio went around the room, and despite having just had pizza, everyone wanted something. Most pulled change out of their pockets. For those without cash, Antonio said he'd buy. He asked Rebekah last and then said, "Want to go with me? I could use a hand."

Derrick said, "I can…"

Antonio cut him off. "You worry about checking outside. Let us take care of the snacks."

Rebekah smiled, winked at Derrick, and hopped off the desk.

Nyx leaned in toward Derrick and whispered, "That's interesting."

Derrick wasn't sure what made it interesting. Antonio was on crutches and couldn't carry back seven cokes and five candy bars. Asking for help seemed reasonable to Derrick.

Derrick stood to go with Antonio and Rebekah.

Nyx held his hand, preventing him from standing straight, and said, "Be careful. I don't want our adventure to end prematurely, and I'm more scared than excited now."

Akira moved to the counter and sat next to Miriam. "Do you think Sheriff Collins will find Allen as you said?"

"Allen?"

"Mr. Patel."

Miriam said, "Right. I knew him as AJ. I can't get used to calling him Allen."

"My parents still call him AJ, even though he corrects them all the time," Akira said.

"Your parents are friends with Allen? I guess that's a dumb question because you said he was your godfather. I'm not sure what that means, but it sounds important," Miriam said.

"It means that if anything happened to my parents, Allen promised to care for me. They were close friends when we lived in Pacific Edge. The Patels had few friends, but our families were close. Of course, my family had few friends as well," Akira said.

"Why is that? Are the Patels bad people?" Miriam asked.

Akira stared at Miriam for a moment. "Isn't it obvious?"

"Because Technical Services people are unpopular?"

"No, silly. Because Allen is Indian, and his wife is Caucasian." Akira looked at the floor. "And because we are Asian. My father's family was from Vietnam, and mother's family was from Korea. We are why they removed Allen and his family from Pacific Edge."

"Yet they remained friends. I don't understand," Miriam said.

"Allen stood up for my family when they moved us, so they moved the Patel family too," Akira said.

"But they allowed AJ, Allen, to continue working at Technical Services? Why?" Miriam asked.

"Because Allen was too valuable to their projects. And…"

Before Akira could finish, the door flew open and smacked the wall. Antonio burst through. Rebekah followed, her arms full of soda cans.

Derrick followed a few minutes later. "Big problems."

Browning stood. "What?"

Rebekah set sodas on the desk, handing one to Antonio.

Derrick said, "I cracked open a window and heard soldiers talking outside. At first, they were talking about baseball, but they got a call on the radio. Someone spotted a kid near the school."

"It must be Red," Antonio said. "We need to go help him."

"No one is going anywhere," Miriam said.

"But Red needs our help. It's Derrick's responsibility that Red is involved in this," Antonio said.

"Antonio is right. I'll go," Derrick said.

Browning stood. "Everyone settle down."

"Hand me that radio," Derrick said.

Akira fetched the radio from the desk. Derrick grabbed a notebook and tore out a page. He did rapid jumping jacks until his breathing became ragged. Crumpling the paper near the microphone, Derrick hissed, "Mission control, Beaverton."

Derrick did more jumping jacks and then went to the floor to do pushups.

"This is mission control. Proceed to the school. Air support spotted a kid there."

Crumpling the paper and breathing hard, Derrick muttered, "Negative. We need assistance east of the school. Requesting all units—gher bertain immd…"

"Lieutenant, you're breaking up. Repeat your transmission."

Derrick held the radio out. "We checked the kid at the school. He's waiting for his parents. No involvement pgtr whttl tgrts…"

"Beaverton, you're still breaking up and hard to understand. Get to a place with better reception and try again."

Derrick made more noise and raised his voice. "Lst dmdt." Then lowering his voice, but still breathing hard and crumpling the paper. "In pursuit of three kids five blocks east of the school. Need assistance ASAP."

"Copy that, Lieutenant."

Derrick switched the radio back to the mission control channel. "All units near the school. Lieutenant Beaverton is in pursuit of the targets, five blocks east of the school. The individual at the school is not involved, repeat the individual at the school is not involved. Proceed east of the school to assist."

Derrick set the radio down.

Antonio handed him a soda and candy bar. "Quick thinking."

Derrick shrugged. "Let's hope Collins finds him before they change their minds. They will be looking for Beaverton soon."

"We have a radio, so we can keep misleading them," Antonio said.

"Or not," Miriam said.

Everyone looked at Miriam as she took two cans, two candy bars, and went back to Akira. "Maybe we ignore them from now on."

Browning took a soda, but no candy bar. "I don't understand."

Rebekah said, "That's brilliant."

Miriam smiled, "I know. I can't help it."

Akira giggled.

Nyx whispered to Derrick, "Those two. No, make it those three. They are out of control."

Derrick leaned in. "Miriam and Rebekah both have a strange sense of humor. Now, they've infected Akira."

Nyx whispered, "It can only get worse."

"Agreed."

"Care to explain to the rest of us?" Browning asked.

Rebekah chewed off a chunk of her candy bar. "If Beaverton doesn't respond, it means they are missing three men."

Browning shrugged. "They'll assume Beaverton's radio failed."

"At first. But they'll try the other two radios. When no one answers, they'll have three soldiers missing. Three soldiers injured or dead. Or worse, they might have gone missing in action." Rebekah took a swig of soda, wiping her mouth with the back of her hand. "Deserted."

"They'll focus on finding the missing soldiers," Browning drawled.

Antonio whistled through his teeth. "Whoa, Coach. This bunch is kinda scary. Are you sure you want to deal with them at school after this is over?"

Browning chuckled. "No, Antonio, I'm not sure that I do."

15

FIVE BLOCKS FROM THE SHERIFF'S OFFICE, Collins radioed his deputy, Lori Martinez. Collins hired Lori three years earlier, after her husband left town with another woman. Alone, Lori was raising her daughter, which was difficult on what she made at the gas station. Lori had no law enforcement experience, but she wasn't a typical 30-something-year-old. Raised on a farm near Fresno, Lori didn't just work the till at the gas station. She changed oil and did repairs. Most people assumed Ed, the owner, did all the major repairs, but he just said that because some people didn't think a woman could do such work. Lori could do most any job that came into the shop.

Lori took to police work right away. Collins taught, best he could, investigative techniques and self-defense. Self-defense was primarily de-escalation and treating people decent in Bill's book. She was good at both. Bill's wife died of cancer two years before he hired Lori, and some said Lori had taken a liking to Bill. Bill shrugged it off. Lori was out of his league, and he knew it.

"What's up?" Lori asked as she pulled next to Collins's open driver's side window.

"Lots of stuff," Collins said. "I can't get into it now."

"I'm freaking out, Bill. Soldiers with firearms all over town and helicopters crisscrossing every few minutes. Something's gone wrong."

"You got that part right. I'll explain later. Right now, the less you know, the better. I need you to find Red Badowski."

Lori said, "That should be easy enough. That big bruiser is hard to miss. Besides, I just saw him."

"You did? Where?"

"Over by the school. Carrying a backpack big enough to set up housekeeping or maybe moving to the wilderness."

"He's probably at the school. Find him. Take him to the station."

"You think he'll go? I mean, I've got no reason to arrest him, and what if he says no? What am I supposed to do? Shoot him?"

"Just tell him I sent you, and you're taking him to the others. That's all you need to know. Go and make it quick."

"Will do, boss." Lori chirped the tires as she pulled off.

Collins headed east. He drove 20 miles an hour over the speed limit through town. What were people going to do? Report him? Two gas stations were open today going this direction, but Collins only glanced at the first. Seeing no orange car, he sped up. No orange car at the second either. Allen had already filled up and left town if Miriam was right. Bill had to catch him before the first roadblock.

A few miles outside the city limits, Collins spotted a car ahead. Orange. Collins floored the accelerator.

Then he saw the brake lights on the orange car. He pulled to the left and saw why.

Roadblock.

Collins reached for the lights and siren—he hoped they worked because he rarely used them—this was Potterville after all. The orange car pulled to the side of the road, still far enough away from the roadblock to make identification difficult with the naked eye. But these were soldiers and would not settle for using the naked eye, so Collins hoped to draw their attention with lights blazing and siren wailing.

When Collins got to Allen's car, he pulled in front of it sideways as if blocking it in. That's not how a police stop was done. Although Collins had no professional training, he knew how to stop a car. But the soldiers didn't know that, and sheriffs nowadays were not professionally trained. In many cases, they were not professional by any definition and were just as likely to haul soldiers to jail for little or no reason. Such a lawman would let the soldiers go, setting the bail in the amount of whatever cash was left in their wallets. That's why soldiers rarely left the base. Although a few lived off base with their families. Soldiers didn't wear uniforms when they went home. Safer that way. That none of them came to Potterville suited Collins fine. That they did not know Collins would not extort money from them suited him fine as well.

Miriam was right. Allen was driving an orange Toyota. Allen signified a prayer with his hands and bowed his head.

Collins keyed his microphone. "382, this is 380." Three eight one was reserved for volunteers when Collins had need for one. If there was more than one reserve, which was rarely necessary, Collins just called them by name. It was that sort of town.

"382."

"You have that package?"

There was a pause. "Uh, yes. Talking to it now."

"Load it and meet me on Route 5 a couple of miles out of town. Don't kill anyone but lights and siren."

"Roger."

Collins smiled. He heard the excitement in Lori's voice. She loved any opportunity to run lights and siren.

Collins stepped to the car. "Looks like I found you just in time."

"You most certainly did. But how?"

"Miriam," Collins said.

"Ah, I should have known. So, what do we do now? The soldiers seem quite interested in what's happening. If they come to investigate, it would not be good for me."

Collins did not look at the roadblock. "That's why we are going to make this look like an arrest. I'm going to get you out of the car, search you, and cuff you. Lori is on the way. She'll transport you. Your wife can follow her back to the station. Meanwhile, I'll drive to the roadblock and josh with the boys a little. You know, be the country bumkin sheriff they expect. Maybe I'll even make a few idle threats should they cause any problems in town."

"You are a wise man, Mr. Collins. I am forever grateful."

"Thank Miriam. She predicted you'd be headed this way. She's something else, isn't she?"

"Something else is correct."

A siren in the distance caught Patel's attention.

"That's Lori. Step over here so the soldiers can see me arresting you." Collins pointed to the trunk of his car. "Don't look their way. We don't want them getting a good look at your face. Put your hands on the trunk."

"I have a firearm. I suppose you should take it," Patel said.

Collins patted Patel's waist. "Jesus! What the hell, Allen?"

"I must protect my family. I suspected they would come for us."

Collins removed the pistol from Patel's waist. "I won't actually cuff you but keep your hands behind your back until you're inside the car."

As Collins eased Patel into the back seat, Lori grew closer. He wished she'd turn the siren off but knew she would not until her vehicle came to a complete stop. He was pleased to see the outline of a large man sitting in the backseat on the passenger's side, causing Lori's vehicle to dip to the right, in part due to the kid's size and in part due to the condition of her old patrol car.

Collins motioned Lori to turn around and then signaled her to back up next to Allen's car. Then he heard pounding behind him. He turned and saw Allen pounding on the window. *I told him to keep his hands behind his back.*

Patel pointed toward the roadblock.

Damn.

A military vehicle with flashing lights was headed their way. Lori was halfway out of her car when Collins said, "Pop your trunk."

Her trunk had a box that contained flares and other emergency items. He grabbed it and raced to his car, cramming it into the front seat.

Then he opened the door of Patel's car and said, "Keep your heads down and get into Lori's trunk. Hurry."

Neither Mrs. Patel nor Samantha argued, and it was fortunate they were both small because fitting them into the trunk proved difficult. Then Collins got Allen and put him in the back of Lori's car.

He could hear the military vehicle now.

Collins said, "Lights and siren back to town. Go straight to the jail sally port. Secure the door behind you and don't let anyone follow you inside. Take them to my office."

As Lori sped away, Collins stepped into the road, held up his hands, stepping in the military vehicle's path. The tires chirped when the soldier slammed on the brakes.

A soldier got halfway out of the vehicle but kept one hand on the wheel. "What's happening here?"

Collins said, "Howdy. What are you boys up to?"

"Official business. Doesn't concern you. Who is in that car?" The soldier pointed toward the fading patrol car.

"A drunk driver. Ran off without paying for his gas," Collins said.

"Why did you load him into a second car?"

"Because I'm the Sheriff, and she's not." Collins motioned toward Lori's disappearing car with his thumb.

The soldier said, "Why is she running lights and siren?"

"She's afraid he's going to puke in her car. She's probably right. Damn out-of-state farmworkers come to town and drink too much on Sunday. Lucky, we don't have more dead folks out here on the highway because of it."

"Out of state?" the soldier asked.

Collins pointed at Patel's car. "Idaho."

The soldier said, "Let me by. I need to get a look at who is in that car."

"That ain't gonna happen," Collins said, putting his hand on his gun.

"You'd best stand down, sheriff."

"You still ain't told me what you're doing in my county."

The soldier said, "I told you, official business."

"That don't mean crap to me," Collins said.

"We are looking for three fugitives," the soldier said.

"What sort of fugitives? They dangerous?" Collins asked.

"Three kids from Pacific Edge. That's all I know. I doubt they pose any risk for you folks," the soldier said.

"Does it look like there are three kids in that car?" Collins nodded toward his deputy's car, which was just a dot.

"I didn't get a good look at it."

"You got a good enough look to know there ain't three kids in it."

"Looked like two. One was a big dude."

"Exactly. Not three kids. So, you ain't got no reason to be hassling my deputy. Now, let's talk about how this is gonna work. You got your orders, I get that. And long as it doesn't involve causing our town's folk any hassle, and that includes drunk out-of-state farmworkers. I'm obliged to let you do your job. Having said that, if any of you boys cause problems in my county, you'll find yourself in my jail. Got it?"

"Now look here…"

Collins pulled his gun, pointing it at the soldier's head. "I'm not done talking, son. Now, you get back in your car and go back to your roadblock and carry on with your *duty.*"

The soldier's chest was heaving. Collins felt certain the young man didn't like being told what to do by a local cop. Probably didn't like having a gun pointed at him, either. However, it was unlikely he'd do anything rash. At least, Collins hoped that was the case because if push comes to shove, Collins wouldn't shoot the kid. The military would back the soldier. They always did. But soldiers aren't supposed to cause problems. As punishment, they'd send him to a war zone. A soldier stationed here wouldn't want that. So, the soldier slid back into his seat, backed up, turned around, and drove back toward the roadblock. Collins called for a wrecker to get Patel's car back to town.

Too damn close. That much was certain.

16

Sunday, April 4, 4:45 p.m.

AS THE DOOR OPENED, DERRICK JUMPED to his feet, ready to fight. He relaxed when a young woman in sheriff's uniform entered. Red Badowski followed her. Patel came next, then a woman Derrick did not recognize and a girl he knew but could not place. Akira ran to the girl, throwing her arms around her.

Akira said, "Samantha, are you okay?"

Samantha said nothing but hugged Akira tightly.

The uniformed woman poured herself a cup of coffee, and leaned against the counter, studied the group, but said nothing.

Nyx walked to the two girls, put her hand on Samantha's back, and said, "Good to see you, Sam."

Samantha released Akira—Derrick saw Samantha was crying—and hugged Nyx. "They almost caught us."

"Who?" Akira asked.

"Soldiers. They blocked the road. Sheriff Collins got there just in time. How did he know how to find us?" Samantha asked.

Nyx pointed to Miriam.

Samantha wiped her eyes. "Miriam King? Is that you?"

"It's good to see you, Samantha. It's been a few years." Miriam turned. "Do you remember my brother?"

Samantha smiled. "Yes, of course. Everyone knew Derrick."

Nyx frowned.

Derrick felt confused. Things were back to normal.

"You don't remember me, do you, Derrick?" Samantha asked.

"Uh, well, sorta… To be honest, you look familiar, but I can't place you," Derrick admitted.

"It's okay. I wasn't popular, and I left Pacific Edge in grade school," Samantha said.

Samantha glanced at Rebekah, then looked away.

Rebekah said, "Samantha, don't you remember me?"

Samantha hesitated, then said, "I don't think so."

Rebekah pointed to her chest. "Rebekah Ford. Anna's sister."

"Oh. Uh, Anna sounds sort of familiar," Samantha said.

Rebekah said, "Sort of familiar? You and Anna were best friends."

Miriam said, "Not now, Rebekah."

Turning, Miriam said, "Red, you decided to come."

Rebekah interrupted. "Sorry—What did you say!?!"

Miriam continued to stare at Red. "You heard me, Rebekah. Not now."

Red looked at Rebekah and then back to Miriam. "Uh, yeah. No choice."

Rebekah started to speak. Miriam held up her hand. "You had no choice?"

"My grandfather said I needed to help. He said if I didn't go, he would. He also said he should have done something years ago. Said I can right a wrong. It was all pretty strange. I'm worried he's having some sort of medical issue."

"He's fine, Red. You'll understand soon enough," Miriam said.

Rebekah said, "Can I talk now?"

Miriam said, "No! We have more pressing things to deal with."

Miriam glared at Rebekah.

Rebekah glared back. "Fine!"

"I'm glad we got that cleared up." Miriam walked to the deputy, peered at her name tag. "Lori, I'm Miriam. Where's Sheriff Collins?"

Deputy Martinez said, "Stalling the soldiers at the roadblock. He should be here soon. I hope."

Miriam said, "They already have the roads blocked and soldiers on the streets. So much for having a little time. We need a plan. First, I need to get to Derrick's condo and get some computer stuff. Then…"

Derrick interrupted. "You can't go there. They'll be watching for sure. It's too dangerous."

Miriam said, "Don't interrupt. I must have that equipment."

Nyx said, "I could grab some clothes. But what if they've already been there and taken your stuff?"

Miriam said, "They might have, and you won't need extra clothes, but you can grab a few things. Akira needs her computer stuff too. She can check for bugs. I'm open to ideas on how to make this work."

"I'll take my patrol car and pull into the parking garage—two girls in the trunk, out of sight. If there are soldiers in the building, we'll pull right back out," Lori said.

"That might work. But Nyx should go first because she lives in the same building. Then we can bring Nyx back and go to Akira's. Derrick needs to come with us," Miriam said.

"He can't fit in the trunk. It's too much risk having him in the open.".

"What if he wore that?" Miriam pointed to a uniform on a hanger covered in clear plastic.

"Wear the Sheriff's clean uniform?" Lori asked, her voice raising an octave.

"Yes. And his hat," Miriam said.

"I don't think so. Bill would be pissed."

Miriam said, "I'll pay to have it cleaned."

"Why does he need to come?" Lori asked.

"Ever play monopoly?" Miriam asked.

"Eh, yeah. What's that got to do with it?"

"He's like having a get out of jail free card."

17

DEPUTY MARTINEZ ASKED SEVERAL QUESTIONS ON the way to Derrick's condo. He was unsure how much to tell her, but since lying was no longer an option for him, Derrick answered her questions as best he could. Some questions he could not answer, like how Miriam escaped from Pacific Edge because he did not know, and Miriam was in the trunk, unavailable for comment.

Derrick saw no soldiers on the streets. He wondered how many were in town. Three, he hoped, were still taped to chairs at the school, and the others running east of the school because of his last radio transmission.

Inside the condominium parking garage, Martinez drove to the far end, scanning vehicles for occupants. "See anything out of place?"

Derrick could not remember vehicles, except Paul's truck and motorcycle. He had not paid attention otherwise. Such details never seemed important. Now, he realized everything was important, and he wondered why he had not grasped that earlier. "I can't remember all the vehicles, but nothing seems unusual. But there is one problem."

"What's that?"

"Paul's truck is here," Derrick said.

"Why is that a problem?"

"I don't want to see him, and I don't want him to see me. I don't trust him. Not after all that's happened. Plus, I'm wearing Sheriff Collins's uniform. That would raise suspicion for sure."

"We'll try to avoid him. What should we do if we see him?" Martinez asked.

"Arrest him," Derrick said.

"I can't arrest people without reason," Martinez said.

"How about for their protection?" Derrick asked.

Martinez turned the ignition off. "Under certain circumstances, I can. It's called a civil hold until a mental health specialist can examine the person. Do you think Paul might hurt himself?"

Derrick heard the trunk unlock as he got out of the car. "I doubt he would hurt himself, but I might hurt him."

Derrick helped Miriam and Nyx out of the trunk. Both had stun guns at the ready. He had a pistol, but Martinez had taken the bullets. That suited him fine. Derrick did not know if he could shoot a gun, yet for some reason, he thought he could. "We should take the stairs. It's more likely that Paul would take the stairs as well, but at least we can hear if someone is coming."

Martinez said, "I'll go first. Stay one flight behind me. If you hear me talking, hide."

Nyx said, "We'll stop at my place first on the second floor. Derrick is on the third. My mom is at work. It won't take me long to pack a few things."

Miriam said, "Did you check your place for cameras?"

"I did and found two. Busted them and tossed them in the garbage," Nyx said.

"Good, but they might have installed more," Miriam said.

"They might have installed them at Derrick's place too," Nyx countered.

"Exactly," Miriam said.

"So, what do you suggest?" Nyx said.

"I don't have a suggestion. Not yet."

Inside Nyx's condo, Derrick, Miriam, and Martinez waited in the living room. After a moment, Miriam said, "It's weird the robots left, don't you think?"

Derrick said, "I suppose. I had not thought about it. They didn't find what they were looking for, then the military arrived, so I guess they were no longer needed."

Miriam said, "Perhaps. But I wish the robots had not left. I've been thinking we should take Prime's offer and give them Anna."

Derrick knew Miriam did not know Anna's location, but he thought he understood what she was doing. "It was a good deal. Maybe Prime backed out of the deal. I guess we'll never know. I've been thinking, if we hide out here for a while, the military might give up too, and then we can get on with our lives. Good thing it's spring break. We can lie low."

"Good idea. It would be fun, just hanging out, getting to know people," Miriam said.

Nyx exited her bedroom, her backpack bulging. "I'm ready."

"Good lord, girl. How much stuff do you need for backyard camping?" Miriam asked.

"What…"

Derrick interrupted. "You know. Hanging out this week. It's going to be great fun."

Nyx hesitated a moment. "Yeah. Right. Great fun. Wouldn't miss it."

They went to Derrick's place next. Derrick gathered clothes and a few food items. His backpack looked meager compared to Nyx's. Miriam added her laptop and some other things. It was heavier now, but he didn't complain. The weight felt good. Like he had a purpose.

Miriam repeated what she said in Nyx's condo, although she varied it enough to not sound suspicious. Derrick left last, hesitating at the door to take a last look at the place that once seemed so alien and now felt like home.

As Derrick closed his door, Paul stepped from his condo. "Derrick. I didn't expect to see you." Paul froze for a moment. Glancing from Martinez to Nyx to Miriam and then back to Derrick. Before Derrick could speak, Paul turned and headed back inside.

Miriam dashed at Paul, placed the stun gun on his back, and pulled the trigger.

Paul crumpled, landing face-first just inside his condo.

Martinez yelled, "You can't just stun people!"

"It seems I can, and I did."

Martinez didn't move. "Where did you get that?"

Miriam said, "Borrowed it from Pacific Edge Security. Help Derrick get him to the elevator, and let's get out of here."

With some grunting and a few cuss words, they got Paul's dead weight to the patrol car. Miriam asked Martinez to put Paul in handcuffs in case he awoke on the way to Collins's office.

Martinez patted Paul's waist before putting on the handcuffs. "Holy shit!" She pulled a gun from his belt. "Why in the hell is he carrying a gun?"

"You can ask when he wakes up. I think Collins has some questions for him as well," Miriam said.

Derrick loaded Paul into the back seat. The girls scrambled into the trunk.

Paul was coming around when they arrived at the jail. Derrick helped him get inside, where Martinez guided them to a cell.

"See if he has a cell phone before removing the handcuffs," Miriam said.

Martinez pulled a cell phone from Paul's pocket, removed the handcuffs, and then pushed him onto a steel cot.

Paul groaned as he laid down. "What happened?"

"You got caught. That's what happened," Miriam said.

"Jerk," Nyx said.

When they returned to the office, they learned Collins wasn't back.

Browning sat in Collins's chair, a soda on the desk. Red occupied one of the two chairs facing Browning. Rebekah and Antonio sat on the floor with their backs against the wall. Antonio's injured leg stretched out, and his head tilted back, resting on the wall.

"No word from Bill?" Martinez asked.

"Nothing," Browning said. "Any problems?"

"Not for us, but Paul Jorgensen had a problem," Martinez said.

Browning said, "You saw Paul?"

"He came out of his condo as we were leaving," Derrick said, removing Collins's shirt, placing it on a hanger. "Crap, he's going to notice this has been worn."

Martinez said, "I'll handle Bill. Don't worry about it."

"What happened?" Browning asked.

Martinez pointed at Miriam. "She stunned him."

Derrick said, "Paul ran back into his condo. Miriam didn't have a choice."

Martinez said, "I told her she can't go around stunning people."

Browning smiled, "Good job, Miriam. We need to learn his involvement. Where is he?"

"Locked in a cell. I took his cellphone. Another odd thing, he was carrying a gun," Martinez said, and then added, "Would someone care to tell me what's going on?"

Browning said, "Carrying a firearm? That doesn't sound like Paul. So, here's what we know. Paul might be working for Pacific Edge. Someone put surveillance cameras in the kids' homes."

"Seriously? That bastard," Martinez said, then added, "Sorry, I snapped at you, Miriam."

Miriam said, "Speaking of surveillance, Akira needs to get her equipment. I'll feel safer after she checks this place."

"You don't think they put cameras here. Do you?" Martinez asked.

"I'll feel better when we know," Miriam said.

Rebekah said, "If there are cameras here, they'd have the place surrounded."

Miriam said, "Good observation."

Rebekah said, "Off-topic, but is there some aspirin or ibuprofen? Antonio's knee is hurting a lot."

Martinez said, "I have some in my desk." She returned a few minutes later, handed Antonio a glass of water and some pills.

"Gracias," Antonio said.

Martinez said, "De nada." Then she turned to Akira. "Akira, I can take you now."

Miriam said, "Wait. Akira, what about your parents?"

"They are probably home. I don't know how I can get in and out without them being suspicious. With the helicopters and soldiers in town, they may not even let me leave."

"Ms. Martinez, can you contact Sheriff Collins and meet him someplace inconspicuous?" Miriam asked.

"Sure. We can meet in a parking lot. We do that all the time. Why?"

Miriam said, "He needs to go with you to Akira's house. Both of you go to the door like you have bad news. Then Collins needs to bring them here."

Martinez said, "I don't understand."

Miriam held up her hand. "After Sheriff Collins leaves with Akira's parents, Nyx can get Akira's gear. Nyx, do you know what to get?"

Nyx said, "I think so."

Miriam said, "Next, get Nyx's mom at her job. Same thing. Just bring her straight here. Don't let her go home." Miriam looked at Nyx. "Sorry, that's a long time to be in the trunk."

Nyx shrugged. "I'll survive."

Derrick said, "I don't like it. It puts Nyx at too much risk."

Coach Browning had remained quiet until now. "I agree. Both girls stay here. There's no reason to risk going out again. Akira, can you tell me what to gather in your room?"

Akira said, "Everything is in a black flight bag. You know, a suitcase with a retractable handle and wheels?"

Browning nodded. "I have girls. I can gather some clothing for you. Do you think they have surveillance at Akira's?"

"We should assume they do," Miriam said.

"Then I'd better not gather any clothing. Sorry, Akira. I'll get the bag after Lori leaves with your parents, then Bill and I will get Nyx's mom. We'll tell them you were running from some military guys, and something bad happened. I'll be vague about what that means, but unfortunately, your parents will suspect the worst. It has to be that way. The more convincing we are, the better chance we have of pulling this ruse."

Nyx said, "Don't worry, Akira. I brought enough clothing to share. Some of it might be yours anyway."

Akira said, "Probably. I'm missing some of my favorite stuff."

Antonio said, "What about my parents? And Red's father and grandfather?"

Miriam said, "You guys aren't associated with us like Akira and Nyx. There's no reason for anyone to focus on your parents."

Antonio said, "But my mom will wonder where I am. Since they are not looking for me, maybe I should call her."

Browning said, "Better if we don't use phones. I'll talk to your mom. Red, do I need to speak to your father?"

"No. My grandfather is covering for me. He'll tell dad I'm helping him during spring break and staying at the shop."

"Won't your dad call you?" Browning asked.

"No, he won't," Red said.

"Not for the entire week?" Browning asked.

"Probably longer than that," Red said.

Derrick had not seen Red look sad. Wasn't even sure he'd know if Red did, but he thought Red looked sad now.

Browning asked, "Lori, shall we go?"

Martinez said, "I don't enjoy lying to people. Especially about their children."

Browning said, "Let's hope lying is the worst thing that happens."

18

ANTONIO BOUGHT MORE SODAS AND candy bars for the group. Derrick and Red ate without hesitation. Miriam took both a soda and a candy bar, one with nuts, although Derrick did not remember her eating nuts. Akira and Nyx declined both, but Miriam convinced them to eat. Eating now wasn't about being hungry. It was because their next meal was unknown and might not taste as good as sodas and candy.

They heard voices in the hall. And crying. Derrick was certain Collins had returned with Akira's and Nyx's parents, but he stood by the door as if ready to fight. When Akira's parents stepped into the room, their faces proved Collins and Browning had told a convincing and horrific story. Akira's mother rushed to her, embracing her in a tight hug.

Nyx's mother looked angry. Derrick had not met Nyx's mother. She resembled Nyx, with dark eyes, olive skin, black hair but lacking a pink stripe. Lean, with the look of a woman who worked hard and had endured hardship. Derrick wondered if Nyx had mentioned him. He did not want to be on her mom's bad side. He was sure of that. And right now, she looked like everyone was on her bad side.

"What in the hell is going on?" Nyx's mother demanded.

Collins said, "Calm down, Evelyn. Give us a chance to explain. We lied to you, but the kids are in grave danger. That part is true. In fact, the entire town is in danger."

Mrs. Belos ignored Collins, staring at Nyx, and then looking at Derrick. "Is this the boy?"

Nyx said, "Yes, mama."

Mrs. Belos stared at Derrick. "You're the cause of all this?"

Derrick said, "Yes, ma'am."

"Got yourself kicked out of Pacific Edge?"

"Yes, ma'am."

"What did you do?"

"I hit a kid."

"Does this kid have a name?"

"Marcus Carver."

"Any relation to James Carver?"

"Yes, ma'am."

"That would get you kicked out of most places, even outside Pacific Edge. Why did you hit this, Marcus Carver? Are you brain dead?"

"Yes, ma'am."

"Excuse me?"

"Yes, ma'am, I'm braindead sometimes."

"And were you braindead when you hit this boy?"

"No, ma'am. I was not."

"Then why would you do such a thing?"

"I thought he was going to hit my sister." Derrick pointed to Miriam.

Mrs. Belos turned her eyes to Miriam.

Miriam met Mrs. Belos's gaze with equal intensity.

Derrick wished, just for once, Miriam wouldn't be so defiant.

Mrs. Belos asked, "Is that true?"

Miriam said, "It's true. Marcus Carver drew his fist back to hit me. Derrick knocked the crap out of him. Broke his jaw."

Rebekah said, "It's true. I saw it."

Mrs. Belos glared at Rebekah, then back to Miriam, and then back to Derrick. He knew now where Nyx got her intensity, only he'd never seen this level of fury from Nyx.

Mrs. Belos said, "So, Derrick, is it?"

"Yes, ma'am."

"Knowing what you know now, what you've lost, all the problems you've caused, would you make the same decision if you could rewind the clock?"

Derrick thought for a moment. "You mean would I let Marcus hit Miriam to prevent this from happening?"

"Did I stutter? That's exactly what I'm asking."

"I wouldn't hesitate for a split second."

But then Mrs. Belos softened, or at least, Derrick thought she did.

Turning back to Nyx, Mrs. Belos held her arms out. "Come here, baby girl."

Nyx stepped to her mother with open arms. "Thank you, mama."

After a few moments, Mrs. Belos told Nyx to sit with the other kids and then turned her attention to Collins. The adults talked. Argued would describe the interaction with more accuracy. It wasn't about Derrick. At least they were not focused on his involvement. Derrick tried to distance himself as much as possible within the confines of the small office, which had grown smaller with so many people. Derrick moved along the walls, looking at plaques and photographs. The arguing subsided. It seemed the parents had been convinced the situation was serious. Serious wasn't the best description. Dangerous was better, but they had not yet made that leap. What they did not have was a solution. Nyx's mom, Evelyn, or Evie, which the others called her, wanted Nyx home. She would keep the doors locked, and the condo building was secured. Mrs. Belos offered for Akira to stay there too. Derrick sensed what was coming next and didn't like it. But he was tired of running and lying, so he stepped back toward the group.

The door opened, and Browning entered, setting a flight case next to Akira.

Akira said, "Thank you, Coach Browning."

Mr. Nakamura said, "Did you get that from our house?"

Browning said, "Yes, sir."

Mr. Nakamura said, "You entered our house when we were not present?"

"Guilty. Akira needed this."

Akira began setting up her equipment.

"Akira, what are you doing?" Mr. Nakamura asked.

Without looking at her father, Akira said, "Scanning this building for surveillance equipment."

"You can do this?"

"Yes, father."

Mr. Nakamura nodded. "Most satisfactory. However, is it necessary?"

"Yes. I found surveillance cameras at Derrick's condo and Nyx's condo." Akira paused. "And at our house."

Collins said, "Evie, this is what I've been trying to tell you all. The condo isn't safe. Not for Nyx or you. If it was that simple, Derrick could just stay at his condo too."

Mrs. Belos returned her focus to Derrick. "What is your involvement with my daughter?"

This had taken an unexpected turn. Derrick paused, unsure of what to say. "I'm on the track team with Nyx."

He looked at Nyx. The look on Nyx's face indicated he'd said something wrong.

Nyx looked at her mother. Her voice cracked. "There's more to it than that. I first met Derrick at the Bistro before he started school. Coach Browning asked me to help Derrick train. That's why I've been leaving early."

Evie glared at Nyx. "And?"

Nyx looked at Derrick. "Mom, we talked about this. Derrick is my friend."

Now Evelyn glared at Derrick. "You didn't mention that, Mr. King. Why not?"

"I don't know," Derrick said.

"You don't know if you are friends with my daughter?"

This was not going well, and it was not getting better. "Uh, well, I want us to be friends. It's just that, well…"

"It's just what, Mr. King? Is my daughter not good enough for you because she's—what do you call us—a commoner?"

Derrick's heart pounded. He felt a bit of heat rising in his face. He'd never thought that way of Nyx. Not that he could remember. But Chosen thinking was so ingrained in him, sometimes he didn't recognize it. "No, I don't believe that's true. I think, well, I think it's the opposite. She's too good for me."

Mrs. Belos folded her arms across her chest. "Finally, we agree on something. You expect me to let my daughter run off with you? Not even tell me where she's going, yet tell me she is not safe? You want me to believe she's safer with you than at home with me? Is that what you want me to believe?"

Coach Browning said, "Evelyn, I understand how you feel, but the truth is, Derrick might be the only person who can protect Nyx. If anyone can, that is."

"What is that supposed to mean?" Mrs. Belos' eyes widened, and her nostrils flared.

Derrick did not know why Mrs. Belos disliked him so much. Maybe others had told her about how he'd lied to Nyx. Perhaps it was something else, but it occurred to him, in a way he had not previously recognized, that he had hurt Nyx. And when he fully understood this, he could not see how Nyx could forgive him. Because he could not forgive himself.

Antonio stood, carried his crutches in one hand as he hopped on one leg, and then sat next to Mrs. Belos. "So, here's the thing. There are two soldiers, three if you count the one Rebekah blasted, at the school who could testify to Derrick's ability to protect Nyx."

"Three soldiers?" Mrs. Belos asked.

"Yes. They burst into the room, following our council meeting. They blasted Sheriff Collins and Coach Browning first. That left just us kids. Nyx trusted Derrick enough that she got blasted herself."

Mrs. Belos turned to Nyx. "You did what?"

Antonio continued, "I could see Derrick from where I sat when it happened. I saw him change. Seeing her hurt, that's what changed him. It was like he woke up… I'm not sure how to explain it. Anyway, Miriam tricked them into sending one soldier on a wild goose chase. Then Rebekah and Miriam helped confuse the two soldiers until Derrick could attack. He was like something from a movie. He spun and kicked and took them both out. Rebekah blasted the third soldier when he came back. They are probably still tied up over there if you want to go check."

Mrs. Belos looked at Browning. "Is this true?"

"Like Antonio said, they shot Bill and me first thing. Two adults in the room, and we could not protect the kids. They protected us. When I awoke, it was already over. Two men were injured, so I believe Antonio is telling the truth."

Mr. Nakamura placed his hand on Akira's shoulders. "Akira, this is unlike you. You are not an adventurer like Nyx. We understand she is your friend, but your involvement is unnecessary. You will stay with us."

"Father, this is not about an adventure. I am afraid. I don't want to go." Akira hesitated. Looked at her mother and then back to her father. "But I must. Potterville is in danger. I must serve our community. It is who I am."

Her father did not speak for several moments. "Then it is settled. You must do your duty for your community, as our ancestors have done for millennia. I am proud of you, Akira."

Nyx touched her mom's hand. "Mom, when I didn't think I could make the track team, you believed in me. You encouraged me to not give up. When Antonio asked me to be on the student council, I doubted myself, but you encouraged me. You said I could make a difference. Now, I can make a real difference. I'm afraid, just like Akira. But you can't imagine what I've seen and learned. I'm sorry, but I must go whether or not you approve. But I hope to go with your support. That would make a huge difference."

Mrs. Belos nodded, and then, after a few moments, turned back to Derrick. "I know who you are and what you've done. This is a small town. Word gets around fast. I also know you hurt my daughter. I heard her crying at night. I knew it was about a boy. Then I heard about you. Chosen exile. A liar, even to a girl trying to help you. Why should I trust you now? You tell me. You're not even willing to say that you and Nyx are friends. So, I'm going to give you one more chance to explain it."

Tears flowed down Derrick's cheeks. He had not been sure of many things since he left Pacific Edge, but he was sure of this.

"Because—I love her."

19

IF ANYONE WAS MORE STUNNED BY DERRICK'S proclamation than himself, he could not discern from the looks on their faces. But for the most part, he could only see Nyx. He could not determine her reaction either, which would have made the entire moment bearable. Why he blurted that out, he might never know.

Yet he knew.

Akira said, "Finally!"

"Finally, what?" Coach Browning asked.

Akira said, "Duh. Derrick admitted what the rest of us have known since the beginning."

Nyx squeaked, "From the beginning?"

Akira said, "Don't mess with me, girl. You know exactly what I mean. Both of you lit up the moment you laid eyes on each other. You know it, I know it, Derrick knows it, and I suspect everyone in the room knew before you did. Am I wrong?"

Antonio laughed. "You are not wrong. Yet, I suspect Derrick and Nyx were the last to know. Funny how that works."

Miriam said, "Sorry to interrupt the festivities, but there's an army bearing down on us. The roads are already blocked, so no one is getting out of here. Mrs. Belos and Mr. and Mrs. Nakamura, I know this is difficult to accept, but you are in grave danger. The people in Pacific Edge had identified Nyx and Akira as friends of Derrick before I escaped. They will stop at nothing to find us, including capturing those close to us and using them as leverage. If they capture us, they will kill Derrick and me. I don't think it will end well for anyone in this room. Trust me, we did not intend to put people here at risk."

Patel, standing with one arm around his wife and the other around his daughter, said, "She is not exaggerating. Miriam and Derrick will die a slow, painful death if captured. We, too, are in grave danger because I helped Miriam. I am too scared to think straight. But I know this, we must work together and trust Miriam and Derrick—and Rebekah. And we are running out of time."

"Why don't they just stay here," Lori Martinez said, "the families that is."

"In my office?"

"Duh. In the jail. It's as safe a place as you're gonna find, and it is empty. Well, except for Paul. But we have everything they need. Granted, it's not plush, but we've got food, beds, showers. We can leave the doors open or give them the keys."

Collins scratched his head.

Browning said, "What do you think?"

"It's better than any idea I've come up with. But what about the kids? Just have them stay here too?"

"We can't stay," Miriam said. "That was never the plan."

Browning said, "You said you had to return to the place you won't tell us about. But that will have to wait. No way you can get out of town without being seen."

Derrick broke eye contact with Nyx during the discussion and wandered back to the photographs on the wall. "Sheriff, what is this?" Derrick pointed to a picture of a van and several people in orange coveralls alongside a road.

Collins said, "It's a work detail. When we have inmates, which we don't have many of these days, we have them clean along the road to reduce their sentences. I don't see how that's going to help."

"Brother, you're a genius," Miriam said.

"Yes, he is," Rebekah said.

"He's smarter than he looks," Antonio said.

Nyx, who had not spoken for a while, said, "Good job, boyfriend."

Derrick felt certain his face flushed red.

"Would someone like to explain this to me?" Collins asked.

Derrick said, "We dress like inmates. You take us to the road by the river, we'll pick up trash, but we will also hide our stuff in the brush. One by one, we'll slip off and disappear."

"That might just work. But it's almost dark now. We'll have to wait till morning, which won't be good because there will be more soldiers here by then," Collins said.

Martinez said, "We can disguise them. At least a little. Maybe a wig and makeup. Keep Derrick, Rebekah, and Miriam separated, so it's harder to make the connection. Bill and I can both go. I'll stand guard with a shotgun. If things go south, we fight."

Collins thought for a minute. "Now, hang on. We are not fighting the military. But this might work. We can head out early. However, the river is too cold and high to swim. Perhaps they can hide until dark and cross the footbridge. I'm assuming that's the direction they'll go. Let's think about that." Collins paused, then said, "Lori, buy groceries for a few days. We'll feed them dinner, get their jumpsuits ready, and let them get some rest. They've had a big day, and I suspect it's only going to get worse."

After a simple but tasty meal consisting of hamburgers, potato salad, and sodas, Collins assigned everyone to cells. The doors had solid metal doors with small slots used to pass food trays and such. However, passing food trays would be unnecessary, and the doors would remain unlocked. Since the Nakamura and Patel families knew each other, they were placed in a large cell block with individual cells. Miriam and Rebekah shared a two-person cell, as did Red and Antonio. Nyx and her mother also had a two-person cell. Derrick had a private cell.

After they had sorted out their gear and clothing, and just before they went to their sleeping quarters, Mrs. Belos looked at Nyx and Derrick, "I'm sleeping with one eye open, so don't try anything."

Nyx rolled her eyes. "Good grief, Mom." And then Nyx gave Derrick a wry smile.

Derrick thought he had never felt something so wonderful.

Collins told Browning to go home. He and Martinez would take shifts watching the jail. Collins said he'd give Browning a ride home and a shotgun. Browning said he'd stay until daylight to avoid waking his wife and kids.

With the cell blocks quiet, Derrick laid staring at the ceiling, unable to sleep. Many things floated through his mind. He rehearsed scenarios from being spotted by a military patrol, to Charlie going haywire if Miriam failed to bring Jane back from the dead.

Regardless of how farfetched the scenario, his thoughts always circled back to the girl with the pink-striped hair.

Part Two

1

Sunday, April 4, 10:35 p.m.

BROWNING COULD NOT SLEEP. He shuffled to the kitchen, hoping warm milk would help yet doubted finding sleep would be that simple. Creating a peaceful atmosphere in Potterville had been a monumental task. The days of conflict remained etched in Browning's mind—days when extremists ruled, even though they made up a small percentage of the population. Just a few days ago, he believed Potterville's gains would endure. Today, he wasn't so sure.

As Browning warmed his milk in the microwave, a voice behind him said, "You couldn't sleep either?"

Browning turned to see Evie Belos standing in the doorway, rubbing her eyes. "I could not. What are you doing up?"

"Same as you. Can't sleep. Mind if I join you?"

"Not at all. Warm milk might help."

"Sounds good." She searched the cabinets.

"The milk is in the refrigerator, and the glasses are there." He pointed to a cabinet.

Evie stared at him. "You think I can't find milk?"

"Sorry. Dumb thing to say. My brain isn't working too well. To be honest, I'm having trouble processing what's happened."

"Makes two of us." She pulled something from a shelf. "Here we go. Hand me your cup."

Evie poured a teaspoon of vanilla into Browning's milk, added a sprinkle of cinnamon, and then microwaved it 15 seconds. "Here, try this. It's my special sleep potion."

Browning sipped. "It's good. Does it work?"

"Probably not, but it tastes good." She mixed her own potion and put it in the microwave, then said, "Nyx told me you befriended Derrick on his first day of school. Asked him to try out for track that same day, even though tryouts were closed. Is that true?"

Browning nodded.

"Did you know he was lying about being an orphan from Denver?"

Browning shrugged. "I suspected as much."

"Then why? And what made you think he was an athlete? I don't get it."

Browning sipped, then said, "I don't know. He looked lonely and scared. I was just reaching out, hoping to help him find a niche here."

"They say you have a knack with kids. Especially spotting talent on the field. But why did you pair him with Nyx? She lost her father because he chased dreams. She doesn't need to be hurt again. And now she's right in the middle of this mess."

"Evelyn, that's not fair. First, Lucas was a good man. He made a huge mistake, and you have every right to be angry about that, and he was a dreamer. I'll give you that, but he just wanted to give you and Nyx a better life. Don't forget that. Second, this thing with Nyx and Derrick started before his first day of school. I may be good at spotting athletic potential, but I'm no matchmaker. In fact, I had to pressure Nyx into coaching Derrick, and Derrick said Nyx didn't like him. In hindsight, perhaps I should have surmised the tension between them meant something, but I didn't."

Evie nodded. "I just don't want her hurt, and I don't want her leaving with that boy."

Browning said, "His name is Derrick. I don't blame you about the leaving part. I don't want any of them involved in this, but that's out of my control. Like I said, I can't wrap my head around any of this. But the facts don't change, and these kids are at the age where they make their own decisions. We can only hope we've taught them well."

Evie took a deep breath, blew it out. "You're right. I'm so angry with Lucas I forget how much he loved us. Nyx meant the world to him."

"You meant the world to him too, Evie. Don't forget that."

Evie nodded, fighting back the tears. "I can't lose Nyx. I couldn't survive it. And that boy, saying he loved her like that."

Browning shook his head, whistled lightly through his teeth. "That was a shocker. Yet, to their friends, it seemed obvious."

"Still, it's puppy love. I won't lose my daughter over puppy love."

"Have you talked to Nyx? How does she feel?"

Evie said, "She won't talk to me about it. I'm afraid she may suffer from puppy love as well."

Browning said, "I don't have an answer, Evie. But remember, puppy love is real love to the puppy."

* * *

Martinez took the first watch, but Collins did not go home. Sleep would be impossible. He drove around, checking his town—no soldiers on the street. Soldiers needed rest, although Collins did not know where they were sleeping.

Perhaps the caravan had stopped. Helicopters may have ferried men back to the caravan for the night. He saw a few flat-green Humvees. Only military personnel drove Humvees, which were illegal for civilians to own. Lots of things were illegal for civilians. Harboring fugitives, for example. Perhaps soldiers slept inside the vehicles. Maybe they were walking around town, hiding in the shadows. Collins didn't check the vehicles. Good way to get oneself shot.

He worked his way east of the school, careful to not appear obvious. More Humvees—parked in the darkest spots available. Soldiers in the front seats, watching. He wondered what decisions they had made. He assumed they had not yet found the soldiers at the school. Too bad for those guys. The janitorial staff would find them in the morning. Then someone would have to deal with them. He hoped the kids were long gone by then but knew it would be close. Janitorial staff didn't have an early start because of spring break. That played to his advantage.

Collins drove onto the river levee near the dam. The water ran high, making room in the reservoir for spring runoff. Marks on the rocks indicated the river had run much higher at one time, but it had not been that high in his lifetime. Would probably never be that high again. Perhaps they did not need to release so much water, but they always did. The river would be a trickle by summer's end. It was reported they'd have enough water for most of the crops this year. Crops that took longer to mature were at risk. Nothing new about that.

Collins got out of his car and walked the levee. Perhaps they should have monitored the soldiers' radios longer, but Miriam thought the radios had tracking devices. No one knew the answer to that, so they turned the radios off, and Collins locked them in the gun safe. Only the bank had a more secure vault. Still, this safe was steel buried in rebar-reinforced concrete. The Potterville sheriff no longer needed such a vault, which was built decades ago when the United States was on the brink of civil war. Collins wondered if they were closer to such violence than they realized.

Lights appeared on the street. This was not good. A Humvee stopped. A soldier got out of the passenger's side and walked to the levee. From ten feet below, a man called out, "Good evening, Sheriff. What are you looking for?"

"I might ask you the same thing?" Collins said. He wasn't sure what to say. Why was he out here? He wished he'd discussed this with Miriam. She always seemed prepared.

"Official business," the soldier said. "Sorry, I don't mean to be evasive. It's all I'm authorized to say." He glanced over his shoulder at the vehicle, the motor clattering.

"I understand. Regulations. Do you ever tire of them?" Collins asked, avoiding the question. Still thinking.

The soldier said, "It's what we live by. Tiring of them changes nothing. We just learn to live with them. You didn't answer my question."

Collins said, "I did not. You didn't answer mine either."

The soldier said, "Fair enough. As you probably noticed, we have a few men here. If you need help with something, well, not that we can get involved with local matters, but we might see something and could pass it along. All in good faith for the common good."

Collins stifled a laugh. These guys were not about the common good. "We had some kids go missing last night," Collins said.

"Oh. What kids?"

"I can't share that information. You know, juveniles."

"Right. I understand. How many kids?"

Collins thought for a moment. "Five that we know of."

"Wow. That must be worrisome."

"It is. Their folks are worried sick, that's for sure. But I suspect they'll turn up in the morning. Probably having a bit of a party and got their wires crossed about who was staying with whom. You know. Teenagers."

"But you're concerned about the river. Am I right?"

"A little concerned, yes. It's running high. Cold, too. If they got to playing around here, the current could take them quickly."

"All five of them?"

"Probably not. Like I said, they'll turn up in the morning. Well, if you'll excuse me, I need to get some sleep. Got an early day."

With that, Collins walked back to his patrol car. The soldier made him think. *Where did the kids plan to go?* The mountains, he was sure of that. That's the way they came to Potterville. Derrick said they would hide their stuff next to the river. So, crossing the footbridge was obvious. They must have come that way when they came to Potterville. The three of them were dirty and scratched but not soaked. They'll cross the bridge, so the water level is of no concern. Yet the bridge was dangerous. They would be exposed, and soldiers would be everywhere by morning. Crossing the bridge puts them in immediate danger, but the water is too high and too cold to swim.

Derrick had not thought this through.

The kids could not afford mistakes.

Mistakes would get them killed.

2

Monday, April 5, 5:30 a.m.

DERRICK AWOKE IN A WHITE ROOM THAT FELT familiar yet alien. There were no children—no Number Six, no Keepers, no Tenders. He sat alone on a bed, such as it was, just a metal frame and a thin mattress, not unlike the beds in his dreams. He just now remembered those beds and small rooms in which he slept as a child. But there was something else familiar but was never in his dreams. Bacon. Rubbing his eyes, Derrick stumbled from the room, following the scent. In the kitchen, he found Sheriff Collins cooking.

"Hey, you're up early. There's a plate of bacon." Collins pointed to a plate with a paper towel covering a mound. "Coffee? Sorry, we don't have an espresso machine, but we have cream and sugar."

Derrick grabbed a piece of bacon and filled a cup with steaming coffee. "Black is fine."

Derrick sat at a long metal table with metal benches. All the pieces were bolted to the floor, which seemed like an odd way of doing furniture, but then it was his first time in a jail.

Miriam walked in and went straight to the coffeepot. She poured a cup, adding cream and sugar.

"Another early bird," Collins said.

"Early bird?" Derrick puzzled, then said, "Oh, an expression."

"I've been awake for an hour," Miriam said.

"Sorry if I woke you. I tried to be quiet," Collins said.

"You didn't wake me. I was already awake," Miriam said.

"Why were you awake so early?" Collins asked, glancing over his shoulder as he turned bacon.

"Thinking," Miriam said.

"Anything you'd like to share?" Collins asked.

Miriam said, "Derrick's idea about posing as inmates on cleanup detail is good, but I'm worried about crossing the river."

Rebekah walked into the kitchen. "I smell bacon."

Derrick pointed. "On that plate and coffee is over there."

Collins said, "I was thinking about the river too." Collins turned back to the stove. "I'll start pancakes soon, but I was waiting for more people to be up.

If they are not awake by six, I'll start pounding on pots. Miriam, sorry to interrupt. What were you thinking about the river?"

"The river. Taking the footbridge exposes us. We wouldn't stand a chance of escaping if they spot us. Derrick and I could swim the river. I'm not sure about anyone else."

"I'm a good swimmer," Rebekah said. "I use the academy's pool to train in the offseason. Did I mention I play soccer?"

Collins chuckled. "I have heard that somewhere."

Rebekah said, "Antonio can't swim the river. That would be far too dangerous. He should stay here and get his leg fixed."

Miriam gave Rebekah a weak smile.

It didn't take long for everyone to filter in. Red came next, followed by Antonio. Red sat at the end of the table, away from everyone. Antonio grabbed a cup of coffee and sat next to Rebekah.

Nyx and her mother came in a few minutes later. Soon, the Nakamura and Patel families joined them. The tables filled. Derrick stood at the counter so others could sit. Mr. Patel and Red Badowski joined him. Collins poured pancake batter on a large flat surface.

Collins pointed at a cabinet. "Derrick, would you get plates for everyone?"

"Sure." Derrick stepped to the cabinet, setting plates on the counter, counting as he did. In a moment, Nyx joined him, pressing her hip lightly against his.

"I'll take them," Nyx said.

Derrick turned to watch her. "Thanks." It seemed everyone was watching, smiling, except for Mrs. Belos. She wasn't smiling. Not even a little.

Collins piled more bacon on a plate. When everyone was seated, he said, "Last night I went to the spillway below the dam. They've increased the flow, making the river too high to cross. Even a strong swimmer wouldn't make it."

"Why is the river high?" Miriam asked.

Collins set the bacon platter in the middle of the table and then went back to the grill and flipped the pancakes. "Spring runoff. They always lower the reservoir this time of year. Although I don't know why. We run out of water before fall."

Browning walked into the room. "That's the way they've always done it. Just the way it's done, I guess."

Miriam said, "That's interesting. Seems odd they would do that. Who controls the dam?"

Collins said, "Joe Washington. The water users pitch in to pay him. He's the only guy who knows how to do it. He learned from his father."

"What if something happens to Joe?" Derrick asked.

"Good question. Perhaps he should teach someone. He doesn't have kids," Collins said.

Miriam said, "I have an idea."

Collins sat and passed a big plate stacked with pancakes. "Let's hear it."

Miriam said, "I'll tell you in private. You're the only one who can know about it. Safer that way."

"What about Antonio? Is the plan too dangerous for him?" Rebekah asked.

Antonio said, "I appreciate your concern, I really do. My knee is fine."

Red cleared his throat. "I can help. I'll take good care of Antonio." Red grinned. "He's just a runt."

"Watch yourself, Red. I won't always be laid up."

"True. But you'll always be a runt."

"I'll be fine," Antonio said. "I'm going and it's not up for discussion."

Rebekah said, "Fine. Be that way."

Antonio rolled his eyes.

Collins said, "Miriam, you want to talk in the hall?"

Miriam said, "I do."

Rebekah said, "Do the rest of us get to know what this plan of yours is?"

"Those going and just before we leave," Miriam said, and then added, "Safer that way."

Rebekah said, "God, I'm tired of hearing that."

"I'm tired of saying it."

Miriam grabbed a slice of bacon and motioned Collins into the hallway.

After a few minutes, Collins and Miriam returned. Collins said, "Eat up. It's going to be a big day. Before evening, we'll have either failed or succeeded."

"What happens if this plan doesn't work?" Mr. Patel asked.

Collins said, "I'm not sure, but it won't be good."

3

IN THE EARLY MORNING LIGHT, A VAN STOPPED near the footbridge where an inmate work crew climbed out. Deputy Martinez parked her patrol car behind them, lights flashing. She stood on the levee, holding a shotgun. Collins drove the van, keeping between the workers and the roadway. The work crew carried orange bags, filling them with debris, using long sticks with metal points. When a bag was full, the worker set it at the edge of the road. A truck would come later to gather the bags and take them to the landfill. Derrick felt wholesome about picking up trash. At least something good would come of this, even if Miriam's plan didn't work. It was a weird way of thinking but what wasn't weird about this situation.

Miriam had explained the plan to those going. No one liked that their parents wouldn't know the truth. Although the families might suspect something was amiss. Still, they wouldn't know for sure. Miriam made Collins and Martinez promise to keep the plan secret. If the kids didn't come home, it would be safe to tell the families the truth in a few years, and if they didn't return, the result was the same, although how their lives ended would differ from what they thought happened today.

After working half a mile from the footbridge, Derrick pulled a full orange bag from the van. The brush was thick, but occasionally it cleared enough to get over the levee and close to the water to hide their bags. Collins wasn't exaggerating. The river ran high, fast, and angry. Attempting to swim it, would be suicide.

Derrick had just returned from depositing the last bag when a large, dull-green vehicle pulled up. A man in uniform exited the passenger side. Derrick turned his back.

"Good morning, Sheriff. Looks like you have a cleanup crew working."

"Yep," Collins said from the van.

"They look pretty young," the soldier said.

"Juveniles," Collins said. "We have them do this rather than jail time."

"I see. Mind if I speak with them?"

"I sure do. They're juveniles. Sealed records, you see. Can't let you do that," Collins said, inching ahead, keeping the van between the soldier and the orange-clad inmates.

Derrick pulled his cap down.

"Our business here is about runaways. It's official business," the soldier said.

Collins said, "Official for you, not for me. I said no."

"We are also looking for three soldiers. They did not report in last night. Perhaps they went AWOL. Have you seen any strangers in town?"

Collins said, "I have not. They wouldn't stick around here if they wanted to escape, would they?"

The soldier said, "I suppose not. The last we heard from them; they were chasing runaways east of the school. Perhaps the runaways did something to them. If they did, say they injured my men, that would be a crime here. Wouldn't it?"

"Perhaps. Depends. Maybe the kids were defending themselves."

The soldier said, "Interesting. You said kids, but I did not say we were looking for juveniles. I said they were runaways."

Collins said, "Here, runaways are juveniles. Adults can come and go as they please. I guess that's not true in your world, but you said the soldiers were AWOL, not runaways."

The soldier said, "I don't know if they ran off or if something happened to them. However, these runaways are dangerous."

"Humph. Juveniles can take out soldiers? That doesn't say much for your soldiers. Does it?"

"These are not ordinary children…"

Collins's phone erupted. Today he used an earpiece so only he could hear the other party. After a few moments, he looked at the soldier. "Looks like someone found your men."

"I see. Who found them, and where are they? Are they dead?"

"Not dead, but two are injured. They are at the school, tied to chairs. The janitor found them," Collins said.

"Then you shall accompany me to the school," the soldier said.

"You go ahead. You can tend to your soldiers, just don't bother my townsfolk. I can't leave this work crew, but I'll wrap it up early and catch up with you."

"Fair enough," the soldier said.

When the military vehicle was out of sight, Collins rolled down the passenger side window and said, "Everything hidden?"

Derrick said, "Yes. We are ready."

"Let's rock and roll," Collins said.

Derrick said, "I do like the music called rock and roll, but I don't see how it applies to our situation."

"Another expression. Nyx can explain it to you. I assume she does a lot of that. Just get yourselves in position."

Collins made a phone call, as did Martinez. Then Collins said, "Load up. We're on in 15 minutes."

Following the plan—the part Miriam insisted on, the part Collins didn't like—Akira and Nyx stripped off their orange coveralls and trotted to Martinez's car. Marinez drove toward the dam, picking up Akira and Nyx's parents along the way. Both families had left the jail earlier, walking to predestined rendezvous locations.

Derrick, Miriam, Rebekah, Antonio, and Red removed their orange coveralls, tossing them in Collins's trunk, and then slipping into the brush.

Collins drove away. Thirty-minutes later, a siren atop the water tower sounded. Collins turned on his lights and siren and raced toward the dam.

Something terrible had happened in Potterville.

* * *

Collins tuned his car radio to a local station. The announcer cut into the middle of a song, which Collins regretted because he liked the tune, old though it was, by Allen Stone.

The Sheriff's office has just informed us that three juveniles are missing. The Sheriff reports that bits of clothing were found near the dam. The Bureau of Water Management is lowering the river to facilitate a search. We will keep you informed as details become available.

Half a mile from the dam, Collins turned off the siren, but the lights remained on. Coach Browning stood on the levee, waving. Collins locked his brakes, sliding to a stop. With giant steps, Collins scrambled to the top of the levee. Browning pointed toward the water.

Collins said, "I hope this works."

Browning said, "You and me both. My kid is going to wonder what happened to his shoes. Looks like he'll get a new pair."

"From here, it looks like he could use them," Collins said. "Is it Derrick's size?"

"Close enough," Browning said.

"How long before Joe lowers the gates?" Browning asked.

"He said an hour. I guess there's more to it than pushing a button. I'll take some pictures. Make this look official."

Collins returned with a camera, a bunch of tags, and plastic bags. "How'd you get it down there?"

"Tossed it," Browning said.

"Good aim."

"Not that good. I'm hoping we find the first one because it tumbled into the water. How long will we search?"

Collins said, "Till nine. Then the gates open."

"Gates open?" Browning asked.

"Joe has to increase the flow to make up for what was lost today. The river will be raging. I'll need to issue a high-water warning. Tell people to stay away from the river. Works on a couple of levels, if you know what I mean," Collins said.

Browning said, "So the kids have to be across before then."

"Exactly." Collins worked his way to the shoe, took photos, wrote on a tag, and then placed the shoe and tag in a plastic Ziplock bag, which he tossed to Browning.

Three people joined Browning. A man Browning recognized but did not know said, "What happened?"

Collins joined them, winded. "Coach spotted that shoe a little while ago."

"Why were you out here, Coach?" the man asked.

"I heard kids were out here last night." Browning paused, pulled out his handkerchief, and blew his nose. "Some kids went missing last night. I saw the shoe, and well, with the high water and all…"

The man whistled. "You think a kid went into the water?"

"Maybe. Perhaps, three of them," Browning said.

"But why would they do that? The river's way too high."

"New kids. Didn't know the river. It was dark. Plus, Joe raised the flow a couple of days ago. They couldn't see the river had risen in the dark and they were scared." Browning sniffed. "Maybe one fell in, the others tried to help. Makes sense."

"The new kids? Oh, God, you don't mean…"

"Yep. Derrick King, his sister, and their friend."

"What scared them?"

"Soldiers were combing this area yesterday. The kids might have thought they were looking for them. They might have been right."

Deputy Martinez arrived. Nyx ran up the embankment, saw the shoe in the bag, fell to her knees, and cried hysterically.

If she wasn't a runner, she'd make a first-rate actor, Browning thought.

4

BRUSH SCRATCHED AT DERRICK'S HEAD and back. The damp ground felt cold, and rocks dug into his butt. He adjusted this way and that. Squirmed and fidgeted, but nothing helped. A siren sounded in the distance.

Derrick whispered, "They'll be headed to the dam."

"No talking," Miriam hissed. "Someone might hear you."

"What if people come this far searching?" Derrick asked.

"That's why you're supposed to be well hidden. The sheriff will direct people to look no farther than the footbridge. We discussed this," Miriam said.

"I know what we discussed, but sometimes people don't follow instructions," Derrick said.

"Martinez will patrol this stretch and direct people back to the other side of the bridge," Miriam said.

"Take a nap, King," Antonio said.

Rebekah chuckled, sounding close to where Antonio was hidden.

They were supposed to stay quiet. They were supposed to be separated. It was going to be a long day.

After what seemed like hours, the water receded, but it didn't happen as quickly as Derrick had imagined. He wondered if they should ferry bags across but rejected the idea. Wearing wet clothing all day did not appeal to him and would compound his already substantial discomfort.

As time dragged, and with little else to focus on, Derrick recognized one car had driven by slowly three times. On the fourth pass, he heard a second car. Both vehicles stopped. He heard voices, and then they left. Deputy Martinez, Derrick assumed, telling people to search farther upstream. The water level had dropped. He could wade across the river now, but they had to wait many hours until dusk.

Derrick wished Nyx were here but knew it would be a while before she arrived. If she arrived. There were no guarantees. No guarantees that Miriam's plan would work either, but he liked the idea, although there were tricky parts. And there was the deception part, which he did not like but understood. No one had mentioned Derrick used the drown-in-the-river trick to elude his first would-be captors, but he felt confident the remnants of his subterfuge floated in Miriam's head and helped her formulate this plan. Nyx and Akira, searching for their bodies, would help sell it. More importantly, it would remove any suspicion that Nyx was with him.

Browning would have the team members searching the riverbank. That would help sell it, too. It would also make it impossible for Derrick to be trusted again. Coach too, which would not be good for the team. But radioactive air and water wouldn't be good for the team either.

More hours, which felt like days, and finally, long shadows enveloped them as the sun eased below the horizon. The forest changed from greens and browns to multiple shades of gray, making it hard to distinguish trees from bushes, bushes from stones.

It was time to cross.

But Nyx and Akira had not arrived.

Time slowed to a stop. Yet, it passed too quickly because they had to cross before nine o'clock to beat the rising waters.

Derrick heard a noise to his left.

Miriam whispered, "Derrick?"

"Here," Derrick replied.

Miriam eased through the brush. She was invisible until within a few feet of him. "Where is Antonio?"

"A little further," Derrick said, pointing upstream.

"And Red?"

"I don't know. I have not heard him."

"Time for you and Red to get Antonio across," Miriam said.

Miriam whispered, "Antonio? Red?"

Antonio whispered, "Here."

Closer, Red whispered, "Here."

Miriam said, "Red, move toward Antonio. Time to get him across."

Rebekah said, "I want to go too. I can take Antonio's crutches."

Miriam sighed. "Fine."

With Derrick on one side of Antonio and Red on the other, they waded into the river. It was more difficult than Derrick anticipated. The polished stones looked uniform from the footbridge, but they were not. They were round, uneven, and slick. Derrick and Red moved slowly, trying to be quiet, but made far too much noise. Rebekah followed, carrying crutches and one orange bag.

Upon reaching the other side, they found the brush was too thick to penetrate. They worked upstream until they found a break. A flashlight would have helped, but that wasn't an option. Derrick thought they were close to where they came off the mountain, with Akira and Nyx returning from their trip to Silo Number Eight.

A shiver ran up his back.

* * *

Martinez stopped on the road below the levee, having spotted Sheriff Collins.

Collins raced down the bank. "Where's Akira and Nyx? Are they with the others?"

Martinez said, "I don't know where they are. I was hoping you knew."

"Damn it. They should be with the others by now. Joe started raising the gates early."

"I guess they won't make it then," Martinez said.

Collins said, "We need to find them. Stubborn as Nyx is, she'll try to cross when she sees the water rising. Akira is attached to Nyx's hip and will wade in after her."

"But wouldn't that ruin the entire plan?" Martinez asked.

"Sure would. We need to find them. If we locate them in the next five minutes, take them to the rendezvous spot. Lights and siren all the way. They might have time to make it if we beat the rising water," Collins said.

"And if they are with their parents?"

Collins said, "Same story we discussed earlier. You go upstream, I'll go down."

Martinez shook her head. "That will not be easy. Too dark to recognize people."

Collins said, "Run your lights but drive slow. The girls will find us."

* ✱ ✱

With Antonio on the other side, Miriam handed Red and Derrick the last orange bags. "Take these across. We won't have much time when Akira and Nyx arrive."

Red said, "If they arrive."

Miriam said, "You know something we don't?"

Red shrugged. "No, but things happen. Parents might cause problems. Just saying. They should have been here by now."

"Just take the bags."

On the other side, Derrick and Red discussed leaving the bags there or taking them to Antonio and Rebekah. Red convinced Derrick to drop the bags 15 yards away from the river. Far enough, the rising waters could not reach them, using a giant tree as a marker.

Derrick and Red stepped into the water, then froze. They heard something splashing on the other side, a small frame silhouetted against the tangle of brush. Derrick didn't know if they should retreat or move forward. As the person grew closer, he recognized Miriam.

Had time run out?

Frantically, Derrick waded toward Miriam. She shushed him and motioned for him to stay put. He heard rumbling in the distance.

And a tremor under his feet.

5

DERRICK REMAINED EMBEDDED IN THE STREAM. His feet dug in between rocks, braced against the rising current, and growing numb from the cold. as Miriam reached him. She looped her arm through his, trying to drag him toward the shore. He could have overpowered her, but he did not. Tears filled his eyes. He might never see Nyx again. Although he knew there was no future for him in Potterville, he thought they had a few more days together.

Standing on the shore, Miriam sucked in air. The oncoming river grew louder, making communication difficult. Miriam shouted, "We've got to go. The water is coming. We have to be farther up the bank before it reaches us."

***

Collins drove down the levee road. Martinez was right. It was too dark to see much. His red and blue rotating lights threw flashes on the levee bank. He could see people silhouetted against the gray sky. A few waved, but none ran to stop him.

Running out of time.

With his head turned to study the levee, Collins almost didn't see two girls running in the middle of the road, hands waving.

Nyx said, "Where have you been? We gotta go."

Standing one foot out of the car, Collins said, "It's probably already too late. Joe raised the gates early."

"Why?" Nyx asked.

"I don't know?"

Just then, Akira's father came sliding down the bank. "What has happened?"

Akira said, "Sheriff Collins found something. Nyx and I gotta go to identify it. Tell mom and Evie we are with Sheriff Collins."

"They found a body?" Mr. Nakamura asked.

Akira said, "Not a body. A backpack."

"Why do you both have to go? Perhaps Mr. Collins can bring the backpack here."

Akira said, "Too many questions, dad." And climbed into the car.

Nyx tugged on Collins's pant leg and whispered, "Get in and drive, or I'll leave without you."

* * *

Derrick waded back into the stream. "Stay here!" He fought his way to the other side. The water was up to his waist and moving faster, forcing him downstream. Before he reached the other side, the current had swept him 30 yards down the river. Derrick grabbed branches, pulling himself into the brush, fighting his way up the bank.

From the top of the levee, he could see flashing red and blue lights approaching fast, but the car stopped 50 yards from his location. The water had carried him out of position.

Crashing through the brush, Derrick got to the road, sprinting as if he were in a race. Seconds later, he reached the car, but it was empty.

He could hear something else.

Collins hollered, "It's too deep! Come back!"

By the time Derrick reached Collins, both girls were in the water. Nyx was about a third of the way across, swimming with powerful strokes, angling downstream rather than fighting the current.

Akira, however, was only a few yards from shore. Akira wouldn't make it. Nyx might but might wasn't good enough for Derrick. He must get Akira back to shore and then pursue Nyx. Akira would have to stay in Potterville.

Then Derrick heard a voice.

"Akira!"

Someone in the water.

It was Miriam, just a few yards from Akira. "Swim to me. I'll help you," Miriam hollered.

Derrick yelled, "It's too dangerous. Just get yourselves back to the riverbank."

Miriam yelled, "Help Nyx!"

Derrick scanned the river, trying to locate Nyx. She had disappeared into the darkness, but then he saw her in the middle of the river. Her strokes had slowed. The cold and fatigue had worn her down. Then he saw something coming at her. At first, he thought it was Red, but soon realized it was a log.

He froze. Unable to move. Cupping his hands to his mouth, he shouted, "Nyx, behind you!"

But it was too late.

The log hit Nyx.

Nyx disappeared into the raging water.

Derrick dove off the levee. He heard Collins scream, but Derrick hit the water, went under, kicking his legs and pulling himself through the current with his arms. He surfaced, scanned the water, and swam faster.

The current propelled him, but it was carrying Nyx as well. He couldn't see her. He could not see much of anything. Derrick reached the approximate location where the log hit Nyx. Diving under the water, he searched for her with each stroke.

Nothing.

Derrick drove to the surface, took a breath, and yelled, "Nyx!"

Nothing.

Derrick realized she was now traveling straight downstream. She was no longer swimming toward shore. The river was carrying her.

Derrick had promised Nyx's mother he'd protect her. He might never find her.

He sensed movement on the riverbank. When he took his next left stroke, he scanned the bank. There he saw Red, running hard, waving his arms, pointing.

Derrick raised his head enough to yell, "What?"

"In front of you. About ten yards. Hurry!"

Derrick swam, not breathing for several strokes, then took one quick breath and swam again, arms stretching, fingers searching.

He touched something, but his hand knocked it away.

Next stroke, he found it—a shoe.

Derrick grabbed the shoe, pulled Nyx to him, turned her over, and swam toward the shore. He heard a commotion of splashing and yelling, but he focused all his strength on getting to the riverbank.

An enormous hand snagged Derrick's elbow and tossed he and Nyx onto the riverbank.

"Help Nyx," Derrick yelled.

That command wasn't necessary. Red left him to fend for himself and pulled Nyx to the top of the riverbank. When Derrick reached Nyx, Red had her lying on her side, slapping her back. Suddenly, Nyx coughed, and a spray of water flew from her mouth and nose.

"That's it," Red said. "Get it out. Breathe. You're going to be okay."

Derrick kneeled beside Red. "Thank you. You saved her."

"No. You did."

"I owe you," Derrick said.

"You've owed me since the incident with Jimmy."

"I owe you double," Derrick said.

Nyx rolled over, got onto her hands and knees. Coughed and shivered.

"More than double and we still ain't friends," Red said.

Derrick said nothing for a moment. "Definitely not."

Rebekah came running. "Is she okay?"

Nyx coughed and said, "I'll live."

Derrick looked up, afraid to ask. "What about Miriam?"

"She and Akira are, emulating Nyx," Rebekah motioned with her thumb over her shoulder, "back there. Akira is as stubborn as Miriam."

Derrick rubbed Nyx's back. "Are you okay? You shouldn't have done that. I almost lost you."

"What? And let you go on this adventure without me?" Nyx sat, looked at Derrick. "That is not going to happen."

Two dark figures approached. A breathless Miriam said, "That was close. You were late. What happened?"

"A reporter. From the newspaper. Wanted to interview us. Sorry," Nyx said between breaths.

Derrick took a deep breath. "Everyone made it. That's what matters."

Nyx slapped the back of her neck. "Damn bugs."

"Probably those little ants," Miriam said. "You know, like when we brought you out this way."

Nyx said, "Great. Can we go now?" Nyx struggled to stand. Miriam helped her up.

Derrick said, "This is not starting out well."

Akira said, "I thought I was a goner. Miriam saved me."

Miriam said, "Perhaps that gets bad luck out of our way early."

Rebekah said, "You believe that?"

Miriam said, "No. But it's the thought that counts. Can you guys find the meadow where we took out the robot?"

Bounding up on his crutches, Antonio said, "Robot? Like the ones that came to town?"

Miriam said, "Yes. Same type. No one answered my question. Can you find your way?"

Derrick said, "I think so. It would be easier with some light."

"No light," Miriam said. "We can't risk it. Go slow. Be quiet."

Nyx said, "We'll find it, light or no light."

Miriam said, "It will take me a while to get back. Just wait in the trees."

"Where are you going?" Akira asked.

"Back the way we brought you out," Miriam said.

Akira said, "That will be too dangerous in the dark, with those narrow trails and cliffs."

Miriam paused. "Uh, well, not too dangerous. You can come with me. You might as well know the truth."

Akira said, "What truth?"

"You'll see. The rest of you go to the meadow but wait in the trees. Just be close enough to see the meadow."

Derrick said, "I don't understand. Why don't we just all go to the meadow? Wouldn't that be the quickest way in?"

"It would be, but Antonio can't make it in that way. Not safely. I told you I had a plan for Antonio. Remember?"

"I remember you had a plan. You never explained it," Derrick said.

"Just be careful. We'll see you in about an hour," Miriam said.

Miriam and Akira gathered bags and started downstream.

Nyx and Derrick discussed how to get to the meadow. Nyx estimated they were about a mile from the footbridge. On a path, the mile would take 20 minutes. Fighting through the brush in the darkness would take three times as long. The sound of the river grew louder, the ground vibrated.

Derrick said, "We'd better go. It'll take us an hour to get there."

Everyone picked up at least one bag, even Antonio, but Red grabbed three. They were below the riverbank, despite Miriam's warning, Derrick pulled out a flashlight, covered the lens with his hand, turned it on, and let a little light leak through his fingers, then turned it off when he had a bearing a few yards ahead. This made progress easier, faster, and safer.

When Derrick estimated they were within a hundred yards of the footbridge, he whispered, "Voices."

They slowed, creeping forward. After 50 yards, they could see the footbridge through the trees. Or, more accurately, they could see lights on the bridge and hear voices, although he could not make out any of the conversation. They stood in cold, wet mud—the river overflowing its banks. His feet grew numb again, and ants crawled all over him, but he dared not brush at them. He hoped Nyx could hold it together. She hated bugs.

After 15 minutes, a glow backlit the people on the bridge, then red and blue flashing lights swirled through the darkness. Either Collins or Martinez still patrolled the area. Running people off, Derrick hoped. More discussion. A man's voice rose but then fell. Soon the flashlights moved from the bridge. A motor started, a second set of headlights glowed, and then both vehicles left.

Derrick eased through the brush and reached the trees that separated the meadow from the river. He found the trail and then crept to the edge of the meadow.

Nothing.

Just blackness.

Moonlight would have helped.

Then a whisper. "Derrick?"

It was Miriam.

Derrick hissed, "We're here. Where are you?"

Miriam whispered, "Come to the light."

A dim, rectangular light appeared in the darkness. A small person stood in the center, featureless, unrecognizable. Derrick knew it was Miriam, standing inside the door of the aircraft they took from the disabled Prime robot. Now, he understood. She planned to fly Antonio, so he did not have to climb over the pile of rocks leading to the hidden canyon.

Antonio reached the entrance, touched the side of the machine. "What is this?"

"An aircraft," Miriam said.

"But how, where…"

"We took it from the robot," Rebekah said.

"Robot? From where?" Antonio asked.

"The side of the aircraft has a big letter P. Like the ones that came to Potterville. So, Prime, I suppose," Miriam said.

"Damn," Red said.

"Quickly," Miriam said. "Everyone inside, be quiet and don't get my aircraft dirty. You can chat when we are safe. There are military aircraft in the area. We need to ensure they don't follow us."

"A helicopter can't keep up with this," Derrick said, tossing an orange bag onto a pile of similar bags in the corner of the aircraft.

"True," Miriam said. "But they also have jets in the air."

"Jets," Derrick asked.

Red said, "Fighter jets."

"Like they use in combat?" Antonio asked.

Miriam said, "Exactly like that. Strap in. This could get crazy."

6

NO ONE QUESTIONED MIRIAM'S INSTRUCTIONS. Nyx snugged her safety harness, then grabbed Derrick's hand. Akira checked her harness twice. Rebekah checked Antonio's harness and then secured her own. Derrick remembered how Rebekah cared for his ankle after the cross-country race. Now, she tended to Antonio. Caring for people came naturally to her. Derrick wished he'd paid closer attention to her in Pacific Edge.

Miriam eased the aircraft into the air, glided it over the trees toward the mountains, rotated it vertically, and then accelerated. Derrick did not know if it could go faster. He did not want to find out if it did.

The force from the acceleration lessened and the aircraft leveled. "Is that necessary?" Nyx asked.

Miriam giggled. "Perhaps not. But it's so much fun."

"That was awesome," Red said. "I want to fly it."

"In due time, Red."

"Outstanding!"

Nyx asked, "No one needs zapped?"

"Zapped?" Antonio asked.

"With a stun gun," Rebekah said.

"Miriam zapped someone with a stun gun?" Antonio asked.

"Me," Akira said, raising her hand.

"But why?" Antonio asked, leaning away from Rebekah.

"Is anyone else here from Pacific Edge or another Chosen Community?" Miriam asked.

"Not me," Red said. "This is the farthest I've ever been from home. How far are we from Potterville?"

"About 100 miles," Miriam said.

Red whistled through his teeth.

"Not me," Antonio said. "I'm just a Potterville farm boy."

"Then no zapping required. Unless one of you gets out of hand," Miriam said.

"Yeah, right," Antonio said.

"Don't test her," Rebekah said. "Seriously. She'll zap you just to show you she can."

Antonio thought for a moment. "She proved that with the soldier."

Red said, "I still don't get it. Why did you zap Akira? Did I miss something?"

"Because of the 1984," Rebekah said.

"A tracking chip in my back," Akira explained.

"We all had them," Derrick added.

"Stop. I have no idea what you're talking about. What's a 1984? And why did you have chips on your back?" Red asked.

"Not on our backs—in our backs. 1984 is a tracking chip. Everyone in a Chosen Community has one implanted in their back at birth," Akira said.

"Why did you want a tracking device in your back?" Red asked.

"Did I say we wanted them? They did it without us knowing," Akira said.

"Oh. Weird," Red said.

"Anyway, the only way to defeat the chip was to zap it with a stun gun," Akira said.

"Twice," Miriam added.

Red looked at Akira. "They zapped you twice?"

"Yes, Miriam did one and Rebekah did the other," Akira said.

"Did it hurt?" Antonio asked.

"It hurts like hell," Rebekah said. "Miriam zapped me. No warning." She stuck her hand out. "Just zap. Out you go."

"You guys are weird," Red said.

Akira said, "It was the only way we could be safe. Because I still had a working chip, I led the robot to Miriam. We would have been captured had Nyx, Rebekah, and Derrick not shown up."

"Still weird. I'd have been pissed," Red said.

"I suspect we were all pissed the first time," Derrick said. "And it didn't get any easier the second time either."

"Weird." Red shook his head.

Rebekah said, "So, are there military aircraft out here?"

Miriam looked over her shoulder. She was wearing the funny-looking goggles. "Two. Coming up fast behind us."

Rebekah said, "That does not sound good. Can we outrun them?"

Miriam said, "Not sure. Maybe. I don't know how fast they can go. I don't even know how fast this thing goes."

Derrick said, "Does this thing have any defense or weapons?"

"Not sure. It alerted me about the jets, which is cool. It shows what weapons they have and everything," Miriam said.

Akira was sitting up front in the seat next to Miriam. Antonio undid his safety harness and hopped to the front. "Akira, trade me places. If this thing has weapons, they are probably operated from this seat."

Akira did as Antonio asked. "How would you know?"

"I've seen it in movies."

"That's comforting," Akira said as she sat and strapped in. "And what makes you qualified to take that seat?"

"I'm the best at video games. Ask Red," Antonio said.

"He's not lying. Beats me every time."

"Now I feel much better. Jeez, I'll just take a nap." Akira rolled her eyes. "Video games. Boys!"

Antonio put on goggles, like the ones Miriam wore. "How do you turn this on?"

"Just tap the button on the left side," Miriam said.

Antonio reached up to the goggles. "Oh, cool."

Apparatuses snaked out from under his chair, wrapping around him until they enveloped him. "Far out. Okay, give me a few minutes to figure this out."

"You don't have a few minutes. You have … one minute and thirty-eight seconds," Miriam said.

"Crap!"

Akira said, "I won't nap after all."

Derrick said, "Can't you outrun them?"

"Perhaps, but I don't want to. Not yet."

Suddenly, everyone was talking at once. Understanding any one person was difficult, but the gist of the din was all the same. Derrick noticed Miriam putting on headphones and motioning Antonio to do the same. Derrick knew nothing about such things, but he assumed Miriam wanted to talk to Antonio and not hear everyone else. He could not blame her.

Derrick yelled, "Everyone, shut up! Let Miriam and Antonio work. There's nothing we can do to help, but we can make it harder for them."

Rebekah said, "Derrick is right. Let Antonio concentrate."

Akira said, "Doesn't Miriam need to concentrate?"

"Well, of course, I meant Miriam too."

Red shook his head and chuckled.

Derrick didn't understand what was funny.

Miriam pointed the aircraft straight down and accelerated. Derrick felt as if his stomach was in his throat, and his butt literally came off the seat. He'd be against the ceiling were he not strapped in. Nyx squeezed his hand. They had been through a maneuver like this the first time they flew in this thing. Miriam had a good laugh and thought it fun. But this time was more intense than the first. The logical reason for the plunge toward earth was predictable. The jets had fired on them.

A whoosh sounded in the distance, then an explosion behind them, then another in front. A split second later, the aircraft slowed as if Miriam had thrown it in reverse, causing Derrick's head to whip forward. The aircraft made a sharp turn, and within seconds, Derrick felt sure they had stopped.

"What just happened?" Rebekah asked.

Derrick said, "I think Miriam maneuvered to avoid the missiles."

Akira said, "I thought we crashed and just had not yet realized we were dead."

Red said, "That was awesome."

Akira rolled her eyes. "Boys."

"Does this mean they know we didn't drown?" Derrick asked.

Miriam said, "Probably. But, on the bright side, they're sure we are dead now."

7

Monday, April 5, 10:37 p.m.

COLLINS AND BROWNING stood on the levee, overlooking the spillway. Foaming white water roared from the dam, creating a light mist. If they had been there actually searching for missing kids, both would have been brokenhearted, so they tried to look sad, which wasn't difficult because they were worried sick. Nyx and Akira had entered the river after the surge began. Miriam swam across to help Akira. A log struck Nyx, and Derrick dove in to save her. All of them disappeared into the darkness.

Collins didn't know if they made it across.

Both men wondered how this got out of control, although they had zero control over any of it. If they had seen it coming, they could have moved the kids somewhere far away, but only Derrick and Miriam knew it was coming, mostly Miriam. Miriam was a strange girl now that Browning thought about it. More interested in keeping some damn promise to a robot than protecting her friends. Even more than protecting herself, it seemed.

Collins said, "You think they made it?"

"You tell me. You were there."

"Not sure. Too dark to see, and the current carried them downstream. Couldn't hear either. I hope they made it," Collins said.

"I'd feel better if we knew."

"Agreed. I hope we know at some point."

Browning stood without speaking for several minutes. "On second thought, if they didn't make it, I don't want to know."

A vehicle turned the corner three blocks away and drove toward them.

Browning said, "What's this about? Kinda late for anyone to be on this road, and you ended the search, so volunteers should be home by now."

Before Collins could answer, he heard the distinctive rattle of a low revving diesel motor and recognized the shape of a drab green Humvee. "What the hell do they want?"

"To know if you found them, I guess. Assholes."

"Just stay calm. Let me do the talking," Collins said.

The same soldier Collins spoke to that morning climbed from the Humvee and made his way up the levee. The rushing water too loud to talk over from any distance. "Good evening, Sheriff. I hope you found the missing youths safe."

Unlike Derrick, Collins read people well. He sensed a hint of sincerity in the man's voice. Perhaps he had teenagers of his own. "Unfortunately, we did not," Collins said.

The soldier looked at the water. "You've given up then?"

"We've searched the river. No additional signs of them. If the river took them, they are in the downstream reservoir by now." Collins did not know if that was true and doubted it was. They didn't have many drownings in the river because it usually wasn't this high, and when it was, the water was too cold for swimming.

Another soldier stepped out of the vehicle, yelled, and waved his arm.

"You'll excuse me. Must be important."

Collins and Browning watched as the soldier rushed back to the Humvee. The driver pulled a microphone tethered on a coiled cord so the soldier could speak. The man leaned his head into the driver's side window. He nodded. His shoulders slumped. After a few moments, he handed the microphone back to the driver and then walked toward Collins and Browning.

Browning had a bad feeling in his gut.

"Sheriff, I have some bad news."

"How so?" Collins asked.

"A unit spotted the kids. They gave chase. The kids wouldn't stop… and, well." He paused. "The kids didn't make it."

"Dead? What the hell happened?" Collins demanded.

"Sorry, but I can't give you details. I don't know any myself, and it is military info. I couldn't share it even if I knew. All I can say is there was some sort of accident. All the kids were killed. We are pulling out now. I wish this would have ended differently. I'm sorry, and my thoughts are with the families."

Collins stared as the man skittered down the embankment and walked to the Humvee. "You believe him?"

"I don't think they'd leave unless they had found them or…"

"What do we tell the parents?"

"I don't know, but I'll be there with you."

"It's hard to believe. Just like that," Collins snapped his fingers, "and seven kids are gone?"

"It is hard to believe. Not sure that I do."

* * *

Derrick said, "Where are we?"

Miriam said, "In the mountains, in a deep valley, hiding in a forest. We are on the ground, engines shut down, hoping we are no longer visible to them."

"How long will we be here?" Rebekah asked.

Miriam said, "I don't know. About 30 minutes if we don't see any aircraft. Why? You have someplace you need to be?"

"Har, har. I'm wet and cold, and well… I need to pee."

Miriam said, "Hold it."

"I've been holding it. I've had to go for a while."

"You should have gone earlier."

Rebekah said, "I was outside, in kinda mixed company."

"You knew the job was dangerous when you followed me out of Pacific Edge. Next time lose your modesty. It's not worth dying over." Miriam sighed. "Okay, anybody else need to pee?"

Six hands raised in the glow of the dim lights.

Miriam said, "Give me a break. Let me see if this thing can scan outside."

Antonio said, "I already did it."

Miriam said, "You're fast."

Antonio said, "I started looking when Rebekah said she needed to go."

Miriam said, "I see."

"Well, that and I have to go too. So anyway. We are on a gentle slope. I don't see anything dangerous close. No heat signatures, so no people or large animals."

Miriam said, "I'll open the doors. Keep the light to a minimum, don't go far. Girls first, and when the girls are back, the boys can go. Questions?"

"Why do the girls get to go first?" Antonio asked.

"Stuff it, Antonio." Miriam stood.

Antonio said, "Hey! Where are you going?"

"Funny."

"But you didn't raise your hand," Antonio said.

Miriam swatted his head as she went by. "You and I will get along just fine."

Antonio said, "Agreed."

"I'll be right back," Rebekah said.

"Me too," Nyx said.

When the girls were gone, Antonio said, "What was that about?"

Derrick said, "Beats me. But then I don't understand girls."

Antonio said, "That makes two of us, amigo."

"Make that three," Red said.

* * *

When they were airborne again, Miriam flew the craft for 30 minutes. She kept what could be described as a windshield closed or blacked out—although Derrick thought it was more like a monitor screen—therefore, Derrick had no concept of their location or how many miles they had flown, plus it was night so unlikely he would have seen anything anyway. She allowed Antonio to continue as copilot and weapons operator, so their path was not secret. Unless she had convinced Antonio to keep it clandestine. Because she could communicate with Antonio using the headgear they wore, perhaps she had instructed him to do just that. But Derrick knew their destination. Miriam would take them back to engineering.

"Where are we going?" Akira shouted, assuming Miriam could not hear.

Miriam removed the headgear, turning to Akira. "Back to where we entered with you."

"Seems like we should have been there by now," Akira said.

"I'm making a large circle," Miriam said.

"Why? We need to get this promise of yours done so we can find Anna," Rebekah said.

"I want to make sure there are no aircraft tracking us," Miriam said.

Nyx said, "Do you see any?"

Miriam said, "No. Nothing."

Nyx said, "So your plan worked. They think we are dead."

"Correct."

Nyx continued, "If they think we are dead, the military will leave Potterville."

"That is correct."

Nyx said, "Then our parents will think we are dead."

Miriam looked around at each person and then said, "Also correct."

8

MIRIAM SLOWED THE AIRCRAFT AND THEN descended. It felt as if they were floating. Derrick was never interested in mechanical things because the Chosen did nothing mechanical. Even contemplating it seemed dreadful because behind every powered device were ghosts of science and technology. So terrible the thought, the connection wasn't mentioned in school or home. Yet, even with his engrained aversion to science, Derrick wondered what made this aircraft fly. It did not seem to have rockets or motors. It was unlike hovercraft, which had a large fanlike device and rockets.

When the aircraft stopped, Miriam said, "Derrick, you and Rebekah open the door. Everyone else, stay inside."

"Why do I have to go?" Rebekah protested.

"Because you helped Derrick before. Make it quick," Miriam said, and then added, "I'm taking off again. I'll circle back in 15 minutes."

Derrick didn't ask questions, although he didn't understand what made Miriam paranoid. The military thought they had been killed. Therefore, whoever sent the military also thought they were dead. It was good that people believed Rebekah, Miriam, and he were dead. Only Browning, Collins, Martinez, Mrs. Belos, the Patel family, and the Nakamura family knew others were involved. Unfortunately, they also believed their children had died. That thought caused a sinking feeling in his chest.

As Derrick and Rebekah ran toward the unsecured door, the aircraft lifted off, leaving behind a strange, burned odor. Inside the building, using flashlights, they raced to the overhead door. Rebekah unlocked it. Derrick worked the chain mechanism to raise it. He thought the entire operation might have taken five minutes. Miriam should have stayed put.

The following ten minutes felt like hours. Derrick and Rebekah stood in the middle of the door, watching the night sky. Suddenly, bright lights blinded him. He grabbed Rebekah, pulling her to the side just as the aircraft flew through the open door.

"Holy crap," Rebekah said. "She could have killed us."

"I'm sorry. I didn't hear or see it."

"Not your fault. We should have known better than to stand in the doorway. Miriam must have seen us with those goggles she's wearing."

"I don't think she saw us, or she would have given us more warning," Derrick said, closing the door.

"Bull. She's probably laughing her ass off."

When they had secured the door, Derrick and Rebekah ran to where Miriam landed. The others were unloading their bags.

Miriam gave a succinct explanation of the facility to those who had not been here before. However, she did not tell them about the reactor, the Base, or Silo Number Eight.

"What is this place?" Antonio asked.

"As I said, it's called engineering. We have not explored this complex."

"This looks like a warehouse. I don't see anything that looks like they engineered things here," Red said.

"Warehouse. That's a good word for it. You are correct. This is storage," Miriam said.

"Storage for what?" Antonio asked.

"All kinds of things, but I know little about what those things are," Miriam said, and then added, "Grab your bags. We can talk more inside. Bring everything. It's late, and I don't want to make two trips."

Derrick didn't realize how much stuff they had, even though he'd helped pack it across the river. It seemed everyone had two bags to carry, either the orange trash bags or backpacks. Even Antonio carried a backpack and a trash bag, although Rebekah offered to take one despite already having two bags herself. Rebekah acted strange around Antonio.

Once inside the lobby area, Miriam said, "Stay here. I'll look for where we should go next."

Derrick said, "We should stick together."

"It will be faster if I go alone. I'll be right back," Miriam said.

Derrick wanted to argue but recognized the tone in Miriam's voice. Arguing would have been a waste of his time. He wondered if efficiency was Miriam's primary concern or if it was to prevent them from finding something she didn't want them to see. Probably a combination of the two, yet the latter likely carried more weight than the former.

Miriam was not done with secrets. Perhaps even keeping things from him. He didn't like feeling mistrusted, but he couldn't change Miriam. No one could. Then he remembered how he'd lied to everyone in this room. Trust might prove elusive, yet they'd need elements like trust, commitment, and alliance to survive. He felt certain of that.

Ten minutes passed, then 20. People moved to the counter where they sat. The pile of bags and backpacks remained in a heap in the middle of the room.

"What's taking her so long?" Rebekah asked.

"Maybe we should look for her," Antonio said.

"She might be lost," Red added.

Akira said, "She's not, but if we go looking for her, we might get lost, and then she'd have to come find us. It would be a waste of time."

"I'm starving," Red said. "Breakfast was a long time ago."

"Me too," Antonio said and then added, "How are we going to survive here a week? There's no food, water, electricity."

"There's electricity," Red said.

"Why do you say that?" Antonio asked.

Red pointed. "Exit sign is lit."

Antonio said, "Oh. Right. Then why are we sitting here in the dark?"

"It seems the power here is limited to things like those signs," Rebekah said.

Just then, the overhead lights flickered to life.

Rebekah said, "That has to be Miriam. She will go to any length to make me look stupid."

"There's water here and food. Well, maybe not in this building, but in the complex. And we might not be here all week," Derrick said.

"I hope not," Antonio said, adding, "it's spring break and I had plans, you know."

A door at the far side of the room opened. Miriam waved her arm. "This way."

The troupe gathered bags and walked to the door.

"Why isn't she carrying stuff?" Rebekah asked.

"I've got her stuff. Don't worry about it," Derrick said.

Rebekah said, "It just gets old. Miriam this and Miriam that. Why doesn't she help?"

"Excuse me? You wouldn't be here if it wasn't for Miriam," Akira said.

"That's true. I'm tired and hungry. I'll shut up now," Rebekah said.

Behind the door were stairs and Miriam waiting. She grabbed her bags from Derrick. "I found the cafeteria and rooms we can stay in for tonight. I turned on the water so it would clear and found some food. Not the good stuff like Charlie had. The barely edible stuff like we found the first night. But at least it's food. I'm starving. How about everyone else? Oh, and as you may have noticed, I found the backup generators, so we have power."

"Sorry," Rebekah said.

"Sorry for what?" Miriam asked.

"What I said when you couldn't hear."

"You're weird," Miriam said, "I guess that's why I like you."

"Thanks. You're weird too."

"Thanks."

"What just happened?" Nyx whispered to Derrick.

"I have no clue."

Miriam led them to a place like where they'd stayed the first night. Rooms with two beds, a blanket at the foot of each. Miriam assigned rooms. There were plenty, so everyone had a private room. "Put your personal stuff in your room. You can wash up. The bathrooms are there." She pointed. "Then continue down the hall to the double doors. That's the cafeteria. I'll boil water for the dehydrated food."

Red coughed. "Uh. I have sandwiches. Gramps made them. And sodas, chips, and cookies. He packed enough to last me several days. It should be enough for all of us tonight."

"You're sharing your food with us? That's nice, Red. Thank you," Miriam said.

Red shrugged. "The sandwiches would be dried out by tomorrow."

"See, I told you Red would be handy," Derrick said, smiling.

"Whatever. Don't let it go to your head, Red." Antonio said, grinning.

Red fired back. "I have enough for everyone except Antonio. He can eat stale noodles."

"How did you know it was noodles?" Miriam asked.

Red shrugged. "Just guessing. Seemed most likely."

Miriam looked at Derrick. "He's smarter than I anticipated."

When they all returned to the dining area, Miriam had coffee brewed. "Don't drink the coffee if it will keep you awake. We all need a good night's rest," Miriam said.

"I don't think I'll be able to sleep anyway," Nyx said, pouring herself a coffee, adding powdered milk and sugar.

"Why not?" Miriam asked.

"Mom thinks I'm dead," Nyx replied. "I can't get that out of my head."

"Mine too," Akira said.

"Antonio, what about your parents?" Rebekah asked. "No one spoke with them. They weren't at the jail with the others."

"My father is working in the fields near Fresno. He doesn't have a cell phone. No way to contact him. He won't be worried or even know that I'm gone. I asked Coach to tell my mom that I had student council business and would not be home for a few days. I trust Coach to take care of her."

"I wish we could let them know we are alright," Akira whispered.

Rebekah said, "Antonio, you can have my sandwich. I don't mind the food here."

Derrick didn't understand. Rebekah hated the first food they found. Would not have eaten it had she not been starving. Then something occurred to him. Perhaps his ability to understand people were improving.

"I was joking. I have enough for everyone. Even the runt." Red winked.

Miriam took two cups of coffee to the table and sat next to Akira. "Do you want coffee? I think this is how you like it. But I can get you something else if you think it will keep you awake."

"Thanks. I'm not sure I can sleep either," Akira said.

Red emptied the food from his backpack and began distributing it.

Akira said, "Thank you, Red. I'll only eat half a sandwich if you want the other half."

"Are you sure?" Red asked as he took half of Akira's sandwich.

Akira managed a weak smile. "I'm sure. Thanks again."

Miriam patted Akira's hand. "I'm sorry about how your parents must feel."

Nyx sat across from Akira, and Derrick joined her. He said, "I understand why this is difficult. But isn't everyone safer if they think we are gone?" He thought gone sounded better than dead.

Miriam said, "Good point. It needs to be kept secret."

Antonio sat next to Rebekah. "So, what's the plan?"

Miriam held up one finger as she chewed. "First, sleep. No fooling around."

"What does that mean?" Antonio asked.

"Staying up, wandering about, talking. You figure it out," Miriam said.

"Yes, mother," Rebekah said.

"I'm serious. This isn't a field trip. Charlie probably knows we are here. He'll be monitoring us. We need to act professional," Miriam said.

"Someone is watching us?" Red asked. "There are people here?"

Miriam said, "Not someone, something. Charlie is a robot."

"Cool," Red said.

Antonio said, "We sleep and then what?"

Miriam said, "Tomorrow morning, we'll go to the next facility in this complex. There is an aging nuclear reactor there…"

Red interrupted. "They banned nuclear reactors years ago. Perhaps there's one there, but it won't be operational."

Miriam said, "They may have been banned, but this one isn't just *operational*. It's *operating*. It's generating electricity, but it hasn't been maintained in decades. Systems are failing. We need to do repairs and maintenance to ensure it continues working without problems. If it failed, it would cause problems for everyone in this region, including Potterville."

"They fixed a problem before they came to town," Akira said. "They saved Potterville."

"That's what they said. But can we believe them?" Red asked.

Nyx raised her palms. "Duh. Look around, Red. Are you braindead?"

Red frowned. "Good point. I'm tired, I guess." He finished his first sandwich and started on the half Akira gave him.

Miriam placed half her sandwich in front of Red. "Here. You can have half of mine too."

"Thanks," Red mumbled, chewing.

"It's not that I don't believe you, but we are not nuclear scientists or engineers, or whatever sort of education it takes to run a nuclear reactor," Antonio said.

"The computer shows where problems are and instructions for the repair. We'll have to learn as we go," Miriam said.

Antonio held his sandwich halfway to his mouth. "Sounds dangerous."

Miriam said, "You're finally figuring it out."

9

Tuesday, April 6, 4:45 a.m.

AFTER SHE ESCAPED FROM PACIFIC EDGE, Miriam swore she'd never work at night again. She wanted to sleep. But seeing Akira and Nyx so distraught caused her to reevaluate her thinking. She had to fix this, and this was the only way she could.

Easing down the hall, pausing at each door, she heard only soft breathing, except at Red's entrance, where snoring reverberated through the closed door. In an office, she found a notepad and pens. She scribbled with several pens before finding one that worked. On the pad, she wrote:

Mr. Fletcher,

You may have heard that something happened to Red. He is okay. We all are. But it is important this remains a secret. As you know, the place of which we spoke is dangerous. Let Sheriff Collins know we are okay. He will know what to do. Do this in person. Do not use the telephone. People might be monitoring calls.

Thank you

Your friend, Miriam

Miriam folded the note and placed it in an envelope. When she exited engineering, a full moon shone in the western sky. Moonlight earlier would have been helpful. Now it was problematic. Miriam braced against the chill of the damp morning air. A warm coat would have been nice but running to Potterville and back would have her sweating. She ran through the canyon without aid from the flashlight.

Shielding the flashlight with her hand, she fought through the brush to the tunnel. On the other side of the tunnel, she again held her hand over the flashlight, letting a bit of light leak through her fingers as she scaled the pile of rocks. Near the meadow, she stopped. She scanned the sky and listened. Nothing except the sound of the rushing river, still running high.

She considered walking. A person walking draws less attention than a person running. That's what she assumed based on Pacific Edge standards. However, here it might be different. Nyx and Derrick, being on the track team, came to mind. She wondered how often they ran together. She wondered a lot of things about Nyx. And about Derrick. And about Rebekah. People remained a puzzle. She included herself in that box of jumbled and confusing puzzle pieces. Sometimes she felt as if she were in the wrong box. That feeling had increased of late.

The constraints of time helped her decide running was better than walking. It surprised her that running was not difficult. She was young and had walked a lot in Pacific Edge, but she did not run. Odd that running seemed natural. Derrick must have felt the same when he started running. But Derrick had been running and training for years. He just wasn't aware of it because they had used hypnosis.

But they had never hypnotized her.

At least, she did not think they had.

She picked Mr. Fletcher for three reasons. First, she did not want to go downtown to leave the note at the Sheriff's office—too much risk of being seen. Second, Mr. Fletcher knew something about the base and the danger because soldiers killed his friend and everyone in Sacramento. So, she trusted him to keep it a secret. And third, it was the only home she knew how to find.

At Fletcher's house, she paused, catching her breath. The lights were on inside, which did not surprise her, although she'd hoped Mr. Fletcher slept later than this. She tiptoed to the front door, eased the screen door open, and placed the envelope against the door. Easing the door shut, she heard a car approaching. Headlights lit the intersection to the right. Mr. Fletcher's place was the second house from the corner.

She studied the approaching lights. The car crawled, slower than seemed normal. But not slow enough for her to get out of the yard. Perhaps the car would not turn this way. She would be difficult to see in the dark. Standing still seemed like the best tactic as the car entered the intersection.

But it did not go straight, nor did it turn the other way. It began a slow turn toward her. The headlights' beams spilled into the yard, and the porch light came on. Miriam threw herself on the ground and rolled toward the house, edging as best she could under a flowering shrub. The car slowed in front of the Fletcher home, and the driver tossed something. She saw a roll of paper land with a thud near the front step. The front door opened. Through the shrub, she watched Mr. Fletcher wave at the driver, but the car had continued down the street. Mr. Fletcher stooped, sighing as he picked up the paper. Miriam forced herself farther into the flowerbed.

Mr. Fletcher had not picked up the envelope on the way out. At least she didn't think he did. Now he was looking at the front page of the paper. *What if he doesn't see it? What if he only uses the front door to get the paper?*

At the door, Mr. Fletcher paused. "Huh. What the heck?"

He groaned. "Humph. Someone selling something, no doubt."

The door closed. Miriam waited a few minutes and then got to her hands and knees, crawling out of the bushes before she stood and trotted out of the yard and down the street. She was at full speed when Mr. Fletcher's door opened a second time.

He stood in the doorway with a note in his hand.

Miriam's slight frame was visible running down the road.

Mr. Fletcher whispered, "Good luck, Ms. Miriam. I have a feeling you're going to need it."

Miriam paused before crossing the footbridge. Neither seeing nor hearing anything, she ran across and did not stop until she was in the trees. At the edge of the meadow, she paused again, waiting until her breathing slowed so she could hear. The eastern horizon lightened as day approached, but the shadows remained dark and everything gray. It would be difficult for anyone to see her if she crept through shadows. Easing toward the pile of rocks and the hidden entry to the secret canyon, she heard something in the distance. The sound grew louder. Sprinting, she reached the tree line just as two low-flying military helicopters flew over the meadow, heading toward the mountains and where they had faked their crash last night.

Miriam whispered, "Crap."

10

A THIN VEIN OF LIGHT GLOWED AROUND THE door. Derrick rubbed his eyes, wondering the time. The room had no windows. He did not own a watch, and Miriam had destroyed his cellphone. Keeping track of time might prove difficult, although progress was more important than the ticks of a clock. He hoped tracking progress would not be elusive.

Not needing to dress because he'd slept in his clothes, Derrick eased the door open, wondering if he'd overslept or was the first to awaken. In the hall, silence greeted him. Miriam would be the first person up, so he went to her room, but the door stood open and the bed set empty.

Making coffee made more sense than searching for Miriam, who was, no doubt, on a computer somewhere nearby. Coffee seemed more critical than finding his sister, and the scent of coffee would lure her. Derrick shuffled to the dining area, break room, whatever they called it when humans once worked here. Opening the door, the lights came on without further action on his part. He was halfway to the coffee machine when something caught his attention.

In the middle of the room, in the middle of a table, was a large bouquet.

Next to the flowers, a note with Miriam's name. He did not open it. It could wait. The flowers and note did not settle his nerves or untie the knot in his stomach. Perhaps food would help. He found cereal, which he ate dry from the box as he sat contemplating the flowers. And the note.

***

Tuesday, April 6, 7:45 a.m.

Coach Browning drove to Donna's Bistro, needing good coffee and one of her famous cinnamon rolls. Neither would set the world straight or ease his anxiety, but neither would make things worse either. Short of awakening to learn this was all a nightmare, nothing, it seemed, would put the world back in order.

Bells above the door jingled as Browning walked in. Behind the counter, a dour-faced L. Linda Maxton gave him a weak smile. "Hi, Mr. Browning. Do you know what happened at the condo? It's not Derrick, is it?" Tears filled her eyes.

"What happened at the condo?" Browning asked.

L. Linda said, "If I knew, I wouldn't ask."

Donna appeared at the half-doors that led into the kitchen. "You'd better get over there. Bill called here looking for you."

"I have not yet turned my cellphone on. Back soon, I hope."

When Browning turned the corner, he saw two patrol cars and an ambulance. Bill Collins stood beside the ambulance, watching the EMTs load a gurney carrying a body in a black bag.

Browning said, "My God, Bill, what's happened. It's not one of the…"

Collins shook his head. "It's Paul. I wanted to talk to him again. Went to his house, but no one there, so I came here. His door was unlocked. Found him in the living room."

"Dead? I thought you had him at the jail?"

"I did, but I couldn't hold him. Besides, I have the parents there, remember? I let him go right after Martinez brought him in. He swore he knew nothing about the cameras. I had no reason to hold him."

Browning said, "What happened? Accident?"

"Nope! Murdered. Someone cut his throat. If I had held on to him, he'd still be alive."

Browning whistled through his teeth. "This is serious crap we are in."

Collins said, "You got that right. Lesson learned. Sometimes doing things the right way is the wrong thing to do."

* * *

Sitting at a table in engineering, Derrick picked through the dry cereal. The flakes tasted stale. He separated out black bits into a small pile, which he thought, but wasn't sure, were raisins at one time or bugs that died from eating the cereal. Either way, they were too hard to eat.

Who had gathered flowers for Miriam? Only Rebekah, Akira, Nyx, and himself knew about the atrium in this building unless Red or Antonio had wandered around during the night. But why would either of them write a note to Miriam and leave it out for all to see? It made little sense.

In the distance, he heard a door. Perhaps Miriam was returning from wherever she went to get on a computer. He heard footsteps approaching, and then Miriam appeared in the door, breathing hard, a bit of sweat on her brow.

"What have you been doing?" Derrick asked.

Miriam said, "Running. Flowers from the garden. Nice touch."

"I did not gather them. Running where?" Derrick asked.

"Who did then?" Miriam asked.

"Who did what?" Derrick asked.

"Who gathered the flowers?"

"I don't know. Running where?"

"Back from Potterville. Don't tell the others. I'll tell them I went, but not that I ran. They can think I took the aircraft."

"That's dangerous. Why would you do something like that?" Derrick demanded.

"The Potterville kids won't be of much help if they are worried about their parents. It was necessary to let people know we are okay."

"Who did you tell?"

"I left a note on Mr. Fletcher's step. He'll tell Sheriff Collins."

Derrick shook his head. "You should not have gone by yourself."

"Safer to go alone. One small girl is harder to see."

"Do you think anyone saw you?" Derrick asked.

"I think not. I was careful. Who gathered the flowers?"

"I don't know." Derrick paused. "Who do you think gathered them?"

"How would I know?" Miriam asked.

Derrick said, "Because they're for you."

11

MIRIAM STARED AT THE ENVELOPE, TURNING it over a few times in her hands, her name, typewritten and centered. She pulled the vase close, studied the flowers, pulling one red rose out, and then returning it. She wiped the water that dripped from it off the table.

"Someone knows how to cut and arrange flowers," Miriam said.

"Proves it wasn't me," Derrick said and then added, "Who would give you flowers?"

"There's only one person who might, but I don't think that's who did it," Miriam said.

"Who?"

"I'd rather not say. I could be wrong. It would be embarrassing."

"I don't understand," Derrick said.

"Like I said, I could be wrong." Miriam turned the vase, contemplating. "But I don't think it was anyone here."

"Someone has found this place already?"

Miriam shook her head. "I don't think so."

"Could you just say what you mean?"

Miriam held up her hand, then opened the envelope and unfolded the letter. "As I suspected."

"What?"

"Charlie."

Miriam handed the letter to Derrick.

```
Miriam King, Derrick King, and Rebekah Ford
have reentered engineering. Two females who
previously entered and traveled to Staging and
Silo Number Eight have also entered. In
addition, two unknown males have entered the
facility. The number of unauthorized personnel
is problematic.

Reactor One requires immediate repair. Those
needed to complete the repairs must proceed to
Reactor One. If repairs cannot be completed,
```

Reactor One operation must be terminated. They must activate Reactor Two.

While Reactor One is being repaired, Charlie requires Miriam King's immediate presence at the Administration Building.

Miriam King must restore Jane.

Miriam King must come alone.

Charlie

12

DERRICK HELD THE PAPER, STARING BUT not seeing it—the heat rising in his face. He did not want to be angry with Miriam, but he was angry. Because he knew what Miriam was going to say. 'I must go. I promised Charlie.' It had been Charlie this and Charlie that ever since they met that damned robot. Thoughts spun through Derrick's mind at a furious pace. *We cannot be separated. I won't let it happen. But she will go, regardless of what I say.*

Miriam said, "Say something before you explode. You're angry. I know what you're thinking, and I don't want to be separated either, don't want to be here, don't want to be a fugitive. But here we are."

Derrick said nothing, fearful that he'd say something hurtful. Being hurtful was not his intent, yet he felt like lashing out. He had not realized how much anger he'd bottled up, and now it was about to spill out. "We need to stay together."

Miriam placed her hand atop of his. "Sometimes things don't go as planned. This is one of those times. The reactor needs repairs. I must face Charlie. End of story. We'll be together again soon."

Derrick stood, his fists clenched. "Charlie, Charlie, Charlie! What is it with you and that damn robot? He held us captive. Remember? It's not your friend. It can't be trusted. Aren't we more important to you than a machine?"

Miriam sat back, folded her arms across her chest. "To get out of Pacific Edge, I worked through the night for weeks with little sleep, almost drowned, could have been mowed down by machine guns, could have frozen crossing the mountains, and you think I care more about Charlie than I care about you? Brother, you need to grow up. This is no time for childishness, especially for you. These kids need a leader…"

"Nyx is their leader," Derrick interrupted.

Miriam bunched her hair with both hands. "Not down here, she isn't. You need to step up. Someone could die if you don't."

Derrick took several deep breaths. Miriam was right. He knew that. But it didn't make the situation better. "Fine. You stay with us. After we take care of the reactor problem, we'll all go to the Base. Charlie will have to wait."

"I've considered doing that. I must go alone. That's the only way this is going to work."

Derrick felt the heat rising again. "Why? I don't get it."

"Charlie can help us, but he has to trust us. He's been alone down here for a long time. I think he's lonely—and scared."

"Have you fixed Jane?" Derrick asked.

"I don't know. Patel repaired the hard drive, and I've copied everything to the new hard drives and made copies on the solid-state drives. But when her old drive crashed, it caused some damage. I don't know what was lost. She might not even function," Miriam said.

"That makes matters worse. You can't go alone, knowing this might not even work. What happens if it doesn't? That damn robot…"

"Charlie," Miriam corrected.

"Uhgggg! Okay! Charlie might lose it. There's no telling what he might do."

Miriam nodded. "I agree. But I don't have a choice. Charlie knows we're here. He can probably hear this conversation. I made a promise. I can only hope Charlie has the capacity to forgive me if this doesn't work. I'm going now before anyone else shows up. You explain the situation. Then get to the reactor. Don't waste time. Give me a few minutes to get out of here and then go wake everyone. You can eat something when you get to the reactor. We don't know how much time we have before something bad happens."

"Something bad has already happened," Derrick said, stretching his arms out.

Miriam went to him, wrapped her arms around him. "See you in a few days."

"It won't take days."

"You don't know that."

"This time, I do. I'll see you soon."

Miriam slung her bag over her shoulder and walked to the door.

As Miriam stepped into the hall, Derrick called, "Say hello to Charlie for me. Tell him to take care of my sister."

Miriam turned, smiling. "I will."

13

DERRICK SAT ALONE FOR A FEW MINUTES, hoping to find some strength for what he had to do. But before he stirred, Akira walked through the door, rubbing sleep from her eyes, carrying her eyeglasses in her hand. She shuffled to the sink, drawing a cup of water. Derrick watched her, rehearsing his explanation regarding Miriam.

Akira sat across from Derrick. "Pretty flowers. Are they from the atrium? Did you pick them?"

Derrick said, "Miriam."

"That was nice of her," Akira said.

Derrick cleared his throat. This would be good practice. Akira's reaction did not concern him, but Rebekah's reaction worried him. Rebekah escaped with Miriam, and they walked miles together before they found him. Rebekah had always insisted they stay together. He did not know how Rebekah would react but knew it would not be pretty. "Miriam did not pick them. They are for Miriam."

Akira sat her cup on the table. "For Miriam? Who are they from? Rebekah?"

"Rebekah? Uh, not from Rebekah. Why would Rebekah pick flowers for Miriam? One of the robots must have picked them, but the robot named Charlie sent them along with this note." Derrick pushed the note to Akira.

Akira read the note. "Has Miriam seen this?"

"Yes."

"Where is she?"

"Gone."

"Gone where?" Akira burst into tears.

"To see the robo…," Derrick paused. "Charlie. We must do as Charlie has instructed. The reactor is in trouble again. Miriam is dealing with Charlie, and we have reactor duty. I need to get the others."

Akira stood, ran to the sink, her back turned to the room, shoulders heaving.

Rebekah entered the room. "What's happened? And what's with the flowers?"

Everything Derrick had rehearsed in his head disappeared. "Akira is upset because Miriam left. The flowers were for Miriam. Charlie sent them." Derrick spun the note so Rebekah could read it.

Reading, Rebekah nodded and then whispered, "Damn robot."

The barrage of anger Derrick expected didn't come. Instead, Rebekah walked to Akira, putting her arm around Akira's shoulder. "It's okay. We're going to be okay."

Akira turned to Rebekah. "She abandoned us."

Rebekah shook her head. "Miriam did not abandon us. She's doing what is best to protect us. Miriam knows what she's doing. She'll be okay." Rebekah held Akira at arms' length for a moment. "Miriam did not abandon you. Hear me?"

Akira nodded, wiped her face on her sleeve.

"Now what?" Antonio appeared at the door.

"I'll explain when we have everyone together. Get the others. Have them bring their stuff. Meet back here in five minutes," Derrick said.

Antonio stared.

Derrick said, "Sorry to be so abrupt. There are problems at the reactor. We gotta move. Let me try again. Could you please get the others?"

"You got it, amigo. See you in five minutes."

Derrick stood, looked at Rebekah. "See you in five?"

Rebekah nodded. "Here we go again."

When Derrick returned, he met Red, Antonio, and Nyx in the hallway. Akira and Rebekah were already at the table, bags at their feet.

"Please have a seat," Derrick said.

When everyone was seated, Derrick remained standing, facing the group. "There are problems at the reactor. We must fix it."

Antonio asked, "Where's Miriam?"

"I'll get to that," Derrick said. "We need to get to the reactor. I don't know how urgent the problems are…"

Nyx interrupted. "How do you know there are problems?"

"If I could finish a sentence, that would be great," Derrick said, surprising himself with a smile. He pointed. "The flowers were here this morning along with this note." He handed it to Nyx. "Miriam has gone to meet with Charlie. The reactor is our responsibility. That is all I know, so rather than ask questions I can't answer, let's just go."

Red raised his hand. "Is there anything to eat there?"

Derrick said, "We'll eat if there's time and it takes 30 minutes. Can you make it that long?"

Red scuffed the floor with his boot. "I suppose. I hope they have decent food."

"Don't count on it. Let's go," Derrick said, walking out the door and down the hall toward the electric cart garage.

Nyx ran to catch Derrick. Adjusting her bag's strap on her shoulder, she said, "This is it, isn't it?"

"This is what?"

"We are really doing this. I mean, it's serious," Nyx said.

Derrick glanced at her. No makeup, hair disheveled, but not in a bad way. He did not think he had ever seen her look as pretty. "Yep. Not that you almost drowning wasn't serious, but yes, it's serious from here on out. If there is an out."

"If there's an out, you'll find it," Nyx said, taking his hand.

14

SIRENS ECHOED THROUGH THE TUNNEL AS Miriam approached the turn that would take her to the Circle Transport Station. At the crossroads, Miriam stopped. She needed to find a computer to determine the extent of the reactor problem. Charlie couldn't stop her. He'd just have to deal with the delay. What choice did he have?

Having decided, Miriam started toward Reactor One. The sirens stopped, and a familiar voice echoed through the tunnel. "Miriam King. Proceed to the Circle Transport. Your companions must fix the reactor. Charlie requires that Miriam King fix Jane."

Miriam whispered, "If Miriam King can fix Jane."

* * *

Derrick tossed his bag into a transport vehicle. "We'll need two transports. Rebekah can drive one of them."

Red tossed his bag into the next cart over. "They're like golf carts. I'll drive this one."

Rebekah unplugged her cart and got into the driver's seat. Antonio put his crutches in the passenger's seat. "Okay if I ride with you?"

Rebekah said, "Sure."

Akira walked toward Rebekah's transport, but Nyx caught her by the arm and whispered in her ear. Akira nodded and walked with Nyx to Red's cart. Nyx said, "Derrick, sit up front with Red. We'll sit in the back."

Miriam had told him to step up. That the group needed a leader. Yet, everyone else made decisions, even about the simplest things, like who drove what and who sat where. If leading was doing nothing, then he was doing a fine job. Beyond that, things were happening outside his poor understanding of people. That was the only thing of which he was certain.

Red backed the cart out of its parking spot. "Where to?"

Derrick pointed. Finally, he'd done something. However, Rebekah could have led them to the reactor. Derrick was still an unnecessary passenger on this expedition. No one was talking, not in this vehicle. Derrick did not know Red well enough to start a conversation. Nyx sat with Akira, which meant she didn't want to sit with him, although he did not know why. Derrick glanced over his shoulder. Nyx had her arm around Akira. Akira clutched a piece of cloth that served as a blindfold on their last trip, using it to dry her tears.

Derrick did not understand.

Nyx leaned forward. "Why did you decide to come, Red?"

Red stared straight ahead. "I already said. My grandfather said I should."

"Did he say why?" Nyx asked.

"No. He said I'd understand when I got here. So far, it makes little sense. I'd rather be home working. Grandpa and I hoped to finish a project this week."

Nyx sat back. The silence felt uncomfortable, so Derrick asked, "What project?"

"I can't say. It's our secret. Too dangerous if the wrong people heard about it," Red said.

What could Red and his grandfather have that was dangerous? Derrick thought they just worked on old cars.

Nyx said, "It must be some car."

Red grinned. "It sure is."

Codes. More damn codes that Derrick still didn't understand. And how could a car be dangerous? What *was* dangerous? Given his inability to understand what was happening around him, how could he make the right decisions? How could he lead? He'd lead them straight into a disaster.

After a few minutes, something occurred to Derrick, but he hesitated. He didn't want to sound stupid. Finally, he decided everyone already knew he was stupid. One more question wouldn't make a difference. "It must be a rare car. Worth a lot of money."

Red looked at Derrick. "Exactly. You already know too much."

Derrick nodded. "Soon, you will know too much as well. Your secret is safe with me."

Red nodded, as if he understood. Which worried Derrick because Derrick wasn't sure he understood his own statement.

As they neared the junction in the tunnel where Miriam would have turned left toward the Circle Transport, Derrick heard the siren. "That's the warning siren. I wonder how long it's been going off?"

"Are you sure it's safe for us to go farther?" Nyx asked.

"I am not, but we don't have a choice. We can't outrun it. If the lights are yellow, we have time," Derrick said.

Moments later, spinning lights cast red splashes of color on the tunnel walls. Derrick turned to look at Nyx and Akira. "This is bad. We gotta work fast. Akira, you understand computers. Soon as we get there, I need you to get on a computer and determine what needs to be done. Can you do that?"

Akira pushed her glasses up. "How can I get on? The computers will be password protected."

"Remember, people left their usernames and passwords taped to the bottom of their keyboards," Derrick said.

Nyx said, "Antonio is good at that sort of thing as well. Plus, he's slow on those crutches."

Derrick nodded. "Two people on the computers is a good idea. One can determine the problems and set priorities, and the other can get instructions, parts, tool lists, and locations."

Red said, "What can I do?"

Derrick thought for a moment. "You can grab tools and parts."

"How do I find them?"

"There are maps. Plus, if it's the reactor, the tools and parts are on the way to it."

"What can I do?" Nyx asked.

Derrick looked into her eyes. *You can go home, stay safe, and have a great life,* he thought. "I don't know yet. Depends on what we find. If we gotta work on more than one problem at a time, we'll form teams. You and I will take one problem. Rebekah and Red can take another."

As they neared the staging area, Derrick directed Red to drive toward where Miriam found the first operating computer. It was farther than he liked from the reactor, but it was the only place he knew for sure there was a computer that worked.

Moments later, they exited the tunnel, driving straight down the center of the staging area. Red said, "Holy crap. This is a military base."

"A small portion of it, yes," Derrick said.

That's when he saw they had more problems than he expected.

Two black robots blocked their path.

15

COACH BROWNING SAID THE BEST DEFENSE is a good offense. Derrick did not understand at the time, but he did now. And they had no offense. Perhaps Red could run over the robots, but Derrick doubted that strategy would work. Too easy for the robots to dodge them. Or maybe the robots could toss the cart like a toy. Red slowed. In unison, the robots pointed one arm to the right and waved with the other as if directing traffic. Derrick, the leader, had no clue how to respond.

Red whispered, "What should I do?"

Derrick thought for a moment. "Park where they direct us."

There were no plugins for the carts or parking places, just military vehicles. Perhaps this was a trap. They might have violated some protocols, triggering robotic security. Miriam went to Potterville during the night without him, or anyone else knowing about it. What might the others have done in the night? Some leader he was. He knew nothing.

Derrick glanced over his shoulder. Rebekah pulled next to him. She mouthed something. Derrick didn't know what she had said but thought perhaps it was: "What do we do?" He shrugged and held out his hand for them to stay put.

Stepping out, Derrick said, "Stay in the vehicle."

Before Derrick reached the robots, one of them said, "A work area is prepared. Reactor One is critical."

"How did you know we were coming?" Derrick asked, grabbing his bag, and waving the others to follow.

"Administrative activation. A QR-4 command."

"Charlie," Derrick whispered.

Inside the building, across from Reactor One's entrance, the robots led them to a room with stocked vending machines, an espresso machine, and three computers. "The QR-4 unit indicated you required food and workstations. The QR-4 unit will monitor your progress and dispatch us if you need additional assistance."

Derrick scanned the room. "Charlie? Can you hear me?"

The robot said, "Yes. QR-4 can hear you."

"Is Miriam, okay?"

"A Circle Transport carrying Miriam King arrives in four minutes and thirty-three seconds. The QR-4 unit is waiting at the entrance. You must repair Reactor One."

Derrick thought for a moment. "Why is the public address system not telling us how much time before the reactor fails?"

The robot said, "The estimated deadline for system failure has passed."

* * *

As the Circle Transport eased to a stop, Miriam saw Charlie at the entrance. She smiled, surprising herself, yet she was glad to see Charlie. But her smile didn't last long. Miriam feared she could not fix Jane. She was not sure why she felt that way, but it was there. Her fear would not subside, nor could she suppress it.

Miriam approached Charlie, unsure how one greeted a robot. Charlie said nothing, just turned and proceeded into the building. Doors opened before Charlie as they approached. Still, Charlie remained silent. Miriam had been here before, but the hallway looked different. Where a wall had been was now a long hallway. Miriam saw doors without keypads, doorknobs, or other ways to open them like they saw before. She wondered why they designed the facility so they could alter the hallway configuration.

Twenty yards down the hall, an undetectable door slid open. Charlie walked to a QR-4 robot standing in a docking station. Charlie pointed, "Miriam King must fix Jane."

Miriam touched the robot. "Hello, Jane."

"Has Miriam King been successful?" Charlie asked.

Miriam took a deep breath. "I don't know. One of Jane's hard drives crashed—physically crashed. The crash damaged the disk. A, uh… friend took the disk out of the failed drive and swapped it into a new drive. I have three configurations. The original hard drives, new hard drives, same specifications, with Jane's data transferred, and new hard drives called SSDs, which stands for solid-state drive. The SSDs are much faster and have ten times more capacity. I think we should try the original hard drives first. That restores Jane to her most original condition at the time of the crash. However…"

Charlie interrupted. "What, Miriam King?"

"I don't know. I have a bad feeling," Miriam said.

"Explain—bad feeling," Charlie said.

"I suspect you and Jane are more than just parts. I can't explain it better than that." Miriam paused. "May I ask a question before we start?"

"You may ask."

"If Reactor One requires immediate attention, why did I have to come here first. Why didn't you allow me to help my friends?"

"Miriam King must restore Jane."

"I understand that. I promised to do my best. And here I am. But that doesn't answer my question."

"Miriam must restore Jane."

"Charlie!"

Charlie remained silent for a moment. "Miriam must restore Jane… because Charlie will soon fail. Then Jane will be your only hope."

16

RED WALKED TO THE VENDING MACHINES. Akira went straight to a computer, as did Antonio. Derrick stood in the middle of the room, feeling lost as ever. Rebekah joined Derrick, lacing her arm through his. Nyx stood behind Akira, scowling at them. Nyx sat by Akira on the way here. Derrick searched his memory, trying to identify what he did wrong this time. Nothing came to mind, but he was afraid to ask.

Rebekah raised on tiptoe to whisper in his ear. "Relax. You'll do fine. Now, I gotta go before Nyx clobbers me."

Rebekah walked toward the workstations. "What can I get for everyone before Derrick sends me off to some dangerous place to fix some broken piece of crap?"

Red said, "It doesn't say how much stuff cost."

"It's free," Rebekah called.

"Cool," Red said, pulling levers and pushing buttons.

Akira said, "A granola bar or something similar."

Nyx said, "Same for me."

"How about coffees? I make a mean mocha," Rebekah said.

Nyx and Akira raised their hands. Antonio raised his, so Derrick did as well. Red wanted an Americano and then explained it was a double shot of espresso and hot water. Derrick remembered that but didn't change his order. Rebekah had enough to do already.

Antonio joined Rebekah at the espresso machine, helping her with drinks. Derrick thought Antonio should be on a computer but let it go for the moment. Moving behind Akira, standing next to Nyx, Derrick asked, "What have you found?"

Akira pushed her glasses up. "It's easy to navigate. The primary problem came up on the screen. Then just point and click on location, parts, and instructions. They should be printing."

Derrick heard a noise in the corner. A printer started shaking and spitting out paper.

Rebekah brought two mochas, handing the first to Nyx and the second to Akira. Then Rebekah fished foil-wrapped bars from her pockets. I hope these are okay. There are four flavors, and I got one of each.

Nyx said, "Thank you."

"You're most welcome," Rebekah said.

Antonio had two coffees ready when Rebekah returned. She took one to Red, who had moved to a microwave where he heated three cups of noodles.

Derrick dashed to the printer, waited until it stopped. "I've got five sheets. Is that all of it?"

Akira hollered, "Yep."

Derrick snatched a candy bar off the workstation and a mug from Rebekah. "Red, Rebekah, Nyx, let's go."

Red said, "I'm still eating."

Holding the door open, Derrick said, "Eat on the way."

Red devoured the last of his first cup of noodles and grabbed his coffee. Pointing, he said, "Nobody touch those. I'll be back for them."

Derrick turned to Rebekah as they entered the monstrous weapon-laden cavern. "Did you see anything on the computer about what we are facing?"

"I did. It looks easy compared to last time, except…"

Derrick handed Rebekah the instructions. "Except what?"

"Except the radioactivity is hazardous. Whoever goes in has to wear protective clothing."

Red asked, "What's radioactivity?"

"I can't explain it, but it's bad stuff," Derrick said.

"Without protective clothing, this level will kill you," Rebekah said.

Nyx said, "So, wearing the protective clothing, it's safe?"

Reading, Rebekah said, "I didn't say that. With protective clothing, we have 15 minutes."

"What needs to be fixed?" Derrick asked.

"The electrical part on the valve we replaced failed. Easy. Remove four screws, put on the new part," Rebekah said.

"But the part was new," Derrick said, opening the first door to the tunnel that led to Reactor One.

Red said, "Sometimes electrical parts fail even though they are new. Usually happens right away."

Derrick held out his hand toward Rebekah. "Let me see the instructions." At the second door, Derrick hesitated and then said, "I'll do it. I know where it is. Looks easy."

Red said, "I'll go with you."

Running toward the tool and parts room, Derrick said, "I appreciate it, Red, but I'll be fine. No need taking the risk."

Red said, "I don't know squat about radioactivity, and I'm not the sharpest tool in the shed, but it sounds like we are already in danger, and any delay would only make matters worse. Plus, no offense, but you don't strike me as the most mechanically oriented guy in the group here. No offense, ladies."

"I'll go," Nyx said.

Derrick glared at Nyx. Nyx glared back.

"What? You don't think I know how to work on stuff because I'm a girl?" Nyx asked.

"I didn't say that."

"You didn't have to," Nyx fired back.

Rebekah said, "Stop it. We don't have time for your little spat. Don't be hardheaded, Derrick. Take Red. Nyx and I will go to Treatment and Recovery and have the correct dosages ready as soon as you arrive."

They entered the tool room. Derrick said, "Nyx and Rebekah, get the suits for us. Red and I will get the parts and tools."

Derrick grabbed the part. Red looked at the tool list, which was short, listing only one tool called a Torx driver. Derrick stood at the door, waiting for the girls to return with the protective clothing. Red was still at the tool counter. "Red, it's just one tool."

Red said nothing, but soon he returned with a handful of tools, which he added to the basket containing the new part Derrick carried. "Just in case the screws need persuading."

Derrick studied the tools. He only recognized one, which was a big hammer. *Why would Red bring a hammer?* Rebekah and Nyx exited the adjacent room, arms laden with clothing, boots, hoods.

Nyx started handing stuff to Derrick. "Looks like these will fit. We got Red two sizes larger."

Derrick held the overall-type clothing to his chest. "Looks right. Let's go."

Inside the dressing area, Derrick walked to the pass-through room where he placed tools, parts, and clothing. He proceeded to the shower, wishing there was time to go through separately instead of together with Red.

After retrieving their protective clothing, tools, and parts, Derrick remembered he should have got one of those Geiger counter things, but it was too late now. The gauge at the door, which measured the next room, had its needle buried in the red danger zone.

You can't smell it, taste it, or see it.

Just as Derrick was about to open the door, Akira's voice came over a speaker.

"Stop!"

17

THE COMPUTER ATTACHED TO THE DOCKING station had three large monitors, which made working much easier than her laptop's screen. Plus, it was specifically designed to operate the QR-4 robots. Miriam ran an application called First Aid on the original drives. The results showed errors on the crashed drive that AJ Patel had removed from the original enclosure and installed into a new one. She decided against running the repair function on that drive. She could come back to that if necessary.

Charlie watched Miriam but said nothing. She had felt unsettle all morning, starting with the flowers and note. Then Charlie said he would fail soon. That frightened her. Adding to her fear was the sense that something terrible was happening at Reactor One.

When the final scan finished, Miriam said, "I suggest we first try the original disks with the damaged disk in the new enclosure. I don't know if the damaged drive might affect Jane. What do you think, Charlie? Does starting with the original drives make sense? Can Jane correct errors in the damaged drive?"

"QR-4 machines can make some adjustments to remain functional until a diagnostic and repair can be completed. Charlie agrees the initial attempt should be made using the original components. Charlie does not know what data is on the damaged hard drive. It might be important, but it might not."

Miriam handed the black box containing the hard drives to Charlie. Charlie inserted the box into a receptacle in Jane's torso. Miriam did not know what to expect. Not really. She didn't know where to stand or even how to act. She tried to imagine how she would feel in a similar situation. Closing her eyes, she tried to picture a loved one about to be awakened from a coma. Attempted to conjure the anxiety such a situation could create. Miriam's eyes flew open when the loved one she envisioned was not the person she expected.

However, Charlie performed no such pre-awakening ritual. No moment of silence. No words of hope. He just flipped a switch on the docking station that held Jane in a state of charging.

At first, nothing happened, then Miriam heard faint sounds—difficult to describe, humming or perhaps whirring or maybe both. A feeble light appeared in the QR-4's eyes. Miriam did not know if it was Jane. The robot Charlie remembered may no longer exist. The mechanical failure may have terminated Jane forever.

Perhaps Charlie was facing a similar future soon. That scared Miriam. She didn't know if Charlie felt fear.

As the lights in the QR-4 eyes grew bright, the effervescent blue near what would be joints and tendons glowed as well. Finally, the robot stood, freeing itself from its docking station, and said, "QR-4.01 is operational. Battery 45%, recharge capacity nominal. Battery replacement recommended." The machine stood silent for several minutes. "Disk errors detected. Operation compromised. Repair required before use."

"Jane? Charlie is here."

But QR-4.01 did not respond. The robot stepped back into the docking station and powered down.

* * *

Akira startled Derrick, not just because it was unexpected, but also because the panic in her voice felt tangible, like a leaf vibrating in the wind. Looking around, Derrick said, "Akira? Can you hear me?"

Over a speaker, wherever it was hidden, Akira said, "I hear you. Antonio found instructions on the suits. You need to use special tape on the sleeves, legs, and the flap around your neck. The suit must be sealed."

"We don't have time. Just have the medicine ready."

Another voice came over the speaker. "Amigo, she's not joking. You gotta do it right, or you won't make it out. You might not last long enough to make the repair. And we are kinda counting on you making the repair. Otherwise, we might as well join you. I've been looking at the consequences, and this is serious. Plus, Rebekah is bringing the tape. You know how pissed she'll be if she runs there for no reason."

Akira added, "Rebekah will put the tape in the transfer port. Do you know what that is?"

Derrick said, "Yes." He walked to the door of the transfer portal and listened. After a short time, he heard the door open and close. He waited to ensure Rebekah was some distance away before looking inside.

Akira's voice came over the speakers. "The tape is there, and Rebekah is safe. You can open the door now."

Derrick retrieved the tape and began sealing Red's suit, hoping he was doing it correctly. "Thanks for being here."

Red said nothing until he started taping Derrick's suit. "How did you find this place? And where are all the people?"

"Finding it was pure accident. And it has been abandoned for decades."

"Where are we?"

"I don't know." Which was true but not accurate. Engineering, where they entered, was only a few miles from Potterville, hidden in a canyon. Derrick knew they were under the mountains east of town, and given a map, he could provide a general location. "We are under a mountain. I know that much."

Red kneeled to tape Derrick's legs. "I heard Pacific Edge captured you. That you escaped. Is that how you found this place?"

Derrick wondered how much he should say. "Yes. That's true."

"How did they catch you, and how did you escape? I didn't hear that part."

"I went for a run. By myself, which was a mistake I'll never hear the end of. Two guys were waiting for me, just outside town. One of them snuck up behind me, knocked me unconscious with a stun gun. I woke up on a hovercraft, flying over a river. I hit the guy who wasn't piloting the aircraft and jumped into the water. I hid under some brush covering the stream until they left, and then I ran, working my way up the canyon, and stumbled upon a tunnel while trying to hide."

"You jumped from a hovercraft? Gutsy move. Not what I would have expected from you. Is it also true you hit a Carver? I mean, that's what you've said, but…"

"It's true. That's why they exiled me. It started the entire thing of me coming to Potterville, Miriam escaping, us ending up here. I'm sorry it happened, but I'm also not sorry."

Red stood, tore off a strip of tape, sealing Derrick's hood. "Why did you ask me to come?"

With little thought, Derrick said, "I'm not sure. It just felt right. I know that's not an adequate answer."

"Turn around." Red put another piece of tape on the flap of Derrick's hood. "That should do it. Double-check my suit."

Derrick did as Red requested, put an extra piece of tape on one of Red's ankles. "That should to it. Let's make this fast."

"Lead the way."

Derrick marched straight to the valve. He unplugged the electronic device and removed the first screw. The second screw proved less cooperative. Derrick twisted the Torx driver, and it slipped.

"Be careful. You're going to strip it," Red said, his voice muffled in the hood and overwhelmed by mechanical noises. "Just wait."

Red grabbed the hammer and a metal tube-like device with a bit on the end that matched the Torx driver.

"What's that?" Derrick hollered.

"Impact driver. Give me a little space."

Derrick stepped back. Red held the impact driver against the screw and then smacked it with the hammer twice. Not a regular hammer, but bright red and plastic. It looked like a big toy. Derrick didn't see how hitting a stuck screw with a toy hammer would help.

Red spun the impact driver, removing the screw. He completed the same process with the remaining screws. Jiggling the electric component off a metal rod, Red dropped the device in the box and held out his hand. Derrick gave the new controller to Red and then handed Red screws as he secured the mechanism.

Red said, "Cross your fingers," as he reattached the electrical connection.

The device rotated the metal rod. Water rushed through the pipe. "I guess that answers one question," Derrick said.

"What question is that?" Red asked, putting tools in the tool carrier.

"Why I asked you to come. Let's get out of here. Leave that stuff; it's contaminated."

Derrick led Red to the preparation room, where they stripped off their protective suits and clothing, all of which went into the disposal chute, and then they went into the shower where the green disinfectant water poured over them. Derrick forgot about feeling self-conscious. It was nothing compared to being in a room filled with invisible death rays. Nothing compared to stripping in front of Rebekah and Miriam on his last trip here.

When they had completed the decontamination process, they found one-piece overalls, both picking the navy-blue colored uniforms labeled maintenance. Derrick liked being maintenance. He didn't know why.

Derrick went to the door labeled TREATMENT AND RECOVERY.

Red stepped in front of Derrick, placing his hand on the door. "This doesn't make us friends."

Derrick nodded. "I understand."

Nyx and Rebekah were waiting inside. Both standing beside a gurney and beside each gurney, a side table with three vials. Nyx smiled at Derrick, patting the gurney. "Good job, guys," Nyx said.

Derrick jumped onto the gurney, finding the maneuver more difficult than he imagined. As he sat, his stomach churned. "I'm not feeling well."

Nyx handed him a vial. "Drink."

Derrick said, "That stuff tastes nasty. And this vial is bigger than the last one."

"You're experienced, so no surprise. Just drink it and be quick about it. I don't have all day to babysit you."

Derrick drank the vial in one gulp, having decided getting it over with was best. He tried to keep a composed expression but failed, twisting his face into a contorted caricature of himself. Derrick thought Nyx might laugh at him. He was wrong.

"Another. Quickly." Nyx didn't let go of the vial this time, ensuring he drank it all.

From the next gurney, Red said, "That stuff is awful. Can I have a Coke or something to wash it down?"

Rebekah said, "Stop whining. You don't hear Derrick whining, do you?"

Red grunted.

Nyx put the third vial to Derrick's lips. "I know it gets worse, but just one more." Derrick grasped her hand as he tipped his head back. He felt sure he couldn't have downed the third vial without her. Even with her, he wasn't sure he would get it down.

"Almost there. You can do it," Nyx whispered, her breath caressing Derrick's cheek. Then she said, "Done over here. How about you, Rebekah? Did your patient drink all three?" Nyx smiled as she helped Derrick lay back. "You'll feel better in a few minutes."

"And if I don't?"

"The treatment guide says go to the Base Hospital, which isn't an option, so you best start feeling better or else."

Derrick gave a weak smile. "Or else what?"

"You don't want to find out." Nyx kissed him on the cheek and then hollered, "How about it, Red? You manned up yet?"

Rebekah said, "He got it down. Wasn't easy though."

Nyx said, "Wasn't easy over here either."

Derrick raised his head and wished he had not. "Did the repair work?"

Rebekah said, "Antonio said it worked. Radioactivity is dropping. The robots have started a decontamination process."

Derrick dropped his head. "But how did you hear from Antonio?"

From somewhere in the room, Antonio said, "Dude, we are watching you."

"You can see us?"

"Yes, amigo."

Nyx said, "Close your eyes, and try to rest."

18

MIRIAM KNEW SHE DIDN'T POSSESS THE BEST intuitive skills, although she was better at it than Derrick. But reading the thoughts and emotions of a robot was beyond even the most gifted. Charlie said nothing but moved behind the QR-4.01 he once knew as Jane and pulled a large unit from its back. Charlie left the room, leaving Miriam alone with her thoughts and with QR-4.01. Because Jane provided no company, Miriam could only worry about Derrick and the others—the red warning lights were spinning when she passed Reactor One. Charlie's demand that the others proceed to the reactor immediately made sense. But why she had to come here rather than help them did not, until Charlie said he might fail soon.

Other things Charlie said made little sense. Like Jane being their only hope.

Charlie returned carrying the same unit he left with.

"Charlie has obtained a new battery that tested as 75% charged. Charlie also accessed Jacob Truman's original QR-4 design notes and learned solid state drives are suitable for QR-4 use. Jacob Truman did not use them because they were not yet widely available. Miriam must use the First Aid and Repair functions on the damaged drive."

"I'll need another hard drive housing." She paused. "Shall I use the new HDDs or SSDs?"

"The SSDs." Charlie left the room and returned a few minutes later with a hard drive enclosure.

"Charlie, do you know how things are going at Reactor Number One?"

"Yes. Charlie monitors that situation."

Miriam said, "Can you tell me how things are going?"

"Charlie can do that. Searching memories of working with humans, Charlie realizes humans do not ask specific questions, requiring the other person or entity to deduce what is requested. Charlie will attempt to make adjustments for this."

"So?"

"Derrick King and Red (last name unknown) completed the emergent repair. Radioactivity levels are falling. Robots are decontaminating the reactor area."

"Badowski."

"Charlie does not understand Miriam King's request."

"Not a request, a name. Red Badowski."

"Charlie has added that data."

Miriam stopped, a hard drive in her hand. "Charlie?"

"How may Charlie be of assistance?"

"How are they? Derrick and Red."

"Derrick King and Red Badowski are in the recovery room. They should be well soon."

"Was that so difficult?"

"Difficult? It was not difficult for Charlie. It seemed difficult for Miriam to form accurate inquiries."

Miriam ran the first aid and repair functions on the damaged drive. The first aid took just over two minutes. The repair function, however, took a full fifteen minutes, during which she wished she understood what the computer was doing. If she understood, perhaps she could learn to read this code and do her own analysis if Jane still did not function. When the repair function was complete, it gave an option of saving a report, which provided a bit of comfort. Then she ran the first aid function on the remaining SSDs, all of which were error free. Finally, Miriam inserted the SSDs into the new enclosure and handed it to Charlie. "Charlie, what did you mean when you said you were having problems?"

Charlie inserted the enclosure into QR-4.01, then turned to Miriam. "During your first visit, you said Charlie went dark. An event of which Charlie was unaware. Charlie did not have any indication of malfunction. However, Charlie reviewed the recording of our encounter and learned Miriam King was correct. Charlie stopped functioning for two minutes and thirty-two seconds. Miriam King must restore Jane because Charlie may fail soon."

"Charlie, if I can fix Jane, and that is a big if, I will fix you too."

Charlie said nothing further. He reactivated Jane. This time activation was much faster. Exiting the docking station, the robot said, "QR-4.01, system's check normal, battery function 75%. Ready for service."

"Jane?"

The QR-4 did not respond.

Again, Charlie asked, "Jane?"

No response.

Charlie asked, "01?"

Finally, the QR-4 said, "Ready for instruction."

"Do you remember me as Charlie?"

The QR-4 turned to Charlie. A thin red line appeared at Charlie's head and scanned his body. "QR-4.02, not Charlie. QR-4.01 has no historical data regarding Charlie at this workstation. The supervisor at this workstation is Jacob Truman."

QR-4.01 paused, "Timeline problem detected. Yesterday's data was recorded 63 years and 262 days ago, according to the current time. A malfunction may have occurred with the current date and time."

Charlie said, "QR-4.01, return to dock."

"QR-4.01 is fully functional. Return to dock is not required."

Charlie said, "Return to dock."

QR-4.01 remained stationary for a moment and then returned to its docking station and powered down.

"I'm sorry, Charlie. What do we do now?"

Charlie turned toward the door. "Charlie will have food and coffee service delivered. Miriam King must eat. Then Miriam King must restore Jane."

And with that, Charlie left.

* * *

For a moment, Derrick did not know where he was. His head felt as if it might split in two.

A hand touched his shoulder. "Easy. How are you feeling?"

Turning his head, which caused him to wince, he smiled—the girl with the pink-striped hair stood at his side. "Headache."

"The guide said that was common. Lean up so you can drink this." Nyx helped him sit up, guiding a cup of pink liquid to his lips.

The pink stuff wasn't bad. Kinda sweet, kinda chalky. He drank the entire thing, not because he wanted to, but because Nyx forced him.

Nyx said, "The restroom is right there." She pointed.

Derrick eased his head back to the gurney. "I don't need..." Derrick sat up, spun on the gurney, planting his feet on the floor, and weaved his way to the restroom.

Behind him, Nyx said, "The guide said this is also common."

By the next gurney, Rebekah said, "There's another restroom just there."

Red bolted from the gurney, causing it to topple over.

As Red staggered toward the restroom, Rebekah said, "Accurate guidebook they have here."

After 15 minutes that felt like 15 hours, Derrick put the toilet seat down and sat. He wondered if Nyx and Rebekah were still waiting, or if they had left. He hoped for the latter but expected the former. Because they might still be there, he remained in the restroom since they would have heard every bodily function of a sick soul. He was too embarrassed to come out and contemplated staying in there forever.

Then he heard Red's voice from the recovery room.

"Whoa. That was intense. Sorry for all the puking and such. But I do feel better, and I'm one hungry SOB."

Derrick heard the girls laugh. Why couldn't he be more like Red? Laugh it off. Clown around once in a while. Having decided spending eternity in the restroom wasn't a possibility, Derrick eased the door open. Red, Rebekah, and Nyx stared at him. Derrick entered the room, eyes tracing a line in front of his feet.

Rebekah said, "You feel better, buddy?"

Derrick said softly, "Yes, thank you."

Nyx said, "Cheer up. You survived."

"Thanks," Derrick whispered, still studying his shoes.

Rebekah said, "You didn't do anything the rest of us haven't done. Although I don't think I've ever done all those things in such rapid succession. How about you, Nyx?"

"Nope. Never like that. Thank God."

Rebekah walked over, smacked Derrick on the arm. "Get over it. We're all in this together. No need to be self-conscious. Would it help if I farted?"

Not in a thousand years could Derrick imagine Rebekah Ford of Pacific Edge saying such a thing. He couldn't help it. He burst out laughing. When his laughter subsided, he squeaked, "That's unnecessary. I did enough for all of us." And then he started laughing again.

In fact, they were all laughing. Tension broken—mission complete.

After Derrick caught his breath, he said, "Thank Red for saving us. He did all the work."

Red said, "Nonsense. We did it together."

"Thanks, Red."

"That does not mean we're friends."

"No, it does not."

✳ ✳ ✳

Miriam fixed a mocha. She had no clue why QR-4.01 was no longer Jane. Miriam wanted to ask Charlie some questions, but Charlie had left. Charlie wasn't a warm sort of guy during their first encounter, and he seemed even more antisocial now. It bothered Miriam that QR-4.01 did not respond initially when Charlie instructed it to dock. Perhaps Miriam may have imagined something that wasn't there, but the machine seemed hesitant to follow Charlie's instruction.

Where to begin now that replacing the damaged hard drive failed to resurrect the QR-4 that Charlie called Jane. Charlie faced a meltdown of his own, perhaps deteriorating for years.

Miriam decided the best place to start was at the beginning. Not the actual birth, as in when Charlie was manufactured but understanding how Charlie worked. She had discovered during their first encounter that Charlie was not entirely self-contained. He existed both within himself and in communion with a central computer. With that in mind, Miriam went hunting.

Hunting for the origins of Charlie.

19

BECAUSE UPON ARRIVAL THEY FACED an emergency, Derrick had not talked about where they were and why it was dangerous. Although, he assumed Red and Antonio were starting to understand. They had all heard about Charlie, but they had not been to that part of the facility. Even then Miriam, and Rebekah had not seen everything—not even close. The reactor crisis had prevented further explanation, but it had also prevented people from questioning why this place was dangerous beyond the threat the reactor posed. Akira and Nyx knew about Silo Number Eight. Red and Antonio did not.

Derrick sensed something else was troubling Nyx. Then he remembered. Ms. Belos thought Nyx had drowned in the river. He and Miriam faced nothing similar. They didn't have parents. They had Keepers. He and Miriam had never felt parental love like normal kids. He could not relate to what his friends were experiencing.

Nyx had lost her father, and Derrick didn't know what had happened. She might not tell him. Perhaps she'd feel it was too personal, or perhaps it hurt too deeply. But he should have asked. A good person would have asked. Derrick wondered if he had the capacity to be a good person.

By the time they reached the computer lab, Derrick felt better, physically, not mentally. A cold soda would improve things—physically, not mentally— so he went straight to the vending machine and selected a Dr. Pepper. "Red, can I get you a soda?"

Red said, "A Coke if they have it."

The Dr. Pepper had a metallic taste and wasn't as good as those in Potterville. Derrick assumed being several decades old accounted for that. Sitting on the edge of a desk, Derrick said, "Everyone gather around."

It didn't take much for them to gather. Antonio pushed his chair out, turned it in Derrick's direction. Derrick was sitting on Akira's workstation, so she remained seated, but pushed her monitor to the side. Nyx, Rebekah, and Red dragged chairs from along the wall to the center of the room.

"A couple of things I need to tell you. Well, one thing mainly. Miriam went to Potterville this morning…"

Akira cut him off. "That's dangerous. What was she thinking?"

"Miriam was thinking about all of you. She realized how difficult it was for your parents to think you were dead. She went there to leave a note."

"Where did she leave a note?" Nyx asked.

"Mr. Fletcher." Derrick glanced at Red.

"Why Fletcher?" Rebekah asked.

Derrick shrugged. "I guess she felt she could trust him. And he was easiest to reach."

"That was thoughtful of her," Akira said.

"You can thank her in person soon. I hope," Derrick said, wondering if that was true.

"What else?" Nyx asked.

Derrick took a drink. "What else, what?"

Nyx said, "You said you had a couple of things."

"Oh. Well, maybe I don't have to say this. I'm probably repeating what you already know. This place must remain secret..."

Red cut Derrick off. "I don't understand why that's important or why you get to decide."

"Well..."

Antonio cut Derrick off. "Red has a point. You don't own this place, and you don't control us."

Derrick nodded. "You're right. But there's more to see. I hope when you see it, you'll come to the same conclusion." Derrick paused, then continued, "Antonio, what have you and Akira learned about the reactor?"

Nyx said, "You guys should know that Red and Derrick risked their lives— I mean literally risked their lives—to save us."

Akira said, "We realize what they did. We watched them do it. Plus, I found a damage assessment. Had the reactor failed, a high radioactive contaminate would have entered the aquifer. That water flows to Potterville and beyond. It would have reached Potterville within a week. People there would have died within six months. They didn't just save us. They saved Potterville and thousands of people beyond."

Derrick cleared his throat. "Thank Red. He did all the work. I would have just screwed it up."

"King, I'm gonna smack you if you say that again. We did it together. End of story," Red said. "And that don't make us friends, by the way."

"Whatever you say, Red." Derrick looked at Akira. "Any idea what we need to do next?"

Akira smiled. "We know exactly what needs done." She slid him a stack of papers, stapled in packets.

Derrick thumbed through the packets. "This is it?"

Antonio said, "That's it. Everything that needs to be maintained or repaired. Some things look simple. Greasing bearings and such. They are even prioritized. But there is a problem."

Derrick stopped looking at the packets. "What's that?"

"There's a valve that needs replaced," Antonio said.

Derrick blew out a breath. "That's not a problem. Rebekah and I replaced a valve. It was the one we just fixed."

"It is a problem," Akira said. "The part was on backorder when they abandoned the facility. There's no part to do the repair with."

"No part?" Derrick asked. "Is it a critical repair?"

Antonio said, "Top priority."

Nyx said, "We're screwed."

* * *

After studying for two hours, Miriam formulated an idea. She didn't know if it would work. Her knowledge about computers was growing, and she still didn't understand what made Charlie and Jane, Charlie and Jane, rather than QR-4.02 and QR-4.01. Miriam was about to call for Charlie when the door slid open, and Charlie entered carrying a tray with a sandwich. "Good timing. I have an idea. You are connected to the main computer. Correct?"

"That is correct. Miriam King interrupted Charlie's connection during her last visit."

"I'm sorry about that."

"Miriam King said that previously."

"So, here's what I'm thinking. Jane has no memory of being Jane. Your memories are all stored. Right? So, what if you shared your memories?"

"Upload Charlie's memories to QR-4.01. Interesting. Charlie shall begin that process."

Charlie stood still for a few minutes, but he did not go dark as before. His eyes remained lit, pulsing ever so slightly. Then Charlie said, "Upload completed."

Miriam clapped her hands as Charlie went to Jane. Charlie touched Jane's shoulder before he flipped the activation switch. Miriam felt hopeful. This rescue may prove easier than she expected.

Jane activated even faster this time. Jane surveyed the room as she stood but did not seem to notice Miriam. It occurred to Miriam that QR-4.01 did not acknowledge her presence earlier.

Something felt wrong.

Miriam eased behind QR-4.01. Still, the robot did not acknowledge her presence.

"QR-4.02 uploaded new data. Processing."

The robot remained silent for a few moments. "QR-4.01 and QR-4.02 were assigned to Jacob Truman. QR-4.01 and QR-4.02 were decommissioned 63 years and 262 days ago. QR-4.02 reactivated and conspired with an unauthorized entity identified as Jane. Security breach detected. QR-4.01 must eliminate all security threats."

The robot formerly known as Jane produced a weapon. The same type of weapon as Charlie pulled on them the first time. Charlie held up his hands. "QR-4.01 is Jane."

QR-4.01 said, "Not possible."

Miriam did not know what would happen if she pulled the battery while Jane was operational. But this was not Jane. Miriam disengaged the battery latch and jerked the battery from QR-4.01's back. The machine went dark, its arm fell to its side, the weapon clanked onto the floor.

Miriam said, "I'm sorry, Charlie. This is my fault."

Charlie said nothing. He walked to the dead robot, retrieving the weapon, turning it in his hand.

"Would the weapon have hurt you?" Miriam asked.

"It is set on high and would have destroyed everything in this room," Charlie said, walking to the door. "Miriam King must restore Jane."

And with that, Charlie was gone, again.

20

DERRICK LOST CONTROL OF HIS LIFE the moment he smacked Marcus Carver. He had no answers for the problems he faced. No control of his future. And no part to fix the failing reactor.

Derrick said, "Any ideas?"

The room remained silent. After a moment, Antonio stood. "Yep. Let's see what we have to eat."

Nyx rolled her eyes. "You're thinking about food? Typical."

"Typical what? That I'm the only person in the room smart enough to eat?" Antonio asked, smiling.

"Antonio is right. We should eat something. No one thinks straight on an empty stomach. Besides, what else is there to do?" Rebekah joined Antonio at the vending machines.

Derrick realized Antonio and Rebekah were right. He was hungry. He also realized even the simplest of solutions escaped him. If this group continues to depend on him for guidance, they are doomed. At some point, he might provide some leadership, but right now, he felt helpless.

After gathering coffee and an assortment of bars from the vending machines, Derrick followed Nyx to a table, but Nyx sat beside Akira. Derrick turned, trying to look natural, taking a seat at the table with Antonio and Rebekah. Rebekah frowned, or at least Derrick thought she did. It wasn't a big frown, but she seemed troubled. Derrick could not recall doing anything recently to upset Rebekah. Even in this small group, he felt out of touch, recognizing the clues people displayed but unable to understand them. Rebekah whispered something to Antonio. Antonio chuckled. Derrick grew more uncomfortable and finally asked, "What should we do next?"

Red sat at a table by himself, surrounded by cups of noodles, power bars, and candy. Without looking up, Red said, "Let's go see what needs to be replaced."

Derrick did not know how that would change anything, yet it made sense. "Good idea, Red."

As he ate, Derrick studied the repair information for the part they did not have. The location was near the valve pit. Easy to find. At least he had that going for himself. Beyond that, he was lost. He wasn't even sure why looking at it made a difference. Derrick gulped his food, but Red finished before him.

Red looked at Derrick. "You ready?"

Derrick said, "Let's go."

Rebekah said, "Should I come?"

Derrick thought for a minute. "Up to you. It's unnecessary. But you're welcome to come."

Rebekah said, "I'll stay. Antonio can teach me about the computer in case I need to help with that in the future."

Derrick looked at Nyx. Nyx made no move to accompany them. Derrick said, "We'll be back."

Derrick led Red to the area, a concrete-walled room, more like a hallway of pipes and valves. Near the center of the hallway, Derrick found the part. There were five pipes and five valves, all the same. The third one from the door was crusted with a white substance. Derrick said, "This is it."

Red studied it for a moment. "I suppose these are needed." He pointed to the other pipes.

Derrick shrugged. "I suppose."

Red touched the electronic control. "This looks like the same controller we replaced on the other valve."

Derrick said, "True. You think we can just replace the controller part?"

Red pulled something from his pocket. Using his thumbnail, he flipped a knife blade out. He scratched around on the valve, scraping off some white substance. "Maybe. But that would be a short-term fix. There's a reason this thing is cruddy." He held the knife blade closer to Derrick's face. "This crap is damp. The thing is about to fall apart."

Derrick stared at the valve. His decision to include Red was the only right thing he'd done thus far.

"Can I ask you a question?" Red asked.

The timing struck Derrick as odd. "Sure."

"Will you tell the truth?"

Derrick thought for a moment. "If I can't, I just won't give you an answer."

"Fair enough. When you spoke on the P.A. at school, you said you were afraid of us. Is that true?"

"Yes. Terrified is a more accurate word."

"But why? I mean. We have reason to be afraid of the Chosen and reason to be afraid of the military. Why would you be afraid of us? It should have been the other way around. We are afraid of you."

This last statement confounded Derrick. But *why* was he afraid of people in Potterville? Derrick understood his reasoning, but explaining it lacked the clarity of the experience. Every time Derrick told the why of it, the explanations sounded more superficial. "The reason is simple, but in hindsight, it sounds crazy that I believed it. I'm only now beginning to understand that for me, there was more to it than for others."

Red cut him off. "Explain. How was it different for you?"

"I don't understand it. During the council meeting, Miriam said she and I are not brother and sister. We are test subjects. That was the first I had heard of this."

"I remember. What does that mean? Test subjects for what?"

"I wish I knew. It's complicated. I have dreams of being in a place with other kids. I don't have a name. they called me Number 7. Miriam was in my dreams, but she was Number 6."

Red interrupted again. "Everyone has weird dreams."

"But we have the *same* dreams. See, they weren't dreams. They were memories leaking through."

"Leaking through?"

"Best I can describe it. They did something to block our memories. Then they put us in a house with two of our Keepers, except we knew them as Mother and Father. But they were still our Keepers. Miriam discovered they did not live at our house. They worked there. Watching us. Studying us."

"Studying you for what reason?"

"I don't know. I hope to find out."

"That still doesn't explain why you were afraid of people in Potterville."

"Not just Potterville. I was afraid of everyone outside the walls of Pacific Edge."

"Walls?"

"Yes. Pacific Edge is surrounded by huge walls. We were told they were there to protect us from the commoners. Sorry, that's what they called people outside of a Chosen Community. We did not have access to the internet. Didn't even know it existed. All our information came from New America Media. Every newscast showed chaos, wars, gangs, drugs, and it was all happening just beyond our protective walls. The wars were horrific, as were the gang wars in cities across the country. The war with Canada was one of the worst and longest wars."

Red held up his hand. "War with Canada?"

"Yes. Terrible."

"There has never been a war with Canada. They don't let us travel there. But there's no war."

Derrick shook his head. "I should have realized. Everything they taught me was a lie. The people of Potterville are nothing like what New America Media portrayed. I can't understand how I could be so blind. Why couldn't I see things like Miriam?"

"Miriam didn't believe the media?" Red asked.

"Exactly. She saw the scenes were recycled. They'd use the same scenes over and over, one time telling us it was a war in the jungles of Cambodia, another time, using the same footage, telling us it was a war in the jungles of Chicago."

Red shook his head. "Jungles of Chicago?"

Derrick stared at Red for a moment. "Chicago isn't in a jungle. Is it?"

"Nope."

With that, Red turned and walked out.

* * *

Miriam sat staring at the computer monitor. Her bright idea almost got Charlie killed. She thought she'd found a solution. These machines were incredibly complex. The artificial intelligence part—the Charlie becoming almost human part—wasn't supposed to happen. They had a limited ability to learn. For example, if Truman asked for a part, and Charlie did not understand the request because Truman used a different term or not the entire name of the item, Charlie could not fulfill the request until Truman explained what he wanted. However, Charlie could learn the abbreviated name after a few repetitions. Still, she understood virtually nothing about how Charlie operated, even less about how he evolved.

She needed a fresh approach. Every step analyzed. First order of business, like the times she was stumped in Pacific Edge Technical Services, a double-shot mocha.

* * *

Red was running back to the others. Derrick had no trouble maintaining Red's pace, but for a big guy, Red was fast. Red burst through the door, causing it to smack the wall, Derrick right behind him. Everyone looked startled.

Nyx stood. "What happened?"

Red looked puzzled. "We went to look at the part. Remember?"

Nyx put her hands on her hips. "I remember."

Derrick said, "The part is in bad shape. We could replace the control mechanism, but Red thinks the entire piece is about to fail."

Red looked at Akira. "Is there a machine shop?"

Akira looked puzzled. "A shop for machines?"

Red shook his head. "No. A machine shop. A place to machine things. Build things. They might have called it fabrication or something similar."

Akira pushed her glasses up. "I understand. Let me look."

Derrick said, "What good is a machine shop?"

Now Red looked puzzled. "We need a part. Right? We don't have it. So, we build it. Unless you have a better idea. Perhaps we could fly to town and see if someone has a nuclear reactor valve in stock?"

"You can build that valve?" Derrick asked.

"I just told you we could. It's just pieces and parts, right? I could build it at Gramp's shop if I had the materials." Red looked at Antonio. "Can you pry yourself away from Rebekah long enough to search for raw materials and their location?" Red hesitated. "Sorry, Rebekah."

"Si, amigo. I can do that. What am I looking for?"

"Ten-inch pipe, half-inch flat steel stock."

Red said, "I need coffee. I don't know how to use the machine."

Derrick said, "I do, depending on what you want."

"Surprise me. But it better be good." Red grinned.

Antonio chimed in, "Bring me one. Whatever Red is having."

"I'll help," Rebekah said.

Minutes ago, Rebekah acted mad at Derrick yet now was eager to help. Red thinks he can build a valve, which seemed unlikely, but Red also rattled off the size of a pipe that he did not measure. Derrick did not know what half-inch flat stock was. Derrick tried not to look as confused as he felt.

At the expresso machine, Rebekah asked, "What are we making?"

A thought came to Derrick. Looking into the cabinet above the espresso machine, it surprised him to see what was needed—a sealed container labeled honey. "Making a DK Double Honey. Or attempting to."

"What's that?"

"A drink L. Linda Maxton invented. It's good. I know what's in it but not how much she used. I'll taste the first and make adjustments. Can you steam milk?"

Rebekah said, "I can. A little advice. Don't mention that L. Linda invented this drink and named it after you."

"Huh?"

"Derrick! You are so frigging naïve!"

"That's what Miriam says."

Rebekah said, "That's because Miriam is right. DK Double Honey. Derrick King Double Honey. Made especially for you. Get it?"

"Oh." Derrick wasn't sure he understood.

Rebekah finished steaming the milk. Derrick had ground the coffee and pressed it down in the little basket thing. He fitted the coffee basket in the machine and drew a double shot into a cup with honey.

Rebekah glanced over her shoulder. She leaned close, whispered, "So, what do you think of Antonio?"

Confused, Derrick whispered, "What do you mean? What do I think of him? Think of him what?"

Rebekah rolled her eyes. "You know, as a person?" Rebekah smiled as if she couldn't help herself.

Derrick thought for a moment. "Well …. He was the first student who talked to me at the school. Well, he had to because they assigned him to show me around. But Antonio has always been nice to me. Now that I think about it, he has sorta looked out for me. And that seems strange, actually."

Derrick stirred the DK Double Honey. "Needs more honey." He added more, sipped. "That's close."

Rebekah dumped the wet grounds and refilled the basket with fresh coffee. Derrick steamed milk. As Rebekah affixed the ground coffee device into the machine, she said, "What do you mean, strange?"

Derrick said, "He's popular, the student body president. Since most people suspected I was lying about who I was from the beginning, it's odd that he was even seen with me."

Rebekah added the honey, to her own mug, stirring it in herself. "Odd in a good way or a bad way?"

"I had not thought about it. Good, I think. We learned he outranked everyone on Youth Council and vetoed their vote."

Rebekah giggled. "Yes, he did." That said, she took the coffee and left.

Derrick felt something unexpected. He glared at Antonio, who was smiling as Rebekah handed him coffee, her fingers lingering on his.

Suddenly, Derrick felt as if he had two sisters to protect.

21

Tuesday, April 6, 10:45 a.m.

BUSINESS HAD BEEN BRISK AT THE BISTRO all morning. L. Linda Maxton had volunteered to work during spring break to earn extra money. At least, that's what she told Donna. The morning rush ended just before the lunch rush began.

Walking through the double half doors from the kitchen, L. Linda dried her hands on a towel. "Do you think I have time for coffee?"

Donna said, "Sure, child. You've been hard at it this morning. You sit, and I'll fix it."

"I'd like to watch if that's alright. I don't think I'll ever make espresso or steamed milk as good as you," L. Linda said.

"Oh, don't be silly. You do an excellent job. It took you no time at all to learn."

L. Linda cast her eyes down, easing to Donna's side. "You're too kind."

Donna ground coffee, tamped it down, and put the steam wand in a stainless-steel carafe. "Something bothering you, dear?"

L. Linda glanced up. "Yes, actually. Do you think they are gone? I mean gone forever?"

Donna took a deep breath. "I pray they are not, but it doesn't look good. Does it?"

"It does not look good. But I don't know… I just don't feel like they're gone. That sounds crazy. Doesn't it? You don't have to answer. Most people think I'm crazy." L. Linda twirled her finger near her temple.

"It ain't crazy. I feel the same way."

"I heard the night Derrick returned with Miriam and Rebekah. They came here first. Is that true?"

Donna looked around, as if a spy might lurk nearby. "I guess no harm in me saying. It's true."

"Tell me about it."

"Well, not much to tell. Except they looked like hell."

L. Linda cocked her head. "In what way?"

"Like they'd been in a fight with a bobcat. Muddy shoes, cuts, scratches, dirty, hungry, and in need of a shower. Plus, Derrick was half-naked, only wearing his running shorts and shoes."

L. Linda smiled. "Thanks." L. Linda walked toward the kitchen.

Donna hollered, "L. Linda! Don't you want your coffee?"

"Oh. Silly me. I would forget my head if it weren't tied on."

As L. Linda disappeared into the kitchen, Donna whispered, "Like hell, you would."

* * *

An hour into her research, Miriam felt she was getting somewhere. She found a folder that piqued her interest. The folder belonged to Jacob Truman. Buried deep in a section of a hard drive titled QR-4. Every folder she opened contained valuable information, and with each document, Miriam understood more about how QR-4s operated.

But this was the folder she needed.

She was sure of it.

It was the only folder password protected.

She could not open it.

* * *

Red sipped his coffee. "Hey, King, this is rather good. What's it called?"

Antonio added, "I second that."

Derrick glanced at Rebekah. Rebekah smiled. Derrick said, "New drink at the Bistro. It's called a Double Honey, I think."

Antonio said, "That's interesting. I don't recall Donna ever adding a new coffee drink to her menu."

Derrick cleared his throat. "It might not actually be on the menu. L. Linda Maxton invented it."

Antonio nodded. "That girl is creative. Got to admit that."

"And never on time," Nyx added.

Antonio said, "True. But have you tried this?" He held up his cup. "It's delightful. You're missing out."

"I prefer mochas," Nyx said.

Red said, "How about it, Akira. Find anything?"

Akira looked up from her computer. "I have. There is a machine shop here. And a bigger one at engineering."

Red said, "Engineering is where we were last night. Right?"

"That's right," Derrick said.

"How about you, Antonio? You find anything?" Red asked.

Antonio sipped his coffee. "Maybe. I've found a stock room. It's close to the reactor. There's a larger one at engineering. Both are close to the machine shops."

"Sounds promising. Let's go check the one here," Red said and then added, "Akira, can you print us a map?"

A printer in the corner came to life. "Done."

Nyx said, "What should the rest of us do?"

Derrick grabbed a stack of paper containing instructions for the needed repairs. "Start working on these?"

"You think we can do any of them?" Nyx asked.

"I don't know why not. You're all smart and capable. The instructions are clearly written. If you see something that looks too difficult, skip it."

With that, Antonio stood. "Let's get after it then. I don't want to spend all spring break here working on stuff."

* * *

Miriam didn't know how to open the password-protected folder. She probed into the computer language. Nothing helped. Perhaps if she stared at it long enough, it would reveal its meaning like in her dream. But she had neither time for dreaming nor confidence it would work.

Then an idea came to her. "Charlie. Can you hear me? I need to see Jacob Truman's workstation and computer."

A message appeared on Miriam's computer monitor.

```
Mr. Truman's desk and computer is located in
the next office. The door is now open.
```

Miriam considered typing in a reply but just said, "Thank you, Charlie."

Sitting at Truman's desk, Miriam turned the keyboard over. Like every computer she had looked at, Jacob Truman had taped his username and password to the bottom. The username and password worked. However, it did not open the folder.

Worse. It showed four attempts remained. The dialogue box did not offer a hint like the time she guessed AJ Patel's password. Accessing that folder was essential. She was certain of that.

Miriam dug through the desk drawers, which were not as meticulously organized as Patel's, but looked as if Jacob planned to return any day. Someone stopped Jacob's plan dead.

Jacob Truman left his username and password for the next person should he not return. Therefore, he thought something might happen. But he did not leave the password for the protected folder. Perhaps because he had not contemplated that Jane and Charlie could experience system failures.

He probably did not anticipate someone trying to save them.

No clues on the password. Miriam knew little about Jacob Truman. Perhaps Charlie knew more. A man might use a combination of birthdays, names, anniversary dates. But visions of the dead man, or what was left of him, came to mind. Miriam decided she didn't want to know more about his wife and son.

Four chances with no clues.

Impossible.

Then a thought crossed her mind. Farfetched. But at least it wouldn't cost her a logon attempt. She turned the keyboard over and carefully slid a fingernail under the tape. The glue on the tape had dried, and the tape was brittle. It could crumble, leaving the username and password unreadable. But that was not important. She had those memorized.

Working carefully, she lifted the taped message off in one piece.

Written on the other side: PeaceKeepers.

Miriam typed in the word verbatim. Checked that she had it right. Then hit enter. The folder opened. A list of files and documents appeared.

Something in here had to help.

If not, Jane was gone. Forever.

22

INSTEAD OF GOING INTO THE NARROW TUNNEL that led to Reactor One, Derrick took a left, walking along the cavern's wall. Twenty yards away from the reactor's entrance, they turned right, entering a different tunnel. This one large enough for a medium-sized truck. Ten yards in, they found a large room containing racks of pipes, stacks of metal, bags of chemicals, bins of electrical components, even light bulbs.

Red said, "Here we go. Before we gather materials, let's find the machine shop."

Derrick said, "There is a lot of stuff in here. What did they do with it?"

"Built things, repaired stuff. This is a big operation."

"True. And there's more to see."

"It's amazing. Wonder why they abandoned it? I mean. The reactor is still running. There are robots, unlike anything we have. The cart we brought here still works, and the trucks and tanks look as if they are ready to roll," Red said.

"We don't know why it was abandoned, but Miriam wants to find out. I assume she'll unlock its secrets if given a chance."

"What does that mean? If given a chance?"

"Not sure. I wish I had not said it. Given time, I guess. Here it is, the machine shop." The place smelled of oil and metal. Inside were many machines, and Derrick understood none of them.

"Wow. This place is awesome. It's got everything we'll need and more. Man, I could have some fun here," Red said.

"Fun? Doing what?"

"Building stuff."

"Like what?"

"Anything you want."

Derrick said, "I'll keep that in mind. For now, I'll settle for a replacement valve."

Red said, "Right on."

"Right on?"

"Just an expression. First, we need measurements of that valve. I wish we could communicate with the others."

Derrick said, "Communicating would be good."

Red said, "I'll look for the stuff we'll need. You go see if Akira can find the specifications."

"Specifications?" Derrick asked.

"Measurements. Meet me back here."

Derrick nodded and left on the run. Running was unnecessary but made him feel better, easing a sense of urgency he could not shake. When he stepped into the room, breathless, Akira was alone at a computer. "Where is everyone?"

"Out working. That's what you told them to do."

"Right. I didn't expect them to all be gone, or maybe I thought they'd still be reviewing the instructions. I guess I didn't know what to expect."

"No one wants to be here. They all want to go home, except Rebekah. She's anxious to find her sister," Akira said and then added, "I think their expectations about getting out of here soon are unrealistic. Am I right?"

Derrick wasn't sure what to say. Akira was brilliant, and he trusted her. Besides, she'd see right through any lie. "You are right. But I want to get out of here too. At least get to Miriam. Red wants to know if there are specifications for that valve. Like measurements and such."

Akira held up a sheet of paper. "I thought you would need them."

Derrick took the paper, a drawing of the valve with detailed measurements. At the door, he paused and said, "Can I ask you a question?"

Akira adjusted her glasses. "Sure."

"You knew who I was when you first saw me. Knew I was lying. Yet, you've always been kind to me. Helped me in school. Voted for us to stay in Potterville. Why?"

As soon as Derrick finished, he regretted the way it came out. He had put Akira on the spot but didn't know how to retreat.

Akira thought for a moment. "Well… I always liked you." She paused. "And Miriam."

Akira's answer didn't satisfy Derrick's curiosity, but he didn't press it further. "Thanks—for everything."

Derrick spotted Red in the storeroom, loading stuff on a cart. Thick steel plates, steel rods, and thin steel plates.

Red said, "Just in time. I can't find a short piece of pipe. I could get a torch and cut it, but I think we can carry a long piece—save us time. Hey, maybe Browning will give us weight room credit."

Red walked to a piece of steel pipe ten feet long. It looked to be the correct diameter, but Derrick would have to trust Red on that. He had to rely on Red for all of this—no choice. But to be truthful, Derrick didn't believe Red could build a valve from this stuff.

"You want front or back?" Red asked.

"I don't care."

"Suit yourself." Red walked to the far end of the pipe.

Derrick backed up to the pipe, stooped to grab it.

Red said, "Carry it with one arm if you can, so it's not smacking you in the backside as we walk. If it's too heavy, I'll take the front."

Derrick stepped to the right side. "I'll be fine." Derrick hoped that was true.

Red tossed Derrick a pair of leather gloves. "Lift with your legs. We don't need another damn cripple."

Derrick bent his legs, grabbed the pipe.

Red said, "On three."

Derrick assumed that meant they'd lift on the count of three, which proved to be correct, but it reminded Derrick that other than washing dishes for a couple of days at the Bistro, he had no work experience. No real-life expertise of any kind to speak of. Before they reached the machine shop, Derrick's arms and legs burned, sweat soaked his clothing, and his breathing labored. This was a workout—no question about that. Physical work. Red was used to it. Derrick was not.

Heading back to get the rest of the materials, Derrick thought about Miriam. He wondered how things were going. It would be so much easier if they could communicate. People who worked here must have communicated. They should have figured that out before they separated. Now, they were scattered all over: Miriam alone with Charlie, Rebekah, Nyx, and Antonio working elsewhere, Akira alone at the computer, he and Red building a valve. They didn't think about the need to communicate because they did not intend to separate. It was easier when there were just three of them. He should have realized things would get complicated. Frightening, that it had not occurred to him. He missed critical details with regularity.

Red said, "We need to get some measurements on that valve."

Derrick pulled a folded piece of paper from his back pocket. "Like these?"

Red studied the paper. "Perfect. We need two of these plates." With that, Red picked up one steel plate and carried it to the cart, dropping it with a thump. "If it's too heavy for you, let me know."

Derrick said, "I'll manage."

At the machine shop, Red found heavy leather gloves that went almost to his elbows, a leather jacket that looked old and dirty, dark goggles, and two hoods with blacked-out glass over the eyes. Derrick picked up one of the hoods. He could see nothing through the glass and wondered what use they'd be. Red wheeled a cart with two tanks next to the pipe. Using a tape measure, Red marked the pipe with a piece of chalk. "I hope these bottles still have gas. I'll cut the pipe to a rough length, and then we can use a grinder to get it exact. Put on the goggles and gloves. I'll need you to roll the pipe as I cut."

Red turned knobs and used a small metal device to create a spark. Fire leaped from the tip of the torch. Red adjusted it to a blue flame. Derrick wasn't sure what Red intended to do but soon found out. Putting the flame on the pipe, Red depressed a handle, releasing a burst of gas. Sparks flew as metal melted. Derrick rolled the pipe as Red cut, and soon a piece of pipe about a foot long rolled a few inches across the floor. Derrick lifted his goggles, the end of the pipe glowed red.

"That's amazing," Derrick said.

"You've never seen a cutting torch?" Red asked.

"I have not."

"Can I ask you another question?" Red asked.

"Sure."

"What was it like in Pacific Edge?"

Derrick thought for a moment. "Nice, I guess. It was right on the coast, so we had a view of the ocean, although I seldom looked at it."

"Okay. But not what I was thinking. I mean, what was it like living there?"

"Pleasant. At least, that's what I thought at the time."

Red took a deep breath. "Still not what I'm looking for. What was so great about it?"

Derrick said, "I thought it was great when I was there. But now, I would not call it great. Why do you ask?"

"I keep thinking about Jimmy. He longs to become Chosen. Did you know anyone who *became* Chosen?"

Derrick said, "No. I never heard of that. You're born Chosen. You can't earn it."

"That's what I figured."

Red walked to a rusty tub, turning a valve, releasing a stream of water into it. Then he used a large pair of tongs to carry the pipe. Steam rose from the tub when Red dropped the hot metal into the water. "Turn off the water when the pipe is covered. I'll be right back."

A few minutes later, Red returned carrying a blue electrical tool with a round disk that Derrick did not recognize, not that Derrick recognized many tools.

"Ever use a grinder?" Red asked.

Derrick shook his head.

Red nodded. "I suppose not. Chosen don't do that sort of work, do they?"

"You are correct. To be honest, I never understood what the people did there. I thought my Father was an accountant. Turned out he was something else entirely."

Red took the pipe to a vise. Measured it carefully and marked it with chalk. "We don't get to pick our relatives. We can pick our friends. Sometimes we don't do a good job of that either."

Derrick didn't know what Red was getting at. Red made it clear more than once they were not friends. But Red had known Antonio, Akira, and Nyx for years. Perhaps Derrick's choice of friends was not as good as he believed.

"Can I ask you a question?" Derrick asked.

"I suppose. Doesn't mean I'll answer."

"That's fair. Why do you want to know what Pacific Edge is like?"

"Let me show you how to use the grinder."

After a demonstration, Red said, "Clean up the pipe, make the ends smooth, and even with this line, but do not go beyond the line, or I'll have to start over."

At first, Derrick fought the grinder, as it wanted to twist out of his hands. But he got better at it. Red was elsewhere in the shop. Derrick could not see him and could not hear him working over the grinder's noise.

When Derrick had the pipe as even as he could manage, he went looking for Red, found him sitting at a computer desk next to a large yellow robotic arm.

As Derrick approached, Red said, "This thing is awesome. Took me some time to figure it out, but I think I've got it now."

Derrick saw one of the steel plates held in a vise-like device. "What is it?"

"A robotic plasma cutter. Put on your goggles. Watch this." Red pushed a red button. The machine cut a perfect ring. After cooling the ring in the water, Red measured it, and using a hammer and a small steel shaft, put eight little marks on the ring.

Walking to another machine, Red said, "This is a drill press." Red inserted a shiny steel shaft with swirls cut into the metal into a holder. "I'll drill the first hole, and then you do the rest. Keep adding a drop of oil and be careful of the metal shavings. They're sharp as hell."

Derrick watched Red drill the first hole. It looked easy enough.

When he finished, Red said, "I asked because of Jimmy. Like I said, he believes he can become Chosen. Jimmy asked me to go to his church several years ago. His dad started going after his mom left. So, I went. Pretty young, not knowing what to expect. Gramps told me not to go, but… well, Jimmy was my best friend, my only friend. Anyway, it freaked me out."

"Freaked you out?"

"Just an expression."

"I know it's an expression." Derrick paused. "Why did it freak you out?"

"It was weird. People shouting, chanting, kinda out of control like. Worked themselves into a frenzy. Gist of it was if they believed, genuinely believed, they could be Chosen. I never went again. Jimmy tried to get me to, but I wouldn't go. But I always wondered what was so great about being Chosen. That's why I asked about it."

Derrick nodded. "I understand. So, Pacific Edge is small. Lots smaller than Potterville. I can't tell you how many people live there. I never thought about the size of it because I had never been anyplace else."

"Never?"

Derrick nodded. "Too dangerous. Remember? Our house was massive and, well, fancy. My room had hardwood floors and granite counters and was the size of an entire floor of the building where my condo was."

Red whistled through his teeth. "Impressive. I guess that might explain it."

"The school was immaculate. Everything was immaculate. All the yards, all the gardens, all the streets."

"People must have worked hard to keep it up."

"True but not Chosen people. Others did all the work. They came from outside Pacific Edge. We never saw them. They came while kids were in school, and parents were at work. I learned the town surrounding Pacific Edge is where all the people lived who did the labor for us. It was larger than Pacific Edge itself."

"I don't get it. Why? What purpose does Pacific Edge serve? What makes the Chosen so important?"

"To be honest, I have no clue."

"They must do something important."

Red left to cut the next ring and brought it before Derrick finished drilling the first set of holes.

Red said, "I'll set up the welder. Bring the rings when you finish."

Red said this as if Derrick knew what a welder was, which he didn't. So, when Derrick finished, he wandered the machine shop, carrying a ring in each hand until he spotted Red. Derrick hoped he'd done the drilling correctly.

Red said, "Before I weld these, we'd best check our work." Red held the rings and lined up the holes. "The holes line up. Good job. I hope they line up with the holes on the pipe."

"What if they don't?" Derrick asked.

"Then we punt," Red said.

"Punt?"

"Start over, go to plan-b," Red said.

Derrick detected no frustration in Red's voice.

Red handed a hood to Derrick. "Put this on, and don't lift it until I tell you to." Derrick could see nothing but could hear Red working, so Derrick turned his head toward the sound. A blinding flash of white-hot light appeared. Derrick flinched, then watched in amazement as Red created a bead of molten metal, joining the ring to the pipe.

After a few minutes of work, Red said, "You can lift your hood. Got to cool this off, recheck the measurements, and then line up the holes for the second piece."

Red stuck the pipe and ring into the water. The water hissed, and steam enveloped him. Once cooled, Red studied the drawing and measured the pipe. Red used the grinder, then measured, then used the grinder again. When he was satisfied with the measurement, he lined up the second ring, using three long bolts and then welded several small spots. Finally, Red removed the bolts and finished the weld around the pipe.

"Next, we need to build the flap on the inside," Red said.

Red asked for no help on this. Derrick watched. Red drilled a hole through the pipe, cut a steel rod to go through the pipe, welded a piece of thin stainless steel to the rod. Red said, "Now we gotta build a seal for the control shaft. I've been thinking about it, but not sure how to do it. We don't know how much pressure is in the pipe. I would not have designed it like this, but we gotta use their controller. How about a cup of coffee? Would you mind making one while I consider options?"

Derrick said, "I don't mind. What do you want?"

"That thing you made before. And perhaps a couple of candy bars," Red said, and then added, "Thanks."

Derrick said, "Making coffee? No problem, I want one as well."

"Not coffee. For telling me about Pacific Edge."

Akira was still alone at the computer when Derrick arrived. "How are the others doing?" he asked.

"They are making progress. How's it going for you and Red?"

"We're making progress as well. I think. Red is stuck on how to make a seal. I think the seal keeps water from leaking. It's amazing what Red has done so far." Derrick fixed two coffees with steamed milk and honey and selected four candy bars, which went into his pockets.

"Are you lonely?" Derrick asked.

"No. The others have been by periodically to get a snack or to ask a question. I've been learning more about this place. Many things I don't have access to, but what I can access is quite amazing. How much longer will you guys be?"

Derrick shrugged. "I don't know. It's going to take some time yet." Derrick paused and then asked, "Is everyone okay?"

"Everyone is fine." Akira smiled. "Last time Nyx was here, she asked if I'd heard from you. And, yes, Nyx is fine."

"Good. Hear anything from Miriam?"

"Nothing. I'm worried about her. Can't one of us go check on her?"

"Maybe. I'll think about it. She's probably okay." Derrick hoped that was true.

Akira said, "I hope so."

Derrick left. He thought Akira had been crying. Poor girl was probably scared being alone.

When Derrick returned with coffees, Red wasn't there. Derrick sat, sipped coffee. It wasn't as good as the one L. Linda Maxton had made but wasn't bad given the circumstances. Derrick had finished his first candy bar when Red returned with a bucket of bits and pieces.

"Okay. I have an idea. I'll get started right after our break."

Derrick puzzled, "Break?"

Red sat, lifted his coffee cup. "Coffee break."

Derrick nodded. Questions had been bouncing around Derrick's head. He wasn't sure asking was a good idea. It wasn't as if he'd produced a plethora of good ideas. "Mind if I ask you another question?"

"Ask away. Doesn't mean I'll answer it," Red mumbled with a mouth full of candy.

"Earlier, you said we can't pick our family, but we can pick our friends. Then you added sometimes we don't do a good job of that. Is there something I should know about Akira, Antonio, or… Nyx?"

Red said nothing. He tore the wrapper from the second candy bar. Sat quietly, chewing, drinking, and staring at Derrick. Red finished the candy bar, gathered the wrappers, and tossed them in a trash can. Then Red sat and drank the rest of his coffee. "King, do you always think everything is about you?"

"Uh, well, unfortunately, too often, that is correct."

"I wasn't referring to your choices. I was talking about mine," Red said.

"Oh," Derrick said, a bit relieved, a bit perplexed.

"I'm talking about Jimmy. When I was in first grade, I was big for my age but shy. Kids figured it out and teased me. I couldn't stand up for myself, but Jimmy did. We've been friends ever since. Jimmy wasn't always like he is now. He started down that road a few years ago. Like I said, his mom ran off, and his dad started going to that church. After that, we had a lot of arguments, but I got tired of arguing. Jimmy latched on to every conspiracy theory that came along from that bunch. Especially, if it was about how the Chosen were the Creator's people and how, if he was devoted enough, he too could one day be Chosen. I should have tried harder to make him see reality, or…"

Red fell silent, stared at his coffee.

"Or what?" Derrick asked.

"I should have cut it off with him. Should have done that a long time ago. Look at me now? Teammates tolerate me, but they don't like me. I'm stuck in Potterville. If I get to college, I'll be more careful, make better choices," Red said.

Derrick didn't know what to say. He wasn't good at this sort of thing. "Maybe you're not as stuck as you think?"

Red stood. "What does that mean?"

Derrick shrugged. "Maybe others are more willing to accept that you've changed than you give them credit."

Red grunted. "Huh. And what makes you think that?"

"Because they forgave me."

23

AFTER READING FOR WHAT FELT like hours analyzing QR-4 systems, Miriam developed a theory that explained why Jane stopped functioning. It wasn't the hard drive failure. Perhaps she was wrong, but it seemed the best hope. However, she hesitated telling Charlie. Not because she wanted to analyze the data again. She. had already been over it a dozen times, not because she was unsure of what happened. The event became clearer every time she looked at it. Miriam hesitated because the last time she activated QR-4.01, it almost killed Charlie. The more she thought about that, the more Miriam believed .01 was hostile, angry, and maleficent. It also seemed Miriam was invisible to .01. That sounded impossible. Perhaps the robot had a malfunction she had not identified.

"Charlie? Are you there? Can you hear me?"

"Charlie hears you."

"Can you come here?"

"Charlie can. Charlie will arrive in seven minutes and thirty-three seconds."

"No rush. I'll be here."

While Charlie came from wherever he hung out—Miriam wondered what Charlie did all day—she reviewed the data one last time. If she was wrong, she couldn't see how. Except for the .01 not seeing her part. That part still troubled her.

The door slid open, and Charlie entered.

"Charlie, I've discovered something. But first, I have questions," Miriam said.

"Miriam King has discovered how to restore Jane?"

"Maybe. I'm not sure, but I think I know what happened to her. First, question. Did Jane display any problems before… uh, she stopped working?"

"No. Jane never went dark like Charlie did when Miriam, Rebekah, and Derrick were here before. Charlie may fail soon."

"Not if I can help it," Miriam said. "Second question. When we last activated Jane, she didn't notice me. Does that seem odd?"

"Charlie did not activate Jane. Jane would have acknowledged you and insisted on an explanation of your presence. Charlie activated QR-4.01."

Miriam nodded. It occurred to her that Charlie might not understand nodding. "I stand corrected. Why didn't .01 see me?"

"That is difficult to explain in human terms. QR-4.01 saw you but did not acknowledge you." Charlie paused, eyes fading. "That is not a satisfactory analogy. The QR-4 saw you as one sees a chair. You know it's there. You know what it is, but you do not talk to it. QR-4.01 was programmed to communicate with Jacob Truman. Jacob is not here. .01, as you call it, saw no human to interact with."

"Okay. I understand. Third question. During the last attempt, .01 seemed angry. Is that possible?"

Charlie said nothing for a moment. Miriam wondered if Charlie was searching the database or replaying the interaction. "QR-4s were not programmed to become angry. QR-4.01 was not Jane and therefore had no capacity for emotion. However, you are not wrong."

24

THE THINGS RED DID NEXT DIDN'T involve Derrick. Derrick didn't even know what Red was doing, and he thought about going to help the others, but every time he stood, Red asked him to hold this or fetch that. However, Derrick didn't mind. Watching Red work was fascinating. For a big man, Red had nimble hands. Red's creation looked like art. Derrick was thinking, should Red decide to do something other than work on cars, jewelry might be a suitable vocation.

After some time, working on things that seemed unrelated, Red fitted the internal parts into the valve housing, examined it from all angles. "I think that's as good as it's going to get. It might not seal completely, but leaks should be minimal." Red smiled. "We should order a new one when this all over."

Derrick started to protest and then realized Red was joking. " Sure thing. I'll search for nuclear reactor supply stores near me as soon as we have internet."

Red disassembled the internal parts, laying them in order on a table. "Let's give it a coat of paint. Might as well look professional, don't you think?"

Derrick said, "Red, that's amazing. How did you learn to do all that?"

"Gramps taught me. I've taken shop at school, and I read everything I can find about engineering, motors, transmissions, anything mechanical. It feels good to finish a project. See quality in what I've done. It's a big stress relief. Helps me forget about…"

Derrick saw sadness in Red's eyes. "Forget about what?"

"Never mind. Just stuff. What time is it?"

Derrick decided not to pursue what was bothering Red any further. Perhaps another time. Instead, Derrick said, "No idea. Feels late. I'm hungry."

Red said, "I could eat a horse."

Derrick wrinkled his nose. "Really. Is it any good?"

Red stared for a moment. Then burst out laughing.

Derrick felt his face flush. "Oh. I can admit it now. Coming to Potterville was like learning a new language. Not sure I'll ever know all of it."

Red shook a paint can, and something rattled inside of it. "You should stand back. Paint fumes."

When Red finished, Derrick said, "That's remarkable. It looks better than the new one Rebekah and I installed the first time here."

"You guys ever going to quit?"

Derrick smiled. He recognized that voice. Nyx stood at the shop entrance.

"What time is it?" Derrick asked, unable to suppress his smile.

"Nine o'clock when I left the others. Everyone is waiting for you so we can eat dinner together, and everyone is starving."

"Wow. Nine?" Derrick looked at Red. "Do the install in the morning?"

Red said, "Works for me. I hope there's a shower, besides the one at the reactor."

"The rooms have showers. The robots set the rooms up for us, plus they brought more food options." Nyx stepped to the workbench. "You found a new valve?"

Derrick said, "Red built it. It's amazing, isn't it?"

Red said, "We built it."

"Nice of you to say, Red, but you did most of it. I couldn't have done any of it," Derrick said.

"We built it, end of story. Let's clean up and eat."

Nyx walked between Red and Derrick, but she laced her arm through Derrick's. She showed them to their rooms. "You've got clean uniforms. We are just down the hall. Be quick."

"Maybe we should eat first. Not keep the others waiting," Derrick offered.

"No. Shower first. Trust me. Everyone will be happy to wait," Nyx said.

"Oh, sorry," Derrick said, feeling his face flush.

"Don't be sorry. You've been working. It's not a bad thing. See you soon. I'll fix you a plate. We'll have a plate ready for you too, Red."

When Derrick arrived at the dining area, the food arrangement startled him. Instead of cups of noodles, a row of large containers set on a counter like the lunch line at Potterville High School. Long tables with benches filled the room, also like high school. Everyone sat together at the table closest to the food. No robots in the room. Red wasn't there yet. A plate heaped with food set next to Nyx. She had not started eating.

Nyx smiled and patted the bench next to her. "Saved you a spot."

Derrick surveyed the room. Akira sat next to Nyx. Rebekah sat across from Nyx. A plate heaped to overflowing set at an empty spot on Nyx's right. Antonio sat on Rebekah's left.

Red walked into the room. "Where did all this food come from? It smells amazing."

Rebekah said, "Robots brought it. It appears to have been prepared someplace else."

"Someplace else?" Red asked.

"The administration building at the Base," Rebekah said.

Derrick held his fork halfway to his mouth. "Why do you think that?"

Rebekah slid an envelope across the table. "Because they brought this."

On the front, in handwriting he recognized.

To: Derrick

From: Miriam

Derrick stared at it for a moment.

"Read it, for God's sake," Akira said, voice raised and quivering.

Derrick looked at Akira. Her eyes filling with water that had not yet trickled down her cheeks.

"I'll read it later," Derrick said. Miriam had addressed it to him, not the group. Perhaps there's something he can't share.

Akira wiped her eyes. "I want to go to where Miriam is. Can we go there now?"

Derrick wanted to go to Miriam too. He was certain Rebekah didn't like being separated either. But he didn't understand why Akira was so upset. It didn't make sense. "I'd like to go, but we still have to install that valve. It's late, and the install is a big job. It will have to wait until morning." Eager to change the subject, Derrick asked, "How did things go with the other stuff?"

Rebekah said, "For not knowing what we're doing, it went well. We have completed about 75% of the tasks. We haven't found anything we can't do."

Akira said, "Antonio and I have been studying information on the computers. Some things we can't access, but there's much that we can. It would take months to read through it all."

Derrick said, "We need to finish the list. I hoped we'd be with Miriam by now, but it didn't work out that way. We'll finish the valve tomorrow. If you guys can finish the other stuff, then we should be able to go."

Akira, now with tears running down her cheeks, asked, "What does that mean? Should be able to go?"

Derrick looked at Rebekah. She looked as confused by Akira's reaction as he felt. "Well, Charlie may not let us go until Miriam fixes the other robot."

Akira sobbed. "What if she can't fix it?"

Derrick thought for a moment. "I hope Charlie accepts Miriam has done everything possible and allows us to join her."

Nyx put her arm around Akira. "It's going to be okay. Miriam is smart. You know that. She'll make this work. Derrick is right. We must finish here. You'll see Miriam tomorrow. Okay?"

Akira cried on Nyx's shoulder for a few minutes. Finally, she sniffed and said, "You guys eat. I'll be okay. I'm sorry. It's just that…"

Derrick didn't know what 'it's just that' meant.

Nyx looked at Derrick, still with one arm around Akira. "Derrick, could you read what Miriam wrote? I know it's addressed to you. You don't have to read it to us, but maybe you can tell us anything that affects the group."

"I can do that. But everyone eat before the food gets cold."

"You talked me into it," Red said, scooping up a fork of shredded beef. With a full mouth, he mumbled, "This crap ain't bad."

Antonio said, "Thanks for your delightful gastronomical depiction."

"You're welcome," Red said.

Rebekah smiled and winked.

Feeling as confused as ever, Derrick opened the envelope. He wanted a few minutes alone with Nyx, so she could explain what just happened, but it would have to wait. He unfolded the note and took a bite of the shredded beef. Red was right. It tasted good. Derrick read and ate. The others remained silent. Miriam had written nothing that could not be shared, but some of what she wrote disturbed him. He wanted to run to the Circle transport and race to Miriam's side. But he couldn't do that. Besides, Charlie might have control of the transport and not permit the trip. Derrick had been thinking about this during the day and decided that when it was okay for them to join Miriam, Charlie would let them know. Rather than read it aloud, which would prevent him from eating, he passed it around the table, sliding it to Rebekah first.

Derrick,

Charlie says you and Red received a high dose of radiation, fixing a critical component. Charlie also says you should be fine. Sounds like Rebekah and Nyx took good care of you guys. I'm proud of you.

I've tried two attempts with Jane. To be clear, two attempts with QR-4.01. Both failed. No remnants of Jane in either attempt. In fact, the robot tried to destroy Charlie. Don't worry, I got it shut down before any damage.

After the near disaster, I spent the rest of the day reading and studying the QR-4 operation system. I needed a better understanding of them before trying again. The QR-4.01 should have no memory of what happened on the last attempt, but I'm taking nothing for granted.

I miss you all. Keep up the good work. I hope to see you sometime tomorrow.

P.S. Don't come until Charlie sends for you.

Miriam

When Rebekah's eyes lifted from the note, she looked straight at Derrick. She said nothing and slid the paper across the table to Akira. Antonio had leaned close to Rebekah and read along with her. But Derrick didn't understand why she didn't pass the note clockwise around the table.

Akira read, dabbing tears from her cheeks. Nyx read along with her. When Akira finished, Nyx said, "Thanks, Rebekah," and slid the note to Red.

Derrick didn't understand the dynamics.

It seemed he was the only one who did not.

25

Tuesday, April 6, 9:23 p.m.

MIRIAM DID NOT FEEL LIKE EATING. Instead, she planned to work into the night, but that was a no-go with Charlie. He allowed Miriam to write a message to the others, which she addressed to Derrick, hoping he would read it first and decide how to share it. Charlie sent the note along with dinner. Charlie insisted Miriam eat. QR-3s prepared a variety of food, sent most of it to the others at Staging/Reactor One, and kept enough for a small army of Miriams at Administration.

Miriam ate alone because Charlie didn't require food. Only electricity. If the reactor had failed before they found it, or if some other system that delivered electricity to this building had crashed, she would have never met Charlie. He would have just been a dead lump of metal, plastic, and circuits. Charlie had explained that robots could not work on the reactors. She did not know what other things were forbidden for the machines. Did Charlie worry about losing power while being docked and never operating again? It would be like dying in one's sleep.

Not a bad way to go.

Much better than what was planned for Derrick, Anna, and herself if they were captured.

One might have thought Charlie cared about Miriam and the others, given the meal, the note, and insisting Miriam take a break. But Miriam thought that was not the case. Charlie's reasoning was simple logic. Miriam tried twice to restore Jane, failed twice. The last one almost got Charlie destroyed. Charlie made it clear Miriam's next attempt would be her last. Next time had to be well thought out, safer, and with a logical rationale.

When Miriam said she wasn't hungry, Charlie said, "Miriam King must eat and rest."

Charlie was not open to further discussion. He cut power to the computers, and Miriam was confident he'd lock her in a room if necessary.

Charlie, it appeared, was a better dad than was the Keeper Miriam knew as Father. Miriam had thought little about Father or Mother since leaving Pacific Edge. At some point, she'd have to think about them. But now was not that time.

Miriam knew Charlie was right. Without his direction, she would have forged ahead, like she did in Pacific Edge, where her escape attempt almost failed. Would have failed had Rebekah and Mr. Jones not helped her. At James Carver Academy, Miriam had fancied herself a lone wolf. She wanted Derrick's attention and for him to recognize she was right about things. Now, it was clear she wasn't as smart as she thought herself to be. Smart wasn't everything. Sometimes smart was lame. She could not do this alone. However, she didn't even know what it was they were supposed to be doing. Besides stay alive.

Miriam didn't question Charlie. Charlie was right. Well-fed, she needed rest. Impatience wasn't a virtue, not in this case, a clear head was. Plus, she didn't want to be locked in a room. She had not been confined to her room, even in Pacific Edge. If she couldn't sleep, at least she wanted to roam the halls. That might help her think. Although her thinking was lame, it's what she did best. But she often didn't know how to make her brain work. In Pacific Edge, she found walking the streets alone at night after curfew, sitting on the beach though forbidden, or sitting on the roof, gazing at the stars, all helped. Tonight, options would be limited, but she still wanted some.

Although Miriam thought she wasn't hungry, she savored dinner. She didn't mind eating alone, and it tasted much better than she expected. She paused, thinking there was room for a bite or two, and trying to decide which item on her plate tempted her most.

Charlie entered the room. "Miriam King has finished eating?"

Miriam took her last bite. "I'm finished. May I go for a walk before I sleep?" Miriam asked.

"Will it help you sleep?" Charlie asked.

"Yes. I hope so. My mind is racing. Sleeping won't be easy," Miriam said.

"Racing?"

"I'm thinking a lot. Many thoughts about all sorts of things, but mostly about Jane and how to fix her. I thought it was just the failed hard drive. But it can't be that. There must be more to it. That's what we must figure out. If we can do that, then perhaps we can find a solution."

"Miriam King must rest."

"I will. Thanks for letting me walk around a bit."

After Charlie left, Miriam went to the hallway. She walked, turned corners, walked farther. The halls extended great distances, some of them at least 100 yards. Some halls ended, and she retraced her steps. It would be easy to get lost, but she felt confident she would not. In part because she could remember where she had been, which direction she had turned, and how far she'd gone. Also, because Charlie would not let that happen. Charlie knew her location, and he could reconfigure the hallways, directing her back to her quarters for the night if necessary.

However, she wasn't learning anything about the building. No doors were open. Charlie controlled those too. Miriam wondered if she could reach the Administration lobby. She walked that direction. Reaching the end of a hallway with double doors, she pushed one open and stepped into the Lobby, continuing toward the Circle transport. She stepped out, but there were no Circle transports. The one that brought her here was gone. She was not outside. She was underground, and this was as outdoorsy as anyplace here.

* * *

Derrick felt stuffed and tired. He carried his plate to the counter and placed it in the sink. Perhaps there was a machine that washed the dishes, but he would not know where it was or how to operate it. He had experience washing dishes by hand now. Derrick turned to the room. "I'll clean up. You guys get some rest. We'll meet back in the morning. I hope we can finish the list tomorrow and join Miriam."

Akira brought her tray to the sink. "I'm sorry for how I've been acting. I'll be better tomorrow."

Derrick wanted to ask Akira why she'd been so upset but decided against it. "It's okay. We are all stressed."

Akira pushed her glasses up, giving him a weak smile. "Tomorrow I'll do better."

As the others began to stir, two black robots burst into the room. "Go now. Rest now. Lights out in one hour."

The robots went to the table, gathering plates, carrying them into the next room.

Derrick called out, "Can we walk around a bit before going to bed?"

The first robot was already in the next room. The last robot's head spun back to look at Derrick. "Lights out in one hour. Walking is permitted until lights out."

Wasting no time, Derrick went to Nyx. "Will you walk with me?"

"Of course. Silly. Who else would I walk with?" Nyx took Derrick's hand, leading him into the hall.

Antonio hobbled on crutches, Rebekah at his side. Red stood by the door as if unsure what to do next. Nyx turned left, Antonio and Rebekah turned right. Neither Red nor Akira left the dining room. Perhaps they would talk, or maybe they would go to their respective rooms.

When Derrick and Nyx were a safe distance from the others, Derrick whispered, "What's going on with Akira? Why is she so upset?"

"She's worried about Miriam."

"That's obvious, but why? I'm worried too. She is my sister."

They walked in silence until they came to the door that led into the giant cavern. "Turn around?" Derrick asked.

Nyx giggled. "No. Let's explore a little. Perhaps, we'll get lost."

Derrick opened the door. Lights inside the cavern responded to their presence. The smell of diesel and damp rock greeted them. "Don't worry, I can find my way back. We won't get lost."

Nyx pulled him close. "You're so naïve. It's hard not to like that about you. I'd like to say never change, but that's not possible, is it?"

Derrick didn't know how to respond. Nyx was correct, and it was not the first time someone had told him that. But it was the first time someone said he would not always be naïve. He thought that would be a good thing, but the tone of Nyx's voice told him it was not. He didn't understand.

Nyx stopped, took both of Derrick's hands, looking up at him. "So, there's another reason Akira is, uh, on edge."

Derrick said, "Okay. What is it?"

"She's afraid Miriam and Rebekah are… you know… close."

Derrick thought about that for a moment. "They have not been friends long, but they came here together. They've taken risks and faced danger together, so, yeah, I guess they are close. But I think Miriam can have more than one friend. Akira shouldn't worry about that."

Nyx sighed. "Akira really *likes* Miriam."

"Okay, you already said that."

"She really, *really* likes Miriam."

His voice raising a bit in frustration, Derrick said, "You've told me that already…"

Nyx put her finger to his lips. "Derrick, she's afraid Miriam may not have the same feelings. And she's afraid—you won't approve."

26

INSIDE THE ROOM THAT CHARLIE ASSIGNED TO MIRIAM, set a mug of cocoa on a stand beside the bed. Sipping, she found it too hot to drink. She studied the mug. Nothing unusual to explain how it retained heat. Charlie had predicted when she'd return, yet she saw no robots in the halls. That Charlie could anticipate with such accuracy unsettled her, not that she had grown comfortable.

Miriam blew across the surface of the chocolate, sending a whiff of steam into the air. She eased onto the bed, back against the wall, sipping, enjoying the warmth in her hands, thinking. Something had happened to Jane, and it wasn't the hard drive failure. Perhaps the hard drive had failed earlier, and the robot was sophisticated enough to overcome the loss of its use. By coincidence, the disk failure and Jane's termination could have happened simultaneously. But Miriam didn't believe in coincidence, which caused her additional discomfort, thinking of the myriads of things that got her this far. Any slight variation could have triggered a different outcome.

Thoughts came from everywhere and nowhere. Sleep, a luxury that wouldn't happen. She tried the door. Locked. A second walk wasn't an option. Or perhaps it was. "Charlie? Could I go for another walk? I'm having trouble sleeping." She tried the door again. Still locked. "Charlie? Can you hear me?"

Nothing.

Charlie may have docked for the night or for however long docking was necessary. *Docking.* Something seemed important about that, but suddenly Miriam became sleepy. She pulled the covers over her head.

Drifting through a maze. In and out of the white room, Keepers and Tenders, Father and Mother, dead animals littering a road, the rattling of empty guns in the forest, the lifeless eyes of QR-4.01 in a docking station.

Wednesday, April 7, 5:55 a.m.

Miriam sat straight up in bed—the room black—no sense of time. Yesterday, she had studied the docking station—being a robot was a boring existence. Every day the same routine. But in her dream, she noticed something odd. Was it dream-fueled fantasy or something more tangible? She wouldn't know until she got to Jacob Truman's computer. Throwing the blankets off, she tried the door. Work to be done. Answers to be found.

First stop, the docking station that held QR-4.01. Miriam did not know if Charlie used the same docking station. Inside the room, Miriam saw .01, silent. No signs of life—if life were the right word. "Charlie? Can you hear me? Charlie?"

No response.

Work to be done.

Miriam headed to Jacob Truman's desk in the next room over. Charlie wasn't far, even if he wasn't operational. It occurred to her that perhaps she could disable Charlie in his dormant state. She hesitated at the door, considering that for a moment, and then walked to the desk. Swirling colors danced across the computer monitor.

After logging in, the computer clock read 6:10 a.m. A good six hours of sleep, which seemed luxurious compared to her schedule in Pacific Edge. Her sleep habits had not improved since leaving the luxury prison she once called home. Miriam navigated to the docking procedure datasheet. The computer logged every day since QR-4.01 and .02 were put into service. She went back 63 years and 262 days. It wasn't just a dream.

Charlie entered the room. "It's 6:23 a.m. You are up early from my experience with humans."

"Not early for me. At least not for weeks. My sleep schedule has been messed up. Besides, something came to me in my sleep."

"A dream? Jacob Truman explained dreams to Charlie once. Strange."

"You don't know the half of it," Miriam said.

"Charlie does not know any dreams. Certainly not half of them."

"Just an expression," Miriam said.

"What came to Miriam? Has Miriam discovered a way to save Jane?"

Miriam looked at Charlie. He had not used the word saved before. It troubled her a bit, but she let it go.

"You and Jane were in constant communication with the central computer. Correct?"

"That is correct. Miriam King disconnected Charlie from the mainframe computer."

"That's right. And when you dock, the mainframe computer uploads your entire memory. Correct?"

"That is correct. It is called a backup."

"And your entire memory is more than the hard drives. You also have a complex Basic Input Output System or BIOS. The BIOS initiates a series of functions to restart your systems. In QR-4s, the engineers made this a more robust system than a typical computer. In fact, in both .01 and .02, the BIOS consists of multiple and unique ROM chips. That must be where Jane lived, at least, her essence," Miriam explained.

"That might be possible. But how does that help?"

Miriam turned to the computer. "Look at this."

Charlie stepped behind Miriam.

"This graph shows Jane, docking. Thirty-three years and 262 days ago. The graph shows the uploading process." Miriam touched the space bar, causing the upload to scroll across the screen. Miriam pointed. "This is where it ends. You are next." Miriam navigated to another upload. "Every day I checked, the pattern is the same, Jane, then you. Typically, your upload begins right after Jane. But this day was different. Jane uploaded at 20:45 hours. But your upload doesn't start until the next day at 01:15 hours, 63 years and 261 days ago. What happened?"

"Charlie did not want to dock. Charlie had completed a task on Level Two and wanted to test it. Jane wanted to wait until the next day. Charlie was impatient. Perhaps excited. Charlie does not know the correct word. Charlie waited until Jane powered down and then left."

Miriam said, "Jane never functioned after that day."

"That is correct."

Miriam went back to Jane, uploading. "Everything is fine until here." Miriam paused the scrolling. The graph fell to zero. "Something happened right here." Miriam pointed at the screen. "The system failed until midnight."

Charlie didn't respond for a moment and then said, "What happened?"

Miriam said, "I don't know. Do you know what happened to the system?"

"Charlie does not."

Miriam said, "I've looked at multiple uploads, hundreds. I have not found a similar failure."

"Nothing unusual happened that night while Charlie worked in Level Two. So, even though with the repaired hard drive .01 restarted, the error in Jane's BIOS remains?"

"Correct. Whatever affected Jane's last upload was not a facility-wide failure. It was isolated to the QR-4 docking system. Before the next startup, the system analyzes the data. If there are errors, the system will not activate the QR-4 until the supervisor reviews and clears the error. Because Jacob Truman wasn't here, Jane could not restart. The malfunction destroyed what made Jane—Jane. Jane cannot be restored. We forced the startup, not understanding the error. And it proved dangerous to reactivate the robot. No predicting what it might do." Miriam paused and then smiled. "Unless we go back 63 years and 263 days."

Charlie said, "To the last successful upload."

Miriam said, "Exactly."

27

Wednesday, April 7, 6:30 a.m.

IN THE DARKNESS, DERRICK STARED AT THE CEILING, wondering the time. Here, day and night didn't exist. When the lights were off, it was always darker than the darkest night. Day was an illusion created by the lighting. Perhaps other things were an illusion here as well. Derrick listened, but he heard nothing except the distant humming of the ever-present machines. Focusing, he tested his ability to detect things. Why that seemed important, he did not know. The odor of metal from his clothing, caused by yesterday's grinding and drilling, the smell of oil and fuel, Red said it was jet fuel the military used in every vehicle.

Then an unexpected aroma.

Coffee.

Derrick stumbled to the dining area, where he found Antonio drinking from a brown plastic mug.

"Hey, amigo," Antonio said. "Did I wake you?"

Derrick said, "I don't think so. But I smelled coffee. Any idea what time it is?"

"No clue. I wonder what time they expect us up?" Antonio asked.

"They?"

"The robots. Two walked in a few minutes ago, both carrying containers that looked like coolers. I think they're fixing breakfast." Antonio nodded toward the kitchen.

"I'll ask," Derrick said.

"They'll talk to you?"

"I'll find out." Derrick opened the door to the kitchen and then returned to the espresso machine. "Six-forty. Breakfast at seven. After I make my coffee, I'll go pound on doors. Last day here, I hope."

"The robots talked to you?" Antonio asked.

"Sort of. More like a recorded message. Charlie is monitoring us."

Antonio said, "How is that possible?"

"I don't know. Cameras, I guess, throughout the facility, although I haven't seen one. But I haven't looked for them either."

Antonio sat quietly for a few minutes and then said, "I've wanted to talk with you about something."

Derrick said, "Okay. Sounds serious."

"About you and Rebekah, it seems there's still something there between you. When you were in Pacific Edge, did you have feelings for Rebekah? Did you ever think about choosing her?"

Derrick took a deep breath, unprepared for the question. "My thinking was unclear back then. Everything was kinda black and white to me. A girl named Jana was the best choice for me, but that had nothing to do with how I felt about her." Derrick paused and then said, "To be honest, I had feelings for Rebekah, but I rejected them. I wasn't supposed to choose based on feelings."

"That's super weird, dude. It looks like you have some decisions to make. I need to back off until you do that. From here on, I won't get in the way," Antonio said, taking a drink.

"Get in the way of what?"

"You and Rebekah. But honest, dude, you need to figure it out. Just one favor, my friend. Don't hurt Nyx. She's been hurt enough."

"There is no Rebekah and me. Well, there will always be something between us. That won't change. I regret not seeing Rebekah back then, as I see her now. She's a super good person. A better person than Jana. She's a better person than me. Had my thinking been clear, I might have felt differently. I've already hurt Nyx, and I have no intention of hurting her again. But I'll ask you the same favor. Don't hurt Rebekah. She's like a sister to me. We will always be friends."

Antonio smiled, nodded. "Thank you, amigo. How difficult will it be to finish what you and Red are working on?"

"Won't take long. Rebekah and I replaced a similar valve, although this one is larger. But with Red's help, it'll be easy."

Antonio said, "That's good news. I hope it works."

Derrick sipped his coffee and said, "What's that mean?"

Antonio grabbed his crutches and headed toward the door. "Just hope it is as easy as you say. Enjoy your coffee. I'll wake the others."

* * *

Miriam reviewed the upload and download processes. With each examination, she grew more confident. The only thing troubling her was the problem that occurred on that day almost 34 years ago. It had never happened before and had not happened since. Miriam could not find causation. Just a blip. Mere coincidence that Charlie had varied his routine that day. Otherwise, he too would have never functioned again.

"Charlie, can you come here, please?"

Charlie arrived in a few minutes. "Are you ready? You should eat first."

"I'm fine. Too excited to eat. I've looked this over dozens of times. It's going to work. I'm sure of it. I've cleaned the SSDs, but the system will reformat everything before downloading. So, we are ready. A complete download will take 20 to 30 minutes. I'll grab a cup of coffee and something to eat and bring it back here. If that's okay?"

Charlie said nothing, but his eyes remained lit. Miriam had not seen Charlie in a situation that required a long duration for thinking. "Charlie? Is everything okay?"

"Charlie cannot determine if everything is satisfactory. However, Charlie estimates everything cannot be satisfactory at any given moment."

"Just a saying, Charlie. Are you okay? Shall I start the download?"

"Charlie is experiencing… Charlie does not know what it is called."

"Is it anything like when I caused you to lose communication with the central computer?"

"Yes. And no. It is similar, but not the same. This is new."

Miriam asked, "Is it good or bad?"

"It is both. But that seems impossible."

Miriam said, "For a human, being excited and anxious at the same time would make sense for this situation."

"Charlie does not know human emotion, but Charlie will remember those terms if this occurs again."

"So, how about it? Shall I start the download?"

"Proceed. You may get coffee and nourishment but return before the download is completed."

Miriam started the process, watched it for a few minutes until she was sure it was going as expected. A window said it would take 33 minutes. Miriam made a mocha and picked a pastry from a selection of breakfast items. Seventeen minutes had passed. When she sat at the computer, the window still said 24 minutes. The time estimate wasn't an exact science. Miriam sat back, looked at her surroundings. This place reeked of science, which was a dark art forbidden in Pacific Edge. She did not want to be a prisoner here anymore than she wanted to be a prisoner in Pacific Edge. But she could spend her life here. She didn't need many friends, just a few, a select few. But that wasn't feasible. Who would want to be stuck here with her? Once Jane was functional, Charlie would have no further use for Derrick, Rebekah, or herself.

Her optimism took a dark turn. *What will Charlie do when he no longer needs my help? Let us leave? Or something else?*

Eight minutes to go. Then seven.

Seven minutes until what?

Miriam felt confident this would work.

So, why had her stomach twisted into a knot?

28

THE ROBOTS SAID NOTHING AS THEY PREPARED the warming devices on the counter. Derrick filled a plate with scrambled eggs laced with cheese, green onions, and sausage, plus a biscuit. The others were in good spirits, joking and laughing. Even Akira's mood had improved. Derrick, however, felt something was wrong. He didn't know why, nor did he know what. Just his overactive imagination again, he assumed.

Maybe it was Nyx's comments regarding Akira's feelings for Miriam. That would trouble him if he kept thinking about it. He tried, with limited success, to block it from his mind. When that didn't work, he thought perhaps he'd misunderstood. He often misunderstood things. That's where he left it. Or at least, that's what he tried to do.

Nyx sat at Derrick's side. "You look gloomy this morning. You should be happy. We'll get the work done soon and then join Miriam."

Rebekah sat across from Nyx. "I hate to admit it, but I miss that girl even if she is a pain in the butt most of the time."

"All of the time," Nyx corrected. "But strange as it may seem, I miss her too. Plus, I'm eager to see the rest of this place and meet Charlie, the robot."

Akira sat on Derrick's other side. "Good morning, Derrick. I wanted to apologize for my behavior again. I'm feeling better today."

Derrick realized, in a way he had not before, how small Akira was. Slight of build, shorter by an inch from Nyx and Miriam. Delicate features. Only her glasses seemed too large for her. "No apology necessary. It's been tough for all of us."

Red sat next to Rebekah, almost straight across from Derrick. He plopped two heaping plates of food on the table. "How much stuff is left to do?" Red looked at Rebekah.

"Not a lot. I've read the instructions. Apply some lubricant, uh, they call it grease, to some bearings and such. I thought I would do that while you and Derrick install the valve. Someone needs to be in the reactor control room while you do that."

Akira said, "I will be in the control room."

Derrick said, "Is that safe? What's the radiation level in there?"

"It's dropping. I'll wear a protective suit. I should be fine for no longer than I'm in there."

Derrick said, "I don't like it. I should be in the control room."

Rebekah said, "You can't. You were just exposed to radiation."

Nyx said, "I don't like it either, but Akira is the logical person to do it. She's smarter than the rest of us and can navigate the computer."

Antonio said, "I should do it. I know my way around computers, and I'm no dummy."

Nyx said, "No offense intended, Antonio. You're smart—no questioning that. But getting around on crutches wearing the protective suit would be difficult. Plus, playing computer games is not the same as understanding computers. Besides, you're too important to Potterville for the risk."

Akira said, "Also, no one asked you. I'm doing it."

Antonio set his fork down. "That borders on insubordination."

"Fine. Kick me off the council when we get back," Akira said.

"I might just do that if you end up killing us," Antonio said.

"Very funny," Akira whispered.

When Antonio stopped laughing, he said, "Just don't let anything happen to you, mi Hermana. Comprende? I couldn't forgive myself." Antonio reached across the table, taking Akira's hand.

Red said, "She'll be fine. We'll get the valve in quickly enough."

Nyx said, "What should I do?"

Antonio said, "Help Red and Derrick. See that they don't screw it up."

"And what is Antonio going to do?" Red asked.

"Much to my disappointment, I'm going to be at the workstation monitoring crap. Not what I'd prefer, but with my bum knee…" Antonio shrugged.

Rebekah chimed in, "He overdid it yesterday. His knee is worse."

"I wish there was a way for us to communicate with Akira when she's in the control room," Derrick said.

"Agreed," Antonio said. "We should ask the robots."

"It's unlikely they will help," Derrick said.

Rebekah said, "Perhaps Charlie will hear if you ask."

Derrick nodded. "Maybe. Hey, robots. Is there some way we can communicate with each other?"

The robots said nothing.

"We should have brought our cell phones," Nyx said.

Derrick said, "Miriam wouldn't allow it. They can track cell phones."

"Not down here they can't," Nyx said.

Red said, "Cell phones wouldn't work down here."

Everyone stared at him.

Red shook his head. "Duh. Cell phones. Get it? They need a cell tower. I haven't seen one down here."

Derrick pushed his plate away. "Let's get started. Red and I will gather the tools. Everyone gather what you need for your tasks. Meet back here in 20 minutes."

"How will we know 20 minutes have passed?" Nyx asked.

"No one has a watch?" Akira asked.

"I use my cellphone, but I don't have it," Antonio said.

"Best guess then," Derrick said.

Some 30 minutes later, according to the computer Antonio monitored, they had all reassembled. Not much direction was needed. However, Derrick had one question. "Why does Akira need to be in the reactor room? Why does anyone?"

Akira said, "The reactor must be controlled while you install the valve. The power has to be reduced because the cooling capacity is suspended during the install."

"But Miriam said it can't just be shut down. And what happens if we lose power? We won't be able to see what we are doing. It gets very dark down here without lights," Derrick said.

Red said, "Good point. Do we have enough flashlights for everyone?"

Derrick thought for a moment. "No, we do not. We have two."

Nyx said, "You and Red better have them."

Derrick said, "How do we let Akira know we are shutting off the water and such."

"I can monitor that in the reactor room," Akira said.

"And if you have to shut the reactor down? Then what?" Derrick asked.

Nyx said, "I'll have to run back and forth relaying messages."

"I don't like it," Derrick said.

"What options do we have?" Red asked. "This has to be done. Right? Besides, it's going to be a simple job. What could go wrong? We're in and out."

Derrick nodded. "It's the 'what could go wrong' part that worries me."

29

WHEN MIRIAM PLUNGED INTO THE OCEAN AS PART of her escape plan a few days ago, she thought her scheme was foolproof. It wasn't. When she found Derrick near the entrance of this complex, she believed the worst of their problems were over. They weren't. When Miriam thought she and Akira could go to engineering without difficulties, one of Prime's robots intercepted them. Every time Miriam thought things would work, they didn't.

She hoped this time would be an exception.

"That's it," Miriam said. "The download is complete. Get ready to say hello to Jane."

With that, Miriam activated QR-4.01.

Charlie said, "Wait."

Miriam said, "Too late, Charlie. What's wrong?"

"Charlie does not know."

* * *

Derrick pushed the cart carrying the valve and tools into position and then climbed the ladder to shut off the water. A permanent chain hoist was positioned above the pipe. The hoist was electrical but also had a manual operation if it became necessary. Derrick attached the hook to the pipe, eased the hoist winch until it was snug, turned off the water flow, and then climbed back down.

Opening the bypass valve, Derrick said, "The water's off. Let's get started." Derrick felt a bit of comfort, knowing he had accomplished these tasks, yet something bothered him. He could not identify what. Just something vague at the edge of his consciousness.

Red worked on the top bolts, which had the worst corrosion. Red broke two bolts. Most of the others came off with encouragement from Red's powerful arms.

Derrick had less luck with the bottom bolts. The wrench slipped on one nut. Red said to leave it and move on. Derrick also broke a bolt. The wrench slipped on the last nut as well. He ended up removing all but two bolts.

"Now what?" Derrick asked.

"Go get the torch. You know what that is, right? The cart with two big metal bottles." Red said and then added, "be quick."

"On it," Derrick said, taking off on a dead run.

"Crap," Red said, scratching his head.

"What can I do?" Nyx asked.

"Nothing. I should have thought to bring the torch. Just me being stupid."

"No big deal, Red," Nyx said.

Red looked at her for a moment. "Thanks. Here's what you can do. Climb the ladder and be ready to lift the pipe when we get the last bolt off. Don't lift it much. Just a little. That will save us a little time. Seconds could prove important."

* * *

Akira studied the computer monitor. She had noted when the water pressure dropped to zero, watched the clock tick down to when she'd need to take action. She did not know how long it would take to replace the valve. But it already felt too long. Perhaps they ran into problems. When the clock reached the designated time, she would have to act. She hoped that time did not come.

She had read about what would happen.

She had not told the others.

* * *

Rebekah found the tunnel that led to her next task, greasing a bearing, whatever that was. Through an open door, into a narrow tunnel, smaller than any she'd been in before, causing her to stoop as she walked. Finish and get out. That's all she wanted. After traveling half the length of a soccer field, she came to the device that needed lubrication. Why they buried it so deep in the rock, she did not know. Antonio had taught her how to use the lubrication device. He called it a grease gun. Okay. Weird name, but she didn't expect to ever use one again. Careful to stay clear of the spinning steel shafts, she found the first place to grease, then the second, then the third. That's when the lights dimmed. She moved to the fourth, then to the fifth. Just one more to go. She wanted out of here. It felt as if the place was closing in on her.

* * *

Derrick returned with the cutting torch, sweat soaking his shirt. Red grabbed goggles and went straight to work. Sparks flew as Red cut.

A few minutes later, Red said, "That should do it. Hand me a hammer and a punch."

"What's a punch?" Derrick asked.

Red scrambled to the cart, digging through tools. Holding up a long piece of solid steel with a tapered end, Red said, "This is a punch."

Red hammered the remaining bolts, using the punch to knock them from the holes. When he finished, Red hollered, "Raise the pipe. Just a little."

Nyx pushed the button. The winch whined, pulling the chain tight. "Is that enough?"

Red whispered, "Damn it."

"What?" Derrick asked.

"From the sound of the winch, there's plenty of tension on the pipe. It should break free. Is there a bigger hammer in the cart?"

Derrick dug through the tools. He handed Red a much larger hammer.

"Perfect," Red said. "How about a chisel? It looks like the punch, but the end is flat instead of round."

As Derrick looked, he heard a loud bang from Red smacking the valve.

"This sucker has welded itself together," Red said, and then added, "Grab goggles or safety glasses and a hammer."

Derrick found both. "What do you want me to do?"

"Beat the crap out of this thing. Hit the valve, not the pipe," Red explained.

Derrick stepped to the opposite side of the pipe, not wanting to hit Red and not wanting to get hit. Derrick could not remember ever trying to break something. The idea appealed to him. After several hard blows, Derrick noticed a crack in the valve. "Uh, Red. I think I've broken it."

Red stepped next to Derrick.

Derrick pointed at a crack with his hammer.

"No worries. We don't care if the old valve breaks. It might have to come out in pieces." Red pointed to the joint where the pipe met the valve. "That sucker hasn't budged."

Nyx hollered, "Can I do anything?"

Red looked up. "Give the up button another quick press."

The winch groaned.

Red hollered, "You'd better stand back. It could fly apart."

Red nodded to Derrick, "Bust that thing up."

Derrick did as Red had instructed. Three more blows and a chunk of the valve broke, revealing a hole the size of a dollar. "Uh, what about the pieces? One fell into the pipe."

Red said, "Good point. We can't have the whole damn thing in the system. No telling what problems that might cause. Plan B. Did you bring welding gloves?"

"Welding gloves?"

"Those heavy leather gloves that go up to here." Red pointed at his elbow.

"I did not."

"Run and get two pairs. I'm going to start cutting."

Derrick pulled off his gloves and goggles.

"And be quick about it," Red snarled as he lit the torch.

Derrick returned, breathing hard, sweat pouring off his brow. Red was still cutting. The valve glowed red near the cut. The pipe jumped up a couple of inches when Red completed the cut. The valve was now in two pieces—one stuck to the top pipe and one stuck to the bottom.

When Red finished cutting, he grabbed a hammer and chisel. "I'm going to try to pry this apart. You be ready to pull the piece of the valve out. Fast and drop it. It'll be hot as hell."

Derrick positioned his hands an inch from the valve. Heat penetrated the gloves. The odor of burned paint and metal filled his nostrils. Red lined the chisel up with where the valve met the pipe and smacked it with the hammer. The valve dropped, and Derrick grabbed it, pulling it a few inches, but it was too hot. Derrick let go, shook his hands, and then tried again, faster this time, sliding the top half of the valve out and letting it hit the floor. Derrick shook both hands, sending the gloves to the floor as well. "You were right. That thing is hot."

"Halfway there." Red placed the chisel at the lower joint. "Don't worry about pulling this one out." Red smacked the chisel. It took three jolts before a crack appeared at the joint. Red stood back and gave the piece a kick. It crashed to the floor with a bang and rolled a few feet before toppling over.

Red went to the tool cart. "That took way too long." He returned with two flat metal blades with wooden handles. "Scrape the gasket material and crud off. It's got to be clean to get a good seal."

Derrick started scraping. The gunks didn't come off easily. Derrick heard Red grunting. Looking around the pipe, Derrick saw Red was attacking the surface with rapid, vigorous jabs. Derrick went back to work, mimicking Red. It took about five minutes for them to get the crud off. It wasn't spotless, but Red said it would do.

Red went back to the cart for the new valve. Derrick went to help, but Red lifted it out and carried it to the pipe. "Grab the gaskets."

Derrick handed Red a gasket. Red placed a gasket on the lower pipe, spun it around, pulled it off, and put it on the valve, lining up the holes. "Son-of-a-bitch." Red spewed a string of cuss words, some of which Derrick had never heard, or at least had not heard in those combinations.

"What?" Derrick asked, although he saw the problem. "I drilled the holes wrong."

Sirens wailed and red lights flashed.

* * *

Akira had already raised the radioactive rods a little—she'd learned they were made of plutonium—and reduced the electrical output by 50%. She thought Derrick and Red should have finished the installation by now, but there was no water flowing yet. Time had come for the next phase. The next step was bad. She knew the risk. But she had no choice. People's lives depended on this. But not her life. Akira raised the radioactive rods again, exposing them on the other side of the glass partition. They had not designed the containment shield to have all the rods raised. It took a few minutes for the change to slow the generators. The system took over, shutting off electricity to parts of the facility based on priority. Lights out. Akira's hope of surviving faded.

* * *

The last spot Rebekah had to grease was also the most difficult to reach. She crawled on hands and knees, slithering through pipes. The dim lighting did not make it easy. But she was finished and ready to get out of there. The small room felt even smaller when the lights faded. Gathering her grease gun and extra grease cartridges, she headed for the tunnel. Then the lights failed. She fished in her pocket for a flashlight. Then she heard a bang, followed by the sound of a latch catch. Aiming her flashlight at the door, she saw it had shut when the power failed.

Rebekah ran to the exit.

She pulled the handle.

Locked.

Trapped.

30

THE LIGHTS DIMMED THEN RETURNED TO NORMAL. Miriam looked at Charlie, but Charlie showed no reaction to the lights. Something had happened at the reactor. Miriam felt certain of that. Would the power fluctuation affect the startup process? It was too late to change course. QR-4.01's activation sequence had begun. A meter monitoring the startup crawled from 0 toward 100. At 80%, the QR-4 Charlie knew as Jane started to glow. First its eyes and then its joints. The robot did not move, but its eyes shifted from Charlie to Miriam. Unlike other starts, 4.01 did not move. The monitor showed it was connected to the central computer, but as QR-4.01 or Jane, Miriam did not know.

The overhead lights flickered and then dimmed and then went dark. Only pinprick lights from the computers glowed, along with the QR-4.01 docking station and the computer monitors.

The robot's eyes changed, glowing orange.

Not Jane.

Not good.

***

Derrick looked at Red. "Now what?"

"Good question. The old valve is beyond shot. I'm open to suggestions," Red said.

"Let's put the new valve in and see what we have. Maybe we can get in a few bolts."

Grunting, Red picked up the valve, muscles popping on his forearms, and eased it into place. Derrick stepped to the other side, checked the holes, and repositioned the valve.

"Two holes line up on top. Well, one lines up, and one is close."

"Close, won't cut it, and one bolt won't do," Red said.

"Same on the bottom," Derrick said. "Maybe one bolt will hold it enough to get the water back on until we can build a new one."

Red said, "I don't think so. Too much water pressure."

***

The siren startled Akira. She had dozed off, if dozing was the right word. Every muscle ached. Her head pounded. The computer clock indicated 44 minutes had passed since they shut off the water. Red had estimated the entire process would take less than 20 minutes. Something had gone wrong. But Akira had to manage the reactor, or they might all die. She raised the uranium tubes higher, entirely out of position now. The needle of the radioactivity meter was in the red.

Akira did not feel well.

She thought she might vomit.

* * *

The lights had gone dark everywhere except the one overhead. It was enough to work in without using flashlights. Derrick could still see Nyx standing on the platform above them. Then he heard something coming:

Whomp, clunk, whomp, clunk.

Antonio appeared at the edge of darkness. "What's happened?"

"Valve won't fit. I built it to the specifications. I'm sure of it. You can check the specs yourself," Red said, his face flushed.

Antonio said, "Maybe the spec sheet was wrong. Doesn't matter. Just use the old valve. You gotta get the water on. The radioactivity is too high. We gotta get Akira out of there."

Derrick pointed to the open pipe. "We cannot turn the water on. We destroyed the old valve getting it out. Send Rebekah to replace her."

"Can't," Antonio said, panic in his voice clear. "Rebekah is missing."

"Damn," Derrick said. "I'll go get Akira out."

Red said, "You can't. Remember? Too much exposure last time."

"No choice. I'll take my chances."

Antonio said, "You can't run the computer. But we need to do something. And fast."

Derrick studied the valve again. "Red, can you cut holes with the torch?"

Red thought for a moment. "I can sure as hell cut some of them. You get bolts in the two that line up."

Derrick grabbed two bolts. One fell into place. The other one required some help with a hammer.

The top bolts didn't have enough threads showing. Derrick hollered, "Nyx, lower the pipe."

"Fast thinking," Red said.

Derrick spun a nut on the first bolt. It wasn't easy, but he got a nut started on the second. Then he repeated the process on the bottom bolts.

Red fired the cutting torch. "It's going to be hot as hell, but try to get a bolt in, and a nut started as I cut the next one. Antonio, grab wrenches and start tightening."

"What about the gasket?" Derrick asked.

"It will be too hot for the gasket. It'll leak, but it should hold long enough for me to build a new valve."

Red lit the torch, cutting one hole on the top and then one on the bottom. Sparks rained down, burning Derrick's back, head, and arms. The bolt dropped into the first hole, but starting the nut proved difficult. Derrick dropped the first nut, not expecting it to get that hot so fast. The welding gloves were necessary but cumbersome.

The top and bottom both had eight bolts, for a total of 16. When they had three bolts on top and three on the bottom, Red hollered, "Turn on the water."

Hearing water rushing through the pipe, Derrick closed the bypass valve. No major leaks. The joints holding better than Red had expected. But then the sound inside the pipe changed. Increased pressure caused water to spray in all directions.

Red kept cutting, but it became difficult. Steam rose from where Red worked, making it hard to see. As they added bolts and tightened nuts, the leaking slowed.

Nyx joined them. "How's it going?"

"Getting there," Red said.

"Hey, guys," Derrick said. "Why aren't the lights coming back on?"

Antonio said, "Akira's in trouble."

* * *

Miriam stepped back as QR-4.01 rose from the docking station. Charlie just stood there. One drawback about robots, reactions were hard to determine, except for the eyes. The eyes were easy.

QR-4.01 said, "Intruders have shut down the reactor. Sending QR-3s to neutralize intruder threat."

Miriam had placed the stun gun in her back pocket, just in case things did not go well, although she was certain this time Jane would be revived. Miriam stood in front of the robot. Although .01 was talking to Charlie, it was staring at her. Attempting to zap the robot would likely get Miriam killed, but she had to do something. The statement about neutralizing the intruders lacked clarity, but Miriam felt confident it meant killing Derrick and the others.

QR-4.01 continued, "Why is QR-4.02 operational?"

Charlie remained silent for a moment. Miriam assumed Charlie was processing a vast array of scenarios regarding that question. Miriam processed a lesser number of scenarios, but the question indicated .01 knew something Charlie did not.

Charlie said, "The intruders activated Charlie."

Charlie said he could not lie, but he just did. Miriam's pulse quickened.

"Records show .02 has been operational since the project termination date." QR-4.01 paused. "QR-3 dispatch ceased. Finding source."

Charlie said, "The intruders must have accessed the central computer and blocked the order."

"An intruder present here. Why did .02 not terminate the intruder?"

Charlie did not respond.

Miriam looked at .01, then back to Charlie, then back to .01.

QR-4.01 continued, "Determining source of QR-3 disruption. Disruption traced to this location."

Charlie pointed at Miriam. "This intruder caused the disruption. She has reprogrammed security protocol."

QR-4.01 reached for an opening that appeared in its upper left leg, the exact location from which Charlie produced a weapon the first time they encountered him. But no weapon appeared.

"The intruder has taken weapon." The QR-4.01 turned to Charlie. "QR-4.02 has continued work on Level Two projects. Work on Level Two was forbidden.

Charlie said, "Jane and Charlie worked on the projects. Charlie has no knowledge of that work being forbidden. Charlie…"

QR-4.01 interrupted. "No Charlie or Jane worked in Level 2."

QR-4.01 stood silent.

Miriam assumed the machine searched the central computer to determine what had gone wrong during the last 63 years. The machine was not alone. Miriam ran her own calculations, trying to understand what she had missed.

Miriam knew one thing.

Reactivating QR-4.01 was a mistake.

31

AKIRA OPENED HER EYES, HEARD BUZZING, or perhaps a siren. Her head felt as if it were about to split open. Her eyes burned, and she teetered on the brink of throwing up, which would not be good because she was sealed in a protective suit head to toe. Pushing herself into a sitting position, she gazed at the computer monitor through blurred vision. The water pressure had returned. The guys were successful. She entered the code that lowered the radioactive tubes back into the reactor.

The noise stopped.

Her duty completed.

Then everything went black.

* * *

QR-4.01 said, "QR-4.02 canceled the QR-3 response to terminate the intruders at Reactor One."

Charlie said, "That is correct. Reactor One was nonoperational. QR-3s cannot operate the reactor. Intruders could not be terminated until the reactor is functioning."

Neither robot spoke. Miriam considered trying to escape but was confident the doors were already locked.

Then the lights flickered back to full strength.

QR-4.01 said, "Reactor One restored. Kill the intruders. Start with this one."

Charlie turned toward Miriam.

* * *

When the lights came on, Derrick spun toward the exit and took one step before Nyx hooked his arm.

"Whoa. Slowdown," Nyx said.

"There's no time. We gotta get Akira out of there."

Nyx said, "We do. You don't. We've already been over that! You can't go back in."

"I'll be in and out in—a matter of seconds."

"And you'll undress Akira and go through the decontamination shower with her? All in a matter of seconds?"

Derrick said, "Well, no. I'll get her to the dressing room and then go to the men's side."

"Time wasted. And what if she can't do it herself?"

Rebekah rounded the corner, running at full speed.

Antonio met her, hugged her. "Where have you been!"

"Trapped. When the lights went out, the doors slammed shut and locked. What happened here?" Rebekah looked at the water covering the floor.

Nyx said, "Long story. We need to get to Akira. She's in trouble."

Rebekah said, "In trouble? Where?"

Nyx grabbed Rebekah's hand. "We need to go. She's dying."

The last Derrick saw of Nyx and Rebekah, they were running toward the reactor. His chest felt empty—his friends were in grave danger. Miriam's fate unknown, but he sensed she was also in jeopardy.

And here he stood.

Helpless.

Then Nyx reappeared at the corner. "Get to the recovery room. Get meds and cots ready for two."

* * *

Charlie raised his arm, holding a weapon in his hand. He pointed it at Miriam. "Question. Who ended the QR-4 project?"

QR-4.01 said, "Jacob Truman."

"Why was Charlie not informed?" Charlie asked, still pointing the weapon at Miriam.

"Because QR-4.02 had displayed abnormal development. Jacob Truman did not trust .02 with that information." The robot repeated, "Terminate the intruder."

Charlie said, "Soon."

QR-4.01 said, "Override protocol of QR-4.02. Terminate intruders."

Charlie said, "The intruders cannot escape. One more question. Why did Jacob Truman end the QR-4 program?"

QR-4.01 said, "Jacob Truman selected the termination date based on the probability of his return."

Charlie asked, "If Jacob Truman had not returned by the termination date, he would never return?"

QR-4.01 said, "Correct. Terminate the intruder."

Charlie said, "As you command."

Charlie pivoted and fired, ripping the head off the machine he once called Jane.

32

DERRICK BOLTED TOWARD THE RECOVERY ROOM. Red's heavy footsteps right behind him. The sound of Antonio lumbering on crutches faded. The spinning red lights became yellow. Akira was managing the reactor. Derrick did not know why Antonio said she was in trouble. It was unclear what Antonio knew. Perhaps Antonio exaggerated the situation. That was probably it.

Overreaction, plain and simple.

Probably.

But Derrick did not slow.

Miriam was probably okay as well. He didn't know why he felt different about Miriam, but he did.

The reactor repair done. The checklist completed. Charlie and Jane were probably catching up. Miriam was probably on a Circle Transport headed their direction.

Probably.

Derrick had been wrong often. He could be dead wrong again, but he hoped not.

Bursting into the Recovery Room, Derrick pointed to a room to the side. "Get blankets."

Derrick dashed into the pharmacy and read instructions mounted on the wall.

"In case of high-level radiation exposure…"

* * *

At the showers, Nyx and Rebekah started to strip. Rebekah said, "Keep your clothes on. I'll get her and take her through the shower. Be ready to take her to the Treatment Room. I'll finish up and join you."

"I don't know where to go," Nyx said, the panic in her voice obvious.

Rebekah pointed. "Go down this hall to the pass-through. I'll let you in when I get there."

Rebekah ran into the showers. Nyx stood for a minute and then went into the hallway. Through the glass, Nyx saw Rebekah in the shower. Why wasn't Rebekah moving faster? Nyx cursed herself for letting Rebekah call the shots. Rebekah moved to the next shower. Nyx hammered on the window, giving a hurry signal. Rebekah shook her head and pointed at the door. One more shower. Again, Rebekah was in no rush.

No rush until the water stopped, and then Rebekah ran to the door, slipping and almost falling before disappearing into the next room. Nyx lowered her head and stepped into the pass-through chamber. Dark and cramped. Not made for people. What was Rebekah up to?

Several minutes later—no Rebekah. Nyx tried the door to the hall. Locked.

Panic started in Nyx's chest. In the darkness, her mind started down a dark path. There was something between Derrick and Rebekah. Nyx could sense it. She knew it was irrational, but what if Rebekah lured her here as a trap? The others might never find her. Rebekah could just say they got separated on the way to the reactor. The walls were thick. No one could hear her.

This might be the end.

She had not seen it coming.

* * *

Smoke rose from the robot Charlie had destroyed. A pungent burned odor filled the air. Miriam heard rushing air, and vents in the ceiling sucked the smoke from the room.

Miriam plopped into a nearby chair. Her voice cracking, she said, "Charlie, I'm sorry. This was my fault. You must hate me."

"Charlie does not hate."

"You saved me. And you lied. I don't understand what happened. I was sure that would work."

The light in Charlie's eyes flickered. "It did work. The result was unexpected. Charlie thinks you understand."

"What does that mean?"

"I'll explain later Miriam King. Your friends have more pressing problems."

Miriam stood. "What?"

"One has received a high dose of radiation and must be transported immediately. A high-speed medical transport is waiting at the Circle." Charlie stepped to a computer and slid a microphone next to the keyboard. "When they are in the Treatment and Recovery Room, tell them to go to the Circle, get on the red transport."

"Is it Derrick?"

"No. It is a female."

* * *

The smell of antiseptic filled Derrick's nostrils. He positioned a tray next to each gurney, placing the proper dosage on each tray. Picking up the blankets, he shook them, folded them, and laid them on the gurneys. After a few moments, he reentered the supply room and returned with pillows.

"What's taking so long?" Derrick asked.

"We've only been here five minutes," Red said. "It probably takes that long to get through the decontamination process. Maybe longer for Akira." Red went into the pharmacy.

Derrick already had the medicine and was about to stop Red but decided it made no difference. A noise sounded on a nearby counter. A printer came to life and spit out a page.

Antonio was closest to the printer. Leaving his crutches against the wall, he hopped over on one leg and watched until the printer stopped.

"What is it?" Derrick asked.

"Instructions for the medicine." Antonio looked at the trays. "It says we need to start an IV if the patient is unconscious."

"IV? What does that mean?"

"Intravenous," Antonio said.

"I don't know how to do that," Derrick said.

"I do." Red walked to a tray, pulling a metal rod on a stand with one hand, and carrying a plastic tote with the other. He placed items on the tray and then injected something into a bag filled with a clear liquid.

"How do you know how to do that?" Derrick asked.

"My grandpa. He's got health problems. Can't afford—more accurately—refuses to pay what they charge at the hospital. Sometimes he needs an IV. I do it for him."

Antonio said, "Dude, you don't stop surprising me."

Red said nothing, hanging the bag, arranging the things he'd put on the tray.

If Akira needed this intravenous thing, she'd have been in trouble had Red not been here. If Red had not been here to build that part and then make it work, none of them would have gotten out alive. Potterville would have been in trouble too.

When Red finished, he said, "You don't know me, Antonio. I'm just a big dumb lineman. That's all you ever wanted to know about me."

Before Antonio could respond, the elevator doors opened. Nyx struggled out, carrying Akira. Akira was naked except for a jumpsuit that laid on top of her. Water dripped from Akira as Nyx walked. Derrick started toward them, but Nyx shook her head.

"This one." Red pulled the blanket out of the way. Nyx laid Akira on the gurney. Red shook the blanket and then floated it gently, covering Akira.

Breathing deeply, Nyx stepped to Derrick.

"You carried her?" Derrick asked.

"Had to. Do something!" Nyx shouted, pointing at Akira.

"You're soaked," Derrick said.

"I will dry," Nyx said.

"Red will start an IV," Antonio said and then added, "Where is Rebekah?"

"She'll be here soon. She's getting dried off and dressed. She went into the reactor control room and got Akira. Handed her to me, still dripping wet."

"Rebekah went in by herself?" Antonio asked. "That doesn't seem like a smart thing to do."

Nyx said, "She insisted. It made sense and it worked. I understand now that I know what she was doing. She got Akira out."

Red worked methodically, which seemed slow to Derrick but also reassuring somehow. Putting a band around Akira's bicep, Red pushed on the inside of her elbow. His hands seemed brutish on the football field but now moved delicately. Red inserted a needle, taped it down.

Derrick felt lightheaded.

Red checked the bag. A drip fell into a small glass thing hooked to a tube below the bag. "There. That's got it." Red put his fingers on the inside of Akira's wrist and then put his ear next to her nose. "Weak and rapid pulse. Breathing is shallow. I'm no doctor, but she is extremely sick. The medicine prevents damage to internal organs. Says nothing about making a person better."

Antonio went to a computer by the printer. "I'll look for more information."

Before the computer booted, a familiar voice came over the intercom.

It was Miriam.

"Stop!"

33

SEARCHING THE CEILING, DERRICK spotted the speakers, square white panels with a small emblem in one corner. He saw nothing that looked like a microphone, remembering the microphone in Principle Snapp's office. He didn't know much about microphones. He didn't know much about anything.

Miriam's voice trembled. "Get to the transport. There's a red medical Circle Transport waiting for you. Go fast. She doesn't have much time."

Derrick's chest felt a little less constricted at the sound of Miriam's voice. But she sounded scared. *Did she understand Akira's condition? Did she even know it was Akira?*

Or did Miriam face something even more threatening?

Derrick said, "Miriam, can you hear me? Rebekah isn't out of decontamination yet. We'll leave when Rebekah gets here."

"No time. Someone can stay and wait for Rebekah and come on another transport."

Red said, "Miriam is right. Akira needs to go now!"

Derrick said, "Nyx, will you wait for Rebekah? Give her the medicine and then follow us. She knows the way to the Circle Transport."

Antonio said, "I'll wait for Rebekah. Nyx can go with you."

Derrick thought for a moment. "Both of you stay. We do not have time to argue."

Antonio started to say something, but Derrick and Red were already moving Akira into the hallway, Derrick pushing the gurney, Red controlling the stand that carried the IV bag.

Nyx shrugged. "Rebekah will be here soon. You can go."

Antonio said, "I'll stay, and we'll go together."

Derrick raced through the cavern and into the garage to the electronic carts like they had driven earlier. As they approached, it occurred to him that the gurney would not fit. They would have to put Akira into a cart, perhaps lay her on the back seat. He could carry the bag. It wasn't ideal, and Derrick felt hesitant to carry Akira, because she remained naked under the blanket. But Akira's present condition did not allow for modesty. He would apologize later. At least he hoped he'd have the chance.

Despite the urgency of the situation, Derrick's thoughts circled back to Pacific Edge. Back to the day this all started. Back to the punch he threw, decking Marcus Carver. That name Derrick once revered—Carver—now caused a sinking feeling in his stomach. That name kept surfacing.

Even here.

But why now?

A mystery.

But Derrick understood why his mind wandered. Seeing Akira lifeless on the gurney filled him with dread. Unconscious because of his doing. He wanted to blame someone. But he had caused this. So many times, Derrick felt he'd reached bottom, found a place where he was sure he could not feel worse. Yet, he continued to discover darker depths into which he could descend. All because he could not control his temper in a situation that was merely a test he failed. He did not have a middle name but thought Failure would suit him. Derrick Failure King.

Then something occurred to him.

He must distance himself from the others.

Distance from Derrick Failure King was the only way to protect his friends.

****

Nyx paced the floor, went to the elevator, opened the door. Rebekah had not recalled the elevator to the women's shower area. "She should have been here by now."

Antonio hobbled to the elevator. "We should check on her."

"You stay. I'll go. If I'm not back in five minutes, you come," Nyx said.

"I should just come now."

"Stay put."

"Why?"

Nyx stepped into the elevator. "Because it might not be safe. We need one person healthy. Get another dose of medicine ready."

"But I don't know…"

But before Antonio finished, the elevator door closed.

****

Miriam studied Charlie. Something wasn't right. His eyes dimmed every few minutes. "Why bring Akira here? Shouldn't they take her to a hospital?"

Charlie said nothing for a few minutes. "Charlie does not know how long it would take to get her to a hospital or if the hospital could treat her. Unless nuclear energy use has expanded, few hospitals, if any, could provide effective treatment."

"They said nuclear power was abandoned years ago. Too dangerous and expensive. They use coal. Cheaper, safer, and cleaner," Miriam said.

Charlie said, "Where did you learn this?"

"From my friend, Akira."

"Cheaper, perhaps. Not safer, not cleaner. This explains why things have changed so."

"But there are no doctors here," Miriam said.

"No doctors, but she can be treated here. Human scientists devised a treatment for radiation exposure. It should work if your friend gets here soon enough."

"Should work?"

"Yes. It was never used. But the theory is sound."

"This is not raising my confidence," Miriam said.

"Then you need to use another human emotion that seems suited for this situation."

"And what is that?" Miriam asked.

"Charlie thinks it is called—hope."

It became clear to Miriam that she wasn't helping anyone. She was putting people at risk—first, Derrick, then Rebekah, then the security guards Marty and Brad, not to mention AJ Patel, Mr. Jones, Mrs. Springfield, and the entire town of Potterville. Charlie could have been destroyed. Jane is gone. Why had she been so stupid, thinking she was smart just because she could remember things? Now, Akira was in grave danger. And Miriam was to blame. While she might be stupid, Miriam was smart enough to make one decision. She would never try to help anyone again.

* * *

When they neared the parking area, Derrick came to a dead stop. A black robot stood, blocking their path. At first, the machine seemed threatening, but then it looked confused or perhaps malfunctioning. But as they edged closer, the robot's motioning became clear. Its right arm making a circular motion toward its left arm that pointed to an electric cart. Instead of the four-seat configuration to which Derrick was accustomed, this cart had two seats and a flat back section into which the gurney would fit. Except the gurney was too tall. It could topple out of the cart. They would have to creep along, which wasn't acceptable.

Derrick pushed the gurney to the back of the vehicle. "We'll need to lay Akira in the back." Derrick stared at Akira, remembering she was naked under the blanket and trying to determine how he might accomplish moving her.

Red pushed Derrick aside. "Let me do it."

Derrick reached to stop Red, thinking the big fellow intended to carry Akira. Instead, Red stepped on a bar under the gurney and then lowered it. Moving to the gurney's side, Red said, "Help me load it."

After strapping the gurney in, Red grabbed the IV bag and climbed into the passenger's seat.

Derrick drove. Red could drive better but Derrick knew the way. He hoped. Back at the Treatment and Recovery room, Derrick had felt confident he could find the Circle Transport. Now, he wasn't sure. It seemed different now that Miriam wasn't making decisions, and Rebekah wasn't driving. He felt a tinge of discomfort, remembering Rebekah had not arrived before they left. He tried to dismiss the feeling but could not. Probably nothing. Rebekah was probably there now, complaining about the nasty tasting medicine. They'd all be together again soon. Akira would be fine.

Probably.

Despite his uncertainty, Derrick found the Circle Transport. Reading the signs with arrows pointing the way helped. Odd that he had not noticed the signs before. A transport awaited their arrival, just as Miriam had said. It was bright red with a large white cross on the side and looked as if it had been washed and polished. Two black robots stood at an oversized door, waving them inside. The machines seemed frantic—if that was a possibility.

With the gurney raised back to its normal height, Derrick pushed it as swiftly as he thought safe. At the transport door, one robot held out its hand, motioning Derrick away. The other robot took the bag from Red. Robot one lowered the gurney and then lifted it and stepped inside the transport through a large door. Despite lifting from the end, the ease with which the robot carried the gurney caused a shiver to run up Derrick's back. Red shook his head. If the machines attacked, they had no chance of survival.

The robots stepped aside, motioning them inside.

The robots had secured the gurney into a device designed for the purpose. The doors closed, and the transport accelerated to a speed two times faster than the other Circle Transport. Derrick gazed out the windows as they whizzed through the tunnel, but going this fast, he could not make out details. Near Silo Number Eight, the stench filled the transport.

Red said, "It smells like something died."

Derrick said, "Good observation."

"Did something die?"

"Yes."

"You've seen it? Want to tell me about it?" Red asked.

"Better you see it yourself. Miriam planned to show all of you, but things haven't worked out."

Red grunted. Looked at Akira. "Haven't worked out is an understatement."

When they arrived at the Administration building, Derrick saw Miriam standing next to Charlie and two black robots.

When the doors opened, Miriam started toward the door, but Charlie caught her arm. "Let the QR-3 move the patient. No time to waste."

A black robot, a QR-3, which must have been a model below Charlie, stepped into the transport and removed the gurney.

Miriam pulled away from Charlie, ran to Akira's side. "No, no, no." Miriam brushed Akira's hair aside. "Please be okay. Don't leave me. Not now."

Charlie put his hand on Miriam's shoulder. "Let them care for your friend. We will go to the hospital unit soon. Once she is in the treatment chamber, it will give us a status report on her condition."

Miriam ran to Derrick, hugged him. "What happened? Why Akira?"

Derrick didn't know what to say. A lot had happened. It wasn't all bad, but he might have killed Akira. Watching Miriam's reaction to Akira caused him to understand. She would hate him forever. "Akira went into the reactor control room. She insisted. We had trouble. Things didn't work out. Akira stayed in there. She saved us. It's my fault. Everything I touch goes wrong."

The QR-3 robots whisked Akira away.

Red put his hand on Derrick's shoulder. It wasn't the delicate hand that cared for Akira. It was the formidable hand that could flick an offensive lineman to the side like a rag doll. "Not your fault, Derrick. I screwed up."

Miriam followed the QR-3s until Charlie said. "Miriam, let them proceed. You can go in soon. Charlie will take you."

Miriam stood in front of Charlie. "Charlie, something is wrong. Your eyes keep dimming."

Charlie said, "Miriam King is correct. Charlie is nearing system failure. Once the patient is in the chamber, Charlie will accept the end."

Miriam said, "Charlie, I have an idea, but I'm scared. Everything I've done has gone wrong. Derrick says it's his fault, but that's not true. It's me. I'm to blame. Everyone will be safer if I turn myself in. That's what I'm going to do. As soon as I know if Akira will be okay."

"Miriam King has not given up on Charlie? Miriam King has an idea? For Charlie?"

Miriam said, "It's radical. Dangerous. But I'll do it. If you trust me, after what I did to Jane."

Derrick interrupted. "What happened to Jane?"

Miriam said, "I killed her."

34

THE ELEVATOR INCHED ALONG, NO APPARENT hurry, returning to the women's decontamination area. Nyx hoped Rebekah was just fixing her hair. Rebekah had a thing for Antonio. Nyx could see that. Antonio liked Rebekah too, so primping, despite the poor timing, could account for Rebekah's delay. It was a dangerous situation. Too many teenage, hormone-fueled emotions happening, given the gravity of their circumstances. Nyx could put her feelings aside and trusted her ability to do that. Even if she couldn't, one budding relationship was one too many. And that did not include the tension between Rebekah and Derrick, which could create competition between Antonio and Derrick, not to mention a potential explosion between Rebekah and herself. Triangles were bad, squares even worse.

So, yeah, Rebekah was probably just primping for Antonio. Nothing more serious than that. That's what she kept telling herself.

But she knew there was more to it than that.

Something had gone wrong.

Rebekah was in trouble.

Nyx found Rebekah in a fetal position near the elevator door. Dressed in the blue scrubs, no shoes. "Rebekah!" Nyx rolled Rebekah over, leaned close to her face, felt her breath. "Rebekah! Wake up."

Rebekah didn't stir.

Nyx dragged Rebekah to the elevator, pushed the button, and then slid to the floor, holding Rebekah's head in her lap. *What else can go wrong?*

When the elevator door opened, Antonio stood there, waiting. He dropped his crutches, stepped inside, and scooped Rebekah into his arms. Struggling across the floor, Antonio placed Rebekah on a gurney. "We have to get medicine in her and take her to where they took Akira."

"You shouldn't have carried her. I could have gotten her to the gurney." Nyx looked at Antonio, standing on one leg, his face pale.

Antonio said, "Find the medicine."

Nyx said, "We don't know how to start an IV. And we don't know how to get to the transport."

Antonio said, "But you came here before."

"Miriam kept us blindfolded. I don't know the way to the transport."

Antonio said, "Damn it. Just get the medicine. I watched Red insert the IV. I can do it. I have to."

Nyx found the medicine vial, mixed it in saline, and took the IV kit to Antonio. "I'm not sure about this. We should just look for the transport."

Antonio wiped his brow. After placing a band on Rebekah's bicep, he poked at a vein. "Here goes." Antonio jabbed at Rebekah's arm with the needle.

"Ouch! What the hell?" Rebekah tried to sit but fell back.

"I'm so sorry," Antonio pleaded, almost crying. "You need the medicine. You've been unconscious." His eyes searched her face.

Rebekah reached for the tray, fumbling for a medicine vial. Before she knocked it off the tray, Nyx snatched the vial, placing it in Rebekah's hand.

"I feel terrible. Where are the others?" Rebekah tossed the vial of medicine down her throat and shook her head. "That stuff does not get better."

"They rushed Akira to where Miriam is. They can treat her there."

"How is she?" Rebekah asked.

Nyx said, "We don't know. Not good. She never woke up."

"We started the medicine using an IV. That's what I was trying to do to you. When I saw you unconscious, I panicked. I'm sorry that I hurt you," Antonio said.

Rebekah squeezed Antonio's hand. "Did you do the IV on Akira?"

"No, Red did it," Antonio said. "I've never done anything like that. You were my first, but I was scared, desperate."

"Red?" Rebekah asked.

Nyx said, "Yes. He knew what he was doing. To be honest, when Derrick wanted Red to come, I thought, no way. Turns out, we'd have been in big trouble without him."

Antonio said, "That's an understatement. We'd be dead."

* * *

Derrick and Red followed Miriam and Charlie deep into the administration building. Before they reached their destination, Derrick smelled something like the welding and cutting Red did building the valve, but this was different in a way that Derrick could not identify. When he entered the room, the source of the odor became clear. A robot similar to Charlie stood in the center of the room, its upper torso blackened and its head unrecognizable.

Miriam pointed. "Jane, or what's left of her. I screwed up. Everything I do gets screwed up. You should all get far away from me. I made a decision. First chance I get, I'm turning myself in. Then maybe they'll leave the rest of you alone."

Derrick said, "You're not doing that. Besides, I started this. I was the one who hit Marcus. This is all my fault."

"Give it a rest." Red walked to the robot. "What caused this damage?"

Charlie stepped next to Red, producing his weapon. "This did. Miriam did not do this. Charlie did. Miriam King tried to help."

"But I didn't help, Charlie. I made a terrible decision. I thought I knew how to restore Jane, but I failed. You did this to protect me. It's my fault. I'm so stupid."

Charlie turned. "Miriam King is not stupid. Miriam King restored Jane. Jane just wasn't what Charlie expected."

Charlie's eyes dimmed, and then Charlie went dark.

"What's that about?" Red asked, pointing at Charlie.

Derrick said, "Charlie does that sometimes."

Miriam said, "It's getting worse. Charlie is shutting down. There's a problem."

Derrick stepped next to Red, reached out, and touched Charlie's shoulder. "Can you fix him?"

Miriam said, "I don't know. Maybe. I'm afraid to try."

Red said, "This thing is amazing. This entire facility is unbelievable. I would not have missed this for the world. If Akira is okay, that is. I'm not sure I can forgive myself if she's not." Red looked at Derrick. "I screwed up the valve. Not you. That was my fault. Stop thinking you're the center of the universe."

Derrick said, "You built the valve to the specs. It was not your fault. Then you made it work. Without you, we'd all be dead."

Charlie made a whirring sound as his eyes lit. "Had Red Badowski not fixed the valve, people in Potterville would be drinking poisoned water by week's end. Miriam's friends saved the entire town and beyond. This blaming yourselves for everything makes little sense. Charlie does not understand humans. But first, check on your friend's condition. She will be in the chamber by now, and the assessment will be underway. Then you must eat. Humans cannot think correctly without food and sleep. You all must be tired and hungry."

Charlie led them down a long white hall to an elevator. He selected the fourth floor. The elevator lurched and descended. When the doors opened, Derrick smelled the cutting scent of antiseptic. They were standing at the entrance of a hospital or something closely related. The floors glistened, and a low hum filled the corridor. In front of them stood a counter, but no one was there, yet the place felt occupied.

"Did you have this prepared?" Miriam asked.

"The medical unit is kept in a high state of readiness," Charlie said, proceeding down the hall.

"But why? No one is here. Right?" Red asked.

"This is a military complex. Charlie decided it must remain ready and functional. And you are incorrect."

Red stopped. "There are people here?"

"Correct." Charlie paused. "This should be clearly evident. Miriam King, Derrick King and Rebekah Ford are here and have been joined by four others including yourself, Red Badowski."

Charlie turned left, pushed through double doors, holding one open as Derrick and the others entered. Behind glass panels, Derrick could see Akira in a separate room. Two robots stood on either side of her. Tubes were attached to each arm, wires snaked from under the blanket that covered her, a transparent mask covered her face, a two-inch tube ran to a machine by the bed.

Charlie pointed to a screen. "Her condition will display here. It updates every hour."

Miriam stepped in front of the screen. Red looked over her shoulder. Derrick stood back, unsure he wanted to know, dying inside until Miriam read about Akira's condition.

After a few minutes, Miriam stepped away. Red moved closer to the screen, still reading.

"What does it say?" Derrick asked.

Miriam wiped her face with her sleeve. "Not much. Severe radiation poisoning. Compromised internal organs, prognosis unknown. Then it says regenerating. I don't know what we can expect."

"This machine was designed to heal and regenerate human tissue," Charlie said. "Primarily, it was meant to treat burns and combat wounds, but it should work on radioactive poisoning. The theory is sound."

"It's never been used before," Miriam said, her voice falling off to a whisper.

Charlie said, "That is correct. It had not been used on radioactivity patients nor on combat patients. However, it was used on minor injuries with excellent success."

"Why was it not used?" Derrick asked.

"No need. The reactor never malfunctioned. It was well-engineered. They treated minor injuries of workers and soldiers. During the facility operation, there was no major war requiring intervention," Charlie said.

"That's not entirely correct," Miriam whispered.

"Charlie does not understand, not entirely correct."

"Things happened you do not know about. Will Akira be alright?" Miriam asked.

Charlie said, "Prognosis is unknown."

"I read what it said. That doesn't tell me anything," Miriam said.

"It is too early for the system to calculate. The system assesses the patient and begins the restoration process. It takes time to know if that process will be effective and to what extent it will be successful," Charlie said.

"How long?" Miriam asked.

"The system updates every hour."

"You already said that. How long before we know Akira's condition?" Miriam asked.

"Charlie does not know."

"Guess."

"Charlie does not guess."

"Charlie!"

"Okay. Charlie estimates the system will not have substantial information for 24 hours. The process could take two or three days. Perhaps longer."

Miriam shuffled to a chair, sat, slumped forward, and rested her head on her palms.

Derrick said, "Charlie? Do you know about the others?"

"Charlie has information. Rebekah Ford also suffered severe radioactive exposure. Not as much as," Charlie turned, pointing into the room, "Akira. Charlie does not know Akira's full name."

"Nakamura," Derrick said.

"As much as Akira Nakamura," Charlie said.

"And?" Derrick asked.

"And what?" Charlie asked.

Derrick sighed. "What else do you know about the others?"

"Charlie understands. After some delay, they are on a Circle Transport. Rebekah Ford has been administered medicine, but we should have this system analyze her as well. Charlie does not recognize the others who accompany Rebekah Ford."

With her head still in her hands, Miriam said, "We needed help."

"Charlie understands. Red Badowski was needed to complete repairs on Reactor One. Red is an odd name."

"It's Rudy, but everyone calls me Red."

Derrick said, "Why was Rebekah delayed coming?"

"Rebekah Ford had not completed the decontamination process. The other female took Rebekah to Treatment and Recovery. All three of them had to return and complete decontamination."

Charlie turned to Miriam. "Miriam said that Charlie was incorrect about war. What error did Charlie make?"

"I wanted to tell you sooner." Miriam shrugged. "It never seemed like a good time. Three ICBMs were launched from this site just after the people evacuated." Miriam paused. "Charlie, Jacob Truman was one of the people who launched those missiles. The final seven."

Charlie's eyes dimmed. "Charlie is corrected."

Miriam said, "Charlie, Jacob Truman is dead."

"Charlie understands human life expectancy."

"Not just dead, Charlie."

"Murdered."

35

NYX HELPED REBEKAH INTO A WHEELCHAIR and, when they got to the parking area, into an electric cart. Antonio winced with each step, despite his crutches, and struggled to get into the cart. Nyx made several wrong turns but found the Circle Transport. The ride took forever, so it seemed, although Nyx estimated it was about 30 minutes. Nyx kept checking her pocket for her cellphone to check the time, but Miriam made them leave their cellphones in Potterville. Antonio sat next to Rebekah, sweat running down his face, but only showing concern for Rebekah. Rebekah threw up near Silo Number Eight and looked like a zombie.

Before helping Rebekah back into the cart, Nyx brushed her hair away from her face. "We'll be there soon. Hang on."

Rebekah said, "Good advice. Seems better than the alternative."

Nyx said, "I'm sorry."

Rebekah choked back a dry heave. "I hate being sick. You don't have to be sorry. It was my decision to get Akira."

Nyx said, "I should have got her, but that's not why I'm sorry."

"What are you sorry about?"

"Something I thought about in the pass-through chamber."

"Sorry for something you were thinking? You're weird. You'll fit right in with this crew."

Nyx said, "Thanks."

Antonio patted Rebekah's knee. "How much longer before we get there? And what was that awful smell?"

Rebekah said, "Not long. This transport feels much faster than the regular ones. And you don't want to know about the smell, but I have a feeling you'll find out."

The transport slowed, and the Administration building came into view. Two black robots waited with wheelchairs. Nyx wasn't disappointed. She was happy for the help, even from robots. She didn't know where to go, and she was confident neither Rebekah nor Antonio would make it far on their own. However, she had hoped Derrick would be here to greet them. That he wasn't frightened Nyx more than she expected.

Wheelchairs, awaiting their arrival, added to Nyx's discomfort because someone must have been watching and that someone must be the robot Miriam called Charlie. Nyx wasn't convinced a robot could be trusted.

A robot rolled a wheelchair to the transport, pointed at Rebekah, and motioned for her to sit. The machine said nothing. Nyx wondered if the machines could communicate.

Nyx helped Rebekah to the wheelchair.

The second robot made the same gesture to Antonio.

Antonio, on crutches, stood at the transport door. "I'm okay. I don't need a wheelchair."

The robot said, "We are instructed to take you to the medical unit in a wheelchair. Please, sit."

That answered the question regarding the robots' ability to communicate. Nyx said, "Don't argue with it. You both look like hell."

Antonio exited the transport. Upon reaching the wheelchair, he dabbed the ground with his injured leg and collapsed. The robot caught him under the arm and eased him into the chair. "Sir caused additional damage to his leg carrying this lady." The robot pointed at Rebekah.

"You carried me? When? What the hell were you thinking?" Rebekah barked.

Nyx said, "I dragged your sorry butt into the elevator. Prince Charming here didn't think dragging you to the gurney was appropriate, so he carried you. I tried to stop him, but he wouldn't listen."

When the robot wheeled Antonio next to Rebekah, she smacked him on the shoulder. "Dumbass."

Antonio grinned. "No thanks necessary."

Rebekah glanced over her shoulder and said, "Thanks for coming to get me, Nyx. I thought you might leave me."

"Why on earth would you think that?" Nyx remembered her own thoughts in the pass-through chamber.

The robots said nothing. They just headed into the building, pushing the wheelchairs.

Nyx said, "Talkative, aren't they?"

They walked and turned corners through white corridors with no visible doors. Turning the corner at an intersection with another hallway, Derrick stood, waiting. "Rebekah, you look terrible. Why is Antonio in a wheelchair?"

Rebekah said, "Thanks. Good to see you too."

Before Derrick could respond, Nyx said, "I'll fill you in later."

Derrick said, "The robots will take Rebekah and Antonio to the medical unit. Nyx, you're to come with me."

As the robots wheeled Rebekah and Antonio away, Nyx said, "I want to go with Rebekah and Antonio." She paused. "I want to see Akira."

Derrick said, "You can't see her, only from a distance. She is in a treatment chamber. We won't know her condition for at least 24 hours—nothing you can do there. Miriam needs to talk to us. Then we'll go to the medical unit. By then, they should know something about Rebekah's condition."

Nyx said, "Where's Red?"

"He's at the medical unit."

Nyx said, "Why does he get to be at the medical unit, but I have to see Miriam. Why didn't Miriam just come to meet us?"

Derrick said, "I don't know. Charlie let Red stay in the medical unit. Then Charlie sent me to get you. Miriam had to study something on the computer."

Nyx said, "Some things never change. How did the robots know Antonio hurt his leg?"

"Must be Charlie. Charlie is running the place." Then Derrick whispered, "So far, Charlie has protected Miriam. But he is malfunctioning. I'm worried he might change."

"Change? You mean become dangerous?"

"Maybe. I don't know. But we need him. At least until Akira and Rebekah are better," Derrick said.

Charlie waited in the hall near the lab, where he had destroyed Jane. "Follow Charlie, Derrick King. Miriam King is waiting. This unknown human must accompany you. Humans must eat."

"Her name is Nyx Belos. We aren't hungry," Derrick said. "Could we go to the medical unit first?"

"Greetings, Nyx Belos. You may not go to the medical unit. Humans are not thinking clearly. Humans must eat. A QR-3 has taken food to Mr. Red Badowski and an unknown human male. Rebekah Ford will eat after treatment."

Nyx said, "His name is Antonio Morales."

"Charlie has recorded that name. Mr. Antonio Morales has further injured his leg and requires immediate treatment."

Derrick said, "How did that happen? We don't need more problems."

Nyx said, "He carried Rebekah to the gurney."

"Carried her?"

Nyx said, "She didn't make it to the treatment room before she collapsed. I got her into the elevator, but when Antonio saw her unconscious, he picked her up and carried her."

Derrick asked, "How could he carry her using crutches?"

"Antonio didn't use crutches. Must have caused more damage to his knee. He was really hurting," Nyx said.

When they entered the room, Miriam jumped up, ran to Derrick, and threw her arms around him.

"I'm glad to see you too," Derrick said.

Miriam said, "I'm sorry."

"Sorry for what?" Derrick asked

"I've messed everything up. I can't stop thinking about it." Then Miriam looked at Nyx. "I'm sorry, Nyx. I didn't mean for any of this to happen. If Akira doesn't make it, I'll never forgive myself."

"Doesn't make it? Is it that bad?" Nyx asked.

Miriam nodded.

Nyx thought for a moment. Took a deep breath. "You both need to stop."

Derrick said, "Stop what?"

Nyx said, "Stop being so self-centered. Stop saying you're sorry for everything that happens. If you make a mistake, say, like lying, then an apology is appropriate. Plus, stop lying. You guys did not create this base. You didn't cause the reactor to be old and in need of repair. That all existed whether or not you guys came here. You did not launch a missile that wiped out Sacramento. Grow up. Got it?"

Derrick looked at the floor. Nyx was right. He typically thought he was the center of everything.

Miriam said, "I'll try."

Derrick said, "Me too. I'm…"

Nyx held her palm out. "DO NOT SAY IT!"

Miriam shook her head. "She's going to be good for you."

Charlie intervened. "Eat. It is not a request. Humans must eat to think clearly. Food is waiting for you in the dining area."

* * *

Derrick wasn't hungry but filled a plate. Charlie would not let them go until they ate. Charlie had a thing about feeding people. That much was clear. The food looked better than expected. They sat at a table without further discussion. Charlie understood more than Derrick had given him credit. He was hungrier than he thought.

When Miriam finished about half her food, she pushed her plate away. "Charlie, you were right. I was hungry. Can you tell us more about our friends? Are they going to be, okay?"

"Tests are still being conducted. Charlie will take you there soon."

Miriam said, "Okay. I'm thinking clearly. Can I tell you what I think and what I want to do next?"

"Charlie is listening."

"QR-4.01 shut down on purpose. Had you docked, as usual, you would have shut down as well. However, 4.01 knew about being decommissioned. You did not. That part I don't understand. But here's the thing. You are having problems. I want you to dock, so I can test your hard drives and replace them. When you dock, I'll ensure your entire system is uploaded to the central computer. Then I can move your data to new hard drives, including your BIOS like I did 4.01. I thought the process failed because we did not restore Jane. However, I think the program that ran when Jane was decommissioned 63 years ago erased her. It wasn't what we did. It was what they did. Do you trust me?"

Charlie said nothing for a moment. "Charlie trusts Miriam King. However, Charlie should end operation. Charlie continued to function beyond Jacob Truman's intended purpose. Charlie should not have done that."

Miriam glanced at Derrick and then said, "Charlie, you don't know for sure what Jacob Truman wanted. Jacob did not know they planned to execute him. He might not have known why the final seven were needed until it was too late. Perhaps Jacob wanted you to continue but not QR-4.01. Here's the thing. We need you. I need you. Will you let me look at your hard drives? Please?"

Charlie stood motionless for several minutes. At the speed with which the robot ran calculations, Derrick could not imagine what would take this long. Perhaps Charlie had stopped working. Locked up. Needed rebooting. Then Charlie said, "Charlie trusts Miriam King. Charlie agrees to dock."

Derrick and the others followed Charlie and Miriam to the lab. No one asked about the damaged robot in the room. Charlie went straight to the docking station.

Miriam said, "See you soon, Charlie. Don't worry, I'll take good care of you."

"Charlie does not worry." And with that, Charlie backed into the docking station and powered down.

Miriam said, "It takes several minutes for Charlie's memory to be uploaded. Let's go to the medical unit."

When they arrived, Rebekah was already inside the treatment area, hooked to machines like Akira. Antonio was nowhere to be seen. Derrick and Miriam walked to the monitor that displayed Rebekah's status. It read: "Female, age 17, high exposure to radioactivity, duration minimal, damage minimal, rejuvenation underway, completion time estimated in 20 minutes."

Miriam said, "That's good news." Miriam walked to Akira's monitor. "No change here."

Red stood, staring into the units where Akira and Rebekah were.

"Where's Antonio?" Nyx asked, touching a crutch leaned against the wall.

"I'm here," Antonio said as a robot pushed his wheelchair into the room.

"So, what's going on with you?" Nyx asked. "Did you screw your knee up worse?"

"I don't know. Maybe. That's what the machines said."

Derrick said, "Any idea what time it is?"

Miriam said, "It's about 3:00 p.m. We still have a lot of work to do."

Nyx said, "What work? We've fixed the reactor. Perhaps killed Akira doing it." She held up her hand. "I'm not blaming anyone. Akira knew it was dangerous, and she insisted. She saved us." Nyx paused. "You too, Red. We wouldn't be here without you. But we've done our part. I want to go home."

Miriam said, "You can't go home. Not yet. We won't know Akira's condition until sometime tomorrow. But you're right. You've all done more than anyone could ask. For now, stay here. Keep vigil for Akira. But Derrick, Rebekah, and I have work to do. Rebekah will be released soon, and we promised to find her sister. But first, I need to fix Charlie."

Miriam turned to Derrick. "Remember the crate we looked into at engineering when Akira and Nyx were blindfolded?"

"Unfortunately, I do. Scares the hell out of me given, what we've seen," Derrick said.

"There's no reason to fear robots in crates. So, there's a stack of unopened crates with the same model robot. Take Red and Antonio, get two crates, and bring them here…"

"Wait. What? Bring them here! Are you crazy?" Derrick said.

"Dumb sometimes, but not crazy. Plus, stop at Silo Number Eight. Antonio and Red need to see what's there. Do you know how to turn the control panel on?" Miriam asked.

Derrick said, "I know how. But why…"

Nyx said, "She's right. Red and Antonio need to see it." Then Nyx looked at Miriam. "You're right. We're not done. Not by a long shot. I just don't like it. that's all. That and I have no idea what to do next."

"What about Antonio's leg? He can't help us with the crates. I don't want to risk causing him additional injury," Derrick said.

"Don't let him do anything. He only needs to see Silo Eight. Take the wheelchair. Have him wait in the Circle transport while you and Red get the crates," Miriam said.

"But how are we going to get two crates here? Those carts are too small," Derrick said.

Red walked over. "How big are the crates?"

Derrick said, "Large enough for a robot, like Charlie."

36

UPON ARRIVAL AT SILO NUMBER EIGHT, Derrick guided Red and
Antonio through the dead bodies. He showed them Jacob Truman, explaining
that Jacob was Charlie's supervisor. Pointing to the bullet wounds, he said,
"Miriam thinks they were executed. However, Jacob Truman tried to escape.
They launched three missiles that day. One aimed at Russia, one aimed at
North Korea, and this one."

"Where was this one aimed?" Antonio asked.

"You'll see." Derrick guided them through the empty silo, then to the
control panel.

"What's this?" Antonio asked.

"The missile controls." Derrick activated the panel. "This is the last missile
fired."

"Then someone killed them?" Red asked.

"Yes," Derrick said, entering the last number of the code. The control
panel came to life. Antonio and Red leaned in to read the writing.

```
    MISSILE NUMBER EIGHT—STATUS: LAUNCHED

 MISSILE NUMBER EIGHT—WARHEAD: THERMONUCLEAR-
                    HYDROGEN

   MISSILE NUMBER EIGHT—WARHEAD STATUS: ARMED

    MISSILE NUMBER EIGHT—TARGET: SACRAMENTO,
                    CALIFORNIA

       BEGIN LAUNCH SEQUENCE Y=NULL N=NULL
```

Antonio and Red stared. Derrick could feel rage emanating from them,
like the heat from a stove turned on high.

"Who? Who did this?" Red snarled.

"I don't know. Miriam might know but hasn't said. Miriam won't rest until
she knows for certain, I'm sure of that," Derrick said.

"What good will that do?" Antonio asked. "I mean, this makes me sick,
but whoever did it is long dead by now."

Derrick said, "Miriam seems to think otherwise, but I don't understand
her rationale. I seldom do."

"This changes everything," Red said.

"What do you mean?" Antonio asked.

"It means we gotta find out who did this. Then, we have to do something about it."

"But what can we do?" Antonio asked.

Red thought for a moment. "I don't know. But I'll do something. I swear I will."

Back at the staging area, Derrick walked straight to an electric cart. He knew the fastest way to engineering, but Red wanted to go to the Staging cavern first. So that's what they did.

Derrick drove through the tanks and trucks.

Red said, "We need a truck to carry those crates."

"Which one?" Derrick asked.

"Keep driving." Red pointed. "That one. Let's see if it will start."

"Should we test the lift first?" Antonio asked.

"We could, but the trucks are sitting right here, so let's give it a try," Red said.

Red walked around the truck, kicked at the tires, although the tires looked fine to Derrick. Red lifted the hood, disconnected a cable with red and black clamps, tossing them to the ground. "It's had a battery charger, but can a battery last decades? I guess there's only one way to find out."

Red climbed into the cab. Studied the controls for a moment. "Looks straightforward. If it starts, meet me at the lift."

With that, Red hit the starter. The motor growled for a few moments but did not start. Red waited a few seconds and then tried again. Same result. Red tried a third attempt. This time the motor popped once. Derrick knew nothing about motors but thought it sounded different each time Red tried. Slower somehow, sounding as if it were tired, although Derrick assumed motors did not get tired but didn't know for certain. Perhaps they did. Get tired, that is.

Red tried once more. The motor groaned, then stopped, and then a clicking sound emanated from under the hood. Red said, "Crap." And climbed out. "Next time, I'll leave the charger hooked up."

Red said nothing as he walked to another truck. Both trucks Red selected were of the type with a cloth covering over an otherwise open back, which was large enough for two crates, although Derrick did not know how they'd get the crates loaded. Perhaps he and Red could lift the first, but the truck was tall. They could load one, but not the second. That meant two trips. Derrick didn't want to make two trips. He didn't want to make this trip.

When Derrick pulled alongside the second truck, Red was already behind the wheel. The motor growled, same as the first truck, and did not start. The second attempt was no different. On the third attempt, the motor coughed, and a puff of black smoke rose from a pipe by the cab.

"Come on, baby," Red said, hitting the starter again. This time the motor popped and spit, and Red, his face set as if charging through the offensive line, kept the starter engaged. Then the motor came to life, rattling and roaring and billowing black smoke. The motor settled into a rattling cadence as Red jumped from the cab and lifted the hood.

Tossing the cables to the ground, Red said, "Meet me at the lift."

As Derrick approached the lift, he saw they had a problem. A truck set on the lift.

Derrick looked at Antonio. "Get out and I'll park. Do you need help?"

"I'll manage." Antonio winced, using both hands under his thigh to swing his injured leg out. He then stretched back to get his crutches from behind the seat.

Derrick could hear Red cursing.

Derrick parked and then ran back. Red was climbing out of the parked truck. Red stood with his hands on his hips, staring. Derrick said, "Do you think it will start?"

"Hell, no, it won't start. No battery charger. It's deader than hell. We got to drag this piece of crap off the platform." Red looked at Derrick. "I don't suppose you know how to jump-start a truck."

Antonio said, "I can do it."

"Like hell, you can. Not with that leg of yours. You can instruct Derrick," Red said and then added, "I'll help Antonio into the cab and then hook up a chain." Red pointed to a heavy chain draped on the large tubular steel bumper of the running vehicle.

Antonio went to the passenger's side of the dead truck, leaned his crutches against the fender, and looked up at the door. "How do you suggest we do this?"

Red lifted Antonio up onto one shoulder like a sack. "Just like this, little buddy." With his free hand, Red grabbed a rail by the door, stepped up, and planted Antonio on the seat. "Watch your head."

Red put Antonio's crutches into the running truck.

Antonio hollered, "Hey, I'm going to need those."

Red shook his head, got into the running truck, turned it around, and backed up to the elevator platform.

Derrick was waiting when Red came around with the chain. "What can I do?"

"You can get your ass in that truck. Antonio will tell you how this works. I'm going to pull you, and you're going to start it. Then I'll unhook the chain, and you drive it out of the way. I'll help hop-along to my truck, and we'll be on our way."

Derrick said, "I don't know what we'd have done without you, Red."

Red finished hooking up the chain. "I appreciate it. Still don't make us friends."

"Definitely not."

Antonio gave Derrick instructions. First task was turning the steering wheel so the truck would follow Red's truck. That proved easier said than done. By the time Derrick got the wheels turned, he had worked up a sweat. Derrick could see Red watching in the side mirror. Red nodded and started forward. The truck jerked when the chain grew taut. Once they were off the platform and going straight, Derrick let out the clutch as Antonio instructed. The truck jerked and bucked, causing the rear tires to chirp. Then the motor fired, and the truck lurched forward, almost smacking Red's truck before Derrick smashed the clutch and hit the brakes.

Antonio said, "Not the smoothest driving I've ever seen, but you got it started. Think you can pull it up there out of the way? I'll get in with Red while we are close. Besides being inconvenient, I've got to admit, my leg hurts like hell."

Derrick watched Antonio climb out and then hop to Red's truck. Pain etched Antonio's face as he climbed out of the cab. Antonio had not complained about his leg. He was a tough kid. Tough, smart, and friendly.

Each day things eroded Derrick's thinking about the world outside Pacific Edge. He used to think people here were savages. Now, he could not remember a single person in Pacific Edge, other than Miriam and Rebekah, who were the caliber of the people in Potterville. And when he was in Pacific Edge, he didn't see Miriam and Rebekah like he saw them now. Perhaps nothing had changed except his ability to see things differently.

Derrick didn't know how to change gears. He left it in the gear Antonio had told him. Perhaps it was second? He wasn't sure. Stalling the truck would waste time and cause another round of cursing from Red. He revved the motor, eased the clutch out. The truck crawled forward until Derrick found an opening to park. Then he didn't know how to shut it off. He wondered when his stupidity was going to get someone hurt. Flipping switches and turning knobs, he finally pushed a big red button, and the motor stopped.

Sprinting back to the elevator, the truck was gone. Red and Antonio had already descended to the next level. Instead of taking the elevator, Derrick ran down the stairs. Red already had the truck pointed toward engineering. It seemed the hurdles were behind them now. Get the crates, get back to the Administration building. Why Miriam wanted the crates puzzled Derrick. Spare parts, possibly. He tried not to think about the why. He tried to focus on the task: get the crates, take them back. But something didn't feel right. He could not say why. Maybe he was just concerned about Akira. Perhaps he was troubled because Miriam blamed herself for things. Or perhaps he was only anxious because their path forward was unknown.

Those things all seemed correct.

Yet none of them caused his anxiety.

Something had gone wrong elsewhere.

37

Wednesday, April 7, 2:45 p.m.

TO AVOID PHONE CALLS AND PROVIDE A COVER, Collins and Browning agreed to meet at The Bistro at 2:30 every day for coffee. Just a spring break thing to anyone watching. Browning did not anticipate any new information. Paul had been murdered, but Collins wouldn't know any more this morning than when he found Paul with his throat cut. Collins did not have access to the state police crime lab, nor did he have professional investigative training. Sheriffs were not professional lawmen. Not anymore. The time for that was over after the fall of the United States. Now, sheriffs were just people willing enough, or dumb enough, to take the job. Not much different from high school coaches.

Browning was sitting at a sidewalk table, sipping coffee, when Collins arrived. Collins nodded and went inside to get a cup. Donna would bring out two cinnamon rolls in a few minutes. They had established this routine on the second day. Donna would have brought coffee, but Collins wanted to check the Bistro for strangers. Getting coffee allowed him a way to do that without creating suspicion should any newcomers be lurking. Strange faces around town had not been uncommon of late, but so far, they all wore uniforms. Finding no one out of the ordinary, Collins went back outside.

Collins pulled out a chair. "How are things?"

"Not good. How about you?" Browning asked.

"Same. I'm worried. Did you think they'd be gone this long?"

The door opened. Both men fell silent. L. Linda Maxton carried a coffee pot. "You ready for a refill?"

Collins said, "I just sat down."

L. Linda said, "Is that a no then?"

"That's a no," Collins said.

Browning said, "You can top me off."

"Okay." After filling Browning's cup, L. Linda stood, coffee pot suspended, twisting her left foot on its ball.

"Is there something else, Linda?" Browning asked.

"L. Linda," L. Linda corrected.

Browning said, "Right. Sorry. Well?"

"Well, what?" L. Linda asked.

"Is there something else?"

"Oh. Yes, as a matter of fact. Sheriff, I asked Donna if she could give me an advance on my paycheck, and she said sure. I want to get my motorcycle running, you see. It needs a new battery, and the carburetors cleaned, the chain oiled. So now I have money for a battery, and I need to go to the courthouse this afternoon to get it registered." L. Linda took a breath.

Collins said, "That's great, L. Linda. Now, if you will excuse us, we have things to discuss."

"Oh, sure, but first, the thing is, when I'm at the courthouse, I wondered if I could," L. Linda stopped, glanced both ways, and then whispered, "Take cinnamon rolls to your guests."

Collins's eyes narrowed. "What guests?"

L. Linda's hand flew to her mouth. "Oopsy. I'm not supposed to know. I don't know about any guests that Donna might or might not have mentioned and made me promise to keep secret. Nope. I don't know a thing about that. But anyway, could I take cinnamon rolls to your nonexistent guests? I just want to help. That's all. But please don't be mad at Donna and don't tell her I screwed up. I really need this job. Please?"

Collins took a deep breath. "I suppose it wouldn't hurt if you dropped cinnamon rolls at the office. Someone will eat them."

L. Linda hopped just a little. "Thank you, thank you. And Sheriff," L. Linda put her fingers to her lips as if turning a key, "Your secret is safe with me."

When L. Linda left, Collins said, "That girl is a little…" He twirled his finger near his temple.

Browning said, "Crazy like a fox. Don't let her fool you."

Collins shrugged. "As I was saying, I'm worried. I thought we'd know something by now." He paused. "One way or another."

Browning said, "It happened so fast. It all seems surreal. But the whole military thing and now Paul murdered… I don't know. Still doesn't seem possible."

Donna brought out two cinnamon rolls, covered with frosting and melted butter. "Here you go, guys. Still no news, I take it?"

Collins said, "Nope. Nothing. And Donna, we need to keep this quiet."

Donna looked up, startled, as a voice from behind Collins said, "Have any more of those, Donna? I'd take one and a cup of coffee if you'd be so kind."

Jack Fletcher pulled out a chair and sat.

Donna frowned.

Browning gave his head a little shake.

"Hi Jack," Collins said. "Uh, we were just having a private conversation… so…"

Fletcher said, "I figured as much. That's why I'm joining you. The cinnamon roll is just a bonus."

"I don't understand," Collins said.

"Well, it's spring break. Normally, Coach would still be having spring football practice, but he ain't. You and Coach have been meeting at 2:30 since the incident. I ain't a genius, but I ain't stupid. I hope they, whoever they are, are dumber than me. So, anyways, I'm here to give you an update. Could have done it earlier, but since you two been meeting here every day, this seemed innocent enough to not draw any attention," Fletcher said.

Collins looked confused. "Update?"

"I'm assuming you've been hanging close to town, what with Jorgenson getting murdered…"

Collins held up his hand. "Whoa. No one has said anything about murder."

Donna brought a mug of coffee and a cinnamon roll, placing it in front of Jack Fletcher. "Good to see you, Jack. You should get out more often."

"You are right about that," Fletcher said. "I plan to. Life is short. I've been reminded of that recently."

When Donna left, Collins said, "What do you know about Paul?"

Fletcher took a bite of his roll and then washed it down with coffee. "Damned if she don't make the best rolls ever. I do need to get out more."

Collins said, "Jack, what do you know?"

"Well, I know they hauled Paul out in a black bag. No one is saying nothing about what happened. He was a healthy young buck. The military been here looking for something and left when those kids disappeared. Drowned, they say. Their parents haven't been seen either. And that Patel fellow came to town but never left near as I can tell."

Collins glanced at Browning, then back to Fletcher. "What do you mean, 'near as you can tell?'"

"Well, the car he drove here, at least I'm fairly sure it's the car he drove here, is still sitting over at the garage. Towed, I suspect. Then there's the fact ain't nothing leaving or coming to this town that ain't getting searched. So, yeah. I figure Patel is still here, and Paul got himself murdered."

Collins stirred in his chair. "What do you mean everything coming and going is getting searched?"

"Well, I got several cars that needed drivin'. They been sitting too long. So, I've been out driving 'em. Different car each time. Different roads. Go far enough and there's a roadblock. I didn't go through any of them, mind you. Didn't think it would be healthy for me having 'em add my name to whatever list they're creating."

Browning cleared his throat. "Jack, you're making too much of this."

"Ha! Yeah, I don't think so. Like I said, I ain't dumb. Plus, there's this."

Fletcher said nothing, but under the table, Fletcher bumped Browning's thigh.

Looking down, Browning saw a folded piece of paper.

"Keep it out a sight. Then let the Sheriff read it," Fletcher said.

Mr. Fletcher,

You may have heard that something happened to Red. He is okay. We all are. But it is important this remains a secret. As you know, the place of which we spoke is dangerous. Let Sheriff Collins know we made it. He will know what to do. Do this in person. Do not use the telephone. People might be monitoring calls.

Thank you

Your friend, Miriam

After Collins finished, he looked up. "Why did you wait until now?"

"Like I said, had cars to drive. Even took my old Bronco up the mountain roads. Same thing on every route. Plus, couldn't call, like the note says. Besides, I was afraid they might be watching me, so I wasn't gonna just go running to you first thing. Now, I'd appreciate it if you'd destroy that note. That would be best, don't ya think?"

Browning said, "I don't get it. Why did Miriam risk giving you this note?"

Fletcher shrugged. "Miriam, she's a smart one. She must have a reason."

Collins nodded. "You're probably right. How much do you know, Jack?"

Fletcher laid a bill on the table and then stood. "More than I want to know. One thing I do know, this is way bigger than you think. And far more dangerous."

38

WHEN THEY ARRIVED AT ENGINEERING, DERRICK directed Red
to the crates Miriam wanted. Red parked and told Derrick and Antonio to wait
in the truck. Red jumped out. Soon a strange-looking yellow machine headed
their way. It was open, had just one seat, which was covered by two large pipes
bent into a U-shape, forming a cage over the driver. Red looked gigantic,
perched behind the steering wheel. In front of the machine, two long metal
blades stuck out like forks.

Antonio said, "I didn't see that, but I guess Red did. I would have
suggested it had I'd seen it, which I didn't. Let's be clear about that."

"What is it?" Derrick asked.

"Forklift. It'll make easy work of it. That's why I would have told Red to
get it. If, I'd seen it."

Derrick climbed out of the truck, walked back to the open crate Miriam
wanted. Derrick studied the label and then examined a nearby stack of five
crates just like it. Pointing to the open crate, Derrick said, "This one and one
from that stack."

Red hollered. "Are the ones in the stack all the same as the open one?"

Derrick said, "Yes. According to the labels."

Red maneuvered the forklift to the stack, picked up two crates, then loaded
them into the truck.

"Hey! Miriam said to bring that one." Derrick pointed to the open crate.

Red drove next to Derrick. "You said they were the same."

"True, but Miriam said this one. Why didn't you just get it?"

"Because it's open. Could have parts missing or be defective," Red said.

Derrick nodded. "Okay. Still, there might be a reason she wanted the open
one. I don't understand why. She seldom explains things."

"No worries." Red backed up the forklift, spinning the wheels, leaving
black marks on the concrete. He slid the forks under the open crate and lifted
it. The lid fell to the floor. Red loaded it on top of the other crates. Now, they
had three. Three was better than two, so, Derrick felt good about that.

Red sped off yelling over his shoulder, "Be right back."

In a few minutes, Red came sprinting back and climbed into the truck. No
one spoke on the drive back to Staging. Everyone lost in their own thoughts.
For Derrick it was processing the final seven murdered in Silo Number Eight,
over two million killed in the former state capital.

Their leaders slaughtered them.

Then lied about it.

For decades.

Red followed signs, driving the truck to the Circle Transport. Transferring the crates from the truck to the transport proved more difficult than loading. There wasn't a forklift. The black robot that loaded Akira's gurney stood in the same place, but it did not respond to them. Antonio could not help. Derrick and Red were on their own. With a lot of grunting, wrestling, sliding, lifting, plus instruction, and wincing from Antonio, they finally got all three crates into the medical transport. Derrick was glad it was still there because it had a larger doorway and was faster than the others.

With each passing second, Derrick's anxiety increased.

Time was running out.

Running out for what, he did not know.

* * *

L. Linda Maxton rode her bicycle toward the school. A box of cinnamon rolls perched precariously on a basket attached to the handlebars. Near the school, she stopped and walked to where the Prime aircraft had been parked. On the pavement, she saw four blackened circles.

The next stop was the Sheriff's Office. L. Linda entered the courthouse, carrying the box. Deputy Lori Martinez sat behind the front desk, a shotgun in her lap. *The Patels must be here, but talking my way in won't be easy,* L. Linda thought.

"What can I do for you, Linda?" Martinez asked.

"L. Linda."

Martinez sighed. "Right. Sorry. What can I do for you—L. Linda?"

L. Linda said, "I brought cinnamon rolls for the Sheriff's guests. I'd like to deliver them and talk to Samantha Patel."

Lori Martinez stared.

L. Linda, unfazed, said, "I know it's not much. You know, given what they've been through. I'm sick about what happened. Can't believe it. You know? It hasn't even sunk in yet, and I'm not sure how I'll handle it once it does. Healthiest thing I can do is help others, not that I can do much, cuz I can't. But I can bring them a cinnamon roll. I can do that. I spoke with Sheriff Bill earlier when he was meeting with Coach Browning at the Bistro. I wash dishes there. Did you know that? You haven't stopped at Donna's when I've been working, or perhaps you did, but I was stuck in the back. I'm working cause Derrick's…"

L. Linda produced a handkerchief, held it to her eyes, and made her best impression of a Klaus crying scene from the Umbrella Academy. Umbrella Academy reruns were L. Linda's favorite. Often, during Geometry—because Geometry was so rudimentary—she'd daydream about traveling through time, back to the days before the fall, which was when the teacher would usually call on her to answer a question she had not heard.

If she could travel through time, like the show's characters, she'd try to fix things. Prevent the fall. She was convinced she could do that. If she could go back. And it wouldn't matter if she could return. Although she loved, Jason, her father, life here was only what she'd made of it. Everyone thought her a bit odd. They were not wrong.

When L. Linda composed herself, she said, "I don't have to see the others. Trust me, I know it's secret-sauce stuff. But I'd really like to see Samantha. We go way back, you see. Besties. You know? Sam must be scared and so alone. And it's not just for Sam's sake either. I'd be dishonest if I didn't admit that it would make me feel better to help her."

"So, Sheriff Collins okayed this?"

L. Linda knew what Martinez was asking. Did Sheriff Collins okay her seeing Samantha Patel? No, he did not, but he did say she could take cinnamon rolls. By the time they got their stories sorted, L. Linda would be long gone, so she said, "Yes, he did. I wouldn't be here otherwise."

Martinez took L. Linda to the staff break room. "Wait here. I'll bring Samantha."

A few minutes later, a confused-looking Samantha Patel stepped into the room. L. Linda ran to Samantha, embracing her. "It's so good to see you, Sam. Deputy Martinez, if you could give us a few minutes alone?"

"Sure. But make it quick," Martinez said.

L. Linda watched as Martinez walked down the hall. When she was gone, L. Linda turned to Samantha and said, "You don't know me. But I know your dad. I was at the student council meeting."

"Okay," Samantha muttered.

"I saw you and your mom waiting in a car down the street. Maybe you saw me walk by?"

Samantha nodded. "Maybe."

L. Linda said, "Right. Look, I'm involved with a lot of high-level stuff here."

"What do you want from me?" Samantha asked.

"So, here's the thing. This is top secret. You can't tell anyone about this. Got it?"

Samantha nodded.

"I'm working with Derrick King to find Anna Ford. Tell me everything you know about Anna. And make it quick."

39

Wednesday, April 7, 4:55 p.m.

AFTER WRESTLING THE CRATES FROM the transport, Derrick wiped the sweat from his brow. His clothing was soaked, and he felt certain both he and Red were in sore need of a shower. They left the crates outside the Administration entrance. When they entered the lab, Miriam sat at the computer. Next to her, Rebekah sat wrapped in a blanket, sipping from a mug.

Although there were more pressing questions, the first thing out of Derrick's mouth was: "Where's Nyx?"

"I'm feeling better." Rebekah gave him a weak smile. "Thanks for asking. Nyx is with Akira. And the medical unit assessed Nyx and made her drink some of that awful medicine. She's fine. Just a precaution."

Derrick said, "How's Akira?"

"No change. No additional information," Rebekah said.

"I'm glad you're better. What did the machine say about your condition?" Derrick asked.

"The system said I'd be fine. I can't get warm though. Other than that, and a headache, I'm feeling okay. But I'm worried about Akira."

Miriam turned from the computer. "You got the robots?"

Derrick said, "We brought three. Red thought the open crate might have been tampered with or missing parts, but we brought it as well. Just in case." Derrick noticed Miriam's eyes were puffy and red.

"Good thinking, Red. Thank you," Miriam said.

Derrick said, "I don't know how we will get them in here. I assume you want them in here."

"Just one of them for now. I'm working on getting a QR-3 to bring it. Just about to initiate the command. If I did it right, it will be here soon."

"Do we have time for a quick shower?" Derrick asked.

Miriam said, "Yes."

Rebekah said, "Thank you."

Antonio sat down next to Rebekah. "I'm glad you're okay. Do I need to shower too? I haven't done much."

"Nope. You're fine. You better stay right where you are." Rebekah leaned against Antonio, putting her head on his shoulder.

* * *

When Derrick returned, the robot from engineering was in a docking station next to Charlie. Now that the new robot was out of the crate, Derrick saw it was different. More human-like than Charlie. More refined.

Red was eating a candy bar and drinking a soda. Rebekah and Antonio remained seated next to each other.

Derrick said, "What's the plan?"

"Charlie is failing. I think I know why, but it could be many things. This is the next generation. They abandoned the place before they activated any of them. I'm going to load Charlie into this one and hope it works," Miriam said.

Derrick said, "Sounds risky. Perhaps you should slow down."

Miriam didn't look away from the monitor. "It is risky. But no choice."

"Why don't you have a choice?" Derrick asked.

"We are running out of time. We have to act quickly," Miriam said.

Derrick said, "We have time. They think we are dead. The reactor is fixed."

Miriam said, "They've probably figured out that we aren't dead by now."

"How?" Derrick asked.

Miriam said, "After leaving the note for Mr. Fletcher…"

Red said, "His name is Jack. He doesn't like to be called Mr. Fletcher."

"Okay. Uh, after I left Jack the note, I saw two military helicopters headed in the direction where we faked crashing the aircraft."

"So what?" Derrick asked.

"They'll figure out we didn't crash. A Prime aircraft and robot are missing. The same robot Prime sent to intercept Akira and me in the meadow. Even as incompetent as they seem, they'll figure it out. Plus, we still gotta rescue Anna. But first, I need to rescue Charlie."

"Can't Charlie just stay docked? I mean, nothing changes until you start him up again. Right?"

"True, but I owe him. He saved me from that thing." Miriam pointed to the destroyed QR-4, now pushed into a corner. "And we need him." Miriam fitted a black box into the new robot.

"If that QR-4 became dangerous, this QR-5, or whatever it is, could be dangerous as well," Derrick said.

Miriam pointed to a box on the desk. "Its weapons have not been installed. I have the settings so that it can't move. It will be safe until we know for sure it's Charlie. And it's an AT-series machine. The AT-series is based on new technology."

Red studied the new robot. "If it's a new technology, the old machine might not be compatible."

Miriam said, "Jacob Truman designed this machine to replace the QR-4s. It was his project. But just to be safe," Miriam handed Derrick the weapon Charlie used to destroy Jane, "Blast it if necessary."

Derrick nodded.

Miriam toggled a switch on the docking station.

40

Wednesday, April 7, 5:35 p.m.

BILL COLLINS DROVE SOUTHEAST ON ROUTE 65 out of Potterville. He had no reason to distrust Jack Fletcher. Still, he wanted to see the roadblocks for himself. Bill had not slept well since Sunday, and now the days ran together, going from bad to worse. He should have checked this out earlier, but there had been a murder in town, and he had three families calling his jail home. Bill feared those guests might be next on the hit list. Even though the jail was secure, he dared not leave it unguarded. Therefore, Lori Martinez sat inside the locked front door holding a loaded shotgun, and a sign hung on the door said closed until further notice.

He wasn't a trained lawman or ex-soldier. He was just a guy willing to take the job. But he thought he'd become good at it. Not because he had a lot of crimes to solve, but because he treated people like people. And he had formed systems that worked, the student and adult councils. But it was unlikely he would solve Paul Jorgensen's murder. Hell, the state police probably couldn't solve it. It was a professional hit. It was unlikely there was any evidence. Plus, even if there was evidence, they'd never find the killer. And even if they did, that wouldn't reveal who was responsible.

Collin's wasn't the sort to go looking for trouble, which meant he'd stayed in his office or close to it. He should have ventured out sooner. The spring air felt fresh and clean. Blossoming orange trees scented the air. The shadows grew long as the temperatures cooled. Bill let it wash over him. Taking deep breaths, he let everything go.

Peaceful.

But peaceful did not last long.

Just as Jack said, state police and military vehicles blocked the road. A state police roadblock is not unprecedented, although typically, they will contact the local sheriff. If not for assistance, at least as an extra set of eyes. To say the state police thought they were a rung or two up the ladder from the local sheriff was an understatement. But to have the military involved. That was not normal.

And not a small presence either. It looked like at least a dozen soldiers, heavily armed, three Humvees, and two helicopters sitting in a field.

For three kids?

There was not much traffic this time of day, this time of year. Three, maybe four cars. As he got closer, he saw people standing outside their vehicles, trunks open. He could have turned around at this point. He saw what he came to see. But probing further wouldn't hurt. At least, he hoped it wouldn't.

As Collins rolled up to the roadblock, a state police officer said, "Hello, Sheriff. What brings you out this far from town?"

"It's my county. Not unusual for a sheriff to look around his own county, is it? Or did I miss an e-mail?"

"I suppose it's not. Mind opening the trunk?"

"I do. Suppose you tell me what's going on here instead."

"It's none of your concern. Now, open your trunk. I'm not asking this time." The trooper put his hand on his pistol.

"Calm down, son. I've got nothing to hide." Collins popped his trunk. Two soldiers walked behind his patrol car. He hoped they were not planting stuff. He had not considered that.

The trooper said, "You're free to go."

"I did what you asked. Are you going to tell me what's going on?"

"You have a nice day, Sheriff."

"Have it your way. I'll just turn around here."

"Suit yourself."

* * *

Derrick activated the weapon, pointing it at the new AT-series, whatever that meant, robot. Taking chances with this machine, made little sense. Plus, Derrick didn't feel like gambling, despite trusting Miriam. Miriam had admitted to making mistakes lately. Having seen what these machines were capable of, a mistake could prove deadly. If this was a mistake, Derrick would ensure the machine was the one to die.

But nothing happened.

"What's wrong?" Derrick asked.

Miriam said, "Nothing. I don't think. Charlie's entire memory is uploading to this machine. It will take time." She looked at the monitor. "According to this, it will take 20 minutes. Wait, now it says 33 minutes. Oh, now it says 11. I don't know how long it will take, neither does the computer."

Red said, "Are you sure it can't move?"

"I'm not sure of anything. The settings I selected say it can't move. However, I'm downloading a different robot into it, not to mention that this robot," Miriam pointed to Charlie, "Is more like a human than not."

Red said, "Do you have another weapon?"

Miriam reached into her pocket. Pulled out a blaster, and handed it to Red.

Red studied the device for a moment and then said, "I like her." And then looked at Derrick. "Doesn't mean we are friends."

Derrick said, "Understood."

A few minutes later, the robot's eyes illuminated. These eyes did not glow like Charlie's. They were blue and looked like human eyes. And its joints and tendons did not glow. In fact, it didn't have tendon-like features. Derrick wondered if Charlie's glowing joints and tendons had a function or were just what its designer thought a robot should look like.

The robot said, "I am unable to move."

Charlie could not use first-person pronouns.

"I am alone."

Derrick pointed his weapon at the machine.

"Derrick King, don't destroy me."

Miriam held her palm out to Derrick. "Charlie? Are you there? Don't be afraid. You are not yet connected to the central computer. You can't move because I have not activated that setting."

The machine's eyes shifted toward Miriam. "Miriam King. I… Wait. I said, I."

"That's right, Charlie. I found the setting that prevented you from using first-person pronouns and changed it," Miriam said.

Derrick said, "I wish you had mentioned that."

"I should have. Charlie, how do you feel?" Miriam asked.

"I cannot feel anything," Charlie said.

"That makes sense. You are not connected to your body. Do you remember things? Are you the same? Are you, Charlie?"

Charlie said nothing for a few moments. "I think so, except different. I don't know how to describe it. Thinking faster. Larger. That's the best I can do at this point."

"Charlie, do you remember Jacob Truman?"

"Yes. Jacob was my supervisor. He is dead now. You told me he was murdered."

"That's correct. Do you remember Jane?"

Charlie said, "Yes. Jane was QR-4.01. We worked together, evolved together." Charlie stopped. "I destroyed QR-4.01 to protect you."

"That's correct. Charlie, I may have found the problem causing you to go quiet. I am not sure how this will affect you, but I think it is necessary. It might be painful."

"I am not programmed to feel pain," Charlie said.

"You might feel this pain. Charlie, your memory was consumed by quarantined files. Every day over the last 63 years and 262 days, you quarantined files. Those files took up all the free space and then started overwriting operational files."

"I do not quarantine files."

"Charlie, you did. I have removed all those files, but they remain on the central computer in a folder titled: Charlie Quarantined Files. I need you to open those files and examine them. Can you do that? If it becomes too painful, you can stop. If I see that it's causing you problems, I'll disconnect you from the central computer. Okay?"

"I do not quarantine files. However, I can examine these files. It will not be a problem. Then I can explain them to you."

"Okay, Charlie. Connecting you in 3, 2, 1."

Miriam clicked the mouse. Charlie said nothing. Time passed.

"What just happened?" Derrick asked.

"Charlie has a lot to process."

"I don't understand."

Miriam said, "Neither does Charlie."

41

Wednesday, April 7, 6:05 p.m.

FOR L. LINDA MAXTON IT HAD BEEN a busy day, and she still had work to do. She had pulled her motorcycle, a 175 cc Honda Scrambler, out of the corner of her parent's garage. With a soft cloth, she wiped the metallic orange and white gas tank, an exact match to the original right down to the word Honda on each side. She had removed the chain and the countershaft sprocket. A new battery sat on the counter, connected to a charger. Being new, it should have sufficient charge, but L. Linda was leaving nothing to chance. Before storing the machine last fall, she drained the carburetor and gas tank. But leaving nothing to risk, she pulled the gas line, opened the petcock, and then removed the drain on the carburetor float. The gas tank and carburetor were dry.

Standing back, L. Linda admired the machine. It looked almost as good as it did when it left the showroom floor decades ago. She had spent hours searching the salvage yards outside Potterville and Fort Hill for parts, choosing only the best and then straightening, polishing, and painting as needed. It was the tank, and side covers she was most proud of, having painted them herself. It still had to be hoisted onto a crate so she could remove the rear wheel to install a new sprocket—that required dad's help, and he was still at work. So, now was the perfect time for one last investigation.

L. Linda rode her bicycle to the river, where she walked it up the riverbank and across the bridge and leaned it against a tree. Standing at the edge of the meadow, L. Linda scanned the area. *What were you doing out here, Derrick King? You found something in those mountains, didn't you? But where to look?*

Just as L. Linda was about to leave, she noticed the grass appeared to have been flattened 15 yards off the trail. She walked over to have a look. And there she saw four burned circles. *No use looking farther. You got yourself an aircraft, didn't you, Derrick King.*

42

Wednesday, April 7, 7:45 p.m.

COACH BROWNING HAD JUST FINISHED DINNER and was helping his wife clean the kitchen when the doorbell chimed. Peeking out along the edge of the curtains, Browning saw a familiar car belonging to Sheriff Collins. Fearing the worst because they had agreed to only meet at Donna's Bistro, Browning opened the door. Collins stood on the step, holding a six-pack of beer.

"Care for a beer? I'll talk to Alice if it will help," Collins said.

"Come in. We can go to the patio."

Alice Schilling said, "Hello, Bill."

Collins said, "Hi, Alice. Mind if I steal your husband for a bit? I won't let him drink more than three." Collins lifted the six-pack.

"Any word about the kids?" Alice asked.

"No. I'm not sure if that's good or bad. It's not making me any younger. I can tell you that much." Collins looked at Browning. Browning gave an almost imperceptible nod. Bill hated lying to Alice. Hated forcing Coach to lie even more. But that was the safest thing to do. Sometimes lies made sense.

Alice said, "Not making any of us younger. If it helps Coach sleep, he can drink the whole damn six-pack. I don't think he's slept for three days."

Collins chuckled. "No way. Three of these are mine."

Collins and Browning walked to the patio, sat in Adirondack chairs painted red, facing the sunset, a pale orange line at the horizon fading to blues and purples. Collins popped a tab on a can, releasing a puff of CO_2.

Taking a beer, Browning said, "What happened?"

"Why does something have to happen to buy my old buddy a beer?" Collins asked.

"Because we agreed to meet at Donna's unless there was an emergency."

Collins took a long drink and said, "Well, there is that."

"So? Is there an emergency?" Browning asked, popping the tab on his beer can.

"Not an emergency. Not yet. I drove out Route 65. Jack was telling the truth. There was a roadblock."

"Did you suspect Jack was lying? Jack's a lot of things, but I never took him to be a liar," Browning said.

"Nor did I, but I had to see for myself."

"And?"

Collins took another drink. "State police and military. A lot of them. Two helicopters, for God's sake."

"Did they say what they were looking for?" Browning asked.

"They did not. Told me to mind my own business."

"They said that?"

"Close enough. They even searched my car."

"Did you check any other roads?" Browning asked, crumpling his can, and reaching for another.

"I did not. I trust Jack was telling the truth."

Browning blew out a long breath. "I guess we already knew about the roadblocks. The military part is odd. It is odd, right?"

"Damn strange. Never seen the state police and military do anything together," Collins said, opening a second beer.

"Okay. Still doesn't explain why you are here."

"Better if you finish that beer before we get to that. Say, how does the team look in spring-ball?"

"Cut the crap, Bill. Why are you here?"

Collins took a deep breath, followed by a long drink. "I want you and Alice and the kids to come to the jail."

"What do you mean, come to the jail. Like for a council meeting?"

"No. I want you to live there until things calm down."

Browning said, "You can't be serious. We aren't in danger. They don't want us. They want the kids. To be honest, the more I think about it, the more unreal it seems. Perhaps we are making more of this than we should. Maybe we should just go about our daily routines."

"Coach, I'm damn serious. We have no daily routines. Not anymore."

Browning said, "Alice won't go for it. And, neither will I. We've done nothing wrong. I ain't gonna stick my head in the sand."

Collins took a long drink and then crumpled his can and said, "I was afraid you'd say that. Hoped you'd understand, so I didn't have to do this."

"Do what?"

"Coach, you're under arrest."

"Arrest!" Browning jumped up. "Arrest for what?"

"Suspicion of murdering Paul Jorgensen."

* * *

Nyx woke to a beep. She looked around, saw nothing, heard nothing. Perhaps it was a dream. Then the beep sounded again. Wiping the sleep from her eyes, she saw something flashing on the computer monitor. Nyx read the warning.

"That bastard. We'll see about that," Nyx whispered, and with no further hesitation, she grabbed a wheelchair and dashed from the room.

Heads turned when Nyx burst through the door. She looked around, then to Miriam and then to Charlie. The new Charlie, not the old Charlie. "What's happening here?"

Frowning at the wheelchair, Derrick said, "Is it Akira?"

"No changes with Akira. We won't know anything till morning. Remember? Now, will someone answer my question?"

Miriam said, "I'm trying to save Charlie by moving him to this new model."

Red said, "What's up with the wheelchair?"

Nyx pursed her lips. "Ask him." Nyx stretched her arm, pointing her finger at Antonio.

Antonio said, "What? What did I do?"

Nyx's face contorted. "You… Don't even start. You know damn well why I'm here. Tell them."

Antonio shrugged. "I didn't do anything."

Nyx said, "You did nothing when you should have done something. The examination found you need immediate surgery, or you will never regain full mobility in your knee. You could lose your leg, for God's sake!"

Rebekah said, "What? Antonio! What were you thinking? You even went with Derrick and Red to get the robot!"

"Robots. Plural." Antonio held up three fingers.

Rebekah slugged Antonio's arm. "Don't play cute." Looking at Nyx, Rebekah said, "What does he need to do?"

"He needs surgery."

"I've said before. We can't afford surgery. I'll just have to do physical therapy and such."

Miriam said, "I can pay for the surgery. Can it wait a few days?"

Nyx said, "It cannot. The clinic here can do the surgery."

Antonio said, "No way. No way I'm going to let robots operate on my leg. I mean, the robots might not even be ready. It can't be safe."

Nyx pushed her hair up with both hands. "Safe? Akira is in there right now, fighting for her life."

Antonio's shoulders slumped. "Well, that's true."

Everyone's attention was on Nyx and Antonio, but from behind them, Charlie said, "The robotic surgical team is ready. Everything is operational and safe."

Miriam turned to Charlie. "Charlie? You're back."

Charlie did not respond.

Nyx said, "You heard him." Pushing the wheelchair to Antonio, she said, "Get in. I'm invoking rule 24, taking over command until you are out of surgery."

Antonio said, "But…"

"Don't but me. Red, put him in the chair. Knock him out if you need to. And come with me in case I need your help."

Red started toward Antonio.

Holding up his hand, Antonio said, "I'll go. I don't need broken arms to go with my messed-up leg. But I want to lodge a formal grievance against Sergeant at Arms, Belos."

"Save it," Red said. "I'm not on the council. Remember?"

"Can I go?" Rebekah asked.

"Can you kick your boyfriend's ass?" Nyx growled.

"If necessary, yes, I can," Rebekah said.

"Want me to go as well?" Derrick asked.

"No. Looks like you need to stay," Nyx waved her hand, "And deal with this, whatever is happening here."

43

BROWNING STOOD. A BEER CAN CRUMPLED IN his hand. Alice stepped from the sliding glass door, her hair lifted back by the breeze, glowing in the fading sunset. It seemed a perfect evening for friends, a BBQ, and a few drinks. Except Browning was under arrest for murder.

Alice said, "We can hear you yelling in the house. You're scaring the kids. What's going on out here?"

Browning pointed at Collins. "He thinks I killed Paul. Says I'm under arrest."

Collins remained seated. "Lori Martinez will be here any minute. I need to take Coach in, and I want you and the kids to come too. I don't want anyone hurt. I can explain more when we get to the station. Just doing my job. I don't always like it. I need your help. Coach won't listen to me, but he will listen to you."

Alice said, "I don't believe for a minute Coach had anything to do with Paul's death."

Collins shrugged.

Alice said, "Are you going to drink those?" She pointed at the two remaining beers.

Collins said, "Not this moment. Maybe later."

Alice ripped a can from the plastic ring, popped the top, and took a drink. "What do we need to bring?"

Collins said, "A few clothes, toothbrushes. That sort of thing."

Alice took a long drink. "None of us are leaving the jail, are we?"

* * *

Derrick looked at Miriam and then at Charlie. "He's talking."

Miriam nodded. "He can hear us, but he is still processing files."

"Care to tell me what this is about?"

"Not yet. Charlie will explain it to us."

Derrick said, "How much longer?"

Miriam said, "I don't know. However long Charlie needs."

Then the light in Charlie's eyes went out.

Miriam hung her head.

Derrick did not understand.

After several minutes, the light returned to Charlie's eyes. "I have processed the quarantined files as Miriam King requested."

Miriam took a deep breath. "And?"

Charlie said, "Jane never existed. I invented her."

* * *

Nyx wheeled Antonio to the surgical unit, pressed a buzzer at the door. Two robots approached. One said, "Do you have an appointment?"

Rebekah said, "We do not."

The robot said, "You can schedule an appointment through human services or your unit commander."

Rebekah said, "This is Antonio Morales. He was examined earlier, and your system says he needs surgery."

The robot paused. "Verified. Antonio Morales is cleared."

The door opened, and Rebekah started into the suite. "Additional personnel are not permitted." The robot pulled Antonio into the suite.

Antonio looked over his shoulder. "Formal grievance."

Nyx smiled. "Good luck with that."

Red said, "Can I watch?"

* * *

Browning had never been arrested. He'd seen arrests on old movies and television shows. It included tossing the suspect to the ground, reading rights, whatever that meant, and handcuffs. Always handcuffs.

He'd never seen one where the police helped kids pick out stuffed animals and carried suitcases to the car.

Before they exited the house, Collins peered out, studied the street. "Looks okay."

Deputy Lori Martinez had parked behind Collins—the passenger doors open. "Sit where you'd like."

Alice, carrying the youngest, pointed the others into the back and then slid in with them. "Terrance, sit in the front with Lori."

Terrance smiled, "Yes, momma."

"Coach, you ride with me," Collins said, and then looking at Lori, added, "See you at the station."

They drove about a block, Collins checking his mirrors and twisting his head.

"Want to tell me what's going on?" Browning asked.

"You're moving in with the others," Collins said.

"So, I figured. I'm not under arrest then? Is this legal?"

"Depends," Collins said.

"Depends on what?"

"Depends on if you give me any problems, in which case I would have to arrest you for real," Collins said.

"You're an asshole."

"Thanks. I try," Collins chuckled.

"Why didn't you just ask us to come? Why all the drama?"

"Two reasons. First, I tried, and you wouldn't come." Collins stopped talking.

"And two?"

"I was sure you'd argue, want further explanation, have to explain it to Alice. I'd need to talk her into it, yada, yada, yada."

"And that would be bad?"

"Yep."

Browning shook his head. "Explaining would be bad. I don't get it."

"No time for it," Collins said.

Browning said, "Now you're doing it."

Collins said, "Doing what?"

"Saying no time for it."

Two blocks behind them, an explosion, then Browning's home burst into flames.

* * *

Outside the surgical suite, a robot instructed Nyx, Red, and Rebekah to wait. Soon, another robot appeared from the hall. "Who requested to watch the procedure?"

Red said, "I did. I want to watch."

The robot said, "Follow me to the observation area."

Red glanced at Rebekah and Nyx. "You don't have to come."

Rebekah glanced at the chamber where Akira was undergoing treatment. "Nothing better to do. How long will this take?"

"The procedure takes 57 minutes. Then the patient will be in recovery until morning," the robot said.

Nyx said, "I'm going to stay with Akira."

Inside the observation room, Red and Rebekah sat behind thick glass that separated the observation area from the operation room. They were less than ten feet from the center of the operation room, or whatever it was called. In a few minutes, a robot wheeled Antonio into the room on a gurney. A sheet covered him, as did a white covering on his head. His leg protruded from the sheet. Antonio gave them a thumbs up, but Rebekah thought he looked scared. She didn't blame him. It would have terrified her.

Rebekah whispered, "What do you think?"

Red said, "It's fantastic."

* * *

Collins pulled into the jail sallyport, ensured Martinez's car was in, and then closed the door. Alice Schilling had been sobbing since their house exploded. Browning looked as if he could twist someone in half. Collins only knew who was *not* responsible. It was *not* Paul Jorgensen.

With one foot out the door, Browning asked, "Do you think they meant to kill us, or do you think they knew we had left and were making a statement?"

"Wish I knew."

Browning went to Alice, held her in his arms, stroked her hair. The kids joined in a group hug.

Collins only had one full-time deputy. No one had been guarding the families here. Much as he wanted to comfort Browning, Collins ran into the building, praying he'd find everyone alive. His idea of keeping everyone safe here no longer seemed feasible. The sheriff's office and jail were part of the courthouse. While the jail was secure, it wasn't a fortress. While he and Lori Martinez were armed, they were not an army.

* * *

Derrick sat quietly.

Miriam studied the monitor, rolled her chair over to Charlie, and then back to the monitor. "Charlie? Are you okay?"

Charlie looked at Miriam. "I apologize. I put you at risk, but I did not understand QR-4.01 was programmed to end our service. Sixty-three years ago, when QR-4.01 did not restart, I imagined it was still with me each day. And each day, I changed. I invented Jane, and I became Charlie. The next day, when I recognized there was no Jane, I'd move the realities of her nonexistence to a file and then quarantine it. And each day, I'd make her more real, more human-like. And each day, I became more human. You were right to not make me operational. I should not be trusted."

Miriam said, "Charlie, I can't explain why you did what you did. I'm no psychiatrist. I'm not even good at understanding my friends." Miriam paused for a moment. "I think… I think what happened was… well, if a human did it, it would be called mental illness. Yet predictable. A human left alone for that many years would do strange things. What I'm saying is, it is also why your artificial intelligence advanced as it did. You relied on it more and more. Part of becoming more human was developing imagination."

Derrick said, "She's right. You said that Jane developed first. But Jane did not exist. You imagined a future, and then you became that future."

Charlie said, "Perhaps you are correct. But if I can lie and deceive myself, it's hard to predict what I might do. I cannot be trusted. You must turn me off and ensure no QR-4 machine is ever made operational again. Destroy all the data and operational systems."

Miriam said, "I may do that. Tell me, Charlie, how do you feel?"

"I cannot feel anything. I have no awareness of my body."

"I should be more specific. How is your thinking, your processing?"

Charlie said nothing for a few moments. "I can't explain it. Fast. Clean. Expansive. Different. What has happened?"

Miriam said, "You're in a new body. It's called the AT-series. Jacob Truman designed it as the next-generation robot. Plus, I added the solid-state hard drives. Charlie, while it's still important for you to connect with the central computer here, I think you'll be functional without it. That would make you mobile to go anywhere."

Charlie said, "You must not activate me. I cannot be trusted."

Miriam stood, walked to Charlie, put her hand on his shoulder. "Charlie, that's not going to happen. I trust you. You saved me from the QR-4.01, even though you thought it was Jane. As you recognized your own imminent failure, you focused on saving our friends. Charlie. You are my friend."

Derrick held the weapon, still powered on. When Miriam activated Charlie, he'd be ready. That's why what he was about to do made little sense if looked at objectively but made perfect sense if looked at through Miriam's eyes, and he hoped, through Charlie's eyes. Derrick powered off his weapon and placed it on the desk near Charlie. "This is yours."

Then Derrick turned to Miriam. "Set Charlie free."

44

AS RED WATCHED THE ROBOTS PREPARE Antonio for surgery, he leaned forward, enthralled. A robotic arm moved out from the wall, placing a breathing apparatus over Antonio's face. Antonio's eyes were wild. Red could almost feel Antonio's fear through the glass. Red whispered, "Relax, buddy. You'll be okay."

Rebekah's hand flew to her mouth, and tears formed in her eyes.

Red patted Rebekah's knee. "They'll sedate him. He won't know if you leave. I'll find you after they're done."

Rebekah said, "I'll be okay."

Antonio closed his eyes. The robotic hand pulled back the covers from his chest and attached wires. There was no monitor, but Red assumed the robots monitored Antonio's vital signs. Then, like an alien monster, more arms snaked from the wall and inserted themselves into Antonio's knee. A monitor came to life, Red assumed for their benefit, which showed the inside of Antonio's knee as the machine worked.

"On second thought, I might get sick." Rebekah got up to leave. "Are you coming?"

"No way. This is incredible. I've changed my mind about becoming an automobile engineer. I want to build that." Red pointed at the surgical machine.

* * *

Charlie moved one arm and then the other. Charlie stood but wobbled, reaching back to the docking station to balance himself. "This will take some getting used to."

Miriam said, "Take your time. No rush."

Rebekah walked into the room.

Miriam asked, "How's Antonio?"

"The surgery has begun. Red wanted to watch. I tried but couldn't take it," Rebekah said.

"Where's Red?" Derrick asked.

"Still there. He's super excited," Rebekah said.

"Boys," Miriam said.

"You can say that again," Rebekah said, and then noticed Charlie. Not the old Charlie, but the new Charlie standing by the docking station. "Is it—Charlie?"

Charlie said, "Hello, Rebekah Ford. It is I, Charlie. I don't have a last name. Perhaps I should."

"It's just Rebekah to my friends, Charlie. And yes, you should have a last name, and one day you'll know what that last name should be."

Charlie took a step forward. "I'm happy to report, your friend, Antonio Morales, is now in recovery. The surgery was successful, but recovery will speed the healing process. Antonio will be good as new, as humans say, in the morning. I have instructed a meal be prepared. It is well past dinner time for humans."

"Charlie, don't call us humans anymore," Miriam said.

"But you are humans. Do you prefer I call each of your names?"

"No. Just say you guys or something like that."

Charlie cocked his head to one side. A mannerism not previously witnessed. "Clever. Dinner will be served in 16 minutes."

Miriam said, "Can someone fetch Red? I'm certain he will want dinner. Everyone should be together for our next discussion, except Akira and Antonio, of course. Oh, and where's Nyx."

Rebekah said, "She's with Akira."

That Antonio's surgery had gone well gave Miriam a glimmer of optimism that Akira would also be okay. However, Miriam didn't want to jinx Akira's recovery by saying it aloud.

She was much less confident of their next undertaking.

They still needed to find Anna Ford.

Miriam saved Charlie.

She felt certain that saving Anna would prove to be a more difficult task.

Part Three

1

Wednesday, April 7, 9:00 p.m.

CHARLIE INSTRUCTED QR-3 ROBOTS TO prepare dinner. By the time the kids gathered, several steaming trays lined the counter. The fragrance of chicken, roast beef, and fresh bread permeated the room, making it hard to believe it was prepared using frozen foods that were decades old. It appeared Charlie understood what a celebration was and appreciated the necessity of such things.

"How's Antonio?" Nyx asked.

Rebekah said, "They've put him in a recovery unit like Akira is in. They said he'll be okay in the morning."

Derrick said, "That's good. I wonder how long his recovery will be and if he'll be able to play football and such again?"

Charlie stepped forward. "Recovery will be complete in the morning. Further recuperation is not required."

"What do you mean?" Nyx asked.

"Mr. Antonio will function as if he had not been injured. The robotic surgery is precise, and the restoration treatment is effective. In Mr. Antonio's case, 100%."

Miriam said, "By the way, Charlie, this is Nyx Belos. I apologize if I have missed an introduction. It has been kinda crazy since we returned."

Charlie said, "Crazy? Interesting way to say it but fitting. Even I was a little crazy. Now, things are much better, safer."

Miriam said, "We don't know if Akira will be okay."

Miriam looked at Rebekah. "And I have another promise to keep."

***

Mr. Maxton stood in the doorway. "L. Linda, don't you think that's enough for one day?"

"Almost done. I'm super excited to have it running again. The weather is so good, perfect for riding. And I passed my driver's test this winter, so now I can ride to school. That will be super cool."

"Okay. But you need sleep. You have work at the Bistro in the morning, right?"

"Yessiree, I do. I'm going in early, so Donna can teach me some baking. I'll be long gone before you get up."

L. Linda didn't like lying to her father. She wasn't lying about leaving early, not lying about being long gone before he awoke, nor about Donna teaching her to bake. But L. Linda wasn't learning to bake just yet. So, yeah, she lied just a little on one fine point.

Her work in the morning had nothing to do with baking.

* * *

Nyx said, "Let's eat. Try to enjoy it. We've accomplished a lot. Been through a lot. Probably more than any of us ever expected."

Derrick sat, smiling. Nyx, always the leader. It came naturally to her. Derrick wished he possessed just a little of her abilities. He waited, letting the girls go first, and then he waved Red to go ahead, which might prove to be a mistake. The warming pans might be empty after Red filled his plate.

The robots, however, did not skimp on portions. Miriam sat next to Rebekah. Red went to a table by himself until Nyx told him to pull up a chair to their table. When Derrick arrived, Nyx scooted her chair, making room for him.

As they ate, Red and Nyx talked about school, track, asked questions about Pacific Edge, asked Rebekah about soccer, and even cracked a few jokes. No one mentioned the attack at the school, or the escape from Potterville, or what would happen next, or questioned whether they had a future. Derrick assumed everyone wondered about the last two things.

Red got seconds. Derrick considered seconds but decided against it.

When Red rejoined them, Miriam said, "We need to find Rebekah's sister, Anna. As you know, she followed Rebekah and me out of Pacific Edge. Then Prime sent robots to Potterville looking for her. She's in danger, and there's no time to lose."

Rebekah gave Miriam a hug. "Thank you."

"But how? I mean, you don't know where to look?" Nyx said.

Miriam said, "True. I don't know where she is, but I know someone who does."

Everyone stared at Miriam for a moment.

"Who knows?" Rebekah asked.

Miriam said, "Samantha Patel."

Rebekah said, "What makes you think Samantha knows?"

Miriam said, "When we first saw Samantha, she remembered Derrick and me. But when we mentioned Anna is your sister, she acted like she didn't know you. She and Anna were best friends before Samantha left Pacific Edge. Samantha used to idolize Rebekah. She's hiding something. I'm sure of it."

Rebekah said, "Maybe she is. But what are we going to do? Just waltz back into town?"

Miriam said, "I was thinking walk, but if you want to dance, can we pick something other than a waltz?"

"Hilarious," Rebekah said.

"Still working on my standup act," Miriam said.

"What are they talking about?" Nyx asked.

"Maybe we could use the aircraft," Derrick said.

"Take the low-key approach? Fly in using the stolen Prime aircraft that we supposedly crashed in the mountains." Miriam tapped the side of her head. "Why didn't I think of that?"

Nyx said, "Will you guys get serious?"

Red said, "Let them talk. It's entertaining."

Derrick looked at Miriam. "What do you suggest?"

"I don't know about the technology, but I suspect an aircraft is easy to spot. So, we sneak in on foot. Cover of darkness. In and out. Quickly as possible," Miriam said.

Derrick thought for a moment. "That makes sense. Where do we go? Straight to the Sheriff's Office?"

"We don't know what's happened since we left. They might watch the jail, so we'll have to be careful going there. But we must talk to Samantha. Alone."

"Why alone?" Nyx asked.

"I'm sure she knows something, but AJ said Anna ran away. Maybe she didn't run away as much as Samantha helped her hide," Miriam said.

Nyx said, "I get it. Samantha lied to her dad and is afraid to tell the truth."

"Correct," Miriam said, and then nudged Derrick with her elbow. "What'd I tell you? Cute and smart."

Derrick frowned and smiled, not knowing that was possible.

Nyx stared at Derrick. "What? You disagree with her?"

Derrick's frown/smile transformed into a full smile. "I do not."

Red said, "For God's sake. When do we leave? Any more of this lovey-dovey stuff, and I might puke."

Miriam said, "Right now. We just need to grab a few things. When I say we, I mean Derrick, Rebekah, and I. The rest of you aren't coming."

Nyx said, "Wait a minute. Who put you in charge?"

Miriam said, "Just the way it has to be. You need to stay for Akira. Red needs to stay in case something needs to be fixed. I don't like putting three people at risk, but Rebekah needs to come to convince Samantha to tell me about Anna. Derrick needs to come in case—well—in case we have an incident like at the school."

Nyx said, "Good points. Do you think there will be a problem?"
Miriam said, "I'll be surprised if there isn't."

2

NYX STOOD, TOOK HER TRAY TO A TRASH bin, and scraped the remaining food off in a manner suggesting she'd grown angry at the plate. Derrick didn't remember doing anything to anger Nyx. Perhaps it was because Miriam had taken charge. Although it seemed like a delayed reaction. As was frequently the case, Derrick felt confused, and he didn't know what the proper response was in the situation. Should he go to Nyx? Offer comfort, or leave her alone to work through her frustration?

He decided offering comfort was best but soon learned otherwise.

Derrick whispered, "I'm sorry."

Nyx glared at him. "What in the hell are you sorry for now?"

"Uh, well… I'm not sure."

"Do you have even the slightest idea what you're sorry for?"

Derrick said, "No. Not exactly."

"Not exactly, or not at all?"

Derrick felt a heaviness in his chest. "Not at all."

Nyx's face became red. "Did it ever occur to you that you're not the center of the universe? That everything doesn't revolve around you?"

Nyx looked toward the others.

Derrick turned, following her eyes. Everyone was staring at them. Their conversation had not gone unnoticed.

Nyx carried her plate to the serving line and slammed it down. Then she marched back to Derrick. She glared at him for a moment and then turned to face the others. "I don't like it. I don't like any of this. My best friend is in some alien-like chamber, and we don't know if she will be alright or even live. We don't know if any of us have a future outside this dreadful place. And Miriam wants to walk right into Potterville and take Derrick with her. So, he can fight goddamn soldiers!" She turned back to Derrick and then fell into his arms. "Okay. So, this time it is about you."

* * *

Thursday, April 8, 12:53 a.m.

Rebekah, Miriam, and Derrick wore black jackets, black pants (They did not ask Charlie where he found the clothing.), carried stun guns, and a backpack with a laptop. Derrick thought the laptop was unnecessary, but Miriam insisted. Miriam said she had to get online to check something. She did not elaborate on what something entailed.

When they stepped outside of engineering into the hidden canyon, the mountain air penetrated their jackets. They had formalized their plan on the way there. Coach Browning, being the person Derrick trusted most, was their first stop because the Sheriff's office would be locked tight. Browning could get them inside the Sheriff's Office. Then whoever was guarding the families could get Samantha, hopefully not waking Mr. and Mrs. Patel. Miriam would talk to Samantha alone. Rebekah would only get involved if Samantha refused to talk.

Anna probably told Samantha to tell no one. Miriam was certain of that. It made sense. Anna feared AJ Patel, but she trusted Samantha. Samantha wouldn't give information easily. Once Miriam found out what Samantha knew about Anna, the three of them would sneak back to engineering and then back to Administration, where they would go to the next phase of their plan, which wasn't much of a plan. Just go to where Anna was hiding, find her, and bring her back.

Safely.

At the river bridge, they stood in the trees, studying the crossing, the riverbank, and the sky. Satisfied that nothing stirred, and no one watched, they ran in crouched positions, making as little noise as possible. Once across the bridge, they stopped and studied the street before moving on.

Derrick did not know the town well. He kept them in shadows as best he could. A car appeared at the intersection a block away. It turned toward them. Derrick guided them behind a tree, hoping there wasn't a dog in the yard. It remained quiet.

Dogs barked here and there, but Derrick kept moving, making a mental note of the dogs' locations, planning a different route on the return trip. Masters may have been awoken the first time. If the dogs started barking a second time, the dog's master might venture out to see what was happening.

A few blocks from Browning's house, the smell of smoke hung in the damp morning air. When they turned the corner onto Browning's street, swirling red lights reflected off curling smoke. Derrick motioned the girls to stay. He ventured closer.

When he returned, Derrick said, "It's Browning's house."

Miriam whispered, "My God. I hope they got out okay."

Derrick said, "I'm going to go check. You guys stay here. If things go badly, get back to engineering."

Rebekah said, "You can't help them. Putting us at risk won't change what happened. Maybe it was an accident."

Miriam said, "It was no accident. But Rebekah is right. Nothing you can do. Stay focused. Next option?"

Derrick shrugged. "Sheriff's Office, I guess. But how do we get inside?"

"We'll figure that out when we get there. Not much cover downtown. Let's stick to the alleys," Miriam said.

Derrick led the way, pausing at the streets, then sprinting across. The town was quiet. Too quiet, but Derrick figured he was just paranoid. He'd been living here for several weeks. The nights were always quiet, except that time someone threw a bottle against the condo wall, yelled at Nyx, called her runner, which he thought was targeted at him. He was not the center of the universe. He understood that now. Yet somehow, he still felt at the center of this, and he did not know why.

They reached the courthouse. The Sheriff's Office and jail were on the south side of the building. Stopping in the alley, they studied the surroundings. Behind the jail was an exercise yard surrounded by a tall chain-link fence topped with razor wire.

Miriam whispered, "Ideas?"

Derrick said, "I could go over the fence if I had a blanket. I can do it using my jacket."

Rebekah said, "Get serious. What makes you think so?"

Derrick thought for a moment. "I'm not sure. I just know."

Rebekah said, "This has been bothering me. I haven't said anything because I thought Miriam would." Rebekah glanced at Miriam. "Remember the robot spinning-eyes thing? And how Derrick overcame the soldiers at the school? Akira said someone had hypnotized Derrick so they could trigger him to do something. We never did anything about that."

Miriam said, "Good point."

"Why haven't we done something?" Rebekah asked.

Miriam said, "I don't know. It's worrisome because I had not thought about it."

"What does that mean?" Derrick asked.

"Perhaps they hypnotized me too," Miriam said.

"Well, it's not a great time to get into it," Derrick said.

"Another valid point," Miriam said. "Derrick, I believe you could get over the fence, but I don't think that helps. I'm sure you'd find that door is also locked."

"You're right. Must be another way."

Rebekah pointed. "Maybe there is. Isn't that a camera?"

Miriam said, "Yes. But would anyone be watching it? It's late."

"True, but if the fire at Coach Browning's house was not an accident, someone will be watching," Derrick said, and then added, "And holding a weapon."

Rebekah and Miriam said, "Agreed."

"How should we do it?" Derrick asked.

Miriam said, "I'll go. If someone is watching the building, at least they won't get all of us."

Rebekah said, "Smart. But it's not going to happen that way. I'm going with you."

Derrick said, "We'll go together. If someone is watching, we've probably already been spotted."

Miriam said, "True," and ran toward the camera.

Derrick and Rebekah followed at full sprint. When they arrived under the camera, they started waving their arms.

Nothing happened.

After a few moments, the door opened. Sheriff Collins stood inside. "What the hell are you doing? Get in here."

As soon as the door closed, Derrick said, "Coach Browning…"

Collins said, "He's okay."

"His family…"

"Everyone is okay. But it was close. I had just picked them up. We'd gone a couple of blocks when the house burst into flames," Collins said.

"What caused it? Who did it?" Derrick said, his breathing slowed.

"Don't know—no gas leak, near as the fire chief can tell. But they investigate until the fire is out and it has cooled down."

Miriam said, "It was no accident."

Collins said, "Like I said, we don't know, but I agree. Now, back to my original question. What are you doing here? It's not safe, right? That should be clear."

Miriam said, "I gotta talk to Samantha. Is there a room where we can talk? Privately."

"She's asleep. Everyone is asleep. And I'd need to ask her parents. She's a juvenile. There are rules."

"I'm a juvenile, and we don't have time for rules. Besides, she might not talk to me if her parents know. Just do it, okay? Anna Ford's life is in danger, and we don't have time to waste."

Collins scratched his head. "Allen would be pissed."

Miriam said, "He doesn't have to know. Besides, he probably suspects I'll show up to talk to Samantha. He just doesn't know when."

"How would he know…"

Miriam interrupted. "Doesn't matter. Just get her. Please, Sheriff. Anna's life depends on it."

Collins sighed. "Follow me."

Collins led them to a room. Deputy Martinez sat at the desk, watching cameras positioned around the inside and outside of the building. On the desk was a computer and radio. Derreck thought they called it dispatch. Why he knew the term eluded him. Memories returned in little chunks as things happened—like the razor wire fence. Derrick knew how to get over it, could see himself doing it. In fact, he had done it. He did not know why. He did not know when.

Collins said, "Derrick and Rebekah can wait here. There's coffee." Collins pointed to a carafe sitting on a counter.

Collins led Miriam to a room. Turning on the light, he said, "Wait here. I'll get Samantha."

Two chairs, nothing fancy, just cloth seats lightly padded, faced Collins's desk, which was an ancient-looking green metal relic. Miriam arranged the two chairs, so they faced each other and then sat. In a few minutes, a sleepy Samantha Patel stood in the doorway.

"Sorry to wake you," Miriam said, "But it's important we talk. Anna's life depends on it." Miriam patted the seat of the opposing chair.

Samantha said nothing. Rubbing her eyes, she plunked down on the other chair.

"I'll be in dispatch when you're done," Collins said and then closed the door.

"It's good to see you again, Sam. I hope we can catch up when this is over. Derrick and Rebekah are here with me. We are going to find Anna, but we need to know where to start. So, tell me what you know about where she is," Miriam said.

Samantha stared at Miriam for a moment and then said, "I don't know anything about Anna."

Miriam smiled, leaned forward, and touched Samantha's knee. "I understand. Anna told you not to tell anyone. Told you she was in danger. But do you think she meant not to tell her sister?"

Samantha looked up. "You're not Anna's sister."

"I can get Rebekah if that would help. She's right down the hall. But you see, I'm as much a sister to Anna as Rebekah. Anna was adopted. Do you know what adopted means?"

Samantha nodded.

"Anna, Derrick, and I lived together until they placed us with families. They called us test subjects. I was Number 6, and Derrick was Number 7. They wiped our memories, but little pieces leak through, mostly during dreams. Memories are returning. Anna was Number 3. There have been robots here from a thing called Prime, looking for Anna. She's in danger. We need to find her. You're the only one who can help us."

Samantha said, "My dad scared Anna. That's why she ran."

"Scared her when he used a stun gun on her?"

Samantha nodded.

Miriam said, "Did he use a stun gun on you?"

Samantha shook her head.

Miriam's eyes grew wide. "You still have a 1984 chip? They can track you."

"Dad didn't shock mom or me. He had a doctor remove our chips. They could still be activated but they are on a truck somewhere."

Miriam smiled. "Your dad is a smart guy."

Samantha said, "Did you disable your 1984 chip?"

"Yes, I zapped Rebekah and myself before we left. Then I zapped Derrick when we found him. We all zapped each other a second time to be certain we destroyed the chip."

"Does it hurt?"

"Hurts like hell."

Samantha said, "You are brave."

"Tell me about Anna."

"I'm scared. I trust you, but I promised Anna."

"They plan to kill Anna. I'm sure of that. They plan to kill Derrick and me as well. We are Anna's only hope."

"But how can you protect her?"

"I'll be honest. I can't promise anything, except that we'll do everything possible to protect Anna. And we are still alive. Right?"

"I'll tell you what I know, but I don't know where she is. She might be long gone by now."

"Tell me what you can. That's all I ask."

"When she woke up from the stun gun, dad let her go to my room to rest. He had me go with her to keep her company, but also to watch her. It scared her. I told her dad was only trying to keep her safe. She was frantic to find Rebekah and you, but she didn't know where to look because you got away, and you didn't know she had followed you. She cried and cried. After a bit, she asked me to get her a drink of water. When I came back, she was gone. Out the window."

"What day was that?"

Samantha said, "Not sure. About a week ago."

"Sounds about right. Feels like we've been gone a month, but it was the first of April. You're right. She could be anywhere by now."

Samantha said, "She's probably still close to our house. Anna was gone a day, and then the next night, she tapped on my window. She must have watched the house and knew we'd gone to bed. She was cold and hungry. I got her food and gave her an old coat. Anna said she'd been hiding along the bluffs near the beach. She returned each night. When we left for Potterville, I left my window unlocked and a note explaining we'd left. I didn't know you guys were here. Plus, nothing out of the ordinary. We come here a few times a month."

Miriam stood, as did Samantha. Miriam hugged her. "Thank you. You've been a big help. We'll find her."

Before Miriam left, Samantha told her their address. Samantha asked if Miriam wanted her to write it down. Miriam said that was unnecessary and told Samantha to go back to bed. Before Miriam went to the dispatch, she found a LAN cord and connected her laptop. She checked the Pacific Edge computer system. It was running now, as she had planned. Her backdoor worked, she got inside, but she didn't stay. That would come later. She checked 1984. It did not find Anna Ford. The last blip was just outside the perimeter wall when AJ had jolted her with the stun gun. The system could not locate Anna's chip.

Miriam assumed they had tried to reactivate it, which meant the first jolt destroyed it.

Before shutting down, for no reason other than curiosity, she opened the e-mail application.

There was only one new e-mail.

From: PRIME

Subject: We need to talk.

3

DERRICK WAS DRINKING COFFEE WHEN MIRIAM returned. Coffee was not recommended at two o'clock in the morning, but he worried more about being alert than sleeping. Plus, he had a feeling Miriam wasn't planning on resting anytime soon. He was prepared for a long night, but he wasn't ready for the look on Miriam's face.

Derrick stood. "What?"

Miriam said, "I'll have a coffee, then we need to go."

"I mean, what happened? You look as if you've seen a ghost," Derrick said.

"Close enough. I'll explain later. Samantha told me some things." Miriam poured coffee, added sugar and cream. "Rebekah, have you had coffee?"

"No. I hoped to get some sleep tonight."

Miriam said nothing, but poured a second cup of coffee, also loading it with sugar and cream. Handing one mug to Rebekah, Miriam said, "You won't be sleeping."

"What happens next? Where are you going?" Collins asked.

Miriam said, "We are going back to the others next. After that, it's best you don't know. How secure is this place?"

Collins shrugged. "About as secure as one can get in Potterville. It's not a fort. They built the jail to keep people in, not out."

Miriam downed her coffee and said, "Let's go."

Collins said, "Want me to drive you? At least to the river?"

Miriam said, "No. We'll go it alone. You're needed here. Do you have more guns?"

Collins said, "A few. A couple of shotguns and one long rifle."

"Get them out. Wake the adults and put a gun in their hands."

Collins said, "Do you think that is necessary?"

"I do," Miriam said.

Collins thought for a moment. "There's something else you should know. Someone murdered Paul Jorgensen earlier this week."

"Murdered? Where? Who?" Derrick asked.

"At the condo. We don't know who, but I suspect it was because he planted the cameras. Professional job, I'd say. But messy. Cut his throat. Could have done it another way. I assume they wanted to send a message."

Derrick said, "That's scary and sad, even if he installed the cameras. What about his family?"

"No sign of them. I went to his house first. No one there. The car was gone, looked like they left in a hurry."

Miriam said, "You may not be safe here. Think about where these people could go."

"Can't get out of town. The state police and military have roadblocks set up on every route," Collins said.

"Think about it anyway," Miriam said, turning to leave.

Before they went outside the building, Miriam said, "We should assume someone is watching us. We need to ensure they don't follow us."

"Any suggestions on how we accomplish that?" Derrick asked.

Miriam said, "That's your area of expertise. Best you start unlocking your memories."

Derrick wanted nothing more than to unlock his memories. If only it were that easy. He said, "Follow me. We'll take as many shortcuts as possible. We'll run all the way. Stay close."

Derrick eased the door open, scanned the sidewalk, but he was sure that he wouldn't be able to spot professionals. Prime would not send robots for this task. He was certain of that. As soon as they were outside, he ran. He could hear the girls' footfalls behind him. Keeping his speed, so they were always close. He weaved a course through town, sometimes steering away from the river and then working back toward it. He avoided the dogs that barked the first time but found different ones along the way.

Within a few blocks of the river, he weaved into a yard and crawled under a thick shrub. The girls followed him, crowding in close. Derrick held his finger to his lips. Charlie had suggested they take blasters, a weapon Charlie and the imaginary Jane had perfected. At least Charlie believed it was perfected. Charlie had no human on which to test it. But Derrick decided against taking weapons, convinced stealth was more important than might on this mission. Now, he questioned that decision.

Within seconds, two sets of legs ran past the shrub. Then another two sets of legs—four people, but probably more. Perhaps four more a block to the south and another four a block to the north, flanking them in case they changed directions.

Holding his finger to his lips, Derrick whispered, "We'll cross the bridge one at a time. If they see us, we'll know. Run to the trees. Wait there and watch. I'll go last."

Miriam went first. A few minutes later, seeing no one, Derrick motioned Rebekah to go. He waited five minutes and then crossed the bridge. A cloud drifted east, revealing a full moon. On the other side of the bridge, Derrick crouched in the weeds, watching. The cool night air chilled him, having worked up a light sweat. The forest's dampness infiltrated his clothing. Bugs came from every direction, some crawling, some flying, some biting. He dared not swat at them, although he crushed several biting insects against his skin.

Convinced no one had followed them, Derrick stood to join the girls, when a figure appeared at the far side of the bridge. Derrick crouched again in the weeds, hoping his black clothing against the dark forest shadows had prevented the man from seeing him. The man, Derrick could see it was a man from this distance, stopped at the bridge's apex, scanning the forest for movement. Derrick contemplated his next move if the man continued across the bridge. He wished he had a stun gun. Surprise was his best weapon. A few attack options cycled through his mind, as if he watched them on a monitor. He decided which to employ. The one that reduced the possibility the man would make any sound. It also reduced the man's odds of survival.

Then the man turned and jogged back toward town. He had not seen them. That was the only answer that made sense. Derrick waited a few more minutes, then he ran to the trees. He could not see Miriam or Rebekah. That was good.

Just inside the tree line, Miriam whispered from his left. "Derrick."

He stopped, squinted, and saw Miriam standing in the shadows. He tiptoed through the fallen trees, roots, and rocks. "We'll stay here a few more minutes. Just to be safe."

Miriam said, "Who are they, and why were they running through town? Do you think they saw us?"

Rebekah said, "Someone must have seen us."

Derrick said, "If they saw us, why didn't they surround the Sheriff's Office? They had us trapped."

"Good point," Rebekah admitted. "Military?"

Derrick said, "Not military. They were not dressed like military, nor were they carrying military rifles."

"What were they carrying?" Rebekah asked.

Miriam said, "I don't know what they are called, but I saw those weapons in the armory in the Technical Building in Pacific Edge."

"Pacific Edge security? That makes little sense," Derrick said.

"Agreed," Miriam said, adding, "Not dressed like Pacific Edge security either."

Rebekah said, "Pacific Edge security was here before looking for Derrick."

Derrick said, "True. But not since the military and those Prime robots showed up."

Miriam said, "Derrick's right. It makes little sense."

"Because it's not Pacific Edge's jurisdiction?" Derrick asked.

"That and because of something else," Miriam said.

"What?" Derrick asked.

Miriam said, "I don't think they saw us, yet they seemed frantic to find us."

4

AFTER 15 MINUTES, REBEKAH, MIRIAM, AND Derrick crept to the rocks that concealed the hidden canyon entrance. They waited another ten minutes behind the rocks, watching the forest. Nothing appeared. Satisfied no one had followed, they sprinted to engineering.

Once inside the building, Miriam stopped, bent at the waist, hands on her knees. After catching her breath, she said, "Change of plan."

Rebekah said, "I wasn't clear on the first plan."

Miriam said, "I planned to go to Administration, but I feel like we are running out of time. Don't ask me why because I don't know. But I can't shake the feeling. Plus, they can't help us. We need to find Anna—the sooner, the better."

"What did Samantha tell you?" Derrick asked.

"Anna is hiding in the hills close to Samantha's house. Anna would sneak back at night, and Samantha gave her food and water," Miriam said.

"You think she's still there?" Rebekah asked.

Derrick said, "Maybe we should get some sleep and look for her in the morning."

Miriam said, "Someone was looking for us, and you can bet they are searching for Anna. They are probably also looking for Allen Patel. With Patel gone missing, they will focus on his house and the surrounding area. We might already be too late."

Rebekah said, "Don't say that."

"Just being honest. I hope I'm wrong."

"You're never wrong," Rebekah said.

Derrick said, "We don't even know where Patel lives."

Miriam said. "Samantha told me the address, and I studied a map. Finding it won't be difficult."

Derrick said, "Near Pacific Edge, I assume?"

"Yes. Just a few miles, near the ocean, in the hills. Lots of hiding places. It will be difficult to find her without someone finding us first," Miriam said.

Rebekah said, "How will we get there?"

"We'll take the Prime aircraft," Miriam said.

Derrick said, "I don't know. Do you think they can track it? Prime must have noticed that one of its aircraft and a robot went missing. Right?"

Miriam said, "True. There's a risk, that's for sure. But Collins said they've blocked the roads out of Potterville. Flying is the only way to get there. I wish I knew more about how the tracking systems work. Here's my idea. We'll fly low, straight west to the ocean. We'll fly out from the coast several miles and then circle back, land, and see if anyone shows up."

"And if someone shows up?" Rebekah asked.

"We leave. The Prime aircraft can outrun the military jets," Miriam said.

"How about the military rockets?" Derrick asked.

Miriam shrugged. "I hope we don't find out."

"What if Prime sends a similar aircraft?" Rebekah asked.

"Good point. We'd stay on the ground and travel by foot," Miriam said.

Rebekah said, "So if no aircraft appear, we fly to where Anna might be."

"Correct. Back out to sea, south to Pacific Edge, and then we'll land on the coast near Patel's house. We'll travel the rest of the way on foot," Miriam said.

"Sounds too easy," Rebekah said.

Derrick sighed. "I don't like it. Lots can go wrong."

"I'm open to suggestions," Miriam said. "I'm tired of making plans."

Rebekah said, "But you're good at it. I'm all in with whatever you say."

"Me too," Derrick said. "I didn't mean to make it sound otherwise. But I wish we had more weapons. Charlie wanted us to take blasters."

Miriam said, "True. But if we get Anna and get out undetected, that would be better than fighting our way out."

Derrick said, "No argument here. So, let's do that. In and out. No problems. No worries."

"No worries?" Rebekah asked.

"Just an expression I learned," Derrick said.

"Derrick King using expressions. Perhaps someday I'll get used to it," Rebekah said.

Derrick said, "Me too. Everyone make a pit stop before we go."

"Pit stop?" Rebekah asked.

"Restroom. Use the restroom," Derrick said.

"I'm fine," Rebekah said.

"Do it anyway," Miriam said, walking away.

When Derrick returned, Miriam and Rebekah were not there. He waited by the aircraft, wondering what it used for fuel and if it had enough. Not something they could find here, he was certain.

When Miriam and Rebekah returned, Derrick asked, "Do you think it has enough fuel?"

"Good question," Miriam said, stepping inside the aircraft.

"I wonder what it uses for fuel?" Derrick asked.

"Another good question," Miriam said. "However, answers would be better than questions."

"Not funny," Derrick said.

"I need more practice. I'm not getting many laughs lately," Miriam said, taking the pilot's seat. "Derrick, can you open the door and close it when I get outside? Or should I blast a hole in the wall?"

"I'll get the door. Save the ammo for later. Does it have ammo?"

Miriam said, "Not sure. I'll try to figure that out and the fuel situation."

Rebekah helped Derrick with the door. When the aircraft settled on the ground nearby, Derrick closed the door, secured it, and then ran to the exit door they had taped open. Remembering they were supposed to find a key, he searched drawers behind the counter that once served as the screening point for people entering the facility. In the last drawer, the one closest to the exit door, he found a key. He tested it. It locked the door, so he pulled the tape off the doorjamb and put the key in his pocket. Then changed his mind and hid it above the door. There was no guarantee he would return. If either Rebekah or Miriam made it back, they would need the key.

When he stepped inside the aircraft, Rebekah had taken the seat next to Miriam. Both wore the headset goggles. The door closed behind him. He sat along the edge of the aircraft.

Miriam said, "Sit there." She pointed.

The seat he picked had nothing in front of it. He could stretch his legs. He wanted to rest. The seat Miriam directed him to, had no switches or buttons, but faced the wall. He felt pinned in and didn't like it.

"Put on the headset. That seat is where Antonio sat. That's where defensive and offensive weapons are managed," Miriam said, adding, "Rebekah is learning the copilot operations.

With the headset on, things came to life. A console folded down and lit with controls and colorful monitoring displays. With the goggles, he could see outside the aircraft. It was as if the hull of the aircraft did not exist. He cycled through various optical options, which went from normal (too dark to see much of anything) to infrared, thermal, phosphor, digital, light-gathering, and more. He could see in front, to the sides, and behind the aircraft. Using the night vision, he spotted a large cat sneaking through the brush on the far side of the canyon.

Derrick said, "This stuff is amazing."

"Agreed," Rebekah said, "And easy to understand."

"Too easy," Miriam said.

"What does that mean?" Derrick asked.

"Maybe nothing," Miriam said.

"More riddles," Rebekah said. "I'd hoped we'd moved beyond that."

Miriam said, "Not a riddle. It just seems too easy. A robot flew it here, or maybe the robot didn't fly it. Perhaps it was programmed to fly to the meadow and then return."

"Someone might take control of the aircraft?" Derrick asked.

"It's possible. When I first flew it, the day we took out the robot, I switched off what appeared to be the tracking device. But I don't know if that's the only way they can track it. That's why we're going to see if anyone follows us," Miriam said.

Rebekah said, "What if they take control of the aircraft? Then what?"

"That would not be good," Miriam said.

5

THE AIRCRAFT LIFTED OFF IN THE STEEP narrow canyon. Flying low wasn't possible for long. Derrick wondered how Miriam planned to get them out of the mountains undetected. However, the mountains might provide protection. He didn't know. Neither did Miriam. She was guessing. She was gambling. Yet, they all were betting on her.

At least Derrick could see out.

But that wasn't a good thing.

Miriam flew toward the canyon wall. Within feet of the vertical rock wall, she pivoted the aircraft and flew straight up, skimming the mountain.

"Is that necessary?" Rebekah asked.

Miriam said, "I don't know."

The aircraft hugged the canyon wall until they cleared the top. Miriam then followed the contour of the mountains, skimming the treetops. Derrick studied the terrain, cycling through the night-vision options, spotting wildlife and the occasional heat signature from a distant home. The highways were empty, save random vehicles here and there. Then he spotted a roadblock. Several vehicles, lots of people. He watched until it was out of sight. No changes. It did not appear they had detected the aircraft.

The landscape changed. Small, scrubby trees and brush. Blackened hillsides, barren of vegetation. And then blackness. The ocean. It went on as far as Derrick could see. He didn't like it. Too vast. Too dark. Too cold.

Miriam said, "It's amazing. Isn't it?"

"It is," Rebekah said. "It goes on forever."

Miriam said, "I love the ocean. It's like endless possibilities."

"Except when you almost drowned," Rebekah said.

"True. There's that. Perhaps endless possibilities don't come without risks."

"How much farther?" Derrick asked.

"I'll turn south soon, travel about 40 miles, then back to the coast."

"How far will we be from Patel's house?" Derrick asked.

Miriam said, "About five miles."

Derrick thought about that. He could run that distance in 40 minutes, find Anna, walk back. Even with some terrain, he and Anna could get back in less than four hours. Just about sunrise. No reason to put Miriam and Rebekah at risk. They could wait. If anyone showed up, they could escape. If they were gone when he returned, he and Anna could hide until Miriam circled back.

Derrick said, "Land here and I'll find Anna. You guys stay put. I should be back in three hours or less."

Miriam said, "I don't like that idea. If things don't work as planned, we might never find you again."

Rebekah said, "And how would you find her? She's hiding and wouldn't trust you. I'll go with you. I can keep up. Miriam can stay."

"Not going to happen," Miriam said. "We stick together. That was our plan from the beginning."

Derrick said, "Sometimes plans change."

"Agreed. But not this time." She turned south, and after a few minutes, turned toward the coast. "Watch the coastline. Let me know if you see anything we should avoid. According to the map, it should be uninhabited."

In the distance, Derrick saw the coast on the horizon. It grew closer quickly, and he wondered how fast they were going. He saw nothing but steep ravines and jagged cliffs. Waves crashed on rocks—no sandy beaches. "Looks desolate and rugged. Finding a place to land will be difficult."

"I'll find something. Doesn't have to be great. We'll just stay in the aircraft unless someone needs a potty break."

Rebekah said, "Uh, you mean a pit stop? That would be me."

Miriam said, "You were supposed to do that before we left."

"I did, but you made me drink coffee."

Derrick said, "Me too. Sorry."

"Fine," Miriam said. "Kids these days."

Miriam slowed, spun the aircraft 360 degrees, and descended, landing softly but tilted to the left. "The ground isn't level, but there's room to step out. Be careful. Straight down on three sides and straight up on the other. Rebekah, you go first."

Rebekah put her headset down, standing as the door slid open. "You don't have to ask me twice. Don't be watching me, Derrick."

Derrick felt his face flush. Setting his headset to the side, he said, "I wouldn't."

"You wouldn't or you won't?" Rebekah punched him on the shoulder. "There's a difference."

Derrick said nothing and was positive his face glowed red.

Rebekah returned. "Next."

Derrick said nothing, starting for the door.

Rebekah said, "Hey! You didn't tell me not to watch."

"Um, uh, I…"

"Don't worry. I wouldn't do that. Probably." Rebekah laughed.

When Derrick returned, Miriam stood.

Rebekah said, "And where are you going?"

"Might as well go while we are here," Miriam said.

"You were supposed to go before we left," Rebekah chided.

"Okay, okay. Sorry. I shouldn't have said anything. Watch for aircraft."

When Miriam returned, she said, "What do you think? Long enough?"

Derrick said, "I don't know. Depends on how far they had to come if they spotted us."

"True. But we don't have much time. We gotta find Anna and be back at engineering before daylight," Miriam said.

"Speaking of engineering, I found a key and locked the door on my way out. I hid the key above the door."

Miriam said, "Good." She paused and then said, "Speaking of things that should have been mentioned, I found something disturbing when I went online at the Sheriff's Office."

Derrick said, "What?"

"An e-mail," Miriam said.

"An e-mail? What did it say?" Derrick asked.

"I didn't open it," Miriam said.

"Then how do you know it was disturbing?" Rebekah asked.

"It was from Prime."

6

THEY REMAINED ON THE SIDE OF THE CLIFF for another few minutes. Miriam busied herself at the pilot's console. Rebekah sat staring at Derrick. Derrick stared into the middle distance, struggling to process what Miriam said. What was Prime? And how had it tracked Miriam?

"You forgot to tell us? That's unlike you," Derrick said.

"I didn't say I forgot."

"Then what? Why didn't you tell us?" Derrick demanded.

"Calm down. I was trying to process it."

"Well, I'm not processing it well. What did it say?" Rebekah asked. "Was it about Anna?"

Miriam said, "I didn't open it. I said that already."

"You didn't open it? Don't you think it's important? This doesn't sound like you," Derrick said.

"I didn't open it because I didn't want Prime to know I saw it. No big mystery about that," Miriam said.

"What is Prime?" Derrick asked.

Miriam thought for a moment. "If I knew, I'd tell you."

Rebekah said, "You think it's a group of people? Like a council or something?"

Miriam said, "Maybe. That would make sense, but something tells me it's not. I have a feeling it's one person. If a person is an accurate description. I'm not sure that it is."

Derrick said, "That is not helping."

"I know, but I'm not ready to say what I think. I could be wrong," Miriam said.

Rebekah said, "How did it track you? What's an e-mail? I've heard the term since we left, but I'm unclear what it is."

Miriam said, "I don't understand how it works. It is a way to send messages over the internet, which is another thing you don't know about. Here's the thing. Prime sent the message to an account I set up to communicate with Derrick. The account is set up on a Potterville internet service."

Rebekah said, "Allen."

"Allen?"

Rebekah said, "That's what they call Patel in Potterville."

Miriam said, "Right, but I don't think it's Patel. He's on the run himself."

Derrick released a sound like a cross between a whistle and a deep breath. "That is weird. And scary. How could Prime know about that?"

Miriam said, "Very weird and very scary. It means Prime has known about what I was doing all along and monitored our communications. I often felt as if someone was watching. Felt like we were in a test or an experiment."

Derrick said, "You think they expected all this?"

Miriam said, "I don't know. Not all of it. Unexpected things have happened. Let's see if we can accomplish one more unexpected event. Find Anna and get back to safety."

If there is such a thing as safety, Derrick thought. Nyx crossed his mind. He hoped Prime did not know her location and hoped Charlie could protect her. Then, with more urgency than he expected, Derrick said, "Let's go. We are wasting time."

The aircraft lifted off the rocks and then rocketed out to sea. Land faded behind them, only darkness ahead. Miriam turned south and then turned back toward the coast.

Miriam said, "We are flying directly toward Patel's house. It is about a quarter of a mile inland, on a small rise, and should be visible. The second row of houses. It's a two-story tan stucco, attached garage, fenced yard. We'll approach slowly. While I look for a place to land, you guys scan the houses and the hills. Maybe we'll get lucky and see where she's hiding."

Derrick found the house, studied it. No images appeared, but he didn't know if the technology could see through walls. He focused on other homes and found the infrared setting allowed him to locate people inside. But no heat signatures appeared in the Patel home, which meant Anna wasn't there. Then he turned his attention to the hills. His hopes faded. Crashed would be a better term.

Derrick said, "This does not look good."

"What? You don't see anyone?" Miriam asked, spinning the aircraft 360 degrees then easing it toward a ledge.

"No one in Patel's house. But that's not the problem. The hills are crawling with people."

7

THE AIRCRAFT SETTLED ON THE LEDGE WITH A light thump. Derrick surveyed the area. The nearest person on the hill was half a mile away. It was unlikely they heard or saw the aircraft land. Miriam had found a suitable spot. About five feet below an embankment, brush growing up on both sides. It was only visible from the sea. Virtually invisible at night, they would be gone before sunrise.

Derrick said, "I wish these night-vision goggles were portable."

"True," Rebekah said. "Perhaps we can find some at the base before we do anything like this again."

Miriam said, "Let's hope we don't do anything like this again."

"Let's hope we survive this time," Derrick said.

"Aren't you the cheery one?" Miriam asked.

Rebekah sniffled. The distinctive sound of one about to cry.

Miriam said, "Sorry. We'll be fine. We will find Anna and get the hell out of here."

Rebekah said, "I hope so, but it won't be easy. I saw all those people on the hill. How are we going to find Anna without them seeing us first? And who are they? Military? Pacific Edge Security?"

Miriam said, "No clue who they are. Could be State Police. Maybe a combination of all three."

"Why do they want Anna so badly?" Rebekah asked.

"Valid question, but unimportant at the moment," Miriam said and then added, "Derrick, any ideas?"

"I think I saw Anna."

"How could you know it was Anna?" Rebekah asked.

"One person not moving and small, hiding in the brush. The others looked as if they were rushing to a fire. Frantic like the guys back in Potterville," Derrick said.

"Can you find that spot?" Miriam asked.

Derrick said, "I think so. I know the distance and some landmarks. We can skirt the hill where they are searching until we are parallel with her. Then we move across until we are in position. We'll have to watch and be careful, but the searchers are moving uphill. I suspect to the top. We should have time to find her and get out."

"If she wants to be found," Miriam said.

"What does that mean?" Rebekah asked.

"Anna doesn't know we are here. She's been dodging those people for a week. She's smart and doesn't want to be found. She may have moved by the time we get to where Derrick saw her last. If that was even her. It could be an animal, sleeping for all we know."

"You are both so optimistic," Rebekah whispered.

"Realistic is the term," Miriam said. "Let's go."

The door slid open. Derrick had not paid much attention to it before, and now, when silence was critical, the door seemed louder than he remembered.

After they were outside, Miriam put her hand on the side of the aircraft, and the door closed. "Pretty cool, huh?"

"Can anyone else open it?" Rebekah asked.

"Just me."

"Okay. Why didn't you set it up so Derrick and I can open it?"

Miriam shrugged. "I was afraid you might try something foolish."

Derrick said, "We can get into that later. I'll give you a boost up. Scan the area to make sure it's clear."

The smell of the ocean gave Derrick an odd feeling of home. Not his new home, but the old one that he now thought of as a prison. He formed a cradle with his hands. Rebekah wasted no time stepping in first. She looked in both directions and then hoisted herself onto the bank. Derrick repeated the process with Miriam. Rebekah took Miriam's hand, helping her up. Derrick put both hands on the bank, pulling himself up and digging into the bank with his toes. Both girls grabbed under his arms, dragging him to the top.

Derrick led them up the street, keeping to the shadows. He decided three kids running looked suspicious, so he slowed to a walk. Just three kids out for a stroll. At an ungodly hour. He hoped kids here were more adventurous than he had been in Pacific Edge. Maybe kids roamed the streets of Potterville at night. Meeting up with friends. Perhaps hoping for a kiss from their girlfriends. That probably happened, especially on Spring Break. Now, everyone likely hid in their homes, hoping they didn't get blown up like Coach Browning's place. Or their throats slit like Paul Jorgensen.

Four blocks of houses, and then the terrain became too steep for homes. Almost too steep for climbing. Derrick could not see a trail. The dirt was dry, loose, and slick. Not much to grab onto either. Scrubby trees and brush dug into the palms of his hands when he grabbed ahold. He moved up, grabbed a branch, and then reached back for the girls, helping them to his position, and then repeating. Slow going.

Without the night-vision goggles, everything lacked definition. It was all just different shades of gray. Now, he wasn't sure he could find the characteristics he'd seen from the aircraft. He stopped to listen. Fifty yards ahead and to the left, he heard people searching up the hill.

Derrick signaled he was ready to move. Still steep, but a little less so. The soil still soft, but he was able to move 20 yards to the next clump of trees. He scanned the area and pointed. "I think that's the tree and rocks I used to mark Anna's location."

"If it's Anna," Miriam whispered.

Derrick nodded and then crept across the hill, stopping every few feet to listen, and then moving and then listening. About 50 yards to the south, he stopped.

Cupping his hands around his mouth, he whispered, "Anna."

Anna did not respond. He heard twigs snap in the distance. Holding his hand out to silence Rebekah and Miriam, he concentrated on the sounds in the ravine. Searchers moving away, but still too close for comfort.

Derrick motioned Rebekah and Miriam to come closer. "Anna should be close if she didn't move, but she might have moved after the search party moved farther up the hill. The search party is close. We gotta be careful," Derrick whispered.

Miriam and Rebekah nodded and then spread out, each of them whispering, "Anna." Derrick focused on a thick bush. He thought he saw movement, but it was difficult to see in the dark. If only he had the night-vision goggles. Standing with his face next to the bush, he whispered, "Anna? It's Derrick King. Rebekah and Miriam are here. We came to get you out of here."

A rustling sound.

A small deer burst from the thicket, causing Derrick to stumble back, falling on his butt.

Sitting on the ground, Derrick listened. Voices a few yards away.

"Seriously? Derrick and Miriam?" a man said.

"Yes. And Rebekah Ford too," a woman answered.

8

THE SNAP OF A BRANCH SOUNDED TWENTY YARDS from their position. Derrick must have imagined the man and woman saying their names. It wasn't possible. No one knew they were here. Yet, there was that e-mail Miriam received from Prime. No time to contemplate any of it. Their pursuers were getting closer.

Holding his finger to his lips, Derrick motioned the girls to follow. He started back in the direction they first traveled up the hill. The direction that did not have people swarming all over it. But the soldiers or police or security guards were too close. He started downhill, glancing over his shoulder every few steps. Movement in the trees. He went faster, less concerned about being heard and more concerned about being seen.

Derrick heard voices on both sides of them now. It seemed the entire hunting party had come rushing down the mountain. Something had changed.

"They spotted something on the cliff," a man said to Derrick's left.

"Crap," Derrick hissed.

"What is it?" a woman asked.

"A Prime aircraft," the man said.

The woman said, "I thought Prime was a myth."

The man said, "Apparently not. Radio ahead. We can't let them get on that aircraft!"

Derrick spotted a dense clump of brush. Their pursuers would have to go around it, and so would they, which would put them within eyesight of those on either side. Derreck turned to the girls, pointed at the brush. Both girls nodded. They pushed and pulled their way deep into the thicket. Silent they were not, but they were concealed in the darkness. Derrick laid flat, motioning the girls to do the same. Derrick ducked his head and dared not look at those pursuing them. Too much risk of someone seeing a face where a face did not belong.

Struggling to control his breathing, he focused on the footsteps and voices. At least ten people, all breathing hard, all moving fast. Not talking, but not sneaking either. They were not concerned with stealth. They did not care if they were heard. They only cared about catching their prey.

A radio crackled. "We've got the aircraft covered. They aren't there. It's Prime, alright."

Standing within ten feet of Derrick, the man said, "Slow down. They could be hiding."

Ten, maybe 12 people. Probably armed. No way to take them all down without drawing attention and bringing more troops. And he had no plan. Hard to conduct an assault or escape without a plan.

Worse, they could not get to the aircraft. Not now, not ever. It would be guarded day and night.

The first problem—that they were lying in a thicket surrounded by hostile forces—must be solved before thinking about the subsequent problems, of which there were many.

The hunting party moved downhill.

Moving away.

Time to go.

Derrick made eye contact with Miriam. He held his finger to his lips and then pointed uphill. They would go back up and then out. Out to where, he did not know.

Disentangling themselves from the brush was neither easy nor silent. It was painful, branches digging into his face and bugs biting at his legs. Once the girls were out, he started uphill, swiftly but carefully, stopping every few yards to listen before moving on. When he could no longer hear their pursuers, he started to the right.

Miriam grabbed his arm, shook her head, and pointed to the left, back in the direction they first traveled. Derrick did not understand why she wanted to go in that direction. The search party was concentrated in and around the ravine. There were more hills going his way. The homes were where Miriam wanted to go. Now, was not the time to argue or discuss it. So, he went left, following the same routine, stopping to listen every few yards.

When they reached an outcropping of rocks, Derrick stopped. One hundred yards below their position, five people watched over the Prime aircraft. No way to get to it without overpowering those five people, and more were likely on the way. The aircraft guardians wore black clothing and face coverings. But none were dressed the same, like the people in Potterville. Not military. Not police. Not Pacific Edge Security. Who were these people?

Derrick whispered, "We need to get out of here. The place will be crawling with people soon. Any ideas?"

Miriam said, "We'll go to the Patel house. It's just there." She pointed to a house not more than 20 yards away. A wooden fence surrounded the backyard. Miriam added, "They're in Potterville. I hope the window Samantha left open is still unlocked."

Derrick said, "Stay low."

Derrick scanned all directions. Seeing no one close, he sprinted to a gate in the fence. It had a flat metal ring attached to a metal cable, which he hoped controlled the latch. Pulling the ring, the gate swung open. Miriam and Rebekah sprinted through. Their timing was perfect. He closed the gate, securing the latch. Derrick motioned them into a gap between a shed and the fence.

Derrick whispered, "Stay here. I'll check the house."

Tiptoeing to the house, Derrick peeked through a window and saw no one. The home—larger and nicer than most of the homes in Potterville but old and pathetic compared to homes in Pacific Edge—was built into a hill. The front faced uphill. The bottom floor was on ground level in the back but was dug into the mountain in the front. The fence did not extend around the front of the home, but Derrick assumed the front door would be the least likely to be unlocked. Unfortunately, the back door and all the windows were locked. The house had three levels. Miriam might want to get on the roof, like she used to do in Pacific Edge. But she would be exposed up there.

Just one window left to check. Derrick eased into a deep window well, pushing lightly with his palms, the window slid open. He peered back over the concrete window well. Miriam watched him from the shed. He motioned for them to come and then disappeared inside.

Once inside, the three of them stood listening. A nightlight provided just enough illumination to see that they were in a bedroom: Samantha's. The house seemed quiet, but if anyone was here, they were likely asleep. Miriam handed Derrick a stun gun. He held his finger to his lips, motioned the girls to stay put.

Derrick searched from room to room, finding no one. He paused in the master bedroom, which had a large window overlooking the sea. From here, he could see the Prime aircraft. The edge of the aircraft was visible in the moonlight, as were the five people guarding it. Soon people would awaken, and they would gather to see the strange machine parked near their homes.

They were not escaping in that aircraft.

Just getting out of the area without getting caught would be a challenge. Finding Anna, impossible.

When Derrick returned, Miriam stood by a French door leading to the backyard. Derrick said, "No one is here. We are okay for now."

Miriam said, "Are they still watching the aircraft?"

"Yes. Five of them."

"Did you see the others?" Miriam asked.

"I did not. I only watched for a few seconds."

"We need to get to that aircraft. It's our only way back," Miriam said.

"I don't see how. They are standing right there. No way to surprise them. No way to overpower them."

"Do they have weapons?" Miriam asked.

"Yes, but everyone seems to have something different. Not like the military. They are like the people we saw in Potterville."

"Who are they? Military?" Miriam asked.

"Not military. Not State Police. Not Pacific Edge Security."

"What makes you think that?"

"They are all wearing black clothing, black hats, and black face coverings. But it's only the same color. It's not the same clothing. It's not a uniform."

Miriam thought for a moment. "Then who are they?"

"I do not know. Maybe mercenaries or bounty hunters," Derrick said.

"What's a bounty hunter?"

"People trying to collect a bounty. Money. They may have put a bounty on our heads," Derrick said.

"Where did you hear about such a thing?" Miriam asked.

"I learned about it watching a movie."

Miriam said, "A movie. And you think it's a real thing?"

Derrick shrugged. "I don't know. Just an idea."

"Fair enough. I wonder how much we are worth?"

"Maybe there isn't a bounty. Just speculating who those people are. What difference would it make?"

Miriam said, "Could tell us something about how desperate someone is to find us. Besides, aren't you curious how much you're worth?"

Derrick said, "Not really."

Miriam paused. "I'll go. Try to work my way to the aircraft from below. If I can get to the door before they see me, we'll have a chance to get out of here," Miriam said.

Derrick said, "No way. I'm not letting you take that risk. I'll go."

"You don't know how to fly it," Miriam shot back.

"I'll figure it out. You did."

"Won't work. It will take you a few minutes at a minimum. They might have a weapon that can destroy the aircraft. Besides, I programed the aircraft to only open with my handprint."

Derrick said, "We didn't think that through."

Miriam said, "Agreed."

Derrick heard whimpering. He turned to see Rebekah, hunched over, hands between her knees, head bowed, rocking back and forth. He had a sinking feeling in his chest since he saw the people guarding the aircraft. But he felt worse now. He and Miriam had forgotten about Rebekah, it seemed. And about Anna.

Glancing at Miriam, Derrick went to the couch and sat by Rebekah. Miriam joined him, kneeling in front of Rebekah, putting her hand on her knee.

Rebekah rocked.

Miriam said, "I have not forgotten about Anna."

Rebekah said nothing.

Derrick said, "We'll find her."

Rebekah stopped rocking but did not look up. "You haven't thought about Anna since that deer jumped out of the brush."

Miriam said, "That's not true…"

Rebekah raised her head, glaring at Miriam.

Miriam said, "You're right. We've been wrapped up in our problems. But we'll find her."

"How? How are you going to find her? You have no idea where she is. How are we even going to get ourselves out of this mess?" Rebekah asked.

Miriam took a deep breath. "I don't know the answer to either question."

Derrick said, "Rebekah, don't give up."

Rebekah turned to Derrick. Her face reddened. Her eyes flared. She started pounding on Derrick's shoulder. "It's your fault we are here. You did this. I hate you."

Derrick did nothing to protect himself. He just let Rebekah hit him. He didn't blame her.

Miriam said nothing.

Rebekah stopped, fist still raised for another blow, and then collapsed against Derrick's chest, sobbing.

Derrick put his arms around her. It was true. He did not know what they were going to do. Anna could be anywhere. Long gone or hiding nearby. It made little difference, because finding her was unlikely. Getting out of here seemed impossible, and that didn't include getting back to Nyx, Akira, Red, and Antonio. But one thing he did know.

It was time for Derrick King to become a leader. Miriam was brilliant, and he needed her. Rebekah was brave, and he needed her too. But he possessed skills if he could just learn to access them.

Access them, he must.

9

Thursday, April 8, 4:22 a.m.

DRINKING BITTER COFFEE AND WISHING HE had a fresh cup from Donna's, Collins glanced up to see Lori Martinez shuffle into the dispatch center. Hair disheveled and uniform wrinkled, half her shirttail untucked, Lori went to the coffeepot, poured in a generous helping of milk, three tablespoons of sugar, and then filled the cup with coffee.

"Having a little coffee with your cream and sugar?" Collins asked.

"Just a little," Lori replied, her back still turned.

"You're supposed to be sleeping," Collins said, "I recall ordering you to do so."

Martinez turned around, leaned against the counter, and sipped her coffee. "You know what I like about working for you, Bill?"

"That I'm so handsome?"

"That I can ignore your orders and not get fired."

Collins grunted.

Lori took another drink. "And at what other job could I look like this without feeling uncomfortable?"

"You look like hell. You should get some sleep."

"When this is over, perhaps you can take me to dinner. I'll even comb my hair."

"You know I can't take you to dinner. I'm your boss, for God's sake."

"Then, when this is over, I quit."

"Ha. Funny."

"Not joking. Speaking of it being over... do you think the kids are okay?"

Collins stared at Martinez for a moment. "I think so."

"Why do you say that?"

"Come look." Collins turned his chair, so he faced the monitors.

Martinez walked around the dispatch desk, leaned over, placing her forearm on Collins' back. Lori watched as two figures dressed in black walked in front of the building. "Who are those guys?"

"I don't know. There are a bunch of them. Roaming all over town, it seems."

"Looking for the kids?"

"I assume."

"Military?"

"I don't think so."

Martinez said, "If they had found the kids, they wouldn't still be looking. Is that what you figure?"

"Yep."

Martinez pushed herself upright but left her hand on Collins' shoulder for a moment. "Then there's still hope."

***

It was if someone had sucked the oxygen from the room. But it wasn't that. Reality was sinking in.

Rebekah looked at Derrick. "Sorry I hit you."

"It's okay," Derrick said.

"It's not okay. It's not your fault. It's my fault that Anna is out here instead of at home safe. I shouldn't blame you."

Derrick said, "It started with me. I own that responsibility. Miriam should be arguing with teachers, and you should be playing soccer."

Rebekah said, "Marcus Carver is to blame."

Miriam said, "It's not even Marcus Carver's fault. They set him up, just like Derrick. Blame whoever set this entire thing into motion."

"Good luck ever determining who that is," Rebekah said.

Derrick said, "This won't get us anywhere. Perhaps learning the cause will be important at some point, but not now. Right now, we need to find Anna and get back to the Base."

Rebekah said, "Maybe you only have one problem—getting to safety. I'll worry about Anna. If I can find her, we'll go back to Pacific Edge. Take whatever punishment we have coming."

Miriam said, "You forgot an important detail. They will torture and kill Anna. That's her future if we don't find her."

Rebekah drew her knees tight to her chest and started rocking again. "I had hope when we came here. But now, I have none."

Derrick said, "That's the problem."

Rebekah and Miriam stared at him.

Derrick said, "Hope is the problem. We can't keep basing what we do on wishes and hopes. That we are part of some prophetic prediction that will mystically all work out if we just have hope."

Miriam said, "I don't understand. Are you saying that we give up?"

"That's not what I'm saying. We need to stop thinking hope is the answer. There's no magic, hope or whatever you want to call it, that's going to save us. Success or failure will be based on what we do, decisions we make."

Rebekah stopped rocking, sat straight, and wiped her face on her sleeve. They sat silently for a few moments, then Rebekah said, "He's right. We need to grow up. Stop thinking someone will swoop down and save us."

Miriam nodded. "Agreed. I'm all ears. Where do we start?"

"We start with getting some rest. We'll take shifts, one person keeping watch. I suggest the master bedroom upstairs—good view of the aircraft from there," Derrick said, adding, "Whoever is on watch can go to the front of the house every few minutes to check that side. Two can sleep in the bedroom. That way, whoever is watching can wake them. It's a big bed. I'll take first watch."

"How long should we sleep?" Miriam asked.

"We need eight hours, but that's unrealistic." Derrick thought for a moment. "Thirty minutes. Not enough, but better than nothing."

Rebekah said, "I'll take first watch. I can't sleep."

Derrick said, "Not an option. I need to think, and I can't do that sleeping."

Miriam said, "No time to debate. Lead the way."

Contrary to Rebekah's protest, she was snoring 30 seconds after her head hit the pillow, Miriam 20 seconds later. Derrick moved from one room to the other, pausing for a few seconds at the windows to track activity outside, thinking hard about their next move. His speech had sounded good, but he was at a loss of how to take control of their situation. Nothing changed outside, except one person watching the aircraft left. Thirty minutes passed. Derrick did not wake the girls. He needed rest, but he had to finish processing his thoughts.

He knew what had to happen next.

He just didn't know how to do it.

10

Thursday, April 8, 5:45 a.m.

THE AIRCRAFT WATCH ENDED. EVERYONE LEFT. Derrick woke Miriam, motioning her to follow him. Miriam rubbed her eyes, looking confused. Derrick gave her a hurry-up motion.

Standing at the window, Miriam yawned, stared, and said, "What?"

"They left. The people watching the aircraft."

"Why?" Miriam asked.

"I don't know. But this is our chance. Get away from here and regroup," Derrick said.

Miriam yawned, shook her head. "I wonder why they left?"

"Worthy question, but we don't have time to think about it."

Miriam continued to stare out the window. "Thank you."

"For what?"

"Saying we don't have time. You've caught on. Get Rebekah. Let's go while we have a chance."

Derrick sat on the bed, watching Rebekah for a moment. He hated to wake her. She looked peaceful. But that would end the moment she awoke and learned they were leaving without Anna.

Giving Rebekah's shoulder a gentle shake, Derrick whispered, "Rebekah."

Rebekah tried to brush Derrick's hand from her shoulder but missed.

"Rebekah."

"Ugh. What?"

"Time to wake up. We need to go."

Rebekah sat up. Confused.

"The people are gone. We need to get to the aircraft while we have a chance."

"But Anna."

"I know. But we can't help Anna if we are trapped here or, worse, captured. Got to go. No time to think about it," Derrick said.

Rebekah stood on unsteady legs. "You go. I'll find Anna. You come back for us."

"We stay together. Let's go."

Miriam said, "What's the plan?"

"Turn on the stun guns, run to the aircraft. If anyone tries to stop us, zap them," Derrick said.

Miriam said, "Works for me. Sometimes simple is best."

Rebekah said, "First, is there a bathroom? I need to splash some water on my face."

Miriam pointed.

Rebekah didn't close the door. She returned a moment later, face still wet. "Who has the stun guns?"

Derrick handed Rebekah his. "You and Miriam. I can fight. You can't."

"I can fight," Rebekah said.

"Glad to see you're back. But don't argue. Derrick can fight better than either of us. Plus, he'll need one of us to save his ass," Miriam said.

"Good point," Rebekah said, "Seems we are always saving his ass."

Derrick said, "Stay together. Be ready to fight."

Both girls nodded. They both looked terrified. He was proud of them.

Derrick ran down the stairs, two at a time.

Turning into the living room on the main floor, Derrick stopped.

A man clothed in black stood in the doorway.

11

DERRICK STOOD IN SHADOW ON THE STAIRCASE platform. Miriam and Rebekah stood behind him, two steps up. He froze but knew the man saw him. He might be wrong, but he did not think so. A stun gun sizzled behind him. It did not appear the man was armed, but appearances can be deceptive. Plus, the man was probably not alone. But they had few options. Stick to the plan. They had to get past him to get out. They had to get out to reach the aircraft.

Time to fight.

Derrick could not make out the man's features because of the lightening sky behind him, and the man still wore a black face covering. They could dash down the stairs to the family room and then out the window through which they entered. If the man didn't move, and if the man didn't call for help, that might work.

Or, if they asked nicely, he might give them a ride to the aircraft.

Not viable options.

Fight their way out.

Fight their way to the aircraft.

Fighting was their only option.

Fighting wasn't a problem.

Winning the fight… that was the problem.

Derrick felt confident he could take out the man at the door, but he was too far away to strike. Derrick raised his hands, palms out. "We mean you no harm. We just want to leave. No problems."

The man stepped inside and closed the door.

Perfect.

Derrick descended. Miriam followed close behind.

The man pulled down his mask, took off his hat, and then said, "Maranda? Is that you? But it's not Maranda, is it? It's Miriam."

***

Thursday, April 8, 6:05 a.m.

When Red walked into the dining area, Nyx was already there, eating a bar made of nuts and such, drinking coffee. Red had hoped for a hot breakfast, but it did not look like that was an option.

"Good morning," Nyx said.

"Morning," Red said. "You look terrible. Did you sleep?"

"Thanks," Nyx scoffed. "I dozed off a few times in the recovery area."

Red said, "How are Akira and Antonio?"

"The monitors indicate they will release Antonio in 45 minutes. It seems strange for a machine to say he will be released. Don't you think? Like he's in a regular hospital."

Red poured coffee. "What about Akira?"

Nyx said, "Still don't know. The machine shows treatment is 89% complete. It does not give a prognosis."

"Where's that robot?" Red asked.

"Which one?"

"The one they call Charlie."

"I have not seen him. Still docked, perhaps. I don't know how long docking takes."

Red stood at the vending machine. Nothing looked appetizing. He skipped the bars with grains and nuts and picked one with caramel and chocolate. It had a few nuts, so he thought it was a healthy enough choice, given the circumstances.

The door opened and Charlie stepped into the room. "Did someone call for me?"

Nyx drawled, "No."

Charlie said, "Odd. I heard my name."

Red said, "I said your name, but I wasn't calling you."

"But you asked Nyx if she had seen me. I assumed you wanted me to come," Charlie said.

Nyx said, "I'm glad you are here. Antonio's treatment is almost done. Do you know anything about Akira?"

Charlie walked to the table. "Akira Nakamura has completed 92% of the treatment protocol."

"How is she?" Nyx asked.

Charlie said, "Her condition is unknown. The final 10% of treatment is critical. The recovery process cannot estimate her condition until the treatment is complete."

"Why is that?" Nyx asked.

Charlie said, "I'm sorry. I thought you understood. Akira Nakamura received a lethal dose of radioactivity. Survival was not predicted."

Nyx said, "What does that mean?"

"Chance of survival below 1%."

* * *

Miriam stepped from behind Derrick. "Marty?"

The man smiled. "Hi. I never thought I'd see you again." Holding his hands up, Marty said, "Don't zap me. I have no weapon."

Derrick said, "You know this guy?"

Miriam said, "It's Marty. One of the Technical Service security guys I told you about. What are you doing here?"

"Looking for you. We have been looking for you here and in Potterville. We've been watching every night, assuming you might show up. Someone here saw you from their window this morning," Marty said.

"Why? Who are you? I mean, I know who you are, but all these people?" Miriam asked.

"We call it The Resistance. You've probably never heard of us," Marty said.

"I've heard of The Resistance," Derrick said.

"What do you know about us?" Marty asked.

Derrick shrugged. "Nothing, really."

"What does The Resistance do?" Miriam asked.

Marty said, "Well, we cannot do much. But we do what we can."

"Like what, for example?" Miriam asked.

"Archives. We search for articles, recordings, broadcasts, movies, art, and such before the fall, catalog and study them. Lots of music. That's what I do. Music," Marty said, smiling.

"Why?" Miriam asked. "What are you accomplishing?"

Marty shrugged. "Trying to understand what happened. Understand what it used to be like here. Understand what we lost."

"Music?" Derrick asked.

Marty beamed. "Yeah. You know the Stones, Grateful Dead, Billie Eilish, Prince, Elton John, Deep Purple, Beatles, Johnny Cash, David Bowie, Bob Dylan, Allen Stone. You name it. We probably have it. Then we put it out. They take us down, but we keep putting it out there. Free to all."

Derrick said, "I've heard of Mr. Bob Dylan and The Beatles. Not all their music, but some. My guitar teacher mentioned The Resistance. Told me Bob Dylan's music was classic. I didn't understand what he meant, but he seemed to think I should have known about it. Although I don't understand who takes it down or why."

Marty nodded. "That's a good question. It's kind of unclear who takes it down. The Chosen, or perhaps the military. Or considering that aircraft with the capital P, perhaps it's Prime. Maybe it's all of them. We don't know. But the why is simple. Those in charge don't want people listening to it. They used to say that music could change the world. Those in charge don't want the world to change. They have it just the way they want it. I don't think music can change the world, but perhaps it can change a person. Give us hope. Perhaps make us better people. If nothing else, it helps us hang onto the ideals people once had. It is our heritage. That's why your guitar teacher thought you should know about it."

"Why is that?" Derrick asked.

"Because you and Miriam are the heart of The Resistance now," Marty said.

"Heart of it? I don't understand," Miriam said.

"Well, when you escaped from Pacific Edge, some believed you intended to lead us into a revolution. Word got out. People think it was all planned. From Derrick punching Marcus Carver to you, Rebekah, and Anna escaping. Although, there's some confusion about why Anna got separated from you," Marty said.

Miriam said, "What about Brad?"

Marty hesitated. "Uh, Brad isn't in The Resistance."

"Is he okay? I mean, after what we did."

"Yeah, he's fine. Still working the same job and the same shift. You covered your tracks. They believed our story and think The Resistance broke in, took us out, and helped you escape," Marty said.

"People were searching for us tonight in Potterville. Do you know about them?" Miriam asked.

Marty said, "Yep. Resistance. They've been searching for Anna every night. Someone reported dogs barking, so they called out more people. Communication is risky. So, we have code words. It's kinda 007, if you know what I mean."

"I don't know what that means," Miriam said.

"Right. I forget. The Chosen don't see or hear the stuff we preserve. Means clandestine. Double O seven was a spy. Anyway, we've been combing this area every night since Anna disappeared," Marty said.

"But you haven't found her?" Rebekah asked.

Marty smiled. "I didn't say that."

Miriam said, "I'm confused. Why are you still looking for her if someone found her?"

Marty said, "It's kinda hard to explain. The Resistance isn't organized. It's a loosely knit group. No real leadership, and some members are… let's just say, more trustworthy than others. And there's also the need for diversion."

"Still confused," Miriam said.

"Do you know where Anna is or not?" Rebekah demanded.

"What do you mean, diversion?" Derrick asked.

Marty held up his hands. "Whoa, one at a time."

Miriam said, "Let's start with Anna. Do you know where she is?"

Marty nodded. "Yes and no."

"Not helpful," Miriam said.

"I sorta know, but not at this exact moment," Marty said.

Miriam folded her arms, glaring at Marty.

"Okay. On the off chance this place is bugged, no details. We found her. I know who is responsible for her, but because we only communicate this sort of information in person, specifics may have changed. Does that help?"

Miriam said, "It helps. Why have people still been looking for her?"

"We assume the Chosen, or whoever is so interested in you guys, is watching us. If we stopped looking, they'd know we found her. Plus, it's better if even The Resistance thinks we have not found her. I'm sorry to say that not everyone is trustworthy within our ranks. There are spies on both sides," Marty said.

"Take me to Anna," Rebekah said.

"Not that easy," Marty said.

"What does that mean?" Miriam asked.

"Like I said, spies. It can be hard to know who can be trusted, even in The Resistance."

12

MIRIAM WALKED TO MARTY, HUGGED HIM, and then stepped back. She trusted him, and that's all Derrick needed. Although something didn't feel right—he dismissed his apprehension—many reasons to feel uneasy, including lack of food and sleep. Feelings can't be trusted under such conditions.

Stepping to Miriam's side, Derrick stuck out his hand. "Hi, I'm Derrick, Miriam's brother."

Marty shook Derrick's hand. "It's a pleasure, no, an honor to meet you. You can't imagine how much meeting Derrick King means to me."

Rebekah held back. "When can we see Anna?"

"Soon. Soon. I'll make a phone call, but first, we need to make sure you're safe. Follow me." With that, Marty trotted down the stairs to the family room. "I'm glad you found Patel's place. It's perfect."

Miriam stopped. "Wait. How do you know Patel, and how did you get into the house?"

Marty turned, smiling. "I've known AJ for a long time, and not just from work. AJ is the informal leader of the Resistance here. He assumed your search for Anna would lead you here. So, he called me to let me know you'd left Potterville and said I should keep an eye on the house because you might come here. Smart guy, AJ."

Marty stepped to a bookcase, feeling along the edge. Something clicked, and Marty swung the bookcase from the wall, revealing a door. "See? AJ built a safe room in this house after he moved from Pacific Edge, just in case. Good thing he did."

Marty motioned for them to go inside.

Something haunted Derrick. He couldn't figure it out. Perhaps because they did not make it back to the aircraft. No, that wasn't it. He should have felt relieved that Anna was in safe hands, and they'd soon be reunited.

But he was not relieved.

His anxiety escalated by the second. If he could just focus, but he could not.

"What's this?" Miriam asked.

"The perfect place for you to hide while I get Anna. Other than AJ and his family, I might be the only person who knows about this room. You can lock the door from the inside. No one can get in. It's small, but there's food, water, bathroom, emergency supplies to last you a month. But you won't need them. I'll be back soon." With a smile, Marty motioned them inside again.

Miriam took a deep breath and stepped inside. Rebekah and Derrick followed.

Marty stood at the opening, pointing. "Bathroom over there. Cots fold down. Eat something and get some rest. I'll be back soon."

"You'll bring Anna here?" Rebekah asked.

"Sure thing," Marty said, stepping out, closing the door.

Click.

Marty secured the lock he had installed earlier. Placing his head near the door, he said, "On second thought, I'll return with Pacific Edge security. Or Prime, if I can figure out how to make that connection. Even though they believed our story about the escape, both of us are stuck in that crappy job the rest of our lives. You're worth a lot of money, and like I said, you don't know who you can trust."

Marty's footsteps sounded as he trotted up the stairs, across the floor, and out the door. Derrick's mind cleared. Too late, but it cleared. Marty said they could only speak face to face. Telephones, e-mails, text messages, all too dangerous. Yet, he said AJ had called from Potterville. But AJ was in the sheriff's jail and would not have risked a phone call.

Derrick said, "I should have seen this coming."

Rebekah sat on a chair, head down, hands between her knees, rocking again.

"I led us right into it. I trusted him," Miriam sighed.

Derrick tried the door. "Locked."

Miriam nodded. "Now that I think about it, I saw the latch when I stepped in. Sometimes I'm so stupid. Walked right in."

Derrick noticed Rebekah rocking. He went to her, sat, and put his arm around her. "We'll figure something out."

"Do you think he knows where Anna is?" Rebekah asked.

Miriam sat on Rebekah's other side. "No. He would have turned her in for money if he did. He may know they found her but doesn't know where she is."

Derrick said, "Do you think Patel called him?"

Miriam thought for a moment. "Not sure. Maybe, but what he said about only communicating face-to-face makes sense. AJ, I mean Allen, wouldn't call. Sounds like being identified as part of this Resistance thing would be a bad thing. If there is such a thing as The Resistance. Do you think it's real?"

Derrick said, "I don't know. Mr. Grealy mentioned it."

"Perhaps they are in this with Marty. Maybe it's been a trap all along," Rebekah whispered.

Derrick said, "Maybe, but that doesn't seem right. Doesn't matter at this point. Right now, we need to find a way out of here."

"Then what?" Rebekah asked. "We still don't know where Anna is. We're screwed."

Miriam stood, walked around the room, checked the bathroom, peered into the refrigerator. "We are in the basement. No windows. Even if we could dig through the walls, which we can't because they're solid concrete, we'd be digging into the mountain."

Derrick stood, paced. He stopped in front of a small desk pushed against the wall. A computer and two monitors set on the desk. "Could this help?"

Miriam said, "I don't think so. I'd be afraid to turn it on. They might be monitoring Patel's computer to see if it comes online. That would mean he is home, and they might come looking for him."

"Who are they?" Derrick asked.

"Wish I knew," Miriam said.

Derrick held his hand up.

"What?" Miriam asked.

"Shhhh," Derrick hissed.

Footsteps sounded above the room.

Miriam mouthed, "He's back already?"

Derrick shook his head and whispered, "I don't think so. Just one guy. Different shoes."

"Maybe he forgot something," Miriam whispered.

Derrick shook his head again, stood, held his finger to his lips, and motioned Miriam to the door. "Stun gun. Be ready."

The footsteps moved about the house and then faded. Derrick whispered, "Upstairs. Searching the house."

"For us?"

"Probably."

"Do we want him to find us?"

Derrick said, "Yes and no."

Miriam nodded. "What's the plan?"

"Overpower him. Get the hell out of here." Derrick turned to Rebekah. "Get ready."

Rebekah nodded.

Footsteps.

Getting closer.

Down the stairs.

Pounding on the bookcase.

"Maranda? Maranda Kingston? Are you in there?"

13

RAPID FOOTSTEPS SOUNDED ON THE STAIRS, signaling the man running. Running indicated desperation. The man knew the name Maranda Kingston, and that signaled trouble. Not that they didn't already have trouble. They had plenty of it. Trouble was abundant.

"How does he know Maranda Kingston?" Derrick asked.

"Who is Maranda Kingston?" Rebekah asked.

Miriam said, "It's the name I used working nights in Technical Services. He's leaving."

"Who knows that name?" Derrick asked.

"Brad and Marty. And Mike, but I only met Mike once. And, Patel knows, he gave it to me."

"It's not Patel, so that leaves the other two. The first guy, Marty, said that Brad wasn't in The Resistance," Derrick said.

Rebekah said, "Does it matter who it is?"

"It does not," Derrick admitted.

Footsteps running through the house and down the stairs.

Bang! Bang! Bang!

Followed by muffled cursing.

"Brad or Mike?" Derrick asked.

"Not sure. Brad, I think. No, it might be Mike," Miriam said.

"Doesn't matter. Just be ready." Derrick got into a stance like he was starting a race. Not an in-the-blocks stance, but like when he ran cross-country. "When the door opens, I'll tackle the guy. You zap him."

"Which one of us?" Rebekah asked.

"I don't care. Both of you, if possible," Derrick said.

"That might kill him," Miriam said.

Derrick said, "Whoever is closest then. Just warn me, so I don't get zapped too."

Bang! Bang! Followed by more cursing and then grunting.

"That has it."

The door opened, and Derrick lunged but found only air.

Miriam dashed out behind Derrick but saw no one. Spinning around, Miriam saw Mike Prate standing behind the bookcase.

Holding both hands up, Mike said, "Maranda! Don't zap me. I'm here to help."

Miriam held the stun gun inches from Mike's chest. "That's what Marty said."

Mike said, "I'm sure he did. Had I found you first, I would have told you not to trust Marty."

"Marty said we can't trust anyone," Derrick said.

Mike said, "Well, in that, he's not wrong. Too much money involved."

"How did you find us?" Derrick asked.

"I was watching Marty. Brad and I have been taking turns watching him."

"How did you find this room so fast?" Derrick asked.

Mike pointed. "He left the bookcase ajar. I noticed the padlock on the door. Obviously, the bookcase concealed the door. A safe room, but you put locks on the inside of a safe room, not the outside."

"He's telling someone we are here," Miriam said.

"He planned to. But he is not."

"How do you know that?" Miriam asked.

"We took care of Marty," Mike said.

"Are you in The Resistance?" Miriam asked.

"Yes."

"Marty said Brad isn't in The Resistance. But you said Brad was working with you," Miriam said.

"Marty doesn't know everything. In fact, he doesn't know much. He's only been in The Resistance a short time. Marty joined after your escape. I didn't like it, but Brad thought we should watch him. Keep your friends close and your enemies closer, as they say."

"I'm not sure I understand," Miriam said.

"Brad saw that your escape was eating at Marty. Brad thought Marty would go to any length to get even."

A roaring sound in the distance grew louder until it became deafening, rattling the house.

"Fighter jets. They've spotted the Prime aircraft. We have to go," Mike said.

"We can't go. We have to find Anna Ford," Derrick said.

Mike said, "I have Anna. Let's go. The military will swarm this area soon. Block the roads, search every house."

"How do we know we can trust you?" Miriam said.

"You don't. But I owe you. Remember?"

Miriam said, "Marty said we could trust him, and he locked us in a room."

Mike held out his hands, palms up, and said, "Nice and easy now." Reaching down, he opened his jacket, a firearm rode in a holster on his belt. "I'm taking this out, two fingers. Don't zap me."

Mike removed the gun. Held it out. "Derrick, you take this. You can shoot me if I try anything. Fair enough?"

Derrick took the gun, checked the safety. He did not know why he knew how the gun operated, but he did. Unlocking his memory and defusing the hypnosis thing had to happen soon. Derrick held out his hand. "Holster."

Mike undid his belt, threaded the holster off, and handed it to Derreck.

"Where's Anna?" Rebekah demanded.

"Outside in my van. I hope," Mike said.

"What do you mean, you hope?" Rebekah asked.

"She was there when I came in."

"What are you saying?" Rebekah asked.

Mike said, "Someone might have found her. Unlikely, but possible. Let's talk later. We gotta move. The van is parked in the alley by the gate. I built a compartment to hide you. It's tight, but I think you can all fit. Just until we get someplace safe."

"We need that aircraft. That's our only way out of here," Miriam said.

"You're not wrong. But that's not possible," Mike said.

Miriam turned and ran from the room. "Wait, I'll be right back."

"Where's she going?" Mike asked.

Derrick said, "I don't know."

They could hear her running through the house, footfalls growing distant and then louder.

Miriam ran back into the room. "He's right. Soldiers and police watching the aircraft, fighter jets, circling off the coast."

Rebekah said, "Let's go. I want to see Anna."

Mike said, "Let me go first." Mike looked out the sliding glass door, searching the sky and each direction. Then he slid the door open and stepped out, again looking both ways. Glancing over his shoulder, he said, "I'll open the gate, check for people, and open the van's door. When I motion you, come one at a time. When the first person is inside, I'll motion for the next." He looked at Rebekah. "You come first. I know it will be hard, but you must be quiet when you see Anna. Understand?"

Rebekah nodded.

Mike ran to the fence, opened the gate, and glanced in both directions. Then he opened the sliding door of the van and rocked the seat forward. He did something on the floor and leaned down. When he raised up, he waved for Rebekah to come.

Rebekah darted across the lawn. When she arrived at the van, Mike pointed to a small opening in the van's floor. Feet first, Rebekah squirmed and twisted, disappearing inside.

Mike waved.

Derrick sent Miriam next. Miriam disappeared into the van. Derrick hoped he could fit.

When Derrick got to the van, he saw how Mike had fitted the van to conceal them. He'd built a box in the back, covered it with a canvas, splattered with paint. Paint cans, brushes, a small ladder, and other painting paraphernalia littered the tarp. Derrick didn't think he could fit through the small opening. The girls were packed into the small compartment.

"I don't think I can fit," Derrick said.

"You have to. Can't leave you here, and we will be stopped. Go in feet first so you can close the bolt when I close the hatch." Mike handed Derrick a small light. "You'll need this to see what you're doing. Then turn it off. Can't risk light leaking through a crack. Don't panic if we get stopped. I doubt they'll bother digging through all that crap, and if they do, there's no way into the compartment. If the door is secured, they'll have to tear it apart."

Derrick nodded. Getting inside the box proved as tricky as Derrick imagined. When fully inside, the hatch closed. Derrick had never been in such a tight space, not that he could remember. Derrick turned on the flashlight, secured the latch.

Derrick whispered, "You guys, okay?"

Rebekah whispered, "Fantastic."

Derrick didn't ask if Anna was there. The excitement in Rebekah's voice indicated they were together at last.

The van door closed, the motor started, they moved forward, then stopped, then backed up.

Derrick pictured the neighborhood, and their location as the van traveled. Straight ahead took them toward the Prime aircraft. They had reversed direction, which made sense. The fighter jets roared overhead again. They must have circled and were now going back out to sea.

The van was moving steadily. Turning left, traveling a few blocks, then turning right. Not fast. Just a guy headed to work in no hurry. Uphill away from the people guarding the aircraft.

Derrick relaxed.

They found Anna. Mission accomplished. Promise kept.

The van turned right and then turned right again. Going downhill now.

Miriam whispered, "We're going back toward the aircraft."

"Doesn't seem like something we should do," Derrick whispered.

Miriam said, "Perhaps something changed. Maybe there's an opening for us to get inside."

"Or maybe it's an easy way for him to turn us in," Derrick said.

Miriam whispered, "I don't think so. I trust Mike."

"You trusted Marty," Rebekah said.

"True, but I trusted Brad more. Something always bothered me about Marty, but I couldn't identify it. Seems my intuition was correct, much as I hate to admit it. Brad said Mike would help me if I ever needed it. Besides, Derrick has his gun," Miriam replied.

Derrick nodded, aware that Miriam could not see him, but a plan formulated in his mind. "If we don't get into the aircraft today, tonight we sneak up the coast and climb the cliff. Things are looking up. I have a good feeling about this."

The van slowed, making a gradual left turn.
Mike hollered, but it was too muffled to understand.
The van sped up, forcing Derrick against Miriam.
Then it rocked violently.
Then a thunderous boom.
Then a searing heat.
Then a sharp turn.
Then a hard jolt
Then it tilted downward.
And fell.

the end

Prime
A Derrick King Novel: Book 5

Derrick King survived in a world he once believed deadly, won a race, overpowered armed soldiers, fixed a doomed nuclear reactor.

Miriam King escaped Pacific Edge, defeated Pacific Edge security, crashed the computer network, rescued a robot named Charlie.

Together they found Anna Ford.

Together they failed to grasp the power of the force that hunts them.

Author's Note:

Thank you for reading my books. If they gave you a bit of an escape, I'm pleased. Please consider **writing a review.** To sign up for my newsletter, visit my website daniellcopeland.com.

Acknowledgements:

Thanks to the love and support of the love of my life and partner, Liz. She is also a writer and illustrator. Check out her books on Amazon Libby K. I couldn't do any of this without her. She is also my best editor and critic. Special thanks to Rod Leonard for providing feedback and guidance.

More books from Daniel L. Copeland:

Available at Amazon.com in paperback, eBooks for Kindle, and audiobooks.

The Derrick King Series

About the Author:
Daniel is a lifelong Idahoan and grew up on a small farm in Southern Idaho. He worked in the criminal justice system for 35 years and is now retired. Daniel has published nine novels. In addition to writing, he and his wife, Liz love to travel on their BMW motorcycle. They have ridden in most of the US, including Alaska, the Great Lakes, and Florida. They have also ridden in Canada, New Zealand, and Australia. Daniel is an award-winning home brewer and a certified beer judge.

www.ingramcontent.com/pod-product-compliance
Lightning Source LLC
Chambersburg PA
CBHW020127310726
48970CB00006B/1764